CHANTARELLE

CHANTARELLE

G.A. MORGAN

ISLANDPORT PRESS

ISLANDPORT PRESS

Islandport Press
PO Box 10
247 Portland Street
Yarmouth, ME 04096
Islandportpress.com
books@islandportpress.com

ISBN: 978-1-939017-63-5
Library of Congress Control Number: 2014959662

Printed in the USA by Bookmasters

10 9 8 7 6 5 4 3 2 1

Endpaper map illustration by Alex Ryan
Cover and back cover artwork by Ernie D'Elia

For Lafcadio, who has always been my hero;
for Oscar, who has always been my wing-man;
and for Tom, who has always been both.

Praise for *The Fog of Forgetting*
Book 1 of *The Five Stones Trilogy*

" . . . [an] emotionally resonant adventure."
—*The Wall Street Journal*

" A complex adventure to curl up with on a rainy summer afternoon."
—*Kirkus Reviews*

"Morgan excels at world-building . . . Filled with the type of
danger and magic that will please fans of Brandon Mull's *Beyonders*
series and C. S. Lewis's *The Chronicles of Narnia.* "
—*School Library Journal*

"In Ayda, G. A. Morgan has created an imaginative world, a beautiful and
dangerous island where myth becomes reality. Readers will be carried along by
this fast-paced adventure, and eager to journey back for the next installment."
—Megan Frazer Blakemore, author of *The Friendship Riddle* and *The Water Castle*

"The reader is compulsively moved forward
by just the right touch of intrigue and uncertainty
about exactly what is going to happen next."
—*Voya*

CHANTARELLE

THE ISLE OF AYDA

Exor

Arena

The Palace ×

Ratha's Aerie

×

Varuna

Broomwash

Rothermel's Wold
×

Lake Voss

Melor

City of
Metria
×

VOSSBECK RIVER

HESTREDES RIVER

Seaborne's cabin
×

Metria

NORTH ATLANTIC

Contents

We are like islands in the sea, separate on the surface but connected in the deep.

—WILLIAM JAMES

THE NORTH ATLANTIC, 1497

The cries from belowdecks have ceased, now that the gale has passed. This part of the passage is always unpredictable, with high seas and treacherous winds, but for some reason, the Captain prefers it. He knows his brother, Miguel, loathes it and will go many leagues to the south—adding days to his journey—to avoid the westerlies that blow like ice from the polar regions. But not him. He has made a reputation of being fearless. There is no one faster sailing from the Azores to these newfound shores. And do not be mistaken: ever since that lucky fool Columbus stumbled onto his discovery for Spain, the race has been on. Treaty of Tordesillas be damned.

His ship, a caravel, is an agile vessel, with light triangular sails and a shallow keel that allow him to travel up the narrower reaches of this new land. His crew is minimal, however, and the ship does not have much room for cargo. It is a dilemma, for he must come home with treasures if he is to have another expedition. And so he chooses the most valuable cargo: human beings and fur pelts. The fur pelts are a gift for his king. As for the human beings, they will be put to use in the castle. Oddities to please the court.

He smiles to himself at the thought of the strange, broad-faced people in his hold, dressed in sealskin and fur. He imagines them mingling among the jeweled, be-satined members of King Manuel's court. They do not speak in any recognizable pattern, communicating through short, guttural clicks of the tongue. But—he thinks back on their bitter parting from their homeland—they weep the same as anyone.

He is disturbed by a sharp knock on his cabin door.

"Desculpem-me, Capitão. Um dos hospedes está doente: um com o bebé."

One of the strangers he has brought aboard is ill. A woman with a small child. He chides himself for risking the passage with a baby, but at the time, he could not resist the notion of becoming an agent of destiny. Now, because of him, a child born in the farthest reaches of the known world will be raised to adulthood in the bougainvillea-laced courtyards of his own childhood. And, when it came to the hour of leaving, the mother's grief at the loss of her husband—how she clung to him and sobbed—moved him. He saw how the man had stroked her hair and whispered assurances in her ear.

A feeling then rose in him similar to one that often overtook him at night, on watch, when the moon dropped low across the dark, tossed sea. A longing—for what he could not say, exactly—but it had something to do with the mournful light on the water, and now this couple and their child. He decided on the spot that it was not for him to break the ties of family. That should be a task for God alone, or, the Captain thought, grimacing, for his King.

"Capitão," the mate insists, drawing him out of his thoughts.

He rises from his dinner to go below and see to his cargo. The mother is valuable, and he is not so hard a man that he would have her suffer. The cabin door swings out, spilling a cone of light onto the dark planks of the deck. The rigging has gone dumb and the seas are quiet—still as glass. The sails hang limp as tea cloths. A wind hole, perhaps? He has never encountered the doldrums so far north.

He takes a lantern from its hook outside the door and lights it. Wisps of mist curl around the light, slender and finger-like at first, then with more heft. He proceeds to the main deck, the lantern casting a yellow orb before him. Chill air bathes his face. He lofts the lantern astern. The orb of light evaporates. Fog rolls off the sea and over the stern like spilled cream. He rubs his forehead in dismay, thinking of the food stores.

Fog is an evil in these parts, lingering like an unwanted fever and turning the tempers and bellies of the crew against one another. It billows around his face, bathing him in cloud-like vapor so that the familiar lines of the deck and the rigging are obscured. Dread creeps into the Captain's blood. Belowdecks the child begins to wail.

He gathers the lantern close to him again and opens the wick to its widest glow, as if its light, alone, could ward off his sudden sense of doom.

Chapter 1

PUNISHMENT

The sun radiated sharp, naked heat onto the rust-colored plains of Exor, and the rock spires that dotted the horizon.

Louis hung at the center of one of these spires, like a small insect on a wall. He was shackled at the wrists, his bare feet scrabbling along a narrow jut of ledge to keep his shoulders from dislocating and his arms from tearing out of their sockets. He wore only a rag of dirty linen, tied at his waist. The remaining exposed skin was burnt and blistered from the sun's unwavering attention; his eyes were swollen with sand.

Since the events at the canyon's edge that had branded him a traitor, he had spent the height of each day like this: hung like a sack of meat for the vultures or any *tehuantl* that could climb. The rest of the time he lay in the blessed dark of a cell, deep in Dankar's sunken dungeons, writhing and burning with fever and pain.

Louis cracked an eyelid, looking for any signs of movement or life on the arid plateau below. *The scribes will be here soon to take me down*, he thought.

The desert rose up behind him in striated plateaus of sandstone that hid the maze of valleys, bowls, mesas, and dry canyons that made up the Dwellings. To the north, the shallow depression of a wadi—a river dried up now—was just visible. Louis traced its contours west, imagining Exor as it must have been long before the Great Battle, in the days when the Fifth Stone was harbored safely on Ayda and trouble had not yet reached her shores.

His throat contracted painfully at the thought of water, of the river—how it must have flowed easily toward the sea until it hit the plateau wall and had to yield. He knew that somewhere north of the plateau the wadi ended in a deep bowl—a former watering hole—unable to progress any farther. It struck him that he and the river were very similar: once full and bursting with life, now dried up and almost blasted out of existence. Dankar was to thank for that.

At the thought of his warden, Louis's swollen gaze passed to the Palace, which lay at the westernmost point of the plateau, overlooking the pit-houses to the east and the scribes' quarters to the north. Somewhere between them lay the warriors' barracks, and connecting them all were labyrinthine tunnels and the underground cells where both he and the Keeper of the stone of Metria were now imprisoned.

He had not seen Rysta since his punishment began, but he guessed she was responsible for the generous treatment he received from the scribes. One could not be in Rysta's presence long without being moved to sympathy. They had been coming a little earlier each day to release him from the cliff. Today, they had carried him out. *Even the scribes pity me, and they have nothing to live for but bending and scraping to Dankar.*

He felt a spasm of anger and screwed up his eyes to shut out the sun. It did no good. He saw it anyway: a hot disc of light burning through his eyelids.

Thoughts of Frankie drifted across his mind, and of her sister, Evelyn, and the boys: Chase, Knox, and Teddy. He recited each of their names to himself, and tried to recall little details about their faces. It helped him pass the time. He did not regret helping them, even though it had led to this. His one comfort in all of this was the fact that they were safe from Dankar, hidden by Rothermel deep in the well-protected forest of Melor.

But for how long?

He knew Melor was burning. He could taste ash on the wind with his swollen tongue—and, his head bucked up, something else. Something sweet. He opened his eyes again and saw a sight that made him think he was dreaming: storm clouds were rolling in from the east, casting dark shadows on the plain. He could see a purple mist falling in sheets across the plain—rain that was evaporating before it hit the ground.

Louis was no stranger to hallucinations, but these clouds and the rain were real. He was sure of it. *This* was Rysta's doing. The water was seeking her.

The clouds soon reached him and opened, showering him with a warm, gentle rain. He lifted his burnt face to it and felt the drops course down his skin, making rivulets between the encrusted blood and sand. For a moment he saw once again the white house on a ledge of granite that fell into the sea, and felt the showers of sea spray foaming the rocks. He pictured the little gap-toothed girl in the yellow T-shirt and the snapping sail of the wooden sailboat he used to love. Ghosts from another life, one he had lived a long time ago, in another land, when his name was Edward.

The cliff grew slippery from the rain, and his feet lost their grip on the ledge. He hung freely for a moment, shoulders screaming. The vision disappeared and in its wake crashed a huge wave of despair. He stopped struggling to reposition himself on the ledge, and instead struck the back of his head into the rock, hoping to knock himself out.

Better to die now, roasted on this spit of sandstone, then go on and on alone.

He had lost everyone.

Not everyone, a small voice whispered at the back of his mind. He remembered the clutch of Frankie's hands at his neck when he'd carried her on his back.

Frankie is out there somewhere.

Louis scrambled backwards on the cliff. His feet found the little ledge again, and took the weight off his arms. The sun rolled slowly to the west behind the rain. Across the desert, mounds of rocks glowed red and beige and orange, and despite his torment, his heart swelled suddenly at the sight of it.

Exor.

He had once come to this island as an outlier, a boy from another world, but he had become a man of Exor. His daylights—his essence, forged from the *atar*, the binding energy in all living things—were tuned to it. He was, he told himself, as strong and uncompromising as this land before him. He had proved this much. And he was no longer exiled here alone, cut off from all he once was and all those he cared about.

Meeting Frankie and the other outliers had changed everything.

Louis shifted on the ledge to ease the pain in his shoulders. He said each of their names again, filling his parched mouth with the sounds. He was not dead yet.

He would see this day through, and every day to come, until he had served his punishment. He would not leave Frankie and her sister and those boys to the mercy of Dankar and the Exorian army. He would not abandon them as he had been abandoned. He would stay alive today and every other day until he found them again.

Chapter 2

STORMY WEATHER

Chase is flying.

Below him is the pitched roof of his grandparents' house: Summerledge, with the pink humps of granite dropping into the sea. Then, the arc of Secret Beach, the Dellemere cottage, Fells Harbor, and Captain Nate's dock. Out beyond, his keen eyes make out small outcroppings of islands, a house here and there, and then nothing but a shimmering, undulating carpet of blue sea. He flies on, into a cloud bank, thick and cottony. It grows darker and harder to breathe. He swoops up to find clearer air, but the dense air presses down, sending him somewhere he knows he doesn't want to go, toward something dark and menacing. He can't see anything.

And then he is falling, plummeting into that endless sea. He lands hard and sinks into the cold, black water, comes up sputtering, just as a wave smacks into him. Wind is whipping the sea's surface into froth. The water is dark. The air is dark. He strains to see—and there it is: a flash of orange. Someone's life vest. He thrashes through the water toward it. The person wearing it is floating facedown in the ocean, bobbing up and down with every rise and fall of the waves.

Chase swims beside it and rolls the person over. He sees Knox's face, his hair streaming out around it like a halo, his life jacket bubbling up behind him—useless.

"*Nooo!!*" he screams. The waves carry the sound away. He grabs Knox by the loop on his life jacket, then sees another orange blob floating nearby, then another, and another. Evelyn, Teddy, and then Frankie. All facedown, not moving. Another cry rises at the back of his throat.

There's a tug at the back of his shoulder. He's being pulled up and out of the water, away from them. He doesn't want to leave them.

"No—stop!" he cries.

Then he hears a voice from far away at first, growing louder.

"Chase. Chase, it's okay."

He opened his eyes. Evelyn was standing over him, shaking his shoulder. "Was it the same dream?"

Chase nodded slowly.

He had been dreaming of flying ever since the rescue that followed Knox's disastrous picnic. They *had* all been rescued—pulled out of the freezing water one by one and transported by helicopter to shore—and they were all fine, except for Frankie. But secretly, he wondered if maybe they had died out there in the water for a minute, and that was why they couldn't remember what had happened.

Chase shook himself and sat up on the sofa in the living room at Summerledge, trying to lose the dark thoughts and the strange, empty feeling in his head that just wouldn't go away, no matter how much he slept.

He got to his feet, and with the movement felt a familiar rush of urgency—a panic, sort of. Ever since they'd come home, more than two weeks ago, he'd had this same feeling upon waking—a feeling that he was forgetting something. Something important. It sat there at the edge of his blank mind, like a word on the tip of his tongue that he could not recall.

"Where's Knox?" he asked Evelyn, looking around the room, the dream not completely expunged.

Different-size pots and pans were scattered across the floor of the living room. It had been raining off and on continuously since they'd been back, and the ceiling was leaking.

"Where do you think?" said Evelyn.

Since they'd been back, Knox had taken to sleeping in his tree fort, spending most of his time in the woods, rain and all.

"I found one of your mom's knives stuck in the tree out there. He's been throwing it. Plus, he has a bunch of food from the house up there, and some weird mushroomy things. I don't think he should eat them until we know what they—"

Evelyn was interrupted by a thundering *swoosh* of water rushing through the pipes overhead. Drops of water pinged into the pans on the floor like a timpani.

"Is he *still* at it?" Chase groaned.

Evelyn rolled her eyes in response.

Knox wasn't the only one behaving strangely; Teddy was inconsolable unless he was in water or could hear it running. He'd been taking a lot of baths, and when he wasn't doing that, he was running the faucets or flushing the toilets or going down to the beach. Between the old pipes and the rain outside, the ceiling was finally caving in, and Captain Nate, their trusted handyman, was nowhere to be found to handle the repairs. They'd only seen him once—at the hospital, where they'd all been taken after the rescue—and then he had disappeared.

"We'll need an ark soon," their mother had joked, trying to lighten things up. But it hadn't worked. Nothing worked. The mood around the house was tense, and it was getting worse.

Both Chase and Knox had apologized for taking their parents' Whaler out without permission, but that wasn't the problem. The problem was that they'd taken Teddy with them, who was only six, and had ended up getting lost in the fog, which was the thing their mother was *most* afraid of.

Grace Thompson had lost her only brother, Edward, to the fog off the Summerledge coast when she was eight years old. It was the Golden Rule in their house that no one—not even adults—could take a boat out unless it was a bluebird, sparkling day, and never, ever alone. Chase and Knox *knew* this. They had been coming to Summerledge as long as they had been alive. It didn't matter that it had started out as that kind of a day. Or that no one—not even the locals, who were used to a sudden roll-in of fog—could have predicted what would happen. Chase and Knox had disobeyed the one rule their mother cared most deeply about, and they had put their little brother and Evelyn and Frankie in danger.

Their mother was nervous and irritable now, jumping at every little thing. She couldn't relax unless she knew exactly where they all were, at every moment. And she cried. *A lot.* Their dad had told them to just give her time. Chase knew his mother was relieved and grateful they were home, but the interim between when they were lost and when they had been found had changed her. She was very unhappy—and it was their fault.

Chase sighed, wondering again what had happened in that interim. None of them could remember anything about the accident, and now Frankie was really sick.

Supposedly the boat had been smashed to pieces, and the best anyone could guess was that it had sheltered them for most of the time, and they'd only gone in the water at the very end. Everyone but Frankie had recovered quickly and left the hospital, but Frankie just kept getting worse. Evelyn had stayed with her at the hospital for the first week, but then had opted to go home with the Thompsons. She said it was because she wanted her grandmother, Fanny Dellemere, to be able to focus on Frankie, but Chase knew it was too hard on Evelyn to watch her sister suffer.

And Frankie was suffering. She was feverish and wouldn't eat; she had strange lesions around her neck and arm that were spreading to other parts of her body; and she threw up constantly. In fact, the doctors kept her barely conscious most of the time, to keep her more comfortable. According to the daily phone reports from Mrs. Dellemere, Frankie was also hallucinating. She muttered strange names to herself in her sleep, and had asked once or twice about her camel.

Jim Thompson was pulling double duty, between being at Summerledge and traveling the two hours to the hospital to oversee Frankie's treatment. All talk of his new job at the lab had stopped. As far as Chase could tell, his dad was not leaving Summerledge again without them.

Once, when his parents thought he was asleep on the sofa, Chase heard his mother say, "What *happened* to them, Jim? They all seem so . . . so *lost*—and what is wrong with Frankie?"

"I don't know, Grace. It's not outside the realm of possibility that the kids might have encountered a barrel out there with some sort of toxic waste in it. I've told you before, the ocean has become a dumping ground. At first we thought it might have been radiation poisoning—"

An anguished gurgle emitted by his mother stopped his father mid-sentence. Chase did not dare move a muscle, but he heard his father change tack.

"I don't think that's it, though, honey; otherwise all of the kids would have more physical symptoms. I think it's something else. Some type of virus . . . although it's unlike anything I've ever seen before. Some of Frankie's cells are mutating at a very rapid rate."

Chase heard a chair scrape across the floor in alarm.

"Are you saying that she—that little girl—has some kind of cancer?" cried Grace.

"No. No, I don't think so. I was suspicious of that at first, but that's not it. What's happening is closer to an infection. A form of bacteria is invading her cells and changing the DNA and the mitochondria. Then those mutated cells replicate with a speed I've never encountered before—"

"I don't understand. Speak English."

"Inside every one of our cells is a power center called mitochondria. Mitochondria use the nutrients and energy in food to provide everything our cells need. If a cell were a universe, its mitochondrion would be like its sun. Whatever Frankie has is attacking her mitochondria and—I don't know how else to put it—*supercharging* them."

"That doesn't sound so bad," argued Grace. "Why would that make her so sick?"

"It *is* bad. Cells can't survive that kind of activity for long. At some point this mitochondrial overdrive will kill the cells. And if enough of Frankie's healthy cells have been overtaken . . . well—"

"What?" Grace demanded.

Silence.

"She'll *die*?"

His dad must have nodded, because all Chase heard was his mother saying "Oh my God" in a dreadful voice.

"I'm doing everything I can to help her, Grace. Everything I can. And she's not defenseless; her body *is* fighting back, attacking and killing the mutant cells. There's a battle being waged inside that little girl's body right now, and if we can help her cells get the advantage, she'll make it."

"Does Fanny know all this?"

"Yes, but she doesn't want Evelyn—or our kids—to know how serious it is. They've been through enough, and it won't help Frankie to have Evelyn at the hospital all the time. Frankie is getting the best treatment available. I've had my lab see to that."

"Jim." Grace's voice had grown deadly calm. "How do we know our kids aren't infected? Maybe it's . . . *incubating*. The boys don't seem like themselves at all. They're so . . . I don't know, shell-shocked or something. Look at Chase. He's exhausted. He's barely been off that couch. And Knox has gone crazy. He's like the guy on TV who eats bugs and drinks his own urine—"

A *whoosh* of water through the pipes brought on fresh *pings* into the pans on the floor.

"—and don't even get me started on Teddy. The only one who seems halfway normal is Evelyn, and she's barely spoken. None of them can remember a thing."

Chase squinted through half-closed eyelids. His mother's face was in her hands.

"I've thought about all of this, Grace, but let's not worry about it for the time being; so far they seem healthy, although I agree they are behaving strangely. It's probably just the stress from the accident. As for the rest of it, I had the hospital take blood samples from all of them. They look normal. I'll test them again in a week, and keep testing and monitoring them—"

"But just so I'm sure I understand: As it stands now, you can't say they're *not* infected," Grace asked, her voice flat.

His dad must have nodded again, because all Chase heard was his mother catch her breath and leave the room, followed by his dad.

After an appropriate amount of time, he walked into the kitchen as if he'd just woken up. His mother bit her lip when she saw him. Her face was blotchy, her eyes puffy from crying.

"Aww, Mom, don't *cry*," Chase groaned, sounding more impatient than he meant to. "We're fine. It's okay. Worry about Frankie if you have to worry."

His mom caught him in a death grip. He was almost as tall as she was now.

"I love you—you know that, right?" she mumbled into his hair. "When we couldn't find the boat and you were missing, I—I thought I would . . ."

"Grace," his dad admonished. "Let's not get into it again."

His mother stood back, still holding Chase's shoulders with both hands. "You sure you feel okay?" she asked.

Chase nodded and gently tried to free himself by stepping backwards. She released him with a small sigh, like it actually hurt to let him go, then added, "Well, at least you're breathing well. I ordered you a new inhaler, but you don't seem to need it."

It was true. Stealing his parents' Whaler and getting lost in the fog and thrown overboard seemed to have cured his asthma—if that was even possible. Again, he wished he could remember more about that day. He wished, too, that he could ask some questions about what his dad had just said about Frankie, but he didn't want to admit he'd been eavesdropping.

He hedged. "Sooo, did Mrs. Dellemere call yet?"

His mother shook her head.

"We'll go visit them tomorrow," she said, sounding like she was going to start crying all over again.

Chase briskly opened the refrigerator, saying, "I'm hungry" to distract her.

He knew it would make both his parents feel better if he could explain what had happened to them out on the boat. But he honestly had no idea what was going on with Frankie—or any of them, for that matter. It was like an eraser had swept across his brain, rubbing out the days they had been lost.

He pulled out some turkey and mayonnaise to make a sandwich and went over—again—what he *did* remember: Knox sidling up to the beach with the Whaler; the picnic at Little Duck. The fog rolling in. Then, nothing but water; water everywhere, filling their mouths, choking and gagging them. Freezing cold. Dark. The wind roaring in their ears. And then, the distant clanging bell of a buoy, a beam of light across the water, moving toward them like a giant flashlight. The *whomp-whomp-whomp*, then the white belly of the helicopter with uscg/ariel written in black. Men in orange suits diving toward them.

Chase spread mayonnaise on two slices of bread and stacked the lettuce and turkey in layers, making a huge sandwich. His stomach rumbled.

He sat down at the kitchen table, in the seat closest to the woodstove, took a bite, and chewed. A log in the woodstove split and crackled, catching his attention. He stared at the flames through the dirty little window at the front of the stove, watching the orange glow leap against the glass. A shiver went through him, cold, like dread. Another one of the weird feelings that kept washing over him for no particular reason since he'd been back.

He glanced up at his parents. They had moved back into the living room, and he could see them hugging each other, framed by the kitchen doorway. Beyond them, his eyes followed the porch roof, the grass, and then the pink humps of granite that gave Summerledge its name. He saw it all, even the pitted tidelines scoured on the granite, with a clarity he had never experienced before the shipwreck.

Chase looked down at his sandwich, thinking about his new, heightened sense of sight. His head was beginning to ache. He had not told anyone what he remembered most vividly about the rescue—and that was what had come *after*.

Captain Nate had been waiting for them when they were dragged into the helicopter bay, and when Chase saw the Captain, a sense of déjà vu came over him that was so strong it had completely creeped him out. And then, when they were onshore and being loaded into ambulances, he had sat up on his gurney to look out of the back window. It was dark and raining and the flashing lights of the ambulances were sweeping the area with an eerie red glow. Several big puddles had formed in the wharf parking lot, and every time the lights passed over a puddle, Chase had seen—clear as day—the reflection of the same thing: a lake, and tall, snowy mountain peaks set against a blue sky. The red light would swoop away across the parking lot, and then come back, and there, like clockwork, were those mountains reflected in the puddles. Chase had watched them flicker on and off until the ambulance drove him away.

He swallowed and took another bite of his sandwich.

Maybe something *was* wrong with him.

Chapter 3

REVELATION

The start of the third week home began as the second one had ended—with overcast skies and a steady downpour.

Evelyn's visit with Frankie and Mrs. Dellemere had been uneventful, except that Evelyn was now quieter than ever. Frankie's condition was stable for the moment, and there was little any of them could do. Jim Thompson had emerged only that morning, smacking his forehead with his palm and mumbling something about his own stupidity and driving off. Grace had taken a quick walk to check on things at the Dellemere cottage, unable to bear the tension—and the dripping and flushing—inside the house for another minute.

Chase, Evelyn, and Teddy were alone in the kitchen, a rare luxury. Since they'd returned, there had hardly been a single moment when they weren't being watched.

"The sun's coming out," Knox said, slamming through the back door.

His hair was darker and reached his shoulders now. He had strapped a woven leather belt, bandolier-style, over a stained T-shirt that looked more gray than light blue—in fact, pretty much all of Knox looked overdue for a bath.

"A lot of stuff's been washed up on the beach," he said. "Check this out."

He opened a large leaf he'd used to collect a cache of round white discs and laid them one by one on the kitchen table.

Evelyn picked up one of the discs and held it in her palm. It was small and gray, a perfect circle. Five narrow slits pierced the sides and bottom of the shell; five feathered ovals rayed out from the center like a flower or a starfish.

"Sand dollars," she said.

"Tons of 'em, everywhere," Knox added.

"I want one!" Teddy said. He was standing on a chair at the sink, turning the kitchen faucet on and off. Their turtle, Bob, was sunbathing on the kitchen windowsill. Teddy hopped down and grabbed a large, very white sand dollar. It broke in his hand. He looked up, his mouth a shocked O.

"It's okay, Teddy," said Evelyn gently. "They're fragile because they're empty shells. The animal that lived inside is gone now. Where I was born, in Haiti, a broken sand dollar means an argument or difference will soon be mended. Look!" She took the fragments of Teddy's sand dollar and shook it. Five little winged bones spilled out.

Knox looked over her shoulder. "Frankie's columns," he said.

Evelyn sniffed. "You mean, *colombes du paix.*" Her eyes shone beneath their dark lashes.

Knox rolled his eyes behind her back. "Oh yeah, that's what I meant to say. I don't speak Haitian, remember?"

"It's French, actually," Evelyn answered, matter-of-fact. "Haitians speak French, and French Creole—and English. And don't roll your eyes again. It's not my fault you only speak one language."

She turned toward him.

"Let's go get a bunch for Frankie—she'd like them."

She grabbed her ratty navy blue sweater from the table and pulled it over her head.

"Bob and I want to go, too," said Teddy.

He picked up his turtle and followed Evelyn out the back door. Bob was not allowed far from Teddy's grip these days, and was looking a little worse for wear.

"Chase, you coming?" asked Knox.

"Nah, I'm tired."

Chase made his way back to the living room and flopped on the couch. Knox marched over and threw a pillow at him.

"C'mon, Chase. Bust a move. It's Secret Beach." He emphasized the S and the B, like Chase was deaf.

Chase opened his eyes and shook his head, then rolled over and put the pillow Knox had thrown at him over them.

"No, thanks—my head hurts," he mumbled.

Knox continued to stare at him for a second.

"Forget you, then," he said, and slammed out of the house after Evelyn and Teddy.

The sky was lighter than it had been in days, with sun breaking through the overcast in warm, blue patches. He caught up with Evelyn.

"Something is seriously up with Chase. Remind me to tell Dad when he gets back."

He jogged down the driveway and bolted left to take the path through the woods that led to the beach.

Teddy carefully jumped over the puddles in the driveway. Evelyn waited for him.

"Why are you doing that, Ted?" she asked, watching him almost clear a large one in the driveway.

"I don't want to mess up the pictures," he said.

Evelyn looked back at the puddle, and did a double take. For a second she thought she saw the reflection of a beautiful city, one with low buildings and round, blue roofs, interrupted here and there by a slender tower. But when she looked back, she didn't see anything except the wake from Teddy's landing.

Evelyn shook her head. Maybe Knox needed to tell Mr. Thompson about her, too.

✢   ✢   ✢

The moment he was truly alone, Chase opened his eyes. His head was pounding. He hadn't told anyone because he just couldn't take any more anxious stares. Dad was so preoccupied with Frankie's illness, and his mom was just a bundle of nerves. Besides, he had almost gotten used to the pain, throbbing behind his right temple. *Almost.*

Today, the pain was accompanied by an agonizing sense of pressure building from the inside. He was seriously beginning to *believe* they had run into a barrel of toxic waste and now he had a brain tumor. Maybe his head would blow off eventually, and the only thing left would be bloody scraps and gray matter for everyone to find.

The constantly dripping, groaning house didn't help matters. He needed to clear his head so he could think. He should have gone with the others to get some fresh air, but as much as he wanted to, he couldn't get his body to obey. So he sprawled out even more on the couch. An unexpected gleam of sunshine fell through the window across his torso—agonizingly bright. He had to squint.

Outside, it looked as if the downpour had passed and, finally, some blue sky was visible from the window. Chase stared through slitted eyes at the ledges that fell into the ocean at the front of the house. He opened his eyes a tiny bit wider. The ledges appeared to be moving; to be precise, *things* on the ledges were moving, on the face of the rock. He sat up and shaded his eyes. The ledge was teeming with gulls—hundreds of them, covering the whole surface of the rock. Chase could make out their markings.

A rap at the window startled him. A gull was sitting on the edge of the porch banister, looking at him out of the side of its head. Then, as if someone had shot a gun, all of the gulls flew off the ledge in one squawking, feathery blast, up into the air. The sound of their cries circled over the lawn, coming closer and closer to the house. They massed on the porch furniture and the railing, and a few swiveled their heads and laid their beady eyes on Chase. They looked like they were waiting for something. Another made a lunge for the window right in front of him.

Chase fell off the couch. He felt a twinge in his temple. The gulls cried louder and stalked toward the window like an army, heads bobbing as they walked. Even though Chase knew the window would protect him, for some reason he felt scared.

He crawled into the kitchen. From the kitchen window and the back door he saw that the gulls were everywhere—perched on the lawn, the shed, circling the house, squawking angrily, hungrily, like they did at the back of lobster boats when chum was thrown overboard. Did they want to eat *him?* What was up with these birds?

He felt another twinge, and his heart beat faster. He didn't want to find out.

He ran upstairs, where one look out the window showed him more and more gulls advancing on the house. He looked out his parents' bedroom window for Knox and Evelyn and Teddy. Where were they?

He raced to the attic, his right temple now throbbing in pain. Chase panted at the top stair—a strange feeling, considering he hadn't needed his inhaler once since their disastrous picnic. The attic was warm and refreshingly dark, and, best of all, out of sight of the birds. Only two small windows in the attic and a small door to the widow's walk led outside.

Chase cradled his head with his arms. It felt as if a wedge were being driven through it. Pain screamed through his skull like a fire alarm. The sound of the gulls' cries was softer because of all the insulation, less frightening, and he tried to calm himself. He sat down heavily on the steps, only to bolt back up again when several loud raps on the window let him know the gulls had found him, followed by intense scratching and pecking on the roof.

The stupid gulls were trying to *get in!*

"WHAT DO YOU WANT?" Chase yelled.

A thrum of white light and blinding pain made him feel sick to his stomach. He lurched over to the door to the widow's walk and looked out of the window. Instead of sky and sea, he saw the same image he'd seen reflected in the puddle the night of the rescue: a lake and the black-and-white peaks of a mountain range covered in snow. Then, he saw a bird flying ahead, and his feet in the snow. The light expanded; he was following the bird, stumbling blind, one foot after another. There was a platform above the clouds, set high in the mountain, a square building with four doors, and a tall, severe-looking woman with long black hair standing before a cauldron, great leaping flames licking up the sides.

Fresh air slapped his face and the vision passed. Chase realized that somehow he had opened the door and was no longer inside the attic. He was standing on the widow's walk that looped around the chimney. He swallowed hard and glanced around him. He was completely surrounded by the gulls—no escape—but they were silent. Watching him. They clung to the railing of the widow's walk so tightly he could see the translucent whites of their talons. Chase rubbed his temple, trying to figure out what to do next.

The wind picked up, ruffling the gulls' feathers, although they remained quiet and unmoving. His bangs blew wildly in his face. He ventured a step along the rickety walk, feeling the metal grille with his foot before he stepped. He'd never been up here before; it was off limits. He wondered if Knox had, since Knox always broke the rules. He put his full weight on his foot. The iron swayed and groaned. He shivered a little in the wind and looked out at the horizon. The pain in his temple had eased enough for him to look at the view.

A fresh set of black storm clouds was rolling in fast from the east, moving in on the blue patch that had broken through. The ocean churned steely gray, and far off he could see a dark patch where rain was already coming down in a sheet across the water. He glanced again at the gulls.

Their heads were now bent under their wings, ready to ride out whatever was coming. Chase smelled electricity in the air, a metallic edge that he knew must be lightning.

A bright flash pulsed in his head. His tongue hit the roof of his mouth and a searing pain struck him full in the chest. The pressure behind his right temple burst in an agonizing shudder. Chase fell to his knees. The widow's walk groaned and shook. He lurched sideways, trying to hold on to the iron rails.

Crack!

Something big and structural split beneath him with a loud creak. Chase felt himself slip and then, suddenly, just like in his dream, he was flying. The ground approached with sickening speed. He wrapped his hands around his neck, waiting for the crushing impact, unable to close his eyes against what was coming. The ground was forty feet, then thirty feet, then twenty feet away when a huge waft of air buffeted him back toward the house. He hit the gutter, then slammed onto the porch roof and bounced off into the lilac bush.

He hit the ground with a *thwomp*. The pain that had been simmering in his head exploded into fireworks of light followed by a parade of images: a cabin in the fog; massive wide trees and a path strewn with pine needles; a man in a green skirt with long tangled hair; a shimmering pool and a skylit cavern. He saw the mountains, the cauldron, and the woman's face again, and a river raging through a deep canyon in the desert. At last, he saw a kind, weathered face, bending down to wrap a necklace with a bead around his neck, and the reflection of a man on a wooden ship, shading his eyes to stare out to sea. And—finally—he remembered the thing he was supposed to do.

Chapter 4

CHANTARELLE

"*C*hase!" Evelyn's voice was hoarse from yelling.

She and Knox had come up from the beach when it began to rain. Teddy was with his mother, checking on the Dellemere cottage. Evelyn hadn't wanted to go. It made her feel strange to visit the empty house, the same way she felt sometimes in the dark: like everything that should be familiar and safe—the crack in the ceiling, the closed closet door—wasn't anymore.

Knox had veered off at the tree fort while Evelyn went up to the house alone.

She was the first to discover that Chase was gone. She read his note on the kitchen table.

Mom/Dad/Everyone:

Don't worry. I'm okay! I'm not hurt. I just remembered something I have to do. I need to ask somebody to do something for me. If I'm not back right away, don't freak out. It may take me a little while. I took one of the bikes. Seriously, I'm fine—

Chase

Evelyn scratched her head, wondering why Chase needed to reassure his parents he wasn't hurt. She searched his room and went out on the porch and toward the other beach to look for him. When she turned back toward the house, something odd about the roofline caught her eye. She went out to the ledge to look at it and cried out.

A black hole in the bricks on the front of the chimney was smoking, and below it, the widow's walk was dangling off the roof. Chase's note started to make sense. He might have been standing on the widow's walk when lightning hit it, and fallen off. The porch roof would have broken his fall, but it was hard to believe he wasn't hurt—or was he? Maybe he wrote the note *before* he went up on the widow's walk. Evelyn was suddenly afraid.

She ran to the lilac bush by the porch and beat at it, looking for Chase's body, just in case. She dug back behind the scrub to see if he'd rolled toward the house's foundation.

"*Chase!*" she yelled again.

She crawled around the circumference of the house but could find no sign of him. This was a good thing, she tried to tell herself, despite the fact that her heart was clanging a warning. Something was not right.

She sped off toward the tree fort to find Knox. The rain was now a fine mist that sprayed her face. The leaves on the trees glistened, and the forest smelled like wet earth and pine.

She found Knox squatting on the floor of his fort, stripping the bark off a small sapling with a stubby-looking knife. He had amassed a collection of rocks and sticks and moss that he had arrayed on the edge of the fort railing. It looked sort of homey, the way her grandmother's cottage did with its collection of stuff on the walls.

"Knox," she said, trying not to sound as frightened as she felt. "Chase is missing."

"Hmm?" Knox answered, distracted.

"Chase. Is. Missing." She tried to keep her voice calm.

"He probably just went to find us," said Knox, not really interested. He was bending the sapling into a bow.

Evelyn shook her head.

"Something's not right—I know it. There's a big hole in the chimney, and the widow's walk is broken. I think he went up there, and now he's gone. I looked for him. He left a note."

Knox shot her a look of disbelief that faded when he saw how serious she was.

"Where would he go?" she asked. She sounded like she might cry.

Knox slipped his knife into the leather sheath attached to his belt, shot to his feet, and jumped from the platform to the ground, not bothering to use the planks nailed to the trunk.

"I'll take a look," he said. "I bet he's around here somewhere."

Evelyn trailed him as he headed back toward the beach, calling out for Chase. He led them off the path and into the woods, past a large outcropping of tumbled rock and a small entrance to a cave. He crawled up the side of the rock and hollered into the cave.

"Chase! Quit fooling around! Evelyn's freaking!"

"Why would he be in there?" asked Evelyn. The cave looked slippery and dangerous in the gloom of the forest.

He shrugged. "We used to hide here sometimes. He was a good hider."

Knox shouted into the cave one more time, listened, and then crawled down. A warm *whoosh* of air blew out of the cave after him. He yelped in surprise.

"What? What is it?" Evelyn shrieked. She clambered up the rock hill, coming even with him.

Knox pointed to the cave. "That cave—I just know it goes somewhere. You can feel warm air coming out of it!"

"Why, of course it goes somewhere," said a deep, gravelly voice from somewhere above them.

Knox and Evelyn recoiled.

"Who's there?" Knox yelled, looking around blindly. He couldn't see anyone. He took his knife from its sheath and brandished it over his head.

"There's no need to be hostile; I'm only agreeing with you," the same voice said, apparently out of nowhere.

Then, to Knox and Evelyn's astonishment, a pile of rubble and moss-covered rock at the top of the cave moved, or, more accurately, *stretched*. In one swift movement, it jumped down and perched on the ledge at the entrance of the cave and revealed itself to be a man—a very small man, but fully formed, and *talking*.

Evelyn rubbed her eyes.

The little man held out his clenched fist and unrolled it slowly, palm up, bowing. He had dark golden skin that was so wrinkled it looked as if he might be made of petrified wood. His hair was long and earth-colored, and he carried a gnarled walking stick. He was dressed in pants, shirt, jacket, and a tight-fitting hat, all stained a mottled combination of browns and grays and greens.

"My name is Chantarelle. I am pleased to meet you."

Knox was too shocked to respond.

"I'm Evelyn. This is . . . Knox," Evelyn mumbled.

Chantarelle continued to hold out his hand, palm up, his long and delicate fingers splayed.

Evelyn hesitated, then extended her first two fingers and took his hand and shook his fingers. He smiled up at her from beneath his creased brow with a wide grin that showed his brownish gums and yellow teeth. He had light brown eyes with wide irises, and it seemed to Evelyn that he had just sprung from the ground, out of the rocks and moss and pine needles, just like one of the *djab*—nature spirits—her Haitian mother had told her about when she was very young. She knew from these stories that when you encounter one of these spirits, you must treat them with great respect. They could be protectors and guides—or dangerous enemies.

Chantarelle returned her stare, and continued to smile between lips barely discernible from his face.

Evelyn took a deep breath.

"We are looking for our friend—his brother," she said, tossing her chin at Knox. "We didn't mean to disturb you. I mean no disrespect, but are you . . . are you—*real?*"

The little man chuckled.

"What a funny question! Don't you trust your own eyes? Why, of course I'm real. As real as you—maybe more."

"But . . . but . . ."

Evelyn was stymied. What *was* he?

She racked her brain for any story she might have heard that would describe a little fellow like this. Her mother had not lived long enough to tell all of hers. He must be a spirit of the trees or the cave, or perhaps he was a more powerful deity. One of the *loa*, the kind that traveled between worlds and came to people in dreams.

Evelyn felt her forehead. Maybe she and Knox had finally caught what Frankie had, and now they were both hallucinating. She collapsed on her knees, eye level with the strange creature. If it hadn't been for his small size and his stained and wrinkled skin, he would have almost been ordinary-looking. Perhaps he was just a very small person, not a spirit at all.

"Are you . . . *human?*" she croaked.

A glint came into Chantarelle's light brown eyes. He cocked his head.

"Ask the right question and you will get the answer you need. Ask a better question."

Evelyn pondered this for a minute. It could be some kind of trick. If she asked the wrong question, Chantarelle might put a curse on her.

"I don't know which question to ask," she confessed.

Chantarelle burst into laughter at this and pounded his stick on the ground. The pine boughs above shook and sent a small shower of needles raining on their heads.

"I cannot tell you how refreshing you are," said Chantarelle, taking a step back so he could wave his stick in the air, eyes dancing. "So many think they know exactly where they are going and how to get there when, in reality, no one knows. Better to admit confusion than certainty—eh?"

Evelyn was still not sure how to respond.

"Never mind your question, dear girl, or the answer," he continued, wiping his eyes. "We shall leave them open for now. But let me ask *you* something: Does it matter so much what I am? Isn't it enough to know *whom* I serve? These are dangerous times. One ought not to make friends lightly; you never know in what guise the enemy might appear."

Evelyn reared back, certain now that she was in the presence of a *loa*—a being that crossed between the natural and the spiritual worlds. Chantarelle was a world-walker, and very powerful. If he took offense at anything they did or said, he might call on other spirits to torment them. She tried to warn Knox with her eyes.

The little man sat back on his bare heels and sighed heavily, all of his previous joy evaporated.

"You have no idea why I am here, do you? Those who count on you had hoped you would have paid attention to the signs."

"Signs? What signs?" grunted Knox, finally finding his voice.

"Signs from the sea and the rain, the earth and the sky, of course," said Chantarelle, shifting his eyes to Knox. He shook his small head and wisps of pepper-black hair escaped from the small gray skullcap he wore on his head. "Did Ratha send you all back for nothing, then?"

Evelyn and Knox were mystified. What on earth was this little man talking about?

"Who the heck is Ratha?" said Knox.

Chantarelle kicked at a hump of moss on the ledge, sending dirt flying. Then he sat back and put his head in his hands.

"The fog has done its work all too well. You have forgotten all about Ayda and your task. You do not remember the Fifth Stone."

His voice rumbled in their ears, as if it came from the very rock they were standing on. He looked up.

"But there is one who has remembered. The eldest . . ." Chantarelle chuckled to himself. "With a swift flight and a good knock, he has come back to his senses."

Knox's lip curled in anger.

"Do you mean Chase? What have you done to him? If you've so much as touched him, I'll kill you!"

He lunged at the little figure, but Chantarelle was too quick. He evaded Knox easily by swinging back up to the top of the rock. The necklace around Knox's neck fell out of his shirt as he moved.

"I've done nothing to him! It was her!" Chantarelle squeaked. "*She* found a way to reach him. *Ratha.* That is her business; I come on the business of another."

"I know you, spirit, from the wise people in my country," said Evelyn, holding up her hands in a calming gesture. "We wish you no harm. Please tell us, what business are you about? *Who* has sent you?"

Chantarelle's gaze skipped off the bead that hung on Knox's necklace and landed on her.

"*Now* you begin to ask the right questions."

Chantarelle jumped down, suddenly grave.

"I am here on matters of great importance. One could say the *most* importance. I come at the will of the *atar*. I come at the call of the Keeper of the Fifth Stone, and I am here to remind you of your promises. Tell me, young man, about the fine-looking necklace you're wearing. Surely you must recall how it came to circle your neck?"

Knox shook his head, frustrated.

"Okay," Evelyn said, and breathed out hard. "You obviously know something we don't. So why don't you tell us who you are and where Chase is; then you can tell us what we need to remember."

Chantarelle cleared his throat.

"I am Chantarelle; I have already told you that. And though you may think me a stranger, I have lived amid this forest and many others for several of your people's lifetimes. You have never seen me, but I have known you, as a fawn or a star or flower might—unnoticed. But I ask you: Just because you don't notice me, does that make me less real?"

Before Evelyn or Knox could answer, Chantarelle harrumphed and answered himself.

"I think not. I have shown myself to you because Ayda is in need of your help."

"What is it with you and this Ayda?" said Knox.

Again, a glint appeared in Chantarelle's eyes.

"I can show you, if you like."

He motioned to Evelyn, who bent down a little closer.

She could feel his breath on her face. It smelled like rich, fertile dirt. She knew instinctively that this creature would not hurt them. He was there to teach them something, like all spirits.

"Do you trust me, child?" said Chantarelle.

Evelyn looked into his warm brown irises, and nodded.

"Don't do it, Ev!" Knox shouted.

But before he could say anything else, Chantarelle drew out Evelyn's necklace from beneath her T-shirt and breathed on the bead.

She swooned and pitched forward. He caught her and laid her gently on her side.

"Evelyn!" Knox yelped. He was beside them in a second, making a flying leap at Chantarelle. "What have you done?"

The little man avoided him easily, sprinting into the woods.

Knox went after him, tearing through the trees. He followed the man's mellow, taunting chuckle from tree to tree, but never caught sight of his quarry. He stopped to catch his breath in a small clearing covered in ferns.

From a short distance away, he heard Evelyn calling to him.

"Knox! Knox! I'm okay."

"I'm over here," he shouted back. "That guy is gone."

Evelyn burst into the clearing, her eyes wide and resolved.

"Knox, we have to find Chase. We have to get back to Ayda before Dankar gets the stone of Metria. We have to help Rothermel and Rysta and Seaborne and Calla—*and Mara!*" Her throat thickened with a sudden lump.

"Okay . . . now you sound as bonkers as the elf," Knox said. "What are you *talking* about?"

"She is talking about those you were once close to—those whom you called your friends." Chantarelle's voice burbled up from somewhere beyond the clearing. "Your kin. *Ayda.* She remembers now; do you choose to, foolish child?"

"I don't know what the heck you're talking about!" cried Knox, pounding at his thighs. "I think I'm going nuts!"

In a blink, Chantarelle was beside him, whacking him on the knee with his small fist. "You are stubborn. You persist where you should yield." He pointed to the ground, indicating that Knox should kneel down. "I am giving you the opportunity to remember what you have lost."

Knox looked down at the man's head. He was shorter than Teddy, but ten times as strong. He had the feeling he'd be outmatched, even if he could ever get the guy to stand still long enough to fight.

Evelyn caught his elbow.

"Don't you see, Knox? That's why we've all been feeling so weird! It's the fog. But you—you're a Melorian. That's why you've been acting like a caged animal. And Teddy, all the flushing and washing; it's because he's a Metrian. And why Chase has been sleeping and dreaming those awful dreams—and *Frankie!*"

She cried out in a flash of understanding, connecting the dots.

"It's why she's sick. She was held captive in Exor by Dankar. He must have done something to her, made her sick." Her voice rose in urgency. "*Ayda,* Knox. You have to remember! The island! We have to get back there. So many lives are at stake. Let Chantarelle breathe on your necklace—you'll see in a minute. Please, we don't have much time."

Knox looked at her and then at Chantarelle, and then back at Evelyn. Her eyes were imploring him. She nodded and mouthed *Do it!*

Chantarelle yanked at his shirt. "Time's a-wasting, child."

Knox gave in. He sank slowly to his knees and closed his eyes.

Chantarelle held the bead on Knox's necklace up to his lips, exhaling loudly.

Knox's vision blurred as Seaborne's face came swimming into view, the first of many images that flipped wildly in his mind's eye, gaining speed and meaning. Knox cried out loud when the image of Tinator, lying dead—or near to death—came to the surface, backlit by a waxing moon. He saw it all—everything that had happened to the five of them since they'd awoken in the fog and come upon the shores of the island of Ayda. He could see Seaborne, just as he was the first day they met him, with his long ropes of hair and the broadsword strapped on his back. He remembered the path up the cliff from the beach that led to Seaborne's cabin, an outpost at the edge of the ancient forest of Melor. He saw the faces of his friends, the Melorians, who had taught them all to survive in the forest: Tinator; his wife, Mara; and their daughter, Calla; and the soldiers, Duelle and Duor. And, alongside them, the great hounds of Melor: Axl and Tar.

He heard Seaborne's voice in his head saying, "There are four realms on Ayda. All who live within them are there because their daylights insist upon it, and they, in turn, are subject to each realm's Keeper." *The daylights*, Knox thought to himself, his excitement growing. *The Keepers.* They were the guardians of the four stones of power on Ayda that ruled the daylights, which were the divided essences of the great life energy—the *atar*—that resides in all living things and connects all life forms to each other. Each realm was named for its stone. There was the green, wooded vale of Melor kept by the mighty Rothermel; the jungles and waterlands of Metria ruled by his sister Rysta; the glaciers and mountains of Varuna that lay beneath their sister Ratha's watchful eye; and finally, the desert plateaus and sandstone canyons of Exor, whose stone was once kept by their brother Ranu. Long ago, during the Great Battle on Ayda, Ranu had been killed, his stone stolen, and his lands usurped by the Keepers' corrupt cousin, Dankar.

Knox's memory of the rest of their time on Ayda came rushing back all at once. He remembered Frankie's capture at the cabin and the sky crossing to the Wold, where he had met Rothermel. He remembered the fight with the Exorians. He saw the flight into Metria on horseback and their exile into Varuna. He recalled the blind panic and the battle at the edge of the canyon in Exor, where Seaborne was almost killed; and then, he remembered Rysta. The Keeper of Metria had come to their rescue and exchanged her life for theirs.

And finally, he remembered why: the Fifth Stone. The stone that contained the full force of the *atar* and balanced out the other four. It could defeat Dankar once and for all, but it had been missing—or lost—for centuries. Ratha and Rothermel believed that Captain Nate had the stone—or knew who had it. They had met on Ayda during the time of the Great Battle, when he was called Caspar. There was no other explanation the Keepers could think of to explain why he had lived so long in the world beyond the fog other than the presence of the Fifth Stone. For this reason, they had sent Knox and his brothers and Evelyn and Frankie back through the fog to convince the explorer to return to Ayda before it was too late. The man—who at the time had answered to the name Caspar—had loved their sister Rysta above all others. If Captain Nate was indeed this man, he would not let her die in Exor. He would not let Dankar take her stone. It all hinged on him—but first he had to know Rysta was imprisoned.

A surge of energy pulsed from the bead in his necklace down to the ground and back again, setting his limbs tingling. And he knew in an instant what it was.

The daylights.

"What are we waiting for?" Knox cried, leaping to his feet.

Chantarelle smiled.

"That is *exactly* the right question."

Chapter 5

DENIALS

Two miles away, Chase was knocking on Captain Nate's door as if his knuckles were made of iron. He held a small bundle in his other hand. The bike he had ridden over was pitched on the grass, the upturned front wheel still spinning. He peered into a side window; it was so dark inside he couldn't see anything. He banged on the door again. No answer.

He circled the house and scaled the fretted boards that supported the small deck at the back of the house. A slate of gray-blue sea rolled out in front of him, coated in mist. Captain Nate's dock lay ahead, stretched across the rocky beach, and his boat, the *Mary Louise,* was tied up alongside the float. Chase peered through the two dusky glass doors that separated the deck from the house.

The Captain's living room opened at one end onto a modest kitchen, with a small refrigerator, a stove, and a round table set for one. A large fireplace was at the other end, flanked by bookshelves filled with—from what Chase could make out— the kind of books you sometimes see in libraries, bound in leather and embossed in gold. There was an armchair in front of the fireplace, a small table with an ancient-looking globe, and a reading lamp. From what Chase could see, the walls were papered in navigational charts. The room was empty, with a deserted feel to it. No

TV. No computer. No lights left on, or any sign that someone had been there recently.

Chase pressed his forehead into the glass, trying to think. If he were Captain Nate, where would he be? The truth was, Chase had absolutely no clue. He'd never given much thought to how Captain Nate spent his time. He'd never even thought of Captain Nate as a real person; he was just a grumpy old guy to steer clear of. He had never considered that Captain Nate might have a reason for being so unfriendly. It was a strange thought, and it reminded him of the few times he'd seen one of his teachers out of school—like at the grocery store or the Y. It was always a shock to realize they did all that kind of normal stuff.

Chase wished now that he had taken the trouble to ask Captain Nate a few personal questions. Gotten to know him a little.

Think, he said to himself. He was a Varunan—Ratha had told him as much—and Varunans were supposed to be master thinkers. He had been chosen for this . . . why? A kind of strangling fury rose at the back of his throat. *Why* had Ratha picked him?

For a second, the thought crossed his mind that he actually didn't *have* to do anything. They were all home now. Safe. He could just pretend that he'd never remembered Ayda or Dankar, Rysta or the Fifth Stone. He could just go back to being a normal almost-fourteen-year-old kid, downloading music and playing video games. Couldn't he?

Chase looked back out over the harbor. The water was still beneath the heavy sky, as if it were waiting for something. He had almost decided just to grab his bike and pedal home when the surface of the water rippled. Chase felt the breeze a second later. It teased his bangs and sent a familiar shiver up his neck.

Ratha.

He exhaled. The truth was, now that he had remembered Ayda and his task, life in Fells Harbor would never be normal again. Every moment felt weighted by his promise to the Aydans. Rothermel had told them that the difference between a life of pain and a life of peace was understanding one's daylights and how one was uniquely bound by them. Chase realized now that nobody—not he, nor Evelyn and Frankie, nor his brothers and his parents—would ever live in peace until the Keepers were free. And for that to happen, Chase had to get the Fifth Stone back where it belonged—to Ayda. At the very least, he had to try. He couldn't pretend he'd forgotten his promise. He had to find Captain Nate.

He walked to the deck railing, mentally going back to what he knew to be true—a trick he used when he took tests at school: go through and put down what you know first, then go back and try to figure out the stuff you don't.

This is what he knew so far:

1) Captain Nate had been at the rescue. He had known where to find them. This was proof positive that Ratha might be right: Captain Nate might be Caspar. He might have the Fifth Stone.

2) Except for one brief sighting at the hospital, no one had seen Captain Nate since the night of the rescue. Where had he gone? Had he run away? Chase doubted that. Captain Nate was many things—scary, weird, a loner—but he wasn't a coward. Maybe he was already back on Ayda. Chase's heart gave a little leap, then fell, because:

3) Captain Nate's truck and boat were here, which meant he had left town by some other means. How would he get to Ayda if not on his . . . *boat?*

"Holy crap!" Chase exclaimed out loud. His eyes shot to the dock. How could he be so dumb!

The *Mary Louise* had been on its mooring for the past three weeks, but now it was at the dock. That meant *somebody* had moved it. Chase couldn't imagine a single person who would have had the guts to touch that boat but Captain Nate.

Jumping over the deck railing and onto the grass, Chase sped as fast as he could down the hill onto the dock. He hit the ramp to the float so hard he lost his footing and somersaulted down the grade, grunting as he landed face-first. His knee was bloody where it had scraped the asphalt strips lining the ramp. He hoisted himself up and hobbled to the boat.

"Captain Nate! Are you in there?"

He listened for a minute, hearing nothing. The back of his neck prickled in fear. It hadn't occurred to him until now that it might be a trick. There might be something dangerous on the boat. If Ratha had figured out who Captain Nate was, maybe Dankar had, too.

"Captain Nate?" Chase whispered. "Where are you?"

Chase lingered on the float for a second or two, then screwed up his courage and put a foot on the edge of the boat. It pitched toward him gently. He took a deep breath and jumped into the cockpit, noticing that the hatch to the cabin was closed.

He leaned into the closed hatch and called in through the hinge.

"Please, Captain Nate, please—if you're in there, I need to talk to you. It's important!"

"If you need to talk, I'm right here," a gruff voice said somewhere behind him.

Chase nearly jumped out of his skin. He whipped around to see Captain Nate standing on the float, carrying a box of food and other supplies with a duffel bag strapped to his back.

"Don't know what you expect, son; that hatch is only made of wood—it can't talk back."

Chase's heart was hammering. Now that he was here, he had no idea what to say. In all his life he had never spent more than a second in Captain Nate's company. He peeked at the imposing man standing with one foot on the gunwale. He had on his customary fisherman's sweater and a black watch cap, and his beard was the same dingy white as his sweater. His eyes were bloodshot and bleached from the sun. One weathered hand clutched the box.

Captain Nate stared back at Chase for a long minute, then cleared his throat expectantly. His tone was fierce. "Boy, my boat is private prop—"

"Captain Nate!" Chase blurted. "I was looking for you. We have to get to Ayda—Rysta, she's in prison in Exor. Dankar wants the stone of Metria, and he'll destroy her—and Melor—to get it. We have to go now! We have to bring them the Fifth Stone!"

Captain Nate jumped into the cockpit and set the supplies down on the engine box. He moved slowly, never taking his eyes off Chase, as if he were dealing with a skittish horse—or a lunatic.

"Slow down, now," said Captain Nate. "You're mixed up. It happens when you've been through a shipwreck. Your mind's disordered and you're not making any sense. Does your mother know you're here? Let's give her a call, eh?"

Chase's eyes widened. Had Captain Nate not heard him?

"No! No one knows I'm here. I—I just got attacked by hundreds of gulls, and then lightning threw me off the roof and my head exploded when I hit the ground, and I *remembered!*"

Chase was yelling now.

"RATHA SENT ME!"

"Whoa, there—lightning? You fell off your roof? No wonder you're confused. You may have a concussion. Let's go back up to the house, and I'll get you some help—"

"NO!" Chase yelled, louder.

How could he get the Captain to give up his act?

"You were *there!* You knew where to find us. You know about Ayda and the fog of forgetting—Ratha told me who you are. You have to listen to me—*please.* They think we're coming back to help them."

Captain Nate stood motionless for a moment or two, then turned his rheumy, light blue eyes out to sea. When he looked back at Chase, his mouth was set tight.

"Listen, boy, you've been through an ordeal, and things still aren't put right, with that little girl still in the hospital. You're not clear in your head. I'll take you back home and that father of yours can check you out. He's a medical man, no? It's probably just the effect of too many days at sea. It can do that, you know, put wild imaginings in your head."

"But I'm *not* imagining it!" Chase felt his throat clench—and, humiliatingly, tears weren't far behind.

Captain Nate had stowed his duffel and was already back on the dock. The rain was falling harder.

"Your mother doesn't need any more worry. She's had enough for one lifetime; let's go up and give her a call." Captain Nate held out his hand as if to help escort Chase off the boat.

Chase stared at him. He couldn't believe what he was hearing. Had the fog made Captain Nate forget, too? It didn't make sense. If he really was the Keeper of the Fifth Stone, the fog wouldn't work on him. So either he was not the person Ratha thought he was, or he was lying.

He's lying, said a woman's voice in Chase's head. Chase clapped his hands to either side of his head. Now he was hearing voices . . . maybe he was going crazy.

"Come along now, Chase," said Captain Nate, his voice stern. "I'm not going to stand in the rain getting soaked through. Let's get inside."

Chase's thoughts tumbled around his head frantically. He had to get through to Captain Nate. Suddenly, he remembered his little bundle, the one he'd packed so carefully before he left Summerledge and stowed in the front basket of the bike. He'd almost forgotten he was still holding it. He gripped it harder.

"Okay. How about this: I'll get off your boat if you promise to listen to me for a minute before you call my parents? I want to show you something and tell you a story. If you don't want to help me after that, I'll go away."

Captain Nate nodded once and ushered Chase up the gangplank. They climbed the steep hill and entered the dark house through the glass doors. The air inside the house felt clammy. Captain Nate lit the fire laid in the fireplace, and it roared to life. They gravitated toward the warmth, letting the fire dry their wet clothing. Standing side by side, Chase noticed how tall the Captain was, and how the man's sweater smelled of wool and mildew and woodsmoke. It was a scent that reminded him of the first night on Ayda, in Seaborne's cabin.

"How about we call your mother now, Chase?" said Captain Nate. The rain beat a loud pattern overhead.

Chase avoided the question by turning to examine the bookshelves on either side of the fireplace. The titles on the books' spines were in a foreign language.

"What language is that?" he asked. "I took Spanish last year, but I'm no good at it."

"You wanted to tell me a story, boy; let's proceed with that, and then you can go home where you belong."

Chase hesitated. Where should he start?

He turned back, watching the flames curl and lick over the dried wood in the fireplace, burning like Melor might be burning now. He decided to just jump in.

He went to retrieve his bundle and untied it, slowly laying out the pile of sand dollars he'd taken from the kitchen, one after the other, onto the mantelpiece.

"I think she's sending us a message," Chase said. "Look."

He pointed to the row of sand dollars.

Captain Nate grunted, eyes tracing the ridges and patterns of the shells.

"Knox says they're all over the beach," said Chase. "I never noticed until today that there are *five* slits in the shell, and five petals at the center." He glanced sideways at the Captain. "Tinator told us once that there are reminders of the *atar* everywhere. All you have to do is look. Do you remember the *atar*? I didn't, until about an hour ago. I didn't remember anything about Ayda. All I remembered was that you were there when we were rescued. I saw your face, in the helicopter. You led them to us. How did you know where we would be?"

"I know fog—and I know what it is to be lost at sea," said Captain Nate.

He crossed to the bookcase and removed a slender, leather-bound book from the top shelf. He passed it to Chase. The pages were filled with spidery handwriting in the same strange language that appeared on the spines of the books.

"It's Portuguese."

"What?" Chase mumbled, not understanding.

"This book, and the others—they are written in Portuguese, not Spanish. This one here is a ship's log. I was born in Portugal, and like you, I had two brothers. We were—all three of us—explorers and navigators. I was once the captain of a ship that went to many faraway places. I am the eldest of my brothers—again, like you. And I was also the most impulsive and inquisitive. I never took to being on land. The sea called to me, and I answered, whenever and for as long as I could. I traveled farther and longer than either of my brothers, through waters known and unknown. Always seeking, always restless. Never sated. I know my way around the ocean—that is how I found you."

Chase looked up from the book.

"I don't believe you. You know more than that: You've been to Ayda. You know about the fog of forgetting. Ratha sent me back through the fog to find you. She says you are the only one who can help."

Chase swallowed, screwing up his courage.

"They're in trouble, Captain Nate. Tinator's dead; the Exorians killed him. And the Melorians—they're about to lose the stone of Melor. And Metria is going to be next. Rysta needs you."

Captain Nate pressed his palms to his face and rubbed his bloodshot eyes. The room fell into deep silence except for the hiss and crackle of the fire consuming the logs, and the *tippity-tap* of the rain on the roof.

Chase waited. A large fire ant scuttled out of its hiding place and down the length of a log, trying—and failing—to escape. He tried again.

"Listen, I don't know what's happened to you, or why you're even here when you should be long dead"—Chase's voice rose—"but those people on Ayda? They *trusted* you. Rothermel said you were like his own brother. And Rysta? I've never met anyone so sad. She loves you still, after everything—even after you ran away and took the Fifth Stone and left them to fight and die! I always knew you weren't nice, but you're worse than that. You're a traitor and a thief and a—"

"Enough," said Captain Nate, cutting him off with a hand. "You need to leave my house, now. I will not stand for this. You know nothing about me. Now, go home—and don't come back, or I will have you arrested for trespassing!"

He brushed the sand dollars violently off the mantel. They smashed into shell and sand on the brick hearth of the fireplace.

Chase was speechless. He looked down at the shattered sand dollars and back at Captain Nate. Anger had sparked the Captain's eyes into life.

"Go . . . now!" he said, pointing at the door.

"You led Dankar to Ayda, and now you are going to let him steal all of the stones?" said Chase. His face was burning.

The Captain didn't reply.

"And I thought I was a coward!" Chase said, throwing the Captain's book onto the tattered armchair in disgust. He moved to the door.

"Ratha thinks you have the Fifth Stone, you know. And if you are lying to me and pretending you don't know anything, and they all die—if *Frankie* dies? It's on you, mister. It's ALL on you. My little brother Teddy is braver than you. He stopped Dankar from killing Seaborne—and he's only six!"

Chase swore and stormed out the door. He picked up his bike and pedaled it furiously back up the road toward Summerledge, fuming. If Captain Nate wasn't going to go back to Ayda, Chase would get Evelyn and Knox and Teddy to help him find the Fifth Stone himself. He'd steal it from Captain Nate if he had to, and then he'd figure out a way to get it to Ratha.

"I tried, Ratha!" he screamed into the air.

A car horn behind him made him peel off onto the sandy shoulder. His front tire spun out and he went flying over the handlebars. He landed in the gully by the side of the road and rolled over on his back, too dazed to get up.

A car door slammed, footsteps, and there was Captain Nate, standing over him.

For the second time that morning, Chase thought he was going to cry in front of this man. He bit his tongue to stop himself. He didn't want to give Captain Nate the satisfaction.

Captain Nate held out his hand to help Chase up.

Chase brushed it away.

"All right, Chase. All right," said the Captain, squatting in the dirt.

Chase sat up.

"I know you led Dankar to Ayda, *Caspar*. Now you have to make it right."

Captain Nate sighed and looked him in the eye.

"Now *that* is a name I have not heard in a very long time."

Chapter 6

PREPARATIONS

Each day, more refugees crossed into Metria to avoid the fighting in Melor. From her vantage point high above the blue rooftops of the City of Metria, Urza looked out the watchtower window as a band of hooded Melorians was escorted into the city by guards. One could always spot Melorians from the way they walked: a long, loping stride meant to cover great distances. Even the small children strode with legs of grown men and women. She wondered if the same could be true for Metrians. Could they be identified by the way their knees swayed and buckled when they walked, as if they were balancing themselves on the deck of a boat?

Ah . . . what did it matter anyway? Urza asked herself. Melorian. Metrian. They were all extinguishable. Dankar advanced on Metria each day, and each day the power of the stone of Metria grew dimmer. If Dankar had the Melorian stone, it would not take much to overthrow the city and find the stone of Metria. Urza shuddered at the thought of Dankar possessing *three* stones of power. There would be no restraining him. All of Ayda, and—should he be able to lift the fog with his new powers—all of the lands beyond would be subject to him. She hoped her daylights would be fragmented before that day, but it felt all too near. Once the Exorian army had reduced Melor to an ash heap, it was only a matter of time before they came here. And then they would go everywhere.

Urza moved across the circular room to another window. Below she could see the domed, blue rooftops of the buildings, separated by narrow canals fed by the flowing waters of the great Hestredes. The beauty of the city filled her with pride—even now, when its walls were cloaked in fear.

Urza paced to the north window. Somewhere, far beyond sight, lay the mountains, and Varuna. She herself had only been as far as the grottoes that lay south of Lake Voss, but she knew from what Rysta had told her that it was the mountains that fed the rivers and lakes. Varuna was an austere and isolated region, and in this, its power was undeniable. The Exorians might lay waste to Melor and Metria, but they would beat themselves senseless against the cold and unmerciful mountains. This idea gave her some comfort. Everything she knew might fail, but her enemy would never conquer the bones of Ayda.

But this was not what she should be thinking of now. Her duty was to her Keeper, Rysta, and to the people of Metria. And when the time came, she would ring the warning and gather them into the hidden chambers below the city. She smiled. The Varunans might have their mountains, but Metrians could swim like dolphins.

But what about the Melorians? said a small voice inside her. *What is to become of them?*

Urza pulled her robes around her in irritation. Rysta had not told her what to do, nor had the Keeper imagined a day when Melorians would need rescue. But then again, Rysta had not told them about many things, including her plan to surrender herself to Dankar in exchange for the outliers.

Or—as many had come to believe—traitors and spies.

There were those in Metria, and more every day, who claimed the children had been sent into Metria by Dankar for just such a purpose. And now that Rysta was gone, there was no one to argue it. Nor had the children reappeared, so perhaps it was true. Perhaps they *had* tricked Rysta into giving up her life, as she had been tricked before by an outlier.

Urza had not yet been born in the days of the Great Battle, when the four stones had been forged and the Fifth Stone had disappeared, along with its Keeper, Remiel, and the explorer Caspar, but she had heard all of the tales. She knew intimately of Rysta's great sadness and shame, and of the love she still felt for Caspar. Bane of Ayda.

Light footsteps on the stairs brought her to attention. The shining helmet of a Metrian guard preceded the person who emerged through the hatch in the floor.

"Hesam," said Urza in greeting. She held up her palm, fingers splayed. "What news?"

"There's been a shift," said Hesam, breathless either from excitement or the steep climb up the tower steps. She removed her helmet, and her long, light-colored hair spilled out over her armored shoulders. A curved sword was sheathed on her belt and the purple tunic of a Metrian soldier flowed beneath her metal vest. She grazed her own fingertips across Urza's.

Urza surveyed her closely, looking for signs of strain.

Hesam blamed herself for the outliers' treachery and Rysta's undoing. It was she who had taught the eldest boy, Chase, how to navigate the river and move around Ayda. She had shown him maps and taught him how to find his place by looking at the stars. When the children had run off with Rysta's necklace, Hesam realized her mistake. She had given the boy just enough knowledge to have a dangerous amount of confidence. She should have left him in the dark. She had been willing to pursue them all the way into Varuna, but Rysta had forbidden it.

Urza could not understand why—and even less so now. She sympathized with Hesam. Ever since the outliers had come to Metria, they had wrought nothing but disaster.

"A shift?" Urza prompted.

Hesam nodded.

"You are sure?"

"Yes, I am sure. Someone is coming. Trying to pierce the fog."

"Can you tell if it is friend or foe?"

Hesam shook her head.

"No. I am not good at that, as you well know."

"None of us are, Hesam. They are one and the same all too often. Come, we must prepare."

Urza touched Hesam's shoulder as she passed toward the stairwell.

Hesam frowned.

"Urza, tell me—do you think it is wise to allow yet another outlier on our shores, even one who supposedly comes bearing such a gift? We have not been lucky with outliers."

Urza smiled. No one had been more surprised than she to hear Ratha's plans to bring the Fifth Stone back to Ayda. For most of her life, Urza had believed the legend of the Fifth Stone to be no more than that: a story told to explain the injustice of what had happened to Ayda. Its loss was more real than its existence. To find out now that it *did* exist; that it was solid and possibly near was almost beyond comprehension. It was like finding out that one could touch a rainbow. However, Urza reminded herself, the Fifth Stone was not here yet. It all still might be just a story. Urza was wary of the wind-talker, and unsure of her own mind in the Keeper of Varuna's presence. It was good to have a confidante in Hesam, whom she knew she could trust in this business.

"We do not have a choice, Hesam. We must do this. We will not trust the outlier, but we must trust the sister of our Keeper, no?"

"I'm not sure about that. What is Ratha's game, anyway? Why should she be mistress of us? Perhaps it would be better just to keep the seafarer here. After all, it is where the Exorians are headed. We can use his gift to defend ourselves against them."

"That is why he cannot stay here," said Urza, descending the stairs. "We cannot risk his—or its—capture."

Chapter 7

AN UNEXPECTED TURN

Knox and Evelyn left Chantarelle in the woods to search one more time for Chase. Knox did a quick scout of the beach. Evelyn took another pass through the house. She waited for Knox in the empty kitchen.

"We'll have to go without him," Knox announced, coming through the screen door empty-handed.

"How?"asked Evelyn.

Knox shrugged his shoulders.

"We'll go to Captain Nate's. He'll know what to do. And maybe Chase is there already. His note said he remembered something he had to do."

"Captain Nate's been gone for weeks! And what about Frankie and Teddy and my grandmother—and your parents? I don't want them to worry about us. It feels wrong to just leave them again."

"We'll think of something," said Knox, sounding more confident than he felt. "Write a note. Tell them we had to go somewhere with Captain Nate. Tell them we're with Chase."

"But that's *lying!*" exclaimed Evelyn.

Knox gave her an exasperated look.

"I think we need to tell someone what's happened," she insisted.

Knox snorted.

"Like they'd believe us. C'mon, Evelyn. Are you in or are you out? Do you want those fireworms to trash Melor and Metria! You were so sure back in the forest; what's happened?"

He was grabbing anything handy to stuff into his backpack: a couple of jam jars, some garden twine and matches, and a long, two-tonged fork they used for the grill. Then he layered in any available energy bars and chip packets and drinks.

Evelyn crossed her arms.

"I'm trying to be *smart* about this, Knox—I mean, we should do some planning. After all, how are we supposed to get back to Ayda? It's not like we have a map. We're not *supposed* to be able to find it. That's why the fog is there. And what if we land in the wrong place at the wrong time?"

"That's what these are for!"

Knox gave her a mischievous grin as he pulled four sharp kitchen knives out of the drawer under the counter. He stuffed them in the bandolier he was wearing. The hilts felt good against his chest.

"Just write the note, Evelyn. We'll go over to Captain Nate's and figure out the rest. If he has the Fifth Stone, we won't be gone very long."

"That's a big *if*—and what about Frankie?"

Knox fingered the hilts of the knives sticking out of his bandolier in a gesture at once so familiar and so foreign that Evelyn had to smile. He looked at her out of the corner of his eye.

"Don't you think it's strange—I mean, Frankie's the only one who's sick and all, and she was the only one of us who spent a lot of time in Exor. I think it's Dankar who's *making* her sick—or maybe it's her daylights. It just feels like it has to be related. If we can get to the bottom of this Fifth Stone thing with Chase, then maybe we can help Frankie."

Evelyn gave him a sharp look. He wasn't kidding.

"Give me a pen!" she said.

He handed her one from a kitchen drawer, and she furiously scribbled a note on the back of an envelope.

Hi everyone,

I was missing my grandmother, so Knox and I are taking the bus over to see her and Frankie at the hospital.

She bit the end of the pen. It was a weak story, but it might buy them enough time to find Chase, and maybe even Captain Nate. She reread it and then, thinking about Chantarelle, added at the bottom:

Teddy: Knox and I found the thing that lives in the cave. It explains everything. If you have any questions, go to the cave.

Evelyn

She knew the note was cryptic, but if they were gone a long time, maybe Teddy—or his mom and dad—would look in the cave and find Chantarelle.

She and Knox slipped on rain jackets and unknowingly followed Chase's exact route to Captain Nate's. They, too, knocked on the door and peered through the dark windows along the door, and then ran around to the deck just in time to see the stern of a lobster boat steaming away, headed toward the open sea.

"I think that's Captain Nate's boat," said Knox, slumping against the house. "Now what do we do?"

"We'll just wait for him to come back," said Evelyn. "He's probably gone to pull his traps. He's been away; he probably has a lot of work to do."

"Maybe . . ."

"I guess we'll know either way pretty soon."

Evelyn went to the front of the house and stopped in her tracks. They had been in such a rush that she hadn't noticed it before: one of the bikes from Summerledge was lying in the back of Captain Nate's pickup.

"Knox! He was here. Chase has been here!" Evelyn shouted.

Knox came loping around the corner of the house. Evelyn pointed to the bike. Their eyes met. Chase must have remembered! He'd beat them here and told Captain Nate!

Evelyn lifted the bike out of the truck bed and patted the seat. She rode Knox double, back toward Summerledge.

"I can't let Rothermel down," said Knox, shifting uncomfortably on the seat behind Evelyn, who was keeping the bike balanced by pedaling hard. "You know what's at stake! Dankar will ruin everything! The Exorians hate Melor. They'll burn down the whole forest and everyone in it. They'll take the stone of Melor! And Rysta—don't you feel bad about her, Evelyn?"

"I know, I know . . ."

She stood to pedal them up a small hill.

"I just think . . . Knox, maybe we could tell your parents. Maybe they could help?"

Knox rolled his eyes.

"Yeah, help us all the way into a padded room. They would never believe us."

They turned into the driveway. On their right, scraggly trees and shrubs poked out of the gloom of the waning afternoon. The sight sparked an idea in Evelyn's brain. She pedaled faster.

"I know! Let's ask Chantarelle!"

"You're right! You're totally right! He'll know what to do!"

Knox almost hugged her in his excitement, but settled for grabbing more tightly at the sides of her T-shirt as she picked up the pace.

They dumped the bike at the head of the path into the woods.

"Chantarelle!" Knox shouted, running quickly toward the little cave. "Chantarelle!"

Chantarelle appeared so suddenly that Knox almost tripped over him.

"Shhh, child! I'm right here!"

"Captain Nate! He left—on his boat," Knox panted.

"Is Chase with him? Does he know?" Evelyn added, catching up to Knox. Chantarelle nodded.

"So it's *done*, then. They're going back with the Fifth Stone!" she cried happily. "Ayda is saved! Chase did it!"

Chantarelle said nothing.

Evelyn repeated herself. "Chase *did* do it, right?"

"I am not exactly sure what you mean by *it*," answered Chantarelle. "If you are implying that the eldest has convinced the man you know as Captain Nate to accompany him back into the fog in search of Ayda, then you would be correct."

"*Right,*" pressed Knox. "Chase did what he was supposed to do. He kept his promise to Ratha. He found the Keeper of the Fifth Stone, and they're going back to Ayda to use the stone to seriously kick some Exorian butt."

Chantarelle cocked his head. "And you would be incorrect."

Knox glared down at Chantarelle's head—what he could see of it in the growing darkness. He hitched the backpack higher on his shoulder.

"What are you saying?"

"I'm saying that your brother has completed one part of his promise: he has found the great warrior, Caspar, who was thought to have died in the Great Battle. He has convinced this man to guide him back to Ayda, yes—"

"All of which is possible because they have the Fifth Stone, right?" asked Knox.

Chantarelle shook his head.

Evelyn stood up, confused.

"I don't understand," she said. "You told us you were here at the call of the Keeper of the Fifth Stone. Are you saying that's *not* Captain Nate? But how? I mean, how could he have lived so long if he's not the Keeper? He *must* have it!"

Chantarelle shrugged; at least, she thought he did. It was hard to see him clearly.

"I did not say the Captain had no knowledge of the stone. But its possession . . . I think not."

Knox rubbed his temples. "So, what you're saying is that Captain Nate doesn't actually *have* the Fifth Stone, but he knows where it is?"

"Perhaps, or at least, he once did. He was sent from Ayda so long ago, at the same time it was lost. I am certain he was party to what happened."

Chantarelle gave each of them a pointed look.

"He is attached to it, that is certain, but *how* is still a question I cannot answer."

Evelyn took a deep breath. "But if Captain Nate isn't the Keeper and he isn't going to Ayda with the Fifth Stone—then they're going back with nothing. Worse than nothing! Right now, the only advantage the Aydans have is the fact that Dankar is as much in the dark as they are. If Dankar finds Captain Nate first, it's over."

Chantarelle receded slightly into the shadows.

"I agree. You are right in thinking it is not as easy as Ratha made it appear. But do not forget: the Captain was once a great leader of men. They do not return entirely disadvantaged."

A rustle of twigs and a sigh revealed that Chantarelle was moving some distance off. He was hard to see in broad daylight; in the late-afternoon dusk, with rain bouncing off the leaves of the trees, it was nearly impossible.

"Chantarelle," called Evelyn. "Don't leave!"

"I was sent to remind you of your promises. The eldest has fulfilled his obligation. The rest is out of my hands."

"But . . . but . . . how can they beat Dankar when he has Exor and Rysta? What if he already has her stone? Chase could be sailing into a disaster!"

Evelyn took a deep, shuddering breath.

"Chantarelle! You must tell us where the Fifth Stone is. You were sent by the Keeper of the Fifth Stone. You have to take us to him!"

"That I cannot do."

"AARRGH!" Knox shouted in frustration. "Why? Why is it such a big secret?"

Chantarelle's answer came from quite a distance away.

"The power of the Fifth Stone is ancient, forged long ago when the fate of the world and all who would prosper by the stone lay in peril. Its ways are mysterious, and its force must only be used at the bitter end, when all other attempts have faded. Once it has been found, and its power used, nothing will ever be the same again—and that's only if it can indeed be found."

"None of this makes any sense!" Knox almost sobbed. "Why would Ratha send us back for the stone if Captain Nate doesn't really have it?"

"We don't know anything for certain, except that Chase and Captain Nate are gone," said Evelyn. "We'll just have to go back to the house and try to explain that as best we can. What do you think your parents will say?"

Knox's shoulders sagged. How could he go home now and just *wait?* He stared blindly at the ground, in silence.

"I can't, Evelyn. I can't leave Chase and Seaborne and the Melorians." He shook his head in the dark.

"I *won't!* I have to go back and fight! I'll steal another boat—or I'll swim!"

Evelyn scanned what she could see of his face. She remembered the night she'd stolen the necklace from Rysta. She'd had Knox's unquestioning support, and knew that he would follow her, no matter the consequences. Knox must have seen the same wild look in her eyes then that she was now seeing in his. She thought about Frankie, so fragile-looking in her hospital bed. But Frankie had their grandmother and Teddy had his parents. Even Chase had Captain Nate. She and Knox had no one but each other right now.

She put her hand out.

"All right, Knox. Whatever you want to do, I'll do it with you."

"Even if it means never coming back—leaving Frankie forever?"

Evelyn paused. "We came back once. We can do it again."

Knox grabbed her hand and pumped it.

"Deal. We'll bike down to the docks and try to steal a boat. Lots of people leave their keys in the ignition—"

He was interrupted by Chantarelle's whisper slipping through the trees.

"Ask me a question, and I will tell you the answer."

Knox and Evelyn exchanged glances. This time they knew what to say.

"How do we get back to Ayda?" asked Evelyn.

Chantarelle's small form seemed to rise suddenly out of the moss and pine bracken on the forest floor. His face was in shadows.

"There is a secret way . . . a long way. You must be sure you want to make the journey."

"Just take me to Ayda—and my brother," said Knox.

"And you . . . do you want this as well?" he queried Evelyn.

She nodded.

Chantarelle led them to the rock outcropping that marked the mouth of the cave where the three of them had first met.

"Remember your words, as you may come to regret them. The way is through here," he said, then disappeared into the mouth of the cave.

"I knew it! I told Chase—this cave goes somewhere!" Knox whispered.

"Yeah, I guess it does."

Evelyn's heart was beating so hard she could feel her shirt shake.

"Knox, you need to know something about me. I'm not good with tunnels and things, ever since the earthquake. I don't like going underground. It brings up bad memories."

Knox stopped in his tracks. He'd forgotten. When Evelyn and Frankie had lived in Haiti, there was a big earthquake. It had killed their father.

"It's okay, Ev, if you don't want to go. I understand."

"I didn't say that—just hold on a minute."

She bent down and swept a pile of tiny pinecones into the lap of her shirt. She pulled off her necklace with the wooden bead that Rothermel had given her and hung it on a low branch outside the mouth of the cave.

"What are you doing?" asked Knox.

"Leaving a trail. I told Teddy to look for us here if we don't come back. Now he'll know we went this way."

"All set?" asked Knox.

"Ready."

They got on all fours and scrambled after Chantarelle into the dark.

Chapter 8

THE WAY BACK

The *Mary Louise* skimmed the pebbled surface of the ocean, easily reaching ten knots, then twelve, out the Eastern Way. Chase took note of the familiar islands he'd known since his babyhood as they flew by under a steady downpour of rain: Goat, Squirrel, the Ducks. They pushed farther into open sea. Captain Nate said few words, his eyes darting back and forth over the small chop, looking for something.

How long would it be before they reached Ayda?

Captain Nate hadn't said much on the subject—only that they had to head in the direction of the fog bank that usually sat far to the northeast of Fells Harbor. The only problem was, they hadn't seen a fog bank. They'd been traveling at a steady clip, and the only thing on the horizon was rain and storm clouds. And soon it would be dark.

Chase tried not to think about Knox, Frankie, and Evelyn, or his parents and Teddy. He hoped the note would stop them from worrying too much, but knowing his mom, it wouldn't work for long.

The boat heaved as it took on some larger swells.

Captain Nate shifted to neutral, stalling the boat. He continued to stare at the water.

"What are you looking for?" cried Chase. "Fog?"

"No—water."

"Water! Are you kidding me? We can't get away from it!"

He looked at the rain sheeting off the roof of the cockpit and beyond to the stern, where their wake was illuminated in a funnel of eerie yellow light.

"I thought you knew where to go. That was the whole point!"

"I never said that," said Captain Nate. "I only said I'd been there. My memory isn't what it once was. Half of a millennium is a long time."

"*Great.* That's reassuring!" yelled Chase over a booming clap of thunder. A millisecond later, a huge bolt of lightning cracked the sky open. Captain Nate stood up eagerly, cranking the wheel to port.

"What's happening?" Chase scrambled to hold on to something as the boat pitched left.

"There it is."

Chase peered over the gunwale. All he saw was more ocean.

"What?"

"The calm patches in the chop. It's called watchwater. You've seen it around Fells Harbor; you've just never known what it is. Swum through it, too, I bet. It's colder than the rest of the water around it."

Chase squinted to see through the sluicing rain. The only thing he could make out was a sheet of gray water being pounded by rain. He had a sudden flash of his father's face, his mother and Knox and Teddy. He saw them gathered together in the kitchen at Summerledge, a fire roaring in the woodstove. He was overcome with doubts. Why had he left his family so suddenly? And then he thought about Evelyn. He might never see her—or any of them—again. The sense of loneliness that came over him was so profound, it made his throat ache.

He turned away.

Captain Nate was watching him.

"It will ease," he said, with more kindness. "It's a particular kind of melancholy. It comes from the watchwater. It's going to take us to Ayda."

"It is?" gulped Chase. The lump in his throat made it hard to talk.

"Whenever a patch of watchwater is crossed, it sends a signal back to Metria—to Rysta. That's how the Metrians monitor the seas, and how they guard their shores. Watchwater moves at random with the tides, although it can be set in a pattern, like a map. Rysta once set it for me, and I could see it, like a smooth trail across the surface of the sea—but I felt it, too, when longing filled my heart. It was an easy course to navigate once I found it."

The Captain squinted as another strobe of lightning lit up the sky. He glanced at Chase out of the corner of his eye.

"I used it to find you when you capsized. Watchwater is easier to see from the air."

Chase said nothing; his heart ached as much as his throat. It was beyond uncomfortable, and he felt like jumping overboard and swimming straight back to Summerledge. He did not know how Captain Nate could stand it.

"How long does it last?" He had to grit his teeth.

The Captain had no chance to reply before lightning crackled again across the sky, turning it into night-day—and there it was, right under a large thundershower. A ribbon of water, clear and smooth as metal, slicing through the churning swells like a thoroughfare through a hilly landscape. Captain Nate had the bow pointed straight down the middle.

"There, Chase—our way back."

Chase hugged himself to stop his teeth from chattering. He couldn't help wondering, back to what?

The storm moved slowly to the west. It grew colder. The Captain threw Chase a flashlight. He turned it on and looked over the side of the boat. Misty curls of fog rose up into the light.

"Look!" he shouted. "Fog!"

"True," agreed Captain Nate. "Not the kind we are specifically in search of, but given our chances, we'll idle here until daybreak."

He made a few calculations and set the autopilot.

"The computer will captain while we get ready."

He nodded at Chase and they descended into the cabin, where the Captain shuffled around, opening tins of what looked like beans and some brown, pudding-like bread. He handed one of the tins to Chase and took another up to the helm, saying, "Best eat something, and then you should sleep. It could be a while yet."

✛   ✛   ✛

Chase didn't know how long he'd slept, but when he woke up, the *Mary Louise* was dead quiet. His head felt heavy on the pillow, and empty. Delightfully empty. Familiarly empty! Like that time they'd woken up in the fog after the picnic to Little Duck. Of course . . . *the fog!*

With a lurch, Chase hurled himself out of the bunk and landed smack on the floor. He climbed up the hatch to the deck, and into a cloud. The fog was so thick it was hard to know if it was dawn or full day. The engines were silent, the boat quietly floating wherever the current took it.

Chase swiveled his eyes toward the helm.

The Captain was slumped over the wheel.

"Oh no!" he groaned, scrambling over to the limp form. *Please don't be dead, please don't be dead,* he chanted under his breath as he lifted the Captain's head, then dropped it with a loud yell. The man slumped over the wheel was the same size as the Captain. Same shape. He was still wearing the dingy wool fisherman's sweater, the dark wool pants—but the hair was different. Darker, and more of it. And the *face.*

Chase did a double take.

It was . . . *younger.*

Chase put his hands over his eyes and rubbed them, hard. He took a deep breath, swung back, and grabbed the Captain's hair, yanking his head up and over so that the man now lay back against the chair, face up. It was weathered and tanned, and still sort of old-looking—but not ancient, the way it had been. The cheeks and lips were fuller and—Chase almost yelled again—this man had no beard!

Chase let go of the Captain's head and accidentally sent it slamming into the console. Captain Nate slid off the chair onto the deck, facedown, still unconscious. Chase gulped a few shallow breaths to steel himself, then bent toward the body again. He had to know who this was, and what the hell he'd done with Captain Nate. He watched the sweatered back carefully, hoping to see some movement, some sign of life.

"If you slam my head like that again, I will feed you to the seagulls," grunted Captain Nate beneath his nest of hair. He rolled over and stared hard at Chase. "Don't ever do that again, boy, unless you want to swim the rest of the way!"

Chase nodded, his jaw dropping. The voice was Captain Nate's and the face was similar—but it was like the fog had erased forty years.

Captain Nate sat up and rubbed his forehead.

"What are you staring at? Have you never seen a man asleep before?"

"Your beard's gone, and . . . and your face," Chase stammered. "You're . . . you're *younger*."

Captain Nate gave Chase an incredulous look, then stroked his jaw. His hand stopped mid-stroke. His fingers searched his chin and upper lip. "What in the world?"

Captain Nate rummaged around the hold under the console and came up with a signal mirror, flat and rectangular. He peered into it, examining his face in sections by moving the mirror around. A huge grin spread slowly across his face.

"It's the daylights, boy! They're getting stronger. We must be close!"

Chase shook his head.

"I don't understand. I know the daylights are stronger on Ayda, but—they can reverse aging?"

"If things are still as I remember, the body does not age on Ayda as it does beyond the fog. It remains strong until the daylights are fragmented. Perhaps, when one comes through the fog, it is only the age of the daylights that matters."

"Maybe," Chase said, sounding skeptical. "But whatever it is, it's going to take some getting used to. You just don't look like Captain Nate. You look like . . . like . . ."

His voice trailed off. He looked like the man they had seen in Rysta's pool in Metria.

"That's because Captain Nate is only a name. I have had many names over the last five hundred years, but the one I was born to, the one you were told, is Caspar de Real."

Chase sized him up. He seemed different in more ways than just his younger face: taller, more determined, with a strong voice free of any gravel or phlegm. A thrill of excitement passed through him. *He was right!* He *had* found Caspar, and would return with him to free Rysta and save Ayda—just as Ratha had asked him to do.

Fog poured into the boat over the gunwale. Captain Nate—or Caspar, Chase reminded himself—stood up.

Chase cupped his hand to catch a handful of fog.

"Do you know that the definition of insanity is doing the same thing over and over again and expecting a different result?" Chase asked.

"What does it mean if you keep doing it, expecting the *same* result?"

"Stupidity," said Chase, "especially when what you want is to get back to a place where one-quarter of the population wants to roast you alive."

Captain Nate caught his eye.

"The Exorians want this? I do not believe it. It was not so in my time. Then, they were the most powerful and brave Aydans. Ranu, their Keeper, was very strong. They are a hard people, but very just. I don't believe they would kill without cause."

"*Just?*" cried Chase. "You gotta be joking! They're crazy, bloodthirsty monsters." Chase quickly described the Exorian warriors he'd seen: their thick, scabbed skin and their blank eyes that only came alive when they were fighting. "They hate Rothermel, and steal from and attack Melor all the time. They killed Tinator!"

"You spoke of him before. I do not know this man. Who is this Tinator—a Melorian?"

Chase nodded. "A great Melorian leader."

The Captain's expression was grim. "Then Dankar has achieved what Remiel hoped to avoid by casting away the Fifth Stone. He has set the hearts of Aydans against one another." His voice dropped to a mutter. "It was all for nothing."

"I don't *get* you," said Chase, deciding to ask the question he had been thinking about silently. "Those people loved you! Why didn't you go back? It's like you don't even care."

Captain Nate grabbed him by his shirt.

The sudden movement made Chase wince. This younger version was very strong.

"How *dare* you say such a thing to me? You know nothing of what drives me. I have spent an age with only one longing in my heart. One thought. The despair you feel crossing the watchwater is nothing compared to my torment. If I had had it my way, I never would have left!"

Chase retreated to a corner of the deck, staring at the Captain, who gazed out across the fog-laden sea.

"Even now I am racked by doubt. I once brought a plague to Ayda's shores; I fear now that we are bringing her to her doom. The Fifth Stone was cast from Ayda for a reason; it was never meant to return. Nor was I. I am breaking a vow I made to someone I respect above all others by going back with you. You may have fulfilled your promise by bringing me thus, but I have forsaken mine."

"What promise? To who?"

The Captain shook his head. "That is not for you to know."

Fog rolled over the boat on all sides, until Chase could barely make out the Captain standing just four feet away.

"Well, if it makes you feel any better, it doesn't look like we'll be bringing anyone anything very soon," said Chase. "It looks more like we're lost."

The Captain laughed—a buoyant sound so sudden and hearty and uplifting, Chase whipped his head back to confirm that it had actually come from Captain Nate. He'd never heard him laugh before.

"Ah, son, you should know by now that I am *never* lost—at least when it comes to navigating on the water."

The Captain maneuvered his way to the edge of the boat, then reached over the side of the boat and dipped his hand in the water.

"Now what?" asked Chase.

"Now we wait."

✛   ✛   ✛

Something was different. Something subtle, like early morning light in a darkened room. The *Mary Louise* wasn't drifting anymore. It was moving with purpose across the surface of the water, despite the fact that the engines had stopped a while ago.

And there was something else.

Chase breathed in. The fog was different, denser and darker, and it stung his nose and lungs. He inhaled again through his mouth. It tasted bitter. *Like ash.*

A rustle nearby told him Captain Nate had joined him at the side of the boat.

"Can you feel it?"

The Captain's eyes were inscrutable, but his voice was tight with excitement. "We're almost there."

Chase tried to answer but his mouth was dry. His throat felt scratchy, and his eyes itched. The fog wasn't just fog anymore; it was smoke. Just like in his dream. Ayda *was* burning. The fog lifted a bit, or drew back, as if the ocean itself was inhaling.

"Look," Captain Nate exclaimed, with a nod to the sea.

Around them, the water lay without a ripple, smooth and glistening, like liquid silver. The boat moved across it in a silence so deep that when bubbles suddenly broke the surface, they sounded like gunshots. Chase stifled a yell. A large school of finger-length fish flashed just below the surface, moving one way, then another, in unison, like a flag waving.

Captain Nate bent over again and put a cupped hand over the side. A small shiver passed through the water. The Captain stood and went to the helm, Chase on his heels.

Just as it had happened before, Chase felt the wind shift, growing stronger. He looked back. A small wake followed them. The boat was going faster—just as the Whaler had done the first time. A gull cried far above them. Another answered.

Captain Nate looked up.

"Ready yourself."

"Where do you think we are?" Chase whispered, hoping against hope that the Captain would not say Exor.

"That is not up to us," said Captain Nate. His mouth was set in a line, the skin around it shadowed white. "Bring up the packs, Chase. It's time."

Chase couldn't see a thing at first, but when he came back on deck after retrieving their bags, the fog had thinned. He sensed they had entered some kind of channel. He thought he could make out a shoreline on either side of the boat. To the east was a sandbar studded with gulls. Then, straight ahead, something more distinct unspooled out of the fog: a pair of immense pillars marking either side of the channel, each one painted blue and capped with a large gold sculpture in the shape of a jumping fish.

The *Mary Louise* passed silently between the pillars. The fog parted enough to reveal a large harbor dotted with several long piers sticking out into the water.

Chase flicked a glance at Captain Nate, whose eyes were glistening.

When he sensed Chase looking at him, the Captain cleared his throat.

"I never thought I would see Metria again," he said.

Chase leaned forward to take it all in. The piers led to a wide pavilion bracketed on either side by the suggestion of large, domed buildings. It was difficult to make them out through the mist, but there it was before him: the barest suggestion of a city, just as Calla had once described it to them—except it was like a memory of the one she had told them about. A ghost. The bright blue buildings, high towers, and gold roofs stood, brooding and gray, in their shroud of fog. Chase had been to the northern regions of Metria, but had never made it so far south before, to the city.

They drifted quietly to the side of the long pier. There were no other boats to be seen, and the city was silent. The Captain leapt off and tied the bowline to a pole, then gestured for Chase to follow.

"Quietly, now—we don't want to call attention to ourselves. And keep your wits about you! We don't know what, or who, may await us. Don't trust anyone, even if they appear friendly."

Chase put a foot on the gunwale and stepped onto the pier. As soon as his foot settled, a charge of electricity shivered through him. He took a deep breath, his muscles tensed, and a profound sense of well-being coursed through him. He recognized it.

Ayda.

A huge grin crept across his face. The Captain's face mirrored his.

"Feels good, now doesn't it? Makes the daylights rejoice."

Suddenly the Captain's eyes narrowed. He dropped to a squat and pulled Chase down next to him.

"Someone's here!"

Chase felt the decking of the pier shudder slightly. For several long seconds, the only thing he heard was the panicked thumping of his own heart, and then he saw a tall, hooded woman robed in blue coming toward them through the fog. He blinked. The figure's bearing was remarkably familiar. Could it be . . . *Had Rysta escaped?*

Chase tried to rise, but the Captain held him back with a firm hand.

The figure came nearer and stopped. A pale hand appeared from the folds of the robe, the palm facing toward them at hip level, fingers splayed. The traditional Aydan greeting.

"You have come back to us," said a musical voice.

"Reveal yourself," the Captain growled.

"It has been many years since this outlier crossed our watchwater, but you, Chase, were on our shores not long ago. Do you not know me? Has fog erased the memory of your friends in Metria?"

The soft voice rose into the air, seemingly disembodied from the speaker. Something in it was familiar, but what? Chase's thoughts were spinning.

"Who are you?" demanded Chase.

The hand emerged once more and threw back the hood, revealing a solemn face with long brown hair piled on her head.

"Urza!" said Chase.

Urza bowed her head slightly in acknowledgment. When she lifted it again, her blue eyes were sparkling as they met Chase's.

"You have done well, eldest—unlike *some*," she said, her eyes flitting momentarily to the Captain's face.

"Once Captain Nate—er, Caspar—heard what had happened, he couldn't get back here fast enough," Chase explained. "And he was able to read the watchwater and the fog and everything so we could find our way here."

"Let's hope he was not followed *this* time," Urza said.

"Urza," the Captain said, "it no longer matters what was. It only matters what *is*. I have come to bring Rysta back to Metria, into the safe confines of this city. I will not leave these shores—or her side—again."

Urza assessed the tall, grim man before her, and then a small smile escaped her pale lips.

"I believe you." She bowed her head slightly toward the Captain, and turned to lead them off the pier. "Follow me."

When the Captain's feet hit land, he knelt on both knees and kissed the ground. As he stood up, his eyes were shining.

"It is good to be home."

Chapter 9

THE UNDERGROUND RIVER

Evelyn had lost track of time. How many minutes, hours, days, had they been walking in the half-lit tunnels behind Chantarelle? It was impossible to tell, for there was no day or night, no change of season or time, so deep were they beneath the earth's surface.

It was very cold at first, and soon it became very hot. She and Knox had abandoned most of their outer clothing on the first descent from the cave opening, and were now climbing in their T-shirts and jeans. At first it had been fun: the tunnel was well built and tall enough to walk through without stooping. Chantarelle trotted ahead, lighting small oil lamps that were shelved in carved-out alcoves along the tunnel. It was not a lot of light, but it was enough to keep Evelyn's memories from preying on her.

She did not like being underground. It felt too much like being buried alive—too much like that night in Haiti when the ground had turned to liquid and their house had collapsed, killing their father. Flashes of that terrible night kept tumbling back into her brain, despite how hard she tried to forget it.

It had been unusually hot, even for Haiti. And quiet. She was asleep when she had been startled awake by a rumbling coming from below—a sound she had never heard before—and it had scared her in some deep way, like the way hearing a lion roar at the zoo makes every muscle in your body want to run. She had reacted to it without thinking, rolling off the bed and reaching to pull Frankie off her bed. They had scrambled under Frankie's bed just as the floor melted away and the roof came hurtling down on top of them.

She stumbled in the dark and fell. Knox fell directly on top of her.

"Umm, ow—Evelyn, you have to tell me when you're going to stop," he said.

Evelyn swallowed back the lump in her throat. Nothing good would come from thinking about that night. The only thing that mattered now was that she and Frankie had survived—and that she had learned something from that experience: survival depends upon controlling your fear, and to do that, you had to learn patience. You had to live beside fear every day, as if it were a wild animal in your house. You fed it little morsels from your memory banks, never too much at a time, just enough to keep it from attacking you.

Her adopted grandmother Fanny had understood this; she knew that Evelyn was living with a wild animal that needed space and time to tame.

Chantarelle stopped and waited for Evelyn and Knox to catch up. He lit three oil lamps and handed one each to Evelyn and Knox. His golden-colored skin matched the flame exactly.

"This is all the light you'll have for a very long stretch, so use it wisely. Don't trip and snuff it out," he said. Then, with a small jerk of his head, he indicated that they should follow him. Almost immediately, the path went downhill with shallow steps and switchbacks. The air was heavy and close.

"Where do you think this goes?" Evelyn whispered to Knox, her breath sputtering the flame. "Can people even breathe down here?"

The fear was pacing its cage, making her heart race. A strange, sulfur stench was wafting up from the dark tunnel.

"Knox, I *really* don't like this!"

She reached out her hand, touching all three sides of the tunnel. The wild thing began to growl. Evelyn dropped one of the pinecones she had stowed in her pocket.

"Watch the oil lamp," said Knox. "It will blow out if there's not enough oxygen down here for us to breathe."

The sound of Knox's voice was reassuring. He sounded so much like Chase.

"Do you think your mother and Teddy found the note?"

Knox didn't answer.

Evelyn dropped another pinecone. She thought about the note she had left on the kitchen table at Summerledge. It made her feel better to know that Teddy might be able to follow and find them, if worse came to worst. Her flame flickered and began to blaze stronger. Chantarelle's shadow stopped again. The tunnel broadened. The air felt fresher, and the flames on all three wicks burned steadily.

"We will rest here and eat," Chantarelle decided.

"Where *is* here?" asked Knox, lifting his lamp to throw a wider arc of light. It revealed a small room with what looked to be more tunnels leading in different directions.

"We are at a crossroads," replied Chantarelle. "There are many beneath the surface of the earth, just as there are aboveground."

Knox snorted.

Chantarelle eyed him.

"You do not believe me, yet it was your ancestors who built these roads beneath the ground—roads that lead to cities and towns and stone gardens, some that once rivaled those on the surface."

"*My* ancestors?" said Knox. "I don't think so. My dad's family came from Germany, and my mom's—hmm . . . I don't know where they came from, but definitely *not* from down here."

Chantarelle turned his attention to Evelyn.

"The boy is dense as granite. I do not mean your familial ancestors. I mean humans—your species—and, though you may find it hard to believe, mine. A very long time ago, before the Watchers, guardians and stewards of mankind, were sent to teach men and women how to live above the ground, our species lived *below* it, finding shelter and warmth and protection in the bones of the earth. It is a refuge humans have resorted to throughout history, when life aboveground grew too dangerous."

Evelyn shivered, remembering how the bones of the earth could rebel and bury an entire city.

"I don't understand you, Chantarelle," she said. "How could people live underground? How did they hunt and farm and go to school and work? It doesn't make any sense. You need light and air and food to live. And if we are related, how come you are so"—Evelyn struggled to find a word other than "short," finally settling on—"different?"

"Wait here," said Chantarelle, ignoring their questions. He and his oil lamp disappeared before Knox or Evelyn could protest.

"Where do you think he's gone off to?" asked Knox.

"I don't know," said Evelyn. "I just hope he comes back. I don't like it down here. God knows what else lives down here, like rats and bugs and snakes." She squatted, searching the ground with her oil lamp for a place to sit.

"How much farther, do you think?"

Knox leaned against the stone wall and shrugged.

"Who knows? What do you make of him—Chantarelle? What is he? He said 'our species.' Maybe people like Chantarelle, and Aydans, are everywhere, and I was always just too dumb to notice them."

Evelyn was quiet.

In Haiti, most of the people she knew believed in magic, but they called it something else. They believed there were all kinds of worlds that existed together—the material world, the middle world, and the spiritual world—and that people could travel between them if they knew how. They used special ceremonies and rituals to do it, and called on their ancestors to help them. Maybe what the Haitians called magic was what the Aydans felt in the power of the daylights. Maybe it *was* all the same thing.

Evelyn closed her eyes and tried to feel the strength of the *atar* flowing in her veins. She tried to hear her daylights call, but got distracted by the sudden reappearance of Chantarelle, who was lugging a bag and a cask of some liquid.

"Here we go—courtesy of those who can't hunt or farm or live without fresh air and sunlight."

He threw the bag at Evelyn's feet and handed the cask to Knox.

Knox removed the stopper and took a sniff. His face broke out in a twisted smile.

"It's beer!"

Evelyn reached up and grabbed the cask.

"He can't drink that; he's too young. There are laws about that."

Knox grabbed it back.

"Knox! You're twelve!"

Chantarelle shushed her.

"It's not beer, it's mead. It's made with honey and wheat and it won't harm him. It's fermented because it must keep for a long time. Besides, it's all we have until we get to the river."

Knox stuck his tongue out at Evelyn and took a big swig.

Evelyn examined the gray-colored slab of food Chantarelle was offering, then took a bite. It tasted musty and bland, with a mushroomy texture. Knox handed her the cask and she took a sip. The liquid was sweet and sparkling. They ate and drank in silence until they were finished.

"I brought more oil to refresh your lamps," said Chantarelle.

"Where do you get all this stuff?" asked Knox.

"I have told you: There is a world down here that parallels yours—or at least, it once did. Even after the Watchers perished and the world was plunged in misery, these underground cities were used to protect people in times of war. There were stockrooms the size of houses, filled with food and weapons and clothing, and pens for livestock. Trees full of fruit and nuts were harvested from the roots down. The way into these cities was hidden, known only by those who were sworn to keep the gateways secret. Many lives were spared because of these underground cities."

"You said this world once paralleled our own," Knox said. "What happened to it?"

Chantarelle shrugged his knobby shoulders.

"The girl is right in thinking that most humans prefer the world of light. As time passed and weapons grew more powerful, more and more chose not to flee underground but to fight aboveground for their lands—"

"But not everyone?" asked Evelyn. "Your people are the ones who stayed . . . the ones who liked it underground!"

Chantarelle nodded.

"Yes, there were those who stayed. They delved farther and deeper and created a vast empire; all the while, the world above slowly forgot they existed. The two became as distinct as day is from night, and all trust and knowledge between them ceased. To you, my people exist now only in fairy tales, dancing at the end of rainbows and hiding in mountains and barns and attics. But it's all there for anyone to read in the history books: We began the same."

"How many more of you are there?" cried Knox, imagining a vast city filled with small people bustling underground, going to work and school and home in an exact reflection of what taller people did aboveground.

"Enough," was the vague reply. "But too few for the future to hold great promise for us." Chantarelle took a long swig from the cask. "And yet, perhaps the same might be said for you, children of the light. Or perhaps history shall repeat itself, and your kind will make life on the surface so uninhabitable that yours and mine will meet again beneath the earth?"

He gave them each a long look, then jumped to his feet.

"We must move on. It is a long way yet to the foundations of Ayda."

☩   ☩   ☩

They stumbled through the tunnel, holding hands, their lamps no longer useful.

"Not much farther," Chantarelle croaked.

His hand was small and warm and relatively dry to Evelyn's touch compared to Knox's sweaty mitt. The air was suffocating. Both Evelyn and Knox were laboring to breathe. The rock floor of the tunnel was uneven and split in places, so they had to leap over cracks that glowed orange from some fire lit far below. Heat buffeted out of the cracks, scorching their legs when they crossed. The light in the tunnel was like the inside of an oven being lit only by the burner.

"Jeez, how far down are we, Chantarelle?" asked Knox. He stopped to wipe sweat off his face. "Is that lava down there?"

"We are deep in the earth, but these cracks go much deeper. Be careful how you jump. Overlanders forget that the sun is not the only thing that heats the earth."

"Overlanders? Is that what you call us?"

"Among other things." Chantarelle sped ahead.

"This must be what asthma feels like," huffed Knox, trying to keep up. "It sucks—makes me feel bad for teasing Chase."

Evelyn didn't reply. She was busy fighting off her own waves of terror. The wild thing inside her had scaled the walls of its cage, trying to escape. She did not think she could stand being underground one more second. It was too much like being buried.

"Knox, I can't do this. You have to get me out of here. I can't breathe."

The panic began to spiral up, up, up, taking over. The tunnel was like a large, menacing hand pressing down on her, like it was squashing a bug. She gulped for air, and the wild thing broke free.

"I CAN'T BREATHE!" she screamed, clawing at her clothes and skin. "I need to get out! Get me out, Knox!"

A sudden motion and Chantarelle was there. He held both of Evelyn's wrists as she tried to escape. He pulled her to his level and searched around her neck for Rothermel's gift.

"Quick, boy, give me your necklace," he shouted to Knox, realizing Evelyn's wasn't there.

Knox yanked the necklace from his neck and gave it to Chantarelle.

The little man breathed on its bead. A scent of pine and fresh air filled the small enclosure. Evelyn swooned.

When she came to, Knox was slapping her lightly across the cheek. She could see the outline of his face in the gloom. He went to slap her again and she grabbed his hand.

"Stop enjoying yourself so much!" she scolded him.

"Blame Chantarelle; he told me to do it. No stinkweed down here," Knox joked, remembering how Seaborne had once gotten Chase to come around when he'd passed out.

Despite his smile, Knox looked worried. "Are you okay?"

Evelyn sat up. "Where are we?"

"Almost there, or so I'm told—but then again, he's always telling us we're almost there. I had to drag you."

"Drag me?"

"Yeah; you may be skinny and all, but, man, you're heavy. I thought I was going to pass out. Hit some corners along the way. You might have some bruises." Knox's voice echoed slightly. "Do you think you can swim?"

Evelyn sat up. "Swim? Where would we swim?"

"Down there," Knox said, pointing.

Evelyn followed his finger with her gaze. They were sitting on a large, protruding ledge, and when she leaned over and looked down, she saw a large pool of water directly below them. It was about forty or fifty feet down, lit by a single pillar of light that came through a hole in the roof above them.

"I'm confused—"

"No need to understand," answered a hump of rock from a ledge a few yards away that turned out to be Chantarelle.

"*Ack*," gulped Evelyn.

Chantarelle's camouflage was something. She'd probably walked by him a thousand times in Fells Harbor and never known he was there.

Chantarelle stood at the brink of the ledge and somersaulted into the lake.

Knox and Evelyn craned their necks over the edge to see him.

"Oh, man, Teddy would *love* this," said Knox.

"C'mon, then!" shouted Chantarelle.

Knox grinned at Evelyn.

"Here goes nothing," he said and cannonballed off the ledge. When he surfaced, he yelped, "It's like a hot tub in here!"

"Thermal springs," said Chantarelle.

Knox swam around for a bit, making big splashing sounds.

"Evelyn? You coming or what?"

"In a minute," she replied, strangely reluctant. She peered down at the two floating heads. After everything they'd been through, this jump was nothing, but Evelyn was tired. The memory of that terrible night in Haiti, combined with the airless trek through the tunnel, had left her exhausted. Her arms and legs felt too heavy to move.

"Evelyn?" Knox's voice called again.

"You must jump, child; you are almost there. You cannot give up now."

The sound of Chantarelle's voice coming from behind her made her start. The little man was dripping a puddle of water on the ledge. Sopping wet, he looked more like a log pulled out of a swamp than a man.

"I'm really tired, Chantarelle. And I'm worried about my sister."

"It is the daylights; only those who are tuned more to the stone of Melor can pass through these tunnels with no ill effects. You are not a child of Melor, Evelyn, but your daylights are strong, nonetheless."

"Do you really think so?" she croaked.

Instead of answering, Chantarelle turned to the side of the cavern and produced his oil lamp. He lit it and turned back to her. The puddle on the floor quivered with his movements. When it had stilled, he gestured toward it.

"Tell me, Evelyn, what do you see there?"

Evelyn followed his hand. She saw a thin pool of water, no bigger than a plate.

"Nothing; a puddle."

"Look closer." Chantarelle held the lamp over the water.

Evelyn crept over and peered directly down at the puddle. She saw a fragment of her own reflection: dark eyes, brown curls. Then, she saw Frankie, lying in the hospital. Her sister's hands played with the striped sheet. Her grandmother leaned beside the bed and took one of Frankie's hands in her own. The candlelight wavered and the image disappeared. The puddle shimmered.

"Bring them back!" Evelyn cried.

"They haven't gone anywhere," said Chantarelle. "They are here, as you are with them, even though you are also here. That is the gift of love. It travels all worlds. It heeds no geography. Tell me—do you need to see your loved ones to know you love them?"

Evelyn chewed her bottom lip with her teeth. "No."

"Then you must know the same applies for them. The daylights connect us all like a fine net, or"—he looked up through his eyelashes—"a system of tunnels. Fells Harbor was there." He pointed behind them. "And Ayda is over there." He pointed ahead. "You did not know until today that a tunnel existed between them—has *always* existed between them—just as you do not see the invisible channels of energy that connect all living things, including you to your sister. Nothing is truly separate, no matter how it may appear on the surface. In time you will see the connections whenever you like—I am confident of this."

"You are?"

"I am. You and I share a special bond, Evelyn. Our daylights are tuned to the greatest of stones, the Fifth Stone—"

Evelyn was flabbergasted. "How do you know? I've felt nothing . . ."

"I recognize a kindred spirit," said Chantarelle. "Do not worry that you have not felt them. The Fifth Stone's call is softer than the others, its gifts more fragile and challenging to earn. When you hear it, you will understand."

Evelyn stared at Chantarelle, looking for similarities between them. The amber light of the oil lamp was reflecting back at her in his dark pupils.

"You are a rare creature, Evelyn. You must take care—"

A whooping cry echoed through the chamber, cutting him off.

Evelyn sank her head between her folded knees, wishing she could feel as carefree as Knox. The wild thing was making a racket in her chest.

"Chantarelle—I—I—have to tell you, I don't feel very brave or special. Most of the time all I feel is . . . really, really *afraid*. I don't know if I'm much good for Knox or anyone in Ayda."

The little man studied her for a minute. Then he spoke directly in Evelyn's ear.

"I know you are afraid—we all are—but ask yourself: Are you willing to let that boy go the rest of the way alone?" Chantarelle nodded his head toward the pool. "He will need you before it is all over, you know."

She looked over the side at Knox happily kicking up froth, circling the pillar of light. She thought about the image she'd just seen in the puddle, of Frankie and her grandmother. She felt torn. Frankie was the only real family she had left. Was it right to leave her? But then, she thought about Knox's father—how he had spent so much of his time at the hospital, looking after her sister, trying to help her. The least she could do was look after his son for a while. Maybe that's how this connection thing worked.

She stood up.

"I'm coming, Knox!" she shouted, and jumped into the pool.

Knox swam over to her with long, quick strokes.

A little splash told them Chantarelle was back in the water, pushing what looked like two logs in their direction.

"Here, you will need these," he said.

"How far is it?" asked Knox.

"Not far," said Chantarelle.

"Then why do we need—" His voice was drowned out by a gurgling that became an enormous sucking sound. They felt a tremendous tug from something beneath the surface of the lake, and the water began spinning.

"What the heck?" cried Knox.

Evelyn started thrashing her arms, trying to swim out of what was quickly turning into a frothing, spinning whirlpool.

"HELP! CHANTARELLE!" she yelled.

"Hold your breath!" cried Chantarelle, "and whatever you do, don't let go of your logs!"

The underground pool circled itself, whirling with increasing speed, taking Knox, Evelyn, and Chantarelle with it, like laundry in a washing machine. The sucking sound grew louder and the lake spun faster and faster, until one by one, they were pulled completely under.

Evelyn held her breath and hugged her log, like she'd been told.

She felt another big tug, heard a rushing sound, and then she was flying through the air, popped like a cork out of a bottle. She catapulted past a steep wall in a cascade of foam and water and splashed into the relatively calm waters of an underground river.

She looked back just in time to see Knox hurtling out of a hole in the wall of the cavern, tumbling in a spectacular cartwheel. Chantarelle came last, expertly riding his log like a boogie board down the plume of froth and onto the river.

"Yeah!" shouted Knox, slapping his hands on the water. "That was AWESOME! We gotta go back and do that again!"

"No way," sputtered Evelyn. "Once is enough for me." She hoisted her torso up on her log.

The river took a bend and narrowed; the water grew colder. Light seeped through the stone in places, and the walls were dripping in spots.

Chantarelle paddled to an embankment and got out of the water. He gestured for them to do the same. When they were on dryish land, he walked to the wall above the embankment and pointed straight up.

"There," he said.

"Melor?" asked Knox. His eyes were shining.

Chantarelle nodded.

Evelyn bit her thumb.

"Aren't you coming with us?"

"No, here our paths diverge. You are but two of many beings I must see to this day." He shot her a sharp look. "Heed what I said, and take care; the ground above is overrun, and you are unarmed. No one expects your arrival, and I do not think I need remind you of how Melorians view strangers."

He waved once, dove into the water, and swam quickly back up the river.

Evelyn hugged herself. She already missed Chantarelle's reassuring presence, small as it was.

Knox grabbed ahold of a crevice in the wall and pulled himself up the wet, mossy wall and into the tunnel. Evelyn followed. Ahead they saw a stream of light. The smell of smoke increased, and, within minutes, they were standing, blinking in the hazy, sunlit, open air.

Chapter 10

REFUGEES

Urza hurried the Captain and Chase through the open pavilion that marked the entrance to the city. Within moments they were immersed in a complicated maze of alleys and waterways connected by footbridges.

Inside the city, the fog was less dense. Urza walked ahead. The Captain followed, taking great, swift strides, as if his long legs had just been waiting for the opportunity.

Chase scrambled several paces behind, trying to take in as much as he could on the fly. The buildings were made of a soft, golden stone that looked like cement or stucco. The roofs were covered in blue tile, and all the doors and shutters of the houses were painted blue. Chase saw no one at the windows or in the streets, but he had the feeling they were there, hidden in the shadows, watching their passage. The air was close and quiet but for the gentle sloshing of water against the foundations of the buildings. Occasionally, Chase saw gold engravings and etchings over the doorways. Several sharp turns to the right and another to the left, and they were in a wide square, at the center of which stood the most remarkable fountain Chase had ever seen.

At the top, which stood at least three stories high, four streams of water poured from the mouths of wide, trumpet-shaped shells, falling onto a shelf that mingled the streams and sent them cascading to the next level in a solid curtain of water, onto slabs of marble pierced with tiny holes. At eye level, the water was transformed again into showers of droplets that emptied into a wide, rimmed basin and filled the square with the sound of rain.

Urza stopped at the base of the fountain, her eyes tracing the falling water. Chase came up beside her and tried to get his bearings.

"Beautiful, is it not?" Urza said, nodding at the fountain.

"Very," Chase breathed.

"See how the water changes shape while its essence remains the same?" she said. Her eyes shifted to Chase's. "It is the way of all things—for better or for worse."

Then, her voice dropped, conspiratorially.

"Tell me, Chase, do you trust that man?"

She bent her head slightly toward the Captain, who was prowling the perimeter of the square, his eyes darting back and forth.

Chase nodded. "I do, yes."

Urza's face remained serious.

"I must know something, Chase, before I take you any farther. Does he have it?"

It took a second for Chase to register what she was asking, and when he did, he felt all of his senses sharpen. The Captain's warning rang in his ears. *Don't trust anyone.*

"What do you mean? I . . . er . . . he—"

She cut him off with a sudden wave of the hand.

"Do not trifle with me, Chase. It is my duty to care for my Keeper and all things precious to her. I have knowledge of all that passed between you and the Keeper of Varuna. If I were going to betray you, I would have brought an army with me to meet you at the pier, to take by force whatever treasures you, or he, possess. Now, answer me truthfully."

Chase conceded her point.

But what *was* the truth? Chase was reluctant to admit that he really didn't know for sure if they had brought the Fifth Stone with them. Had the Captain been holding something in his hand when he'd put it in the water? If so, it must be pretty small, but it was *possible*. After all, he'd never seen a real stone of power before. Maybe they were all really small.

He lowered his voice "I, uh—I think so . . . ?"

Urza nodded approvingly.

She circled the fountain in the direction of the large building, skirting the impressive facade and ushering Chase and the Captain through a small side door, unnoticeable from the square.

They passed through a narrow, dark hallway and into a broad, open room with high ceilings and white walls. Sheets of light poured into the room from long horizontal openings in the walls. Once Chase's eyes had adjusted to the brightness, his jaw dropped: groups of Melorians were huddled across the expansive room, more than Chase had ever seen together in one place. It looked like a vast refugee camp. Most were women and children, from what he could see, even a few babies, but not all. Here and there, Chase saw the telltale bronze of a helmet, the flash of a knife hilt, the harnesses filled with throwing weapons. He tried not to stare.

"What has happened?" the Captain asked, his eyes roving across the woven blankets and baskets, the quivers of arrows. "Why have they all gathered here?"

"Most of the Wold has been abandoned and much of the forest burned. Our forces have kept Dankar at bay at our northern borders. Rothermel sent many of his people to Metria for protection."

Chase scanned the faces of the Melorians, but did not recognize anyone. "Where are the others?"

"Most Melorians refused to leave their lands, preferring to fight the Exorian army head-on. We have sent our soldiers to aid them as best they can, but little news reaches us here, so far from the battle. There is a rumor that long ago, Rothermel created safe places throughout Melor, and that his people can find safety there. I believe it to be true."

"But you have no idea who's still alive?" Chase's voice was wild with anxiety. He saw Mara and Calla's gold-flecked eyes and Seaborne's grin flash before him. His Melorian family. "And what about Rothermel?"

Urza looked down at her feet. "We have had little news."

For the second time that day Chase mentally kicked himself for not remembering his task sooner.

The Captain addressed Urza in an urgent whisper.

"Where are the Metrian forces?"

"Amassed at the northern borders of Lake Voss, where Melor and Varuna meet. We have been able to guard our positions from there," she said.

"I will need armor and weapons and transport up the river," said the Captain. "It is my intention to move on to Exor as soon as possible."

The Captain flicked an eye at Chase.

"The boy has completed his task. He has brought me hence and will now stay here in sanctuary. He owes a prior debt to the Melorians; now he may repay it by protecting their families as they once protected his."

"What?" Chase objected. "No! You can't leave me here!"

"Chase," Urza admonished. "I have heard that the daylights cannot speak as clearly beyond the fog, and your behavior makes me think it is true. Yours have grown confused. Do not give way to the extremes of emotion. It preys upon the balance and makes you weak, which is what Dankar wants. Emotion drowns out wisdom. Remember the fountain? Be true to your essence. Calm yourself, and listen to your daylights; then you will know where you are truly needed, and where you can do the most good."

"But—," he objected.

Urza went on, addressing Captain Nate.

"I see that your daylights have remained strong despite the many years away from Ayda, Caspar. This, and the boy's trust in you, makes me dare to hope that you have returned to us with a gift—one that rumor had banished beyond all thought. You should go forth with the knowledge that although the Keeper and her necklace have been stolen, the true stone of Metria remains hidden. We fear for it, as we do not know how long Rysta will be able to keep its location secret."

A silent look passed between Urza and the Captain. Who knew how long Rysta could hold out under Dankar's torments?

"You will be taken to Voss, as you wish," said Urza, "but the boy is to come with you. Ratha has requested it."

"Yes—," Chase started to say, then stopped himself when he saw the dark look on the Captain's face.

"What does she want with him?"

"All I know is that she is waiting for you both."

This did not improve the Captain's mood. "And arms? I can't fight Dankar with my bare hands."

Urza swept past Chase, her robes whispering across the tiled floor.

"That is for Ratha to decide. My task is to deliver you to Voss."

The Captain glowered at Chase, then bent down to hiss in his ear.

"Don't look so pleased with yourself, boy; sometimes the cat chokes when he eats the canary."

✛   ✛   ✛

They were to wait with the refugees in the main hall until nightfall, when they would move. Urza disappeared into the inner recesses of the building. The Captain threw himself down in a corner and slept, one arm crossed over his face.

Chase spent this time trying to glean as much information from the Melorian refugees as he could, but found it no easy task. Babies and children were scooped up and hidden from sight as he approached. The women retreated beneath the privacy of their hoods, shaking their heads when he tried to ask about Mara or Calla. Chase knew how tight-lipped the Melorians could be around strangers, but this was extreme even for them.

Discouraged, Chase sat down on the floor off to the side of the room and leaned against an ornate column decorated with silver etchings. He sat, motionless, watching the light filter through the long slit at the top of the wall as it changed with the position of the sun. The afternoon wore on with nothing to mark it but the entry of several Metrians, in their telltale blue and purple robes, carrying steaming bowls of rice and fish. Chase's stomach was grumbling. He helped himself and ate the rice in hungry fistfuls.

The atmosphere in the room relaxed a little with the meal. Chase noticed with a pang that the Melorians passed small parcels of dried meat and bars of rolled grain amongst themselves, the same food Mara had fed them on the long trek through Melor from Seaborne's cabin, after Frankie's capture. How long ago that seemed now. Beyond the fog, it had only been a matter of weeks, but time on Ayda was different. It collapsed on itself, just as Ratha had once shown him by folding and unfolding her fan. Beyond the fog, time seemed to stretch out in one long line, one day passing to the next, from birth to the end of life. Here, the days and years folded on top of one another, like folds of a fan, so that it felt as if everything that had ever been done to him, or would be done to him, was happening now.

Chase tried to picture his life before this—before Ayda and Dankar and any knowledge of the daylights or the Fifth Stone. Their house at 320 Elm Ridge Road; the day they left for Summerledge; their rusty car and the bikes falling off the rack. Teddy in his flippers and swim goggles. Had there ever been a time when all he had to worry about was nosy neighbors, fitting in at school, and being the new kid?

Chase stared blankly over the heads of the Melorians, dully aware of their protective hoods, the deadly weapons arrayed at their feet or in their harnesses, kept perpetually sharp for battle. Before Ayda, the only battle he'd ever participated in had been in a video game. The kind where no one ever really dies, and the worst thing that happens is someone tells you to stop playing. How lucky he had been! Would he ever have another chance to go back home, to Elm Ridge Road? And what would he say if he did? No one would ever believe what he had done over summer vacation.

Chase shut his eyes, leaned his head back against the column, and sighed.

"There's a saying in Melor that for every sigh, a thought dies that should have been spoken."

Chase's eyes shot back open, landing on the faces of a Melorian man and a small boy, close to Teddy's age, by the look of him. The man, presumably his father, held out a rolled grain bar.

"Here. You were staring at it with such longing. You must be hungry."

He squatted beside Chase and lifted his palm, fingers splayed.

"My name is Adhoran, and this"—he nodded to the child—"is my son, Bron."

Chase met the Melorian's fingertips with his own.

"I'm, uh . . . I'm fine, really," said Chase. "I was just thinking about the last time I ate one of those. A friend gave me one, and I was just wondering about her . . ."

Adhoran studied Chase's face.

"You are one of the outlier children, are you not? One of the five who washed ashore not long ago at the edge of Melor, and were found by Seaborne?"

Chase's heart thumped louder at the sound of Seaborne's name.

"You know Seaborne?"

"I know Seaborne, yes, as do all Melorians, but I have not seen him for some time now, not since he went into Varuna, a journey from which he did not return—"

"But he did!" Chase cut him off. "He did! We were all captured by Exorians and they took us to Exor, and—"

Chase stopped short when he saw the grim expression on the Melorian's face.

"No, it's not like that. We escaped; *he* escaped. We . . . I . . . left him with Rothermel on the beach in Exor."

Adhoran grimaced.

"Then you have answered my question. You *are* one of the outlier children come to Ayda from beyond the fog."

Chase nodded, afraid to say more.

The little boy leaned into his father's shoulder.

"I have a little brother just about your age," Chase said to Bron, trying to change the subject. He pictured Teddy and wondered what he was doing. Then he thought about Evelyn and Knox. What would they think when they read his note? He tried not to think about his parents.

Adhoran's eyes traveled from Chase across the room to the prone figure of the Captain, stretched out on the floor. He gathered his son close.

"I see there is much that you will not say. So do not speak; listen. In Melor, there is a rumor of the outlier children. It is said that you bring bad fortune and a scourge of fire. Many in this room, even, believe that you are demons brought to our shores to defy the Keepers and steal their stones."

Chase's jaw worked furiously.

"But . . . but that's not true. Why would they think that?"

"People who use blame often do not think. Let your actions determine your fate now."

He excused himself with a bow of his head and lifted his son into his arms.

Chase watched them cross the room, his thoughts nagging him. He remembered Rothermel's words the first time they had met him: *Dankar has found a way to bring outliers to our shores.* But Rothermel was wrong. It wasn't Dankar who had brought them here; it was Ratha. For hundreds of years, she had been searching for the person who might have the Fifth Stone, laying all manner of nets, only to catch Seaborne and Louis—and who knows how many others—but never the person she wanted.

Until now.

✛   ✛   ✛

The light in the room faded to twilight. Out of the corner of his eye, Chase saw Captain Nate stand abruptly, his whole manner suddenly alert and on guard.

Urza entered the room and crossed in front of them, not breaking her stride or saying a word. They fell in behind her, silently passing through an archway, into a low tunnel, and out onto the embankment of a canal, where several small, one-man boats were bobbing on their lines.

Out of the gloom, four Metrian soldiers emerged, holding paddles. The Captain settled himself quickly into one of the boats.

Chase almost toppled his boat before regaining his balance and lowering himself into the small aperture at the center of the craft. Fully seated, he rode just above the surface, his paddle easily scooping the black water even with his elbows bent. He concentrated on making the slow, steady strokes he'd learned in Metria, the kind that barely made a sound.

A furred half-moon rose into the deepening night, providing barely any illumination. The lack of light and the steady mist rendered the little flotilla nearly invisible as it made its way up the canal. Chase thought about earlier times when he had been on a river—when he'd lost Teddy on the Hestredes. He was glad that Teddy wasn't here this time.

He had a flashback to the night in Melor when they were attacked by an Exorian warring party. He saw his little brother racing in between the scarred legs of the Exorian soldiers, the forest in flames around them. He remembered the exultant look on Knox's face as he had leapt into battle after Seaborne and Calla.

Whatever awaited him this night, it was good to know that *both* of his brothers—and Evelyn and Frankie—were safely back home. Reaching his paddle down into the water, Chase consoled himself with another thought: at least Knox would never have to know that the Melorians had turned against them.

Chapter 11

AT HOME

Grace and Teddy swung into the kitchen at Summerledge through the screen door. The rain had finally stopped, and the sun was doing its best to dissolve the gray cloud cover.

On the walk back from Secret Beach, Grace had convinced Teddy to put Bob back in his bowl and give him a rest. She wasn't sure how much longer the turtle would survive Teddy's attention, and she didn't want to think about how Teddy—or Knox and Chase, for that matter—would react if Bob died. She felt as strung-out and weary as Bob these days, and only wanted calm, peaceful days for the rest of the summer. The sun breaking through the clouds made her feel like it might just happen that way.

She watched Teddy climb the back stairs to his bedroom, feeling a pang at the sight of his little legs, and a stab of guilt. It still made her quake inside to think of her children and Evelyn and Frankie adrift in the fog, and then floating in that icy water. By all measures, they should not have survived.

She shook her head to clear it. She couldn't let herself think about it, or the whole day would be wasted in a slog of depression. The important thing was to focus on the fact that they *had* survived.

"Chase! Knox! We're back!" she sang out, a little forced. "The sun is coming out. Do you want some lunch?"

She turned back around toward the kitchen, surprised again at how, even after all these years, she still half-expected to see her brother Edward standing there. He would look completely different now, of course. Not the boy she remembered. She wondered what he would have looked like had he lived.

Another wave of grief hit her. She bustled around the kitchen to avoid it, grabbing lunch meat and carrots out of the fridge. She went to place the food on the table and stopped short, seeing the notes.

"Oh no," she said, and sat down, her knees weak. Something bad was happening again; she just knew it.

The flush of the toilet overhead sent water rushing over her head. In the living room, she heard the *ping* coming from the pots on the floor.

"Teddy!" she yelled up the stairs, needing to have him in her sight before she went back for the notes.

✢   ✢   ✢

"Lemme go," said Teddy. "I know where they went."

He squirmed his hand out of his mother's death grip and dove into the woods by the side of the driveway.

"Wait for me, Ted!" she yelled after him. "Let's check the tree fort!"

Grace was trying to stay calm despite the rising panic in her throat.

Chase, Knox, and Evelyn were fine, she tried to reassure herself. They had left notes, after all, even though none of what they had written made any sense. She had called the hospital. Neither Jim nor Fanny had seen Knox and Evelyn. She had read both notes to her husband, and described the state of the widow's walk. He was on his way back to the house now. The only good news was that Frankie's condition had not changed. At least she was not getting any worse.

"He's not there," said Teddy, marching ahead in his rain boots.

He had packed his own backpack with clothes and food, and insisted that Bob come along.

Grace was too distracted to argue.

"How do you know?"

"Because he's not. I just know. They're at the cave."

"What cave?" asked Grace.

"You know, Mom"—Teddy scooted around a pine tree and dove into the thick of the woods—"by the rocks."

Grace's memory twinged. She had not thought about that cave in more than thirty-five years. She and Edward used to have pretend tea parties on the ledge outside of it. They used acorn hats as cups. How could she have forgotten?

Then again, she had been a small girl at Summerledge, only eight years old when her brother had been lost at sea. She had not returned for more than twenty years. In that time, she had buried all of her memories of Edward in a manageable container deep inside of her. It was hard enough to go on without him; she found it impossible when surrounded by memories of him. She had avoided Summerledge for all those years because of it, and it was only after Chase was born that she'd thought she could stand it.

"Over here, Mom," said Teddy, his little voice carrying authority. He seemed so much older since the accident. Bob's head stuck out of the mesh pocket on the side of his backpack.

"I remember, Ted," she answered.

They made their way up the jumble of rocks and onto the ledge. It was clear someone had been here recently. They could see the marks in the moss and pine needles.

"Mom," cried Teddy, "look!" He yanked Evelyn's necklace off the pine branch overhead and pulled his own from under his sweatshirt. "It's a clue!"

Grace looked at the necklaces in Teddy's grubby little fist. Of course she'd seen them before on all of the children, at the hospital. She figured they had made them as part of a friendship ritual.

"I wonder whose it is?"

"They went in, Mom. I know it," said Teddy, getting on all fours and sticking his head in the cave. "Knox! You there?" he yelled.

A warm *whoosh* of air answered his call.

Grace pulled him back and cradled him in her lap.

"I don't think so, Teddy. They wouldn't go in there. It doesn't go anywhere."

Teddy wrestled out of her arms and stood up.

"Yes, it does. It goes to Ayda. That's where they went."

"Ayda? What's that?"

"It's a place . . . where my friends live. That's where they went."

Grace smiled at him. She was used to imaginary friends. She used to have one when she was Teddy's age: a little man dressed in green and brown and gray who carried a walking stick. She called him Chantarelle, and he lived in these woods. She used to save parts of her breakfast for him.

"Hmm," she said. "Well, perhaps your friends are hungry. How about you unpack your backpack and we'll leave the food here for them? Then you and I will go back to the house and make lunch, and wait for Daddy? I think we might need to call around to find your brothers and Evelyn."

"No, Mom!" said Teddy. He stamped his foot. "They went in there. If you want to find them, we have to go to Ayda. That way!" He jabbed his finger at the cave entrance.

Grace sat back, unsure of what to do. There could be a wild animal in the cave, but then again, it was summer, and the chances it was burrowing were slim. What harm would it do to go a little ways into the cave? At least that way Teddy could find out for himself that it went nowhere.

"How about this, Ted: We'll go in a few feet and see?"

Teddy nodded and dropped again to all fours. He scrambled quickly into the cave. Grace stood at the entrance and looked in after him.

"Mom!" she heard him yell.

"What?"

"It goes down—and look!" His head popped back out of the entrance. He held out a small pinecone. "They left us a trail!"

Grace looked at the pinecone in Teddy's hand, and then down at the necklace she was holding. Could it be possible? Had Chase, Knox, and Evelyn left the necklace here on purpose as a signal? And if so, why? What was the important thing that Chase had to do? Why had they all left again?

"Mom?" Teddy asked, looking up at her from the cave's mouth, his blue eyes wide with excitement.

Wherever they had gone, Grace was not going to sit at home like last time—and the time before that when she had waited for Edward. This time, she was going to find them.

"Let's go," she said.

Chapter 12

A BITTER WELCOME

"Is this *really* Melor?" Knox asked. "I don't recognize anything."

The air was thick and hazy around them, lit from above with a greenish glow. It stung their eyes and left a bitter taste in their mouths.

Evelyn squinted to see through the haze.

"I don't know. I can't see anything through all this smoke."

Knox caught her eye.

Smoke meant fire. Fire meant Exorians.

"Do you think we should look around?" she whispered.

Knox nodded. "Carefully; no sound. Use hand signals."

They picked their way down the ledge. Haze still hovered above them, but eventually their vision improved. What they saw was shocking. Under the sickly green glow, the forest floor was charred black; massive stumps of burnt trees poked out at odd angles. Not a leaf or a limb remained of the old forest. No life or wind stirred the burnt ground, and no sound but a faraway stream disturbed the deathly silence.

Melor was as desolate as the moon.

"We're too late!" Knox cried in a great, agonized *whoosh*, then, to his surprise—and Evelyn's—he burst into sobs.

Evelyn took in the devastation without a word. She had seen ruin before, but this was something else, something so malicious it made her hair stand on end. The ancient and beautiful forest they had used for shelter, for food, for protection, so lush and wild, and home to all manner of animals and birds and people, was now a bleak graveyard. It had been incinerated; not a tree or a bush or a pinecone had survived.

"This is evil," she breathed.

Beside her, Knox gave another angry, anguished shudder. Evelyn patted his back. His narrow shoulders under her palm reminded her that he was only twelve. It was easy to forget sometimes; he could be so full of himself.

She sighed, trying to think of something to say that would comfort him. It was not all that long ago that she had looked out, dazed and unbelieving, on her own city laid to waste.

"Knox, the forest will grow back. The daylights are strong on Ayda. Rothermel wouldn't let it stay this way forever; he'll fix it—the way Mara helped our hair grow back . . . remember?"

"Unless Rothermel is dead," Knox snuffled, "and Dankar took his stone."

"Don't say that, Knox," she whispered. "Don't even think it! Besides, even if it's the worst possible thing and Dankar has the stone of Melor, we came here to find Chase and Captain Nate, right?"

Knox lifted his head; his eyes were pink and watery. "Right."

She took a deep breath.

"Okay, Melorian, tune in to your daylights and figure out where we are, while I look around. And be quiet!"

"Do you think Chantarelle will come back?" Knox asked hopefully, nodding toward the rock ledge.

"I wouldn't count on it, Knox. I think from now on, we have to assume we're on our own."

She crouched down to begin sifting through the soot and ash, looking for something solid from which to build a slingshot. She didn't want to say it out loud, but for all they knew the forest could be full of Exorians. They would need weapons.

⁜　⁜　⁜

"Evelyn!" Knox shouted hoarsely from some distance away.

She crossed to him quickly.

"What happened to 'No sound, only hand signals'?"

Knox was bouncing on his toes, staring up at the face of the rock ledge.

"I think I recognize this from before. I think we're near the sky crossing! If we keep the river on our left and walk north, we might find it. Then we can make our way to the Wold."

Evelyn looked at the rock face, dubious. "Are you sure?"

Knox bit his lip. "No. I mean, yes. I don't know." He slumped against the rock, crestfallen. "I don't know anything. It's all wrecked."

"Hey, I think you're right; I think I recognize this," Evelyn said encouragingly. "It must be the Vossbeck down below us, and this is part of the ledge Tinator made us climb. We can't be more than a mile or two from the sky crossing."

It occurred to her that the sky crossing would have been burned along with all the trees, but she decided not to mention that. It was better that they keep moving.

They walked in silence for quite a long time, single file, their eyes scanning the barren landscape for any signs of movement. Evelyn anxiously searched the charred tree stumps, looking for remnants of a platform. Every now and then she stooped down to pick up a slingshot stone and pocket it. As she stood up again, Knox stopped her with a raised hand.

"Do you hear that?" he whispered.

Evelyn strained her ears. Nothing. She shook her head.

"Something's coming toward us, running fast."

Knox's eyes roamed the surroundings for a hiding place. About twenty paces off, he saw the outline of a massive tree trunk with a small hollow cavity burnt into its side, about four feet up. If the tree was hollow inside, it might be big enough to fit both of them. He grabbed Evelyn's hand and pulled her toward the stump. She stumbled, momentarily caught off balance, and tripped.

Knox listened again. They weren't going to make it. Whatever it was, it was coming toward them—fast. It was hunting.

"Run, Evelyn!"

Knox yanked her to her feet and they sprinted for the tree cavity. Knox reached up and pulled himself into it with one hand, effortlessly, as if he'd been lifting his own weight like that his whole life. He reached down to grab Evelyn's hand to help her up.

She gave a frightened yelp just as a giant black shadow flew from the smoky gloom and tackled her to the ground. She didn't have to turn over to know that the sharp teeth and deadly jaws of a large cat—the vicious *tehuantl* of Exor—were poised over her head, panting hot breath on the back of her neck. She waited for the bite—the pain—wishing she had said good-bye to Frankie, but instead, she felt a rough tongue lick the back of her head.

Then, she heard Knox laughing.

"Somebody missed you!" he said.

Evelyn rolled over, coming face-to-face with a dog's giant muzzle. Whiskers tickled her cheek as he bent down to lick her again.

"Tar!" she cried in relief.

"Where's Axl?" Knox asked.

"He is on the other side of the river," a cold voice rang out. "I see you know the hounds of Melor and they know you. You should be grateful for it. Tar has saved your life. Had it not been for him, one of the many arrows trained on you would have found its mark."

"What do you mean?" cried Knox. "I'm Knox, and this is Evelyn. We are friends of Melor!"

"We know of you, outlier. If not for the hound, we would have killed you on the spot."

The outlines of several hooded Melorians emerged from behind blackened tree stumps. A few whizzed down on ropes from their hiding spots atop the highest tree trunks. Evelyn and Knox were quickly surrounded. The Melorians wore ponchos and hoods, and their faces were painted black.

One approached with his sword drawn. He raised the tip to Knox's throat.

"You're making a mistake! We're *not* the enemy!" cried Evelyn, putting her hand up protectively.

"Says who?"

The same detached tone told them they were dealing with the Melorian who had shouted from the gloom.

"Says Rothermel! That's who!" Knox growled. "Ask Seaborne or Mara or Calla; they know us!"

The man's sword hand flinched at the sound of the familiar names, but he did not lower his blade. His dark brown eyes bore into the two children from under his hood. After a moment, he stepped back.

"Bind them!"

A pair of Melorians wrestled Knox's arms behind his back, tying his wrists—and then Evelyn's—together with rope. She was shackled to Knox at the waist, and then they were blindfolded.

"*Great*—just great. We make it through stinking tunnels and almost drown in a giant whirlpool to get back here, for this!" Knox's sarcasm rang through the black forest. He was rewarded with a shove from behind.

"Shhh!"

Evelyn stumbled next to him.

"How are we supposed to walk when we can't see anything?" Knox grunted as he was shoved from behind again.

"Silence!"

They marched as quietly as they could, given the circumstances. With the blindfold on, Knox became increasingly aware of his other senses. His ears twitched with the sound of small twigs breaking; had they entered a different part of the forest? The smell of burnt timber was not as strong here, and though he could not see anything, he knew that the Vossbeck ran to his left, which meant they were heading northeast, as he and Evelyn had planned to do.

"Where are you taking us?" he demanded.

More silence.

Knox grunted again in frustration.

"What did you expect?" Evelyn whispered. "They're Melorians."

It was true; even in the best of times, Melorians were not exactly chatty.

They walked on until a yank on their bonds brought them to a sudden stop. Hands fumbled at their wrists and the knots that tied them together at the waist.

"About time!" cried Knox, pushing up the blindfold when he was free. "We're *friendlies!* Jeez—"

Then, he froze.

They were standing at the edge of a squared-off pit, at least twelve feet deep. A thatched blanket of pine boughs and bracken had been folded back from where it camouflaged the mouth of the pit.

"What's this?" he breathed.

"It's a *tehuantl* trap," said the tall, helmeted Melorian with the flat voice. "We use it to catch unwanted Exorian beasts that stray into our land."

"We aren't Exorians," squeaked Evelyn. "We're outliers—from beyond the fog. Knox is a Melorian!"

"Is he now? Well, any Melorian baby can take a good fall without injury," the Melorian said, shoving Knox in the back, launching him over the edge and into the pit.

"KNOX!" shrieked Evelyn.

"I'm okay," he called back from the bottom.

"How dare you?" She turned on the Melorian. "We came here to help you!"

"We've had enough of your *help*." He chucked his chin at the pit. " Are you a Melorian, too? Will you jump, or should I push you?"

"I-I-I can't believe you," argued Evelyn. "After all we've been through to get here—"

The man put his hand on her back, ready to shove her.

"Leave her alone!" yelled Knox. "Go ask Rothermel about us, you idiot!"

Evelyn glanced over her shoulder at the group of Melorians and the brawny figures of the two hounds, pacing several yards away.

"Axl! Tar," she pleaded. "*Tell* them."

The hounds stopped prowling and sat down on their hind legs, thumping their tails on the ground.

A wave of fury came over her, so strong it banished the wild thing to the very farthest reaches of its cage. She cursed herself for letting down her guard and once again allowing others to lead her into trouble. She had known better once upon a time. Becoming friends with the Thompson boys had made her too trusting. She threw a sorrowful look at the hounds. The Melorian shoved her again.

"Don't touch me!" she snarled at him, and turned to lower herself down the side of the trap. She let go and hit the bottom with a thud.

The Melorian yanked the blanket of thatch over the opening.

"Hey! What are you doing?" Knox shouted. "No one will know we're here!"

"Then you'd best hope a *tehuantl* doesn't land in there with you," said the Melorian.

He dropped the corner of the thatch, casting Knox and Evelyn into darkness.

Chapter 13

RISING TIDE

"Rise and shine, sailor."

Captain Nate's young-old voice penetrated Chase's dreamless slumber. He had fallen asleep at some point during the night, rocked by the fluid hand of the Hestredes and the steady rhythm of the Metrian paddlers.

He started, straightened up, and squinted into the heathered glare of the rising sun. His neck hurt from sleeping while sitting up. Around his boat the river swirled and eddied, a flat metallic color. Soft mist lay on the surface of the water. Between it and the glare, Chase could barely make out the small, floating mounds of the other boats. He stretched as best he could in the small aperture of his boat, trying to get his blood back into circulation. His legs came to life at last, filled with pins and needles. He shook them. The little boat rocked, and he nearly capsized again.

"Hold on to your rigging there, Chase—it's not far now. You've been asleep for most of the journey. We towed you half the night."

Captain Nate swept his paddle in a light, easy stroke and came abreast of Chase. His face had lost much of the surliness it had worn in the city.

"Are we in Varuna?"

Chase's voice was thick with sleep. On a distant shore he heard a monkey squall; another answered. They must still be in Metria, he reasoned. As far as he knew, there were no monkeys in Varuna.

"The border is just ahead, not an hour's paddle, and beyond lies the open water of Lake Voss," said Captain Nate.

The previous night their small fleet had paddled unseen through the silent city. They had navigated the narrow canals, shrouded by a creeping mist that bathed the city's foundations in darkness. Now and then candlelight would flare briefly in a window: a signal arranged to lead the paddlers through the maze of waterways and into the great harbor, where the *Mary Louise* was moored in a hidden berth. Moving together with swift, deep strokes, Captain Nate, Chase, and their companions had paddled up the southern neck of the Hestredes, heading north. Chase must have fallen asleep soon after that, because he remembered no more of the night.

"Melor is not far," said Captain Nate, nodding into the rising sun. He pointed with the butt of his paddle to the opposite side of the river, hidden in the mist.

Chase glanced sideways at him. This new, younger Captain Nate still squinted like he did back home. The wrinkles around his eyes were the same, but the rest of his face—the rest of *him*—was different. If Chase hadn't known what they were paddling toward, he would have said that Captain Nate looked almost *happy*.

"You're in a good mood," he ventured.

"Yes, that is true. I am happy to be here. I never thought I would see these sights again."

"Or Rysta?" Chase asked.

Captain Nate grimaced, as if the name caused him pain. He nodded once, curtly, then added, "And Ayda. I have dreamed of her every night since I was exiled. And if you do the math, you will know that it was a very long time ago. Too many nights."

Chase didn't have to do the math; Captain Nate was at least five hundred years old. But somehow age didn't seem to matter with all things related to Ayda.

"So you *were* exiled? By who? Everyone here thought you were killed in the Great Battle."

Captain Nate looked momentarily taken aback.

"Not *everyone,* surely? Ratha suspected I was alive; perhaps others did as well."

Chase considered this question in silence. He was pretty sure Rysta had guessed the Captain was still alive, since there had been an image of him in her reflecting pool in the caverns. At the very least, the Captain had been on her mind. He wondered if there was anyone else who knew about him. Dankar was bent on getting rid of the fog that surrounded Ayda. Maybe he suspected that the Fifth Stone was beyond the fog. Chase shivered a little inside at the thought of Dankar landing in Fells Harbor with an army of Exorians.

Captain Nate interrupted Chase's train of thought, pointing again with his paddle. The Metrians had fallen behind them, giving them privacy.

"You will remember from the maps that the Hestredes divides Varuna to the west and Melor to the east, but this is nonsense. No sailor worth his knots cares anything about lines on paper: The same water fills all the indentations and crevices of the earth and flows between them, circling endlessly, unless some idiot builds a dam or blocks it in some way." His eyes flashed. "Do you know what they call a sea that cannot move?"

"No."

"Dead. A dead sea. And it's the truth. If water can't move, it dies. Just like everything else. Imagine what would happen if your blood was dammed up inside your body; that's what happens to a sea when it is not allowed to move."

"My dad told me that our blood is salty because we evolved from salt water. We have the same amount of water in us that the earth has on its surface," said Chase.

"He is right. All life comes from water. It's the earth's womb. We're born from it, we carry it inside us, and those of us who are lucky move along it the rest of our days."

Captain Nate bobbed quietly next to Chase for a moment, watching the flat disk of sun rise like a nickel through the mist.

"It is a great gift to be called to the stone of Metria."

"Varuna's not so bad," Chase countered.

Captain Nate laughed, a booming, hearty laugh that skipped over the river and resounded on the shore.

"Shhh," Chase chided, surprised.

"And there we have it, Chase, the everlasting curse of our kind. We decide that what is right for ourselves is right for all, and if someone disagrees, we call them stranger, and become filled with mistrust. I am Metrian, you are Varunan, and that fact alone would have us at odds if not for the truth that we are more alike than we are different. Human history is a story of self and other: a story of war. We forget that we walk the same earth on two legs—that we sleep and eat and love and die, as all humans have since the days when the Watchers were sent to guide us. There is no difference between us except how we think about ourselves."

He gave a hard little laugh.

"Human beings and their thoughts about things! As if their thoughts ever made anything even half as useful as a tree . . ."

He came alongside Chase's starboard side.

"Tell me, Chase—do you know the real reason we have maps?"

"Umm . . . so people can find their way around?" Chase asked, taking two quick strokes to port.

"You would think that, but long ago people found their way with the stars and the rocks and the curvatures of the land, before any notion of maps. The *real* reason is because there's always some warring fool who wants to rule over everyone and everything—and the only way he or she can be sure they've done it is if everything has been divided into neat little parcels and put on a map!"

Chase had never thought about it that way.

"Like Dankar."

Captain Nate nodded. "Like Dankar—but he is not the first. Nor will he be the last, I warrant."

The mist on the river was rising. Captain Nate watched it swirl and lift, then went on.

"When I was a younger man, I took long voyages to find lands unknown and claim them and any riches for my king. I wonder if they have taught you in school what it means to claim something?"

"No," Chase answered. "I learned it here."

He told Captain Nate about their first day with the Melorians, at Seaborne's cabin, when Tinator had made him fight Knox for his sword.

"This man Tinator taught you a great lesson," said Captain Nate. "There is always bloodshed when one kind seeks to own or rule over another. People do not give up their freedom or their treasures easily, believe me."

He wiped his brow with the back of his hand. For a moment, he looked as aged and weary as he had before they had passed through the fog.

"I was no stranger to killing in those days, before I came here. I won glory and fame in my country for it, for expanding my country's empire into the New World that Columbus had stumbled on. But we were not the only ones who wanted riches. All of Europe was determined to find a passage west to the Orient. There was a great race to profit from the bounty of these new unbroken lands. Do you know what happened then?"

Chase shook his head.

"The pope, who was in those days considered to be God's emissary on earth, divided the sea by holy decree from north to south—*on a map!*" Captain Nate frowned over his shoulder at Chase.

"As if such a thing could be done. My country was allowed all lands to the east of that line, and our neighbor, Spain, was given all lands to the west. We were encouraged to lay claim to them, and to conquer any and all who lived in those lands. I took whatever I could trade for or steal—timber, furs, blubber, spices, seeds—"

He surprised Chase by slapping angrily at the water with his paddle.

"History is a record of fools doing the bidding of others—or, more exactly, the Others. And I should know; I have been in their service all my cursed and overly extended life. I could be considered their . . . masterpiece."

Chase thought about the Others, remembering what Rysta had told them about her father, Remiel. According to the legends on Ayda, Remiel was one of ten Watchers sent by the creator, the godhead whom the Aydans called the Weaver. The Watchers were meant to steward humankind and their daylights, so that life could thrive on Earth. But Remiel and his brothers broke the one vow they had made to the Weaver by falling in love with human women and bearing half-human, half-Watcher offspring. And so all of the Watchers except Remiel were destroyed by the Weaver as punishment, and their children cursed. These children were given the name "the Others." They lived in the lands beyond the fog and were twisted, stunted half-immortal beings who hated their human blood, yet continued on through the ages in one guise or another, accumulating power, taking advantage of the weak.

Remiel's children—Rothermel, Rysta, Ratha, and Ranu—had escaped this fate and come to Ayda to live peacefully. But then, one of their cousins from beyond the fog—Dankar—had found them by following Captain Nate, or Caspar, as he was called then, to Ayda. Captain Nate had brought the Weaver's curse here.

Chase watched the easy dip and sweep of the Captain's paddle, wondering what the man had been doing all these years, hidden away in Fells Harbor with his secret. If Captain Nate *did* have the Fifth Stone, who had given it to him? How had the captain found Ayda in the first place? And why had he never brought the stone back? He said he'd made a vow. To whom?

Was it the same person who had exiled him? Who would have that kind of power? And how could they give a stone of power to a human?

None of it made sense.

Chase's eyes roamed the distant shore, looking for anything familiar. They must be in Varuna by now, but there was no telltale sign. The landscape looked unbroken along the banks of both sides of the river. A bird flew out of the tree canopy, heading north. The sight of it lifted Chase's spirits, and he felt a coolness at the back of his neck, as if someone had laid a hand there. His eyes followed the bird's flight pattern, tracing its way toward the distant mountain peaks. His thoughts crystallized so fast that his head almost snapped back: there was only *one* person who could give away a stone of power, and that was its Keeper. If Captain Nate had the Fifth Stone, it must mean that its Keeper had *given* it to him! Remiel was the Keeper of the Fifth Stone—or he had been until he died—so it must have been him.

Remiel.

The last remaining Watcher . . . and the Captain had known him! Talked to him, received orders from him . . . If Remiel had trusted Captain Nate, then surely Chase could trust him?

He grinned crazily at the Captain, elated by his realization. Suddenly, the battle with Dankar seemed totally winnable.

The Metrians were coming up from behind, paddling quickly.

"To the western shore, now," one of them commanded.

Captain Nate dug his paddle into the water. The Metrians fanned out around them.

"Look alive, Chase!" The Captain nodded towards the shore.

The mist was still heavy on the water, but Chase caught a glimpse of something—or someone—moving along the banks of the river.

"Is it—?"

A whizzing sound, and then a flaming spear came flying at them through the mist, giving Chase his answer. It landed with a *thwack* into the hull of one of the Metrians' boats, setting it on fire. The Metrian drove his paddle straight into the water and rolled his boat over, resurfacing, dripping.

Another spear landed. Another boat rolled.

"The Exorians can't swim, so thankfully, this is the worst they can do," the Captain said. "We can see the spears coming and go under."

"But I don't know how to do that," said Chase, watching in alarm as yet another Metrian boat rolled into the water. "I'll fall out!"

A flaming Exorian spear sank into the stern of the Captain's boat.

"Captain!" Chase shouted. The Captain rolled his boat easily.

"Come, remove the spear for me," he cried, water streaming off his sweater.

Chase yanked the spear out of the Captain's stern, almost capsizing himself. Its sharp tip was no longer burning, but it looked just as deadly. He gave it to the Captain.

The Captain dislodged himself from the narrow seat opening and placed a foot on each side, balancing expertly on the tippy edges. He waited a moment, eyes scanning the mist, then threw the spear.

"You never know, we might hit one," he said, sitting back down and picking up his paddle. "Give them a little of their own medicine."

"What do we do now?" Chase was embarrassed by how scared he sounded.

The Captain's expression was grim.

"Keep the mist between us and them, and don't stop. Paddle to the far shore. They will not dare to follow us into Varuna."

He cast another look toward the mist-shrouded enemy.

"They've broken the Melorian line. I fear it's worse than we thought."

Chapter 14

REUNION

Knox and Evelyn sat at opposite ends of the *tehuantl* trap, their backs against the dirt wall. After a while, their eyes adjusted and they could just make each other out.

"I don't understand," said Knox. "Where is Rothermel? Do you think—?"

Knox didn't want to say out loud what he was thinking. Maybe Rothermel was gone.

"Grow up, Knox," said Evelyn. She wrapped her arms around her knees. "We have to take care of ourselves. The Melorians don't trust us."

"That can't be true!" cried Knox, standing up. "Are you going crazy, too?"

"The opposite, actually. I'm just being realistic."

"Well, while you're being *realistic*, I'm gonna get us out of here. I'm not waiting around for some *tehuantl* to crash in here."

He ran his hands across the wall. It was smooth and very hard and dry. He tried to scoop some dirt out with his fingernail. It crumbled into dust. He might be able to make a foothold.

"Help me, Evelyn," he grunted, digging harder.

"Help yourself," she snapped.

She was thinking about Frankie and her grandmother. She never should have believed Chantarelle. She should have stayed with the people she knew. And all that stuff he said about her daylights and the Fifth Stone—it was probably a trick. There was nothing special about her. He just said it to get her to keep going.

"Evelyn, *please*—you're freaking me out," Knox grunted, scraping at the dirt walls of the pit with all his strength. "We have to get out and find Chase and Captain Nate. I can't do it without you. Don't be this way."

"What way?"

"I don't know—all angry, like you're possessed or something. Just be normal. *Nice.* The way you always are."

Evelyn stared at the ground between her feet. There was a faint pattern of shadows where the light was coming through the thatch. It looked like a tangled web of dark lines that stretched across the whole floor of the trap, like a network of fibers. She tried to trace the outline of one all the way from her foot to the wall. Then, she traced another from her sneaker to where it circled around itself and evened out, and ran straight into Knox's foot. She noticed he had a hole in the canvas of his sneaker where his white sock poked through. She followed the line back to her own foot.

It wasn't Knox's fault things always turned bad. It was just the way things were. And he was right: they were friends, even if their connection was as loose as the shadow line that ran between them. She sniffed and stood up.

"What do you want me to do?"

"I think I might be able to reach the edge if I stand on your shoulders," said Knox. "Kneel down with your back towards the wall."

Evelyn gave him an incredulous look but knelt down as he asked.

Knox put a sneakered foot on one shoulder and then, leaning slightly into the wall, raised his other foot and put it on her other shoulder.

"Okay, Ev. Stand up."

Evelyn grabbed his ankles and got on one knee. She tried to lift him from a lunge position, but lost her balance.

Knox toppled off her shoulders and fell backwards onto the dirt.

"You're too heavy," she panted. "I can't lift you."

Knox didn't reply. He lay back on the ground looking up at the woven patchwork of light through the thatch cover. There had to be a way out of here. His eyes swept the smooth dirt walls for any irregularities that he could use to make a ladder. He looked for tree roots or pebbles—but the Melorians were too good. They had carved this pit as cleanly as a glass bowl. He laid his palms on the dirt floor, feeling the coolness of the earth beneath them. He rolled over on his side and pressed his ear to the ground, not knowing what it was he thought he might hear. He was aware of the thrum of his own heartbeat; and as he lay there listening to his own pulse against the cool dirt floor, he felt a surge of warmth travel up from the earth and through him. He was suddenly aware of how different the dirt beneath his cheek and palm felt. He could feel every particle: individual grains that together formed solid mass. He felt how alive the earth was—not cold and inert at all. And with that sensation came the awareness of his own mass, and the small particles from which he was made. Tiny atoms. Weightless.

"Let's try again, Ev," he whispered, not wanting to jinx this feeling. His daylights were telling him what to do.

"It's no use, Knox. I'm not strong enough."

"Ssshhh—don't say that. You are," urged Knox. "Just trust me. Try it one more time."

Evelyn knelt down again. Knox repeated his movements, placing one foot on one of her shoulders, and the other on her opposite shoulder; only this time, he did so with his newfound awareness. He leaned into the wall of the pit, feeling every grain of earth beneath his palms. He felt lightness in his body and concentrated on sending it down through his feet into Evelyn. All of his energy was focused on moving upwards, into the air.

"Try and stand up now," he said, his feet balancing easily on her narrow shoulders.

Evelyn did as he asked, and, to her amazement, was able to rise to her feet.

"What did you do?" she cried.

"It's my daylights," said Knox. "They're doing it. They're making me light."

Standing to his full height atop Evelyn's shoulders, Knox was able to grab the top edge of the pit and claw back the thatched cover. Then, he lifted himself out and onto the ground, grateful to see the haze. He turned over on his stomach and grinned down at Evelyn, who was watching him, her eyes wide.

"When we go home, you need to join the circus," she said.

Knox laughed. "Sit tight. I'm going to weave some kind of rope and get you out."

"That won't be necessary," said a flat voice from behind him.

It was Duelle, a coil of knotted rope around his shoulder.

"I see your claims of being a Melorian have some merit," he said, catching Knox's eye. "I was told to come and get you, but I see you have no need of me. Good. A true Melorian must rely on his own wits and strength. None other."

He cracked a small smile and threw Knox the coil of rope. Together, they yanked back the thatch and pulled Evelyn out.

"Oh, now look who wants to be friends," she said, glaring at Duelle.

The Melorian removed his hood and sheepishly held his palm out, fingers splayed, in the Aydan greeting. He was much younger than both Tinator and Seaborne, with the dark skin and hair, brown eyes, and sharp features that distinguished the Melorians. He wore the harness and weapons of a warrior, including a sword at his hip, but he still looked young.

"My apologies," he said. "I did not understand."

"I bet," grumbled Evelyn, not lifting her palm. "Did Rothermel set you straight?"

The Melorian pressed his lips together, a gesture that was vaguely familiar. He lowered his palm and introduced himself.

"I am Duelle, son of Duon. I acted in haste. I am sorry."

Evelyn and Knox exchanged glances.

"You're *Duon's* son?" said Knox. Duon was one of the Melorian soldiers who had trained him when he first came to Melor. Duon was a friend—a mentor. "Didn't your father tell you who we are?"

"There are many rumors of the enemy at work in Melor," said Duelle. "It is difficult to know what to believe, and we have learned caution in these dangerous times. We do not know who to trust. We barely trust ourselves—"

"Well, you can trust us. I already told you that," snapped Knox.

Duelle nodded once.

"So I am to understand. Please, forgive me. Perhaps if you had lost as much as we have, you would find it easier to forgive me."

He gestured for them to look around the blackened forest.

Evelyn frowned. It was hard to argue with that.

"It's okay."

"I guess we can forgive you," Knox agreed. "But don't pull that kind of thing again."

"Let's start over," said Evelyn. She lifted her palm, fingers splayed.

✥   ✥   ✥

They followed closely behind Duelle, covering some distance before the forest as they had once known it—green and leafy—suddenly appeared, as if an invisible line had been crossed that took them back into a time before the burning.

On the forest floor, yellow moss competed with ferns just unfolding their fronds. The air was clean, with no residue of smoke. Large meadows appeared between stands of green trees, and birds darted in and out of the grass.

Duelle stopped and inhaled deeply.

Knox and Evelyn came to a halt behind him, their heads down. Something in the grass caught Evelyn's attention. She stooped down to pick up a small blueberry.

"I think I know where we are," she said.

Knox swiveled his head around to take in a 360-degree scan, then cocked his head. "Where?"

"The *berries*, Knox. Remember? Tinator told you not to eat them because the Melorians do not pick, eat, or hunt anything that lives here."

Knox beamed, cratering his dimples.

"The glen where it's always spring! That means we're close to the village. Hey, Duelle! Are you taking us to the village?"

"The village is deserted."

"Where did everyone go?"

"Some were sent to Metria for protection; others remained here, hidden in plain sight, to fight the enemy."

"Frankie and I always wanted to see the Wold," said Evelyn sadly. "Mara and Calla made it sound so pretty."

Duelle's perpetual scowl softened.

"You know of my home then."

Evelyn nodded.

"This glen is sanctuary for all," Duelle went on. "If you are ever beset upon or injured by the enemy, find your way here. I know of no Melorian who is not refreshed by time spent here."

"That's good to know," said Knox.

He inhaled deeply and felt a surge of energy pulse through him. It was so strong it almost propelled him into a dead run. They traveled on, single file, deeper into the forest, through the fresh green and mellow gold of the springtime glen. Within minutes, however, strong, healthy trees gave way to carcasses of petrified, gray trunks poking out of a swampy murk. Moss hung like beards along the limbs of the lifeless trees. Knee-high grass grew in dusky patches, grabbing at their knees with its sharp edges. The air was thick and smelled of rotting vegetation.

Evelyn stopped mid-stride, clutching at her chest.

"I remember this place, too," Evelyn panted. "I *hate* this place. It's like every bad thing that ever happened to you is happening all over again."

Duelle nodded, his lips set in a grim line. They had reached the deathfield.

Evelyn's knees gave way. She sank into the stinking grass, gnawing on her lip.

"I can't walk anymore. I'm too tired," she said, as a blankness came across her face. She pulled up her knees and sank her head between them.

Knox stared at her uneasily.

"What's happening to her?"

He felt a strong repulsion to the deathfield, but nothing like this.

"She must have evil memories for someone so young," said Duelle, looking at Evelyn with more kindness than he had expressed up to this point. "There is no line between the shadow and the light in the deathfield. It is all shadow. You are lucky to have endured so little darkness in your life, or you would feel its effects as she does." He sighed heavily.

"No Aydan ventures into the deathfield willingly—not even Melorians. We do it because we must. Wait here; I will be back."

"Here?" Knox asked, edging behind Duelle. He didn't want to stay one extra minute in this place. He looked at Evelyn.

She was cradling her head in her hands, rocking.

✛   ✛   ✛

Evelyn pressed her palms into her wet eyes, trying to stop herself from seeing the faces of her mother and father. For a moment it felt as if she were back in the apartment, in Haiti, hiding with Frankie under the iron bed frame as the walls fell on top of them. All the anger and detachment she had felt earlier evaporated. The wild thing began to pace inside her. She thought she heard her father's voice—distant and muffled as it had been the night he died, when it came to her through the wall.

Then, she heard her name. More specifically, she heard *Frankie* say her name.

She raised her head, assuring herself she was still in the deathfield. She looked around for Knox, but she was alone. Her knees sank deeper in the foul-smelling mud as she tried to stand up. Tree limbs crowded in over her head, dripping their beards of moss. The air was dank and gloomy, until, suddenly, the moss hanging overhead began to glow. Clumps of it pulsed and flickered, and then broke off to swim in the air around her. A larger tuft spread out in front of her, like fretwork, shimmering.

"Evelyn," said Frankie's voice again.

Had Frankie left the hospital and followed her here through the tunnel? She remembered the trail of pinecones she had left. Evelyn searched the swamp.

"Frankie?" she said hopefully.

"Evelyn." Frankie's voice came from the shimmering light hovering in front of her.

"Where are you?" Evelyn stared into the light. "How did you get here?"

"I don't know," said Frankie's voice. "I heard you crying, and I came to find you. Don't cry, Evelyn."

The light grew brighter, and the small pinpoints coalesced. The vague outline of Frankie's form became visible in the light, so lifelike that Evelyn could see her sister's missing tooth. She sprang up to hug her, but her arms swung and crashed together. It was Frankie's form, but Frankie wasn't really there.

"Are you okay?" Evelyn asked.

"I'm fine. We're waiting."

"Waiting for what?

Frankie's head turned, as if to speak to someone unseen behind her.

"To be told where to go," said Frankie.

"Is Gran Fanny there?"

Frankie's apparition wavered.

"Rysta is here, Evelyn."

"Rysta?" Evelyn echoed.

That piece of information was almost as confusing as the fact that Frankie was using her full name over and over.

"Where? Where *are* you?"

"In between places," said Frankie. "Where you wait. Rysta says to be careful; there's darkness ahead. She says for you to tell her brother she is here."

Frankie's voice was fading, and the little lights that outlined her began to drift and spin in the air.

"Wait! Frankie!" Evelyn shrieked. "Don't go!"

She thrashed around the murky grasses, trying to catch the little lights, as if they were fireflies.

"It's all right, Evelyn. You'll know where to go when you need to."

"I want to go with you!" yelled Evelyn.

"I'm just waiting, Evelyn; I'm not going anywhere yet."

The lights spun off into the darker air and reattached themselves to the tree branches in clumps. They stayed illuminated for a moment longer, then dulled, becoming just moss again.

"She's over here," Evelyn heard Knox say.

And then she saw him, loping beside a tall, helmeted figure who moved easily through the stunted tree trunks and murky water. The helmet gleamed around his creased, brown face, and beneath it flowed a tangled thicket of black hair peppered with gray. The bronze of his belt and its amber-colored buckle shone in the dimming light.

Evelyn felt a little leap of joy.

Rothermel.

"Best not to linger here," Rothermel said to her kindly, as he pushed through the long grass. He picked her up as easily as if she had been Teddy's size.

"You're here," she breathed.

"Of course, child," said Rothermel. "And so are you . . . I am most impressed." He clutched her closer and beamed at Knox. "It is a wonder."

Evelyn stared back at the beards of moss.

"I saw Frankie. In the lights. She said Rysta was with her. She told me to tell you."

"It's all right now, Evelyn. Hang on."

He moved them quickly to the edge of the swamp, toward a shallow ledge and a wall of rock, coated with lichen and slime.

Knox's shoulder accidentally brushed against the slime-covered wall, leaving a green stain on his sleeve. Swarms of mosquitoes bit his face.

"There now, that will be better," Rothermel said, lowering Evelyn so she could stand. His bright eyes studied them both.

"Twice now you have made your way to Melor. I am honored."

Knox was bouncing with excitement. He swatted a mosquito.

"We came as fast as we could. The fog made us forget, and then we had to walk for what seemed like days underground, and then we got thrown in that *tehuantl* trap—"

"Yes, Duelle told me," said Rothermel.

Knox frowned. "I can't believe what the Exorians have done."

"It is their nature," replied Rothermel. "Or at least, it is now. In my brother's day, Exorians had respect for the green and growing things of the earth. Not anymore."

He squatted and leaned against the dripping rock. "They have no mercy." Rothermel sighed and surveyed the swamp.

"So, Knox, Evelyn, how do you like my home?"

"Uh, it's . . . umm . . . cool . . . ?" Knox fibbed, licking the blood off his arm where he had squashed the mosquito. "It's not what I expected."

Rothermel smiled at the boy's fabrication and leaned against the wall.

"Perhaps you will like this better."

A deep rumbling came out of the ground, as the entire wall behind Rothermel split apart with a groan. A column of light blazed through the opening, setting alight thousands of unseen beads of moisture hanging on the tips of the moss and lichen.

They went through, and emerged into a giant grove of trees. Plate-sized shelves of fungus laddered up their bark like steps, and a rich smell of pine and earth took the place of the putrid smell of the swamp. The gap in the wall closed behind them.

"Welcome to the very heart of the Wold—to my Keep and castle," said Rothermel. "Does this suit you better?"

"It's beautiful," gasped Evelyn.

Knox nodded dumbly.

They passed through the grove, moving toward a hillside, stepped and layered with flowering bushes and tall grasses. A gentle, inviting light, like that of early summer, shone down. At the foot of the hill, Rothermel stopped them and spoke.

"Before we enter, I must know how you managed to come back through the fog this time. Such a thing has only been done once before in my memory, to our near ruin. If there is some form of artifice or betrayal in your return, speak now. And speak the truth."

His words were plain, but they were uttered with a force that sank deep into their bones and rooted them to the ground.

Knox had the feeling that depending on what they said, they might never move again.

"Actually, we didn't come back through the fog," Evelyn explained. She pointed to the ground. "We went *under* it—under everything."

"Chantarelle brought us," explained Knox.

Rothermel chuckled—a rumbling laugh that released the odd internal weight pinning down their arms and legs.

"So Chantarelle has shown you his tunnels, has he?" said Rothermel. "These are strange times indeed! Not many have had the privilege."

He bowed to them.

"Please, enter."

They scaled the hillside and quickly found themselves in an expansive meadow. To their left lay a cluster of long, narrow, thatched houses, set in groups of four, with open windows and doors. A small group of Melorians tended to their work outside the buildings, and here and there, a goat or cow roamed between them.

Toward the center, a patchwork of gardens was being weeded by hooded Melorian children. And at the farthest edge from where they stood, there was a great pile of boulders that appeared carelessly heaped, one upon the other, until they created a crest, higher than the highest stump. It was there that Rothermel led them.

He took them up a flight of rough-hewn stairs and into an enclosed chamber that opened on one side to a view of the clearing. He nodded at Knox and Evelyn to sit.

They sank, gratefully, onto the clean-swept stone floor, suddenly more tired than they had ever felt before. Knox yawned widely and Evelyn leaned against his shoulder.

Sleep was the only thing they longed for now.

Chapter 15

VOSS

The Metrian company passed into Varuna with minimal damage from their skirmish with the Exorians.

"Be glad we passed when the mist was rising," said Captain Nate, "or it could have been much worse. The Exorians did not expect us."

The smooth waters of Lake Voss spread before them just as the morning sun rose fully into an overcast sky. The surface had a dilute, pearly sheen, and the water against their paddles looked more green than blue.

The paddlers stuck close to the shadows of the eastern shore, the low profile of their small crafts providing good camouflage. Captain Nate took the lead, his eyebrows drawn into a deep V over eyes that reflected the color of steel. A cold headwind blew down from the mountains and swept across the lake. A chill went through Chase that was not altogether from the wind. Soon he would see Ratha again, and the thought made him both excited and terrified.

The wind began to kick up chop. The Metrians and Captain Nate moved easily against it, but Chase struggled to keep his strokes deep and even. The exertion was keeping him warm; otherwise, his teeth would have been chattering.

The shore of the lake did look familiar. Sparse scrub opened onto shallow, gray beaches littered with granite boulders. He and Knox and Evelyn and Seaborne had been captured by Exorians on one of these beaches, pawns in Ratha's grand scheme.

Chase examined the back of Captain Nate's head, wondering again if he had the Fifth Stone on him. He hoped for the Captain's sake that he did. Chase didn't want to be anywhere near Ratha if she got angry.

Captain Nate dug his paddle into the lake abruptly and came to a stop, allowing Chase to drift closer. Water slapped noisily against the hulls. When their bows were even with one another, he leaned over and spoke in a low whisper.

"You've had words with Ratha before. You know how persuasive she can be. Keep to yourself and let me do the talking. As you said before, we do not know her endgame. You have brought me back to Ayda, as she requested. That is all. Your task is complete. Do not let her fill your mind with pictures. Use your daylights to anchor yourself, and if all else fails, hold your breath."

"Hold my breath?" Chase was perplexed. "What will that do?"

"It will stop her from getting inside your head."

Chase frowned. Could it be as simple as that?

The last time he'd seen Ratha, she had shown him a terrible vision of his mother throwing herself off the rocks at Summerledge. If holding his breath meant she couldn't do that again, then he was happy to try it.

"How long am I supposed to hold my breath? I can't do it forever."

"You're a Varunan by lights, right? Try it. It might surprise you how well you can calm your breath. It's the wind of the body, after all."

Sudden movement ahead silenced them. Something white fluttered upshore, where the massive foot of the mountain range dipped sharply into the water. To the left was a rockfall that tumbled into the lake, as if a large hand had taken a spoon and dug into the skin of the mountain, leaving the rocky under layer exposed. Overhead, hidden by cloud cover, gulls circled, calling to one another. It was a lonely, misplaced sound so far inland.

The Metrians circled together. Chase grabbed ahold of Captain Nate's boat, eyes wide with fear. An unsettled feeling had swept over the lake and passed through the paddlers, filling them with dread.

"Steady, son," whispered Captain Nate.

In the distance, a figure, clad in white, appeared.

Chase recognized him. It was Calyphor, the ancient Varunan who had flown him down from Ratha's aerie. Calyphor lifted his palm in the Aydan salute. Chase and Captain Nate returned the gesture. The Captain's expression had turned even more grim, if that was possible, and dangerous. He slammed his paddle across Chase's boat, startling him to attention.

"You have your orders: Keep quiet, no talking, hold your breath. Are we clear?"

Chase nodded.

Captain Nate withdrew his paddle and dipped it into the water, heading toward Calyphor. Chase and the Metrians followed.

When they reached the first few boulders closest to shore, Chase and the Captain got out.

A Metrian came alongside Chase's boat and lashed it alongside his own; another did the same with Captain Nate's. The Captain raised his hand in farewell. The Metrians answered by raising their paddles in the air, then dug them into the lake and swiftly retreated, towing the two empty boats—Chase and Captain Nate's only transport—behind them.

"Aren't they coming with us?" whispered Chase.

"No. They will return to Metria. This part of the journey is ours alone."

Chase's stomach flipped over. The butterflies in it zoomed and flapped wildly.

Captain Nate made his way to shore, hopping from boulder to boulder.

Chase followed him as well as he could, but thoughts were spinning and colliding in his head with dizzying speed. His heart was racing, and he felt like he might vomit all those butterflies. The lake's surface seemed to fall away beneath him, and the sudden vertigo paralyzed him with fear.

He remembered this strange feeling from Ratha's aerie. His daylights were reacting to being so near to their Keeper. He took several deep breaths.

When he looked up again, Deruda, Calyphor's partner, was there to greet him, her clear eyes revealing nothing. Beside her stood three people whom Chase did not recognize: two women and a man. They were the smallest of all the Aydans that Chase had met, and so pale that their skin had a bluish cast. They wore gray fur robes that brushed the ground and covered their clothing completely, but their heads were bare. Chase could see feathers and beads woven in braids throughout their dark hair. One of the women raised her palm in greeting. Chase looked directly at her, and in a jolt of recognition, saw that her eyes were purple.

Welcome, Chase.

The woman had said his name, but he hadn't seen her lips move.

"Varunans!" he whispered excitedly to Captain Nate. "You never see them!"

Captain Nate cut him off. "Shhh . . . remember your orders."

Chase clamped his lips together and took a deep breath in and held it.

The Varunan woman who had greeted him cocked her head, watching him closely.

You have kept your promise, child of Varuna. Do not fear.

Her voice rang out in Chase's head.

"You must come," she said simultaneously, out loud, to the Captain.

Captain Nate was watching Chase's face. When the Varunans turned their backs, he bulged out his cheeks.

"Hold your breath, or they'll get inside your head and wreak havoc."

Chase nodded, and gulped in air.

The Varunans led them through a passageway between a maze of boulders indiscernible from the shore. Chase turned back in time to see Calyphor and Deruda take wing and fly up into the sky.

The cry of gulls somewhere above became frantic.

Chase took another gulp of air. In moments, they were inside a shallow cave in the mountain.

"Wait here," the Varunan male ordered, also speaking aloud.

Do not let the fisherman leave, the same voice commanded in Chase's head.

Captain Nate bowed courteously to him and the man retreated.

Chase exhaled loudly.

"Can you hear them?" he cried, pointing to his head.

"No, Chase. I am not a Varunan. It is a specialized skill—one I am none too fond of."

"Can *I* do that?"

"I don't know; can you?"

Chase closed his eyes and concentrated on the word "Hello."

He opened them.

"Did you hear anything?"

The Captain shook his head.

"Oh, well," said Chase, looking around instead.

The cave was large, but shallow, and lit only by the sun's weak reflection off the lake as it filtered through the rocks. It was gray and cold and barren, so different from the golden caverns and grottoes of Metria.

"It suits her," mumbled Captain Nate. "Not a breath of warmth in her."

"Seaborne doesn't like her either," said Chase.

"She has never been very likable, but this latest act—shipwrecking a boatful of children—is beneath contempt."

"You may not approve of my actions, but they have proven to be effective," a cold, high voice whistled into the cave. "For here you are."

Wind rushed through the boulders in deep, low blasts, horn-like. Light seemed to leap off the lake in silver shards that stabbed at their eyes. Chase's heart hit the roof of his mouth and he forgot all about holding his breath.

Ratha stood before them at the mouth of the cave, her robes shimmering in ever-shifting colors, like the edges of a cloud at sunset: purple, green, orange, pink. Her jet-black hair fell like a curtain to her fingers from the small topknot on her head.

Hello to you, too, she said to Chase, without speaking. Her strange, purple, translucent eyes flicked across his face.

Chase felt as if the ground beneath him had turned to liquid. His knees gave way and he stumbled. In his mind's eye he saw the aerie in the clouds. The cauldron burning beside the square, four-sided building. Then he saw Summerledge, and then the Captain's living room, the fire burning in the grate. The images came and vanished so quickly, it was as if his memory was being flipped open like pages in a notebook.

His eyes shot to Ratha. Was she scanning him?

"Hold your breath!" whispered the Captain.

Chase gulped in some air and held it, feeling better almost immediately. Ratha's lips tightened, and she shifted her glance back to Captain Nate.

"Long have you eluded me, Caspar de Real, son of Jean and Marta, but I see now that I was not fishing with the right bait."

Captain Nate did not reply.

Chase sensed Ratha's gaze.

She studied him for a moment beneath half-lowered lids, then spoke.

"Chase, you have proven your loyalty. You have honored your daylights and earned my trust. You have brought the fisherman and his treasure back to us."

She glided toward them, her feet hidden by her long robe.

Chase felt sick again. He took in a slow, deep breath and tried to save it.

Ratha was face-to-face with Captain Nate. She was almost his height. To Chase's astonishment, Captain Nate did not break her gaze.

Chase tried to watch her face, but his own dizziness, amplified by the swirling, shifting colors of her robe and the glittering light, made it difficult. He gulped in another breath and held it.

The Captain's mouth was a thin, white line, his jaw clamped in fury.

"Fine sister you are, Ratha, sacrificing your kin to the likes of Dankar. Have you learned nothing from the past? You have sent your sister to her doom, and us along with her."

Ratha's face grew still and pale.

Pressure began to mount in Chase's head. He had felt it before, at Summerledge, before he fell off the roof.

"Do not speak to me of Rysta's suffering, fisherman. What do you know of it? What do you care?" said Ratha, spitting the words like venom. "Rysta has suffered far worse, for far longer, on your account, than she has in her time in Exor. She has mourned you for five hundred years, bathing her wounded heart in salt. She thought you were dead. Do you think now she will rejoice that you live?"

Ratha's voice turned mocking.

"You—alone among men with the power to come and go to Ayda as you please; you, who can read the watchwater and the fog; you, who could have stoppered her tears and come to her aid in a single journey—*chose* to not ever do so. Do you think she will be *happy* to know that you have come back now?"

Captain Nate exhaled sharply, as if Ratha had kicked him in the gut.

"But she *did* know he was alive!" cried Chase. "She could see him in her pool! We saw him. Evelyn thought he was Dankar."

"Evelyn thought I was Dankar?" Captain Nate repeated, shocked.

"Rysta *let* herself be taken captive," Chase went on, forgetting his orders. "Why would she have done that unless she knew the Captain would come back for her? She will be glad to see him. I know it!"

Ratha stepped away, her robes flickering.

"Ah, I see now that it was not only the wrong bait that kept you from our shores, but also an internal defender."

She turned her cold eyes on Chase. He had the sensation of looking in an iridescent mirror without seeing his own reflection.

"But do not be confused on one point, Chase: Rysta surrendered to Dankar for *you*—for you and your brothers and your friends alone. Not him. She wanted to see you safe, free of Dankar's treachery, and that is why she went into Exor."

Ratha turned back to Captain Nate.

"So you see, Caspar, it was not I who sent Rysta to Dankar; it was them. *Your* kind. Humans. Always the same story."

"Yes, that is like her," said Captain Nate, his voice soft.

Ratha resumed her place at the mouth of the cave, backlit by the bright afternoon light.

"And now it is time for you to repay her kindness."

She extended her hand.

"Give me what was once my father's and is now rightfully mine."

Captain Nate's left hand hovered by his pocket.

"Give me the Fifth Stone, Caspar," said Ratha.

Captain Nate dropped his hand.

"I don't think so, Ratha. Not yet . . . I may need it to rescue Rysta."

Ratha laughed her cold, frightening laugh. The temperature in the cave seemed to drop.

"Do you think I or any Aydan would let you wander into Exor with the Fifth Stone? Give it to me now! Then we will have no quarrel. *I* will use the stone to vanquish Dankar and find my sister."

Her eyes roamed over the Captain, searching him.

Chase's attention ping-ponged between Captain Nate's drawn lips and Ratha's fierce expression. What could Captain Nate be thinking? Could the Fifth Stone really be small enough to fit into his pocket? Why didn't he just hand it over?

Captain Nate put his hand on his belt.

"Hear me, Ratha. You were not there when the Fifth Stone was cast away. You see only your own power when you imagine the Fifth Stone and what you would do with it. But the Fifth Stone does not belong to any one Keeper. It is of the world, and beyond the world, and was sent from Ayda for a reason. Your father believed it to be a danger."

"Are you saying that I would use the Fifth Stone against my own?" hissed Ratha.

"I am saying that you do not know *what* you would do with it. You are an Other, like Dankar—like all those who claim a Watcher as kin. The Fifth Stone was not meant for you, or else your father would have given it to you. He knew better. Just as the Weaver divided the *atar* so that life might thrive, so did your father divide the governance of the daylights so that Ayda might survive.

"You know this to be true, Ratha." His tone was plaintive now, wanting her to understand. "The Fifth Stone is not to be used as a weapon—by *anyone*. It is meant only to exist. In peace. As ballast for the daylights. It has no purpose here."

She glared at him with her strange, reflectionless eyes.

Wind rushed into the cave, billowing her dark hair around her head in a furious tangle. Sand and gravel began to eddy at their feet.

"You are a fool, Caspar. I already have a great weapon at my disposal—or have you forgotten? If you will not give me the stone willingly, I shall *take* it."

The wind blew harder around the small enclosure of the cave, gaining speed and force, making it hard for Chase to stand. He heard Captain Nate yell above the torrent.

"I AM GOING TO EXOR TO FETCH YOUR SISTER, RATHA! HELP ME!"

As if to answer, she pursed her lips and blew through them. The wind blasted into the cave with the force of a tornado. Chase and Captain Nate were thrown against the back wall of the cave, gravel pelting their faces. Ratha locked her eyes on Captain Nate, her lips still pursed. The Captain clamped a hand over his mouth and nose, but before Chase could do the same, he instinctively inhaled and breathed in a mouthful of Ratha's poisoned air.

Immediately he was hit with an image of Frankie in the hospital, as vivid and real as if he had been standing there beside her sickbed. He saw her round, golden face, her curly brown hair, dank and snarled against the pillow, her eyes moving beneath their closed lids, as if she were dreaming. Her upper lip and forehead were coated in sweat, and her fingers played frantically with the blankets as her mouth moved without sound. A small machine blipped frantically beside her bed. Her eyes blinked open and locked onto Chase's.

Then, in an instant, Frankie was gone, and in her place, Chase saw Evelyn and Knox, trapped in a hole in the ground. A dark, hooded figure stood above them. Then, he saw Teddy, his face dirty with grime and sweat, crawling on his hands and knees in what looked like a tunnel. He was wearing his old school backpack. Behind him was their mother, squirming her way through the narrow space. Dirt and pebbles rained down on both their heads.

Ratha's voice shrieked out loud, drowning out the clamor of wind and rubble: "They are all in danger, Chase! Only the Fifth Stone can save them. You must get it from him. If he does not release it, they will all die!"

"Don't believe her, Chase!" the Captain shouted, loosening his grip over his mouth and breathing in. "Stop this now, Ratha."

Ratha raised a hand and the wind in the tunnel blasted faster around them. The Captain screamed in agony, as if someone were stabbing him.

Ratha moved backwards toward the mouth of the cave, her eyes locked on Captain Nate. He doubled over, slamming his fists into his eyes as if to beat out whatever it was that Ratha was showing him.

"Yes, Caspar, she is dying!" The wind railed in Ratha's voice. "She will not last much longer in Exor. There is no time left for any of them! They will all perish because of you."

Captain Nate and Chase fell backwards onto the ground and curled into themselves to protect their faces. The gravel tornado clawed at their skin as if it would shred it from the bone.

"CHASE—MAKE HER STOP!"

Chase had no idea what he meant.

"Your daylights!" shouted the Captain. "Use them!"

Chase buried his head into his chest, happy to oblige, but not sure what to do.

"Talk to her, man! In your head!" yelled the Captain through gritted teeth. "She'll flay us alive here! She's your Keeper!"

Chase screwed up his face, talking to Ratha without speaking.

Please, Ratha, don't do this. We're all on the same side!

It didn't work. The grit and gravel sliced through their clothing. He tried again, less nicely: *Listen to me—he's right! Your father wouldn't want this. Your mother didn't want this!*

A fresh clump of gravel pelted his face. He tried again.

He's right! They gave the stone to him, not to you! Your father didn't want you to have it! Your father trusted him; why won't you? STOP IT!"

The wind shrieked one more ear-blasting gust and then died as abruptly as if a door had been shut. When the grit settled, Chase dragged himself to his knees and looked around. They were covered in a fine white dust. The cave was empty. Ratha was gone.

Captain Nate's face was bleeding and his eyes were red.

Chase leaned back against a boulder, breathing hard.

"Why won't you just give it to her?" he panted. "What does it matter, anyway? What can we do here that she can't?"

He shook his head, and dust billowed around him.

"She showed me stuff . . . Knox and Evelyn—I think they're in trouble, and Teddy, and my mother, too. They're somewhere underground." He gulped. "And Frankie looks bad—"

"I saw them, Chase," choked Captain Nate, "and Rysta, too. But you must understand: I can't give her the Fifth Stone. I wouldn't. Not for anything—"

"Why?"

"For all the reasons you said. It was placed under my protection long ago, and I vowed to conceal it, even if it meant my death. If you think what just happened was bad, you cannot imagine what would occur should Ratha obtain the Fifth Stone. I would die—and I would let you die—before I surrender it to anyone, let alone allow it to be used."

"Then what was the use of coming here at all? Why bring it?"

The Captain was silent for a minute.

"I never said I brought it."

Chase's mind went utterly blank in an effort to process this latest piece of information. He stared at the man beside him, struggling for words.

"I don't understand. What the hell are we doing here then? I mean, you said—"

"What *exactly* did I say?"

Chase traced their past conversations as quickly as his shocked brain would allow.

Looking back, he had to admit that there was always the suggestion, the hint, that Captain Nate had the Fifth Stone in his possession, and was willing to bring it back to Ayda, but Chase had never actually seen it, or, more importantly, felt it. Chase was certain that the Captain knew more about the Fifth Stone than anyone else—but as for having it on him . . . Who could say for sure?

He buried his face in his hands.

"Oh, man. We're done for."

Captain Nate hoisted himself up, resolute.

"Look—you came all this way because you believed in an idea. I need Ratha to continue to think I have the stone so that I can make a deal with her to get me into Exor, and that means you have to watch yourself—and your thoughts. You're too easy for her to read."

He gave Chase a severe look.

"You can't let her in there, Chase, even though she's your Keeper. Not now. There's too much at risk. For now, hold your breath and keep telling yourself I have the Fifth Stone. I have to get into Exor—and I can't do it alone."

Chapter 16

AN UNEXPECTED MEAL

When they had slept a little, Knox and Evelyn were ready to tell Rothermel what they knew of their rescue beyond the fog, and the weeks of forgetfulness. Knox described meeting Chantarelle, and how the little man had jogged their memory. He told Rothermel everything he knew about Chase and Captain Nate, and then about his and Evelyn's underground journey.

Rothermel was keenly interested in Frankie and the strange sickness that had befallen her.

"No one else has suffered in this way?" he asked. "Not Chase or the little boy?"

Knox shook his head.

"Have you ever heard of this kind of sickness here?" asked Evelyn. She was feeling better. The black chill of the deathfield had retreated now that they were in Rothermel's Keep. It was hard to be afraid of anything here.

Duelle was at the cave's entrance, eyes sweeping the grounds below.

"No," answered Rothermel, "I have not, but perhaps in Exor they know of it, for I am certain that is where it comes from: It is a curse of Dankar's that plagues her daylights and weakens her vessel. But it is curious to me that this sickness has *grown* in strength in your lands and not the reverse. I had not thought that the evil of Dankar could reach so far across the fog."

"Rothermel," Evelyn said, "I don't understand what I saw back there. Where *are* Frankie and Rysta?"

Rothermel was quiet for a moment, then explained.

"What you saw was Frankie's spirit—her daylights. They are stuck between this world and the next. It is not uncommon. Sometimes the daylights will leave a body temporarily if there has been a terrible wound or shock. They seek shelter in the trees of the deathfield until they may return—or move on."

"That's what she and Rysta are waiting for?"

Rothermel nodded once.

"Yes. If the vessel dies, the daylights will be free to become something else. If it lives, they will return in the form you know as your sister's, until they are permanently fragmented."

"But they *aren't* dead, right?" she asked in a tight, little voice.

"No," said Rothermel. "But they aren't truly alive either."

Evelyn's face fell.

"They are not suffering. It is more like . . ."

He struggled for words.

"I think it is more akin to when you and Knox were in Chantarelle's tunnels. You weren't here, but you weren't there. You were *somewhere,* but *where* was completely unknowable to those who had not traveled that way before. It is like that."

She considered what he was saying, thinking once again of the stories she'd been told of the *loa,* the intermediaries between the spirit world and the real world. An uncertainty was nagging at her. She realized what it was.

"But we had Chantarelle to guide us; is it the same for Frankie and Rysta?"

Rothermel's gold-flecked eyes lit up.

"Yes, Evelyn, I like to think so; but one may only know for sure when one is on that particular journey—"

A sharp sound from below brought Duelle to his feet, bow drawn.

Rothermel recognized the source. His lips edged up at the corners.

"Now, here is a better welcome for you."

"Where are they?" cried Seaborne's voice, ringing out against the rock walls, followed by the man himself, much as they remembered him, armed additionally with Tinator's massive crossbow.

"Come here, you fog-ridden scalawags! I thought I was done with you for good," he blustered, holding his arms out.

Evelyn and Knox bounded over to him.

He enveloped them in a giant bear hug.

"Ah, 'tis good for my daylights to have you both back, to be sure. I had not trusted my hope to ever see you again."

His eyes roamed the cave.

"Have you come alone then?"

"Yes," said Evelyn. "But Chase is here somewhere. He came a different way."

Knox quickly filled him in.

Seaborne absorbed his story, and asked, "So did you leave the little ones at home then?"

"We did."

He pounded them both on the back.

"Then you have learned something since I last saw you! I am glad."

He stepped back to get a better look at them, taking in their jeans, sweaters, and torn and dirty rain jackets.

"You look very well, indeed! Taller, I think, and more warmly dressed than the first time, but those ponchos won't do. You'll be spotted a mile off. You'll be needing your Melorian garb back."

"It's so good to see you!" said Knox, hiding his shock at the change in his friend's appearance.

Seaborne looked as if he hadn't eaten since they'd last seen him. His collarbones stuck out sharply from beneath his weapons harness, and sinew and veins were visible just beneath his skin. He had on his blue woolen officer's coat over the familiar green, wrapped skirt, but it was so worn and shredded it could not have offered him much warmth. His face beneath the scruffy beard was gaunt and sported a nasty red slash across the nose and cheekbone.

But his blue eyes twinkled familiarly when he smiled.

"Likewise, lad, likewise." Seaborne's eyes grew misty. "How *is* our Teddy? I have not passed a day without thinking of him. I am glad he is safe. Means I have one less of you to worry about."

Knox thought about Teddy and his turtle, how he had been flushing the toilet all the time.

"He misses Metria, I think."

Seaborne grinned.

"Ah, well, he is a boy after my own heart."

He turned to Evelyn.

"And, Evelyn, how is Frankie?"

Evelyn told him.

"Ah, I'm sorrier than I can say to hear she's unwell. It pains me to think of her suffering," he said soberly.

Then Evelyn described meeting Frankie—or her daylights, at least—in the deathfield.

"Crikey," said Seaborne. "That's not a sight one sees every day."

He gave Rothermel a strange look, then turned back to Evelyn.

"Well, at least she is being well cared for and kept out of this blasted business."

"How are Calla—and Mara?" asked Evelyn, afraid Seaborne might have his own bad news.

"You may see for yourself."

Behind him, Calla and her mother, Mara, strode single file into the chamber, their faces shielded by hoods, the points of their throwing knives glinting below the hems of their ponchos. They lifted their palms in greeting.

Knox threw himself at Calla, hugging her. She was thinner and less substantial than he remembered. She stumbled backwards.

"You have forgotten our ways, son of Melor," said Calla, frowning as she righted herself.

Knox pulled back, stung.

Calla smiled. "I am joking, Knox!" She quickly wrapped one arm around his neck and the other around Evelyn, pulling them close. She pressed her cheek against their bent heads. "I have missed you—more than you know!"

"Us, too," said Knox into her shoulder.

Mara stepped forward and lowered her hood. Her dark eyes were subdued, and the skin beneath was bruised-looking, as if she had not slept in many days. She, too, looked hungry. The scar along the ridge of her jawline was white and gnarled like driftwood.

"Melor has great need of warriors now, outliers," she said earnestly. "The forest is falling. Many Melorians have fled to Metria; more have been fragmented."

"We know," Evelyn said sadly. "I'm so sorry."

"Regret is no help to us now, nor is grief. Each morning we open our eyes to an uncertain sunrise; each night when we close them, we make peace with what has come before. This is what you must know now that you have returned. There is no time for lessons or practice anymore. If you stay here, you must fight as one of us. The stone of Melor must be kept from Dankar at all costs." Her eyes flashed. "Do you understand?"

"Yes," said Knox.

"We understand," said Evelyn.

"Then you are most welcome," said Mara.

She gestured to Calla, who retrieved two fur-lined Melorian ponchos for Evelyn and Knox. Rothermel furnished a weapons harness, a set of throwing knives, a bow, and a full quiver of arrows. He gestured for Knox to take them.

Knox began to arm himself, his face split into a broad smile.

"It feels so good to be home," he crowed.

Evelyn smiled at him. His happiness was catching.

Rothermel nodded to Mara.

Mara reached under her poncho and unhooked a pair of curved throwing blades from her belt. A frayed leather loop hung from the ends of each knife, and the dark bone handles were worn thin with use, but the edges of the blades looked freshly sharpened, and deadly.

She held them out unceremoniously to Evelyn.

"May you live to see better days, girl-child."

Evelyn shot a puzzled look at Mara and then at Rothermel, who indicated that she should take the knives.

She grabbed the extended handles cautiously; the leather loops fell easily around her wrists. Her grip fell effortlessly into the handle grooves that Mara had left behind. The blades felt light and true in her hands, as if they had been made for her.

She glanced up at Mara's face.

"What will you use?"

Mara's tired eyes skipped across the faces of Evelyn, Knox, and Calla, and came to rest on the reassuring visage of Rothermel.

"Since the passing of Tinator, my daylights grow more restless in my vessel; they long for the unbound state from which they shall see this world renewed. My fate lies here now, with my Keeper, with whom I still find some measure of peace. My time as a warrior has ended. You and Calla are to be my blades now."

"Mama," Calla said softly, shaking her head under her hood. "No."

Mara shushed her and stepped away.

Evelyn suddenly realized how very fragile, and very human, Mara was. She had always seemed so strong and untouchable before. Evelyn's heart swelled with a fierce protectiveness. She looked down at the curved blades in her hands and knew, without knowing how, that she could wield them. She stowed the knives and raised her palm.

"I swear by my daylights that Dankar shall not enter these woods."

Mara pressed her own fingers to Evelyn's and bowed her head.

"I believe you."

✛   ✛   ✛

After a brief meeting, Seaborne, Calla, Knox, Evelyn, and Duelle set out from the Keep that night. Since there was no way to hear word of Chase, or Captain Nate, or their hoped-for cargo, the Melorians would not risk relaxing their guard. They left Mara under Rothermel's protection, and in the company of Axl and Tar.

The party headed north, toward the Broomwash and the borderlands of Exor, to relieve a troop of Melorians that had been posted there since the last full moonrise.

Calla did not speak of what had passed between her and her mother before they left, but her companions knew enough by the pace of her stride. Even Seaborne hung back, not daring to approach her. Calla was in search of a battle, and she would have it one way or another.

There was little food to be found in the Broomwash, and less and less along the way, since the fires had consumed much of the forest. They passed through the charred, smoldering remains of what had been the largest Melorian village. Regular walls of stone shone in the dim light, revealing places where houses had once stood.

"They were made of wood and wattle, and roofed with thatch," said Seaborne in a hushed tone. "They went up like a lit torch."

"What happened to all the people?" whispered Evelyn.

"Most escaped, but some stayed to defend the village. They were not so lucky. The Exorians fragmented them all. It has been a bitter fight now that Dankar has Rysta. The forest is dry and acts like tinder to their match. We lose ground every day."

Knox swallowed. It was hard to see the extent of the damage in the dark, but he could smell it. A stinging, roasted smell.

Calla led them through a maze of great tree trunks, burned black and limbless, poking up into the night sky. Seaborne stopped by one enormous tree, gouged and hollowed by flame, and pulled out a handful of charred bark. He smudged it across his brow and cheeks, painting them black. His eyes glowed white in the half-lit gloom.

"Camouflage," he whispered, and smeared some on Knox's and Evelyn's faces.

"What about *tehuantl?*" asked Evelyn as they began walking again.

"They've moved off," answered Seaborne. "There's barely a mouse left in this rubble fit for eating." He shifted the crossbow on his shoulder.

"There's always . . . us," said Knox.

"Aye, they've had their fill of that, too. We're too gristly now, and cunning."

Knox glanced up at Seaborne's skeletal face and winnowed arm muscles. He looked about as close to starving as somebody could get without actually starving.

"So what *do* you eat?"

"Anything we can," said Seaborne. "Roots, leaves, bugs—the occasional fish when I can get to the shore. My cabin is gone now, you know. Burnt to the ground. I've been living in the woods with Calla and her mother. We make do."

Ahead, the black shadow that was Calla stopped and gave the hand signal for full alert. Duelle moved silently to her side. A strange rattling sound was reverberating through the husks of the trees. Everyone froze.

Seaborne reached behind him and removed his sword from the steel scabbard that hung on his back.

"Stay here," he hissed, and silently made his way forward toward Calla. Something made him jump back, startled. He slashed at the ground, then leapt up on the nearest reachable tree trunk.

Knox and Evelyn traded looks. They hadn't anticipated the fighting to start so soon.

Knox slowly slid one of his throwing knives out of his harness; Evelyn unhooked her knives from her belt loops and grasped the handles. Knox saw—or, more accurately, sensed—something moving along the cinders of the forest floor; it looked like massive tree roots come to life.

"Ev, I think it's a—"

"Snake," Evelyn finished for him, just as more slid by accompanied by a rattling sound. "Rattlesnakes." She looked warily at Knox. "What do we do?"

"I don't know," he groaned.

The snakes didn't seem to care much about them, making straight for the spot up ahead where Calla and Duelle stood like statues.

The rattling sound increased. Backlit by the half-moon, multiple large snakes rose up like arrowheads, three feet from the ground. Their silhouettes darted and weaved as one.

"Why does everything have to get so freaking big on Ayda?" cried Knox.

Seaborne leapt from his perch with a yell, and somersaulted in the air. He landed behind the line of pulsing, swaying snakes, slashing at any available necks with his sword.

The snakes' rattles shook angrily, like enormous bees buzzing in the air.

Seaborne was quick and deliberate. Heads rained on the ground before they could strike.

Calla and Duelle pirouetted back to back, their blades scything the air.

Knox threw one of his knives, but it went wildly astray and almost hit Duelle, who blocked it with his sword.

Evelyn spun her knives as she ran, gaining momentum, and attacked. Within seconds, the covey of snakes had been dispatched

"Looks like it's snake for dinner tonight," said Seaborne, surveying the heap of carcasses on the forest floor.

"It wasn't the snakes I had to worry about as much as Knox," said Duelle. "That knife almost got me in the ribs."

"He's out of practice, that's all," said Calla, bending down to collect the rattlesnake carcasses.

Seaborne chucked Knox on the shoulder and went to help her.

A chilling rattle-cry, nearer and louder than all the others, made them freeze mid-bend.

Not two feet behind Knox rose the slender rope-like torso of yet another snake—larger than the rest—gleaming silver and black in the gloom. It rose higher and higher until it faced them at eye level, easily within striking distance for a snake that size.

Seaborne mouthed *Don't move.*

The snake opened its mouth wide, exposing two pearly drops of venom hanging like sap at the tips of its fangs. It reared its head back.

Knox closed his eyes.

Fwhupp!

A pair of sharp, curved knives whizzed through the air, cleanly cutting the snake in three pieces. The bottom part collapsed to the ground, while the other two pieces were thrown a few feet from the rest.

Evelyn pushed past Knox and knelt down to retrieve her knives.

✜   ✜   ✜

Seaborne, Calla, and Duelle gathered as many decapitated snake carcasses as they could carry. Knox and Evelyn wanted to help but Calla waved them off.

"They still have a nasty bite after they're dead," she explained. "If we had time and more light, we would bury the heads, but for now, stand up there." She pointed a ways off to a mound of fallen trees barely visible in the gloom.

Knox and Evelyn touched as little earth as possible as they made their way to higher ground.

Seaborne, Duelle, and Calla followed soon after, snake carcasses draped over their shoulders like scarves.

Seaborne used his machete to strip the skin off each one before he handed them around.

"Dig in," he grunted, tearing bites off the raw meat and chewing.

"Wouldn't it taste better if we cooked it?" said Knox, bringing a snake to his nose and sniffing it. "It's gross this way."

Seaborne swallowed. "No fires. Just eat."

Evelyn used one of her knives to chunk off a bite of her snake. She popped it in her mouth and chewed.

"I've had worse," she shrugged, and cut herself another piece.

"What about the poison?" asked Knox, still not convinced.

"Eat it and don't complain, lad," Seaborne admonished, "or I'll eat yours. You may get nothing else for several days."

Knox took one look at the Melorians, hungrily devouring the meat, and sighed. He brought the dead snake to his lips. He tried not to think about the fact that it had been slithering along the ground only minutes before.

"Here goes nothing," he said, and took a bite, working his jaws to break down the stringy fibers. Evelyn was right. It wasn't too bad: bland, with a rusty aftertaste, similar, he imagined, to what a dusty tire might taste like.

"Definitely does *not* taste like chicken," he mumbled.

Evelyn laughed, a sudden surprising sound that raised the heads of the Melorians.

Calla gently nudged her.

"It is good to see you more contented, Evelyn. It pleases me that you return to us so well."

Calla's words were genuine, but they had a sobering effect on both Knox and Evelyn. The ravenous faces of the Melorians, amid the remnants of their ruined forest, were bleak reminders of who had suffered more since they had last been together.

Knox did not complain again.

Chapter 17

THE TRUTH

Captain Nate and Chase dragged themselves to the water's edge. The lake glittered in the cold sunlight.

Chase plunged his head and neck into the icy water, drinking deeply. The water was so cold it burned as it went down his throat. He came up, spluttering.

Captain Nate splashed water on his own face, washing the grit and dust out of his mouth and nose.

"What now?" asked Chase, when he had caught his breath.

Captain Nate shushed him with a look.

Chase narrowed his eyes and glanced out across the lake at the tops of half-submerged boulders that stuck through the surface. Standing on top of one, as still as death, was Ratha. The air around them was so quiet that Chase could hear the sound of a drop of water splashing on the pebbles at his feet as it fell from his face.

"I'm glad you came to your senses and didn't kill us in there," said the Captain, his voice ricocheting across the water like a gunshot.

Ratha cocked her head.

"You humans fear death to your detriment. Perhaps you would act more wisely if you understood that one life is as significant as one wave is to an enormous ocean—even your life, Caspar, as lengthy as it has been, is but a mote in the eye of the wind. It is not for my sister's life or for mine, or even for all the lives on Ayda, that I would see Dankar defeated. It is for balance of the *atar* and the good of all; it's not just for one or two or even a thousand lives that I want the Fifth Stone."

Chase had a vision in his mind's eye of the shifting, ever-moving surface of the sea, and a wave gaining height and energy as it traveled toward shore, only to crash on the beach and recede, blending back into the waters from which it was born. An endless cycle.

"Why don't you just tell her the truth?" he whispered.

"Shhh," Captain Nate hissed.

Ratha's robes shifted in irritation.

"You do not carry the stone on your person, Caspar. This much I now know. Your mind is not as cloaked as you would like to think. But I am convinced you know a great deal about it, which leads me to reason that you have hidden it elsewhere."

Her robes shifted again, the light glancing upon them with a strobe-like effect. Suddenly, she was before them, eye to eye with Captain Nate. Her skin was so pale that Chase could see the blue veins pulsing at her temples. Her eyes locked on to Captain Nate's.

This is it, thought Chase. He remembered what Seaborne had told them on the glacier: *Ratha could use your own mind to kill you.*

"Captain Nate," he whispered, "c'mon—"

He was cut short by the sharp jut of Captain Nate's elbow in his ribs.

Ratha's eyes flitted over Chase's face and then returned to the Captain. She lifted a long, white finger and tapped it to Captain Nate's forehead, punctuating her words.

"Tell me, fisherman—shall I use the power of Varuna to leach the truth from your skull? It would not be hard, you know, to steal your little human secrets from you. I know you know where the Fifth Stone is, and I could compel you to tell me."

Her glance fell upon Chase again.

"Or perhaps I could make you tell me in some *other* way."

The pressure began to mount in Chase's head, combined with a pain behind his eyeballs.

Captain Nate looked at Chase and then back at Ratha.

"I am going into Exor, Ratha, and I want you to help me," he said.

"Well, I want *you* to help *me*," she said.

"I won't do it," he said.

"Not even for him?" Ratha flicked her eyes in Chase's direction.

The pain intensified. Chase dug his fists into his temples.

"Seaborne was right about you!" he shouted. "I'm a Varunan; you're supposed to *help* me—not hurt me!"

The pain in Chase's head exploded and he saw stars. Blood spurted from his nose.

Captain Nate remained calm.

"If you hurt the boy, you will never get what you want. I will shatter my own vessel first, and this will all have been for nothing."

"I will do as I like, as you have done for all these years," she hissed.

Chase steeled himself to open his eyes and look at her. When he did, it was as if a laser stabbed him in the eye. Chase felt vomit spider up the back of his throat. He grabbed at Captain Nate's sweater to stay upright.

"Don't ever give the Fifth Stone to her—I don't care if she kills me! Don't give it to her!"

Captain Nate caught him.

"*Enough*, Ratha. I will do as you ask. Leave the boy alone."

The pain in Chase's head began to ease. He was surprised to find himself sobbing against Captain Nate's chest.

Ratha was pacing. She stopped in front of Chase. He resisted the impulse to run.

"You—Chase—can you not see that I desire only what my father desired before me: To sacrifice what must be sacrificed for the good of all things? I do not wish to hurt you, but if it will move us closer to ending this, I will do so."

She walked on. A breeze fluttered from her robes across the water, sending a ripple of small waves across the lake's surface. She seemed lost in thought. When she returned, she stopped just short of Captain Nate, searching his face.

"After all the damage you have caused, Caspar, plunderer of sea and souls—why do you insist on more? Why won't you just tell me what you know?"

Captain Nate rubbed his face with his hands, which were covered in flecks of Chase's blood. When he lowered them, he looked unimaginably old, more like the man Chase had known back in Fells Harbor. Broken and beyond grief.

"Ratha," he confessed, "you may think I have escaped the ills that have befallen Ayda, but believe me, I have suffered alongside you each and every moment of my endless days. I have lived generations knowing that I am to blame for what has happened on Ayda, and what may yet occur—" His voice was strained.

"There has been no fog to wipe my memory—and no mercy of death. Believe me when I say to you now: I stand before you because I *am* trying to set things right. And in order to do so, I cannot tell you what I know—*yet*."

Ratha contemplated Captain Nate in utter stillness. An eternity seemed to pass before she spoke again.

"I believe you to be sincere."

"I am," said Captain Nate. "And to prove it, here is my offer: If you will take me into Exor, I will surrender to you all knowledge of the Fifth Stone once your sister is safely back in Metria. I will not resist you. You may take the information as painfully as you wish."

Chase's eyes shot to the Captain.

"But you will not hurt the boy, nor any of his kin, ever again," he added.

Ratha's expression was unreadable; she stirred and the tension eased, like air being released from an overfilled balloon.

"Very well then," she said. "I accept your bargain, Caspar. I shall assist you in retrieving my sister, and in return you will render to me the contents of your mind *and* your life. Both shall be mine to use as I see fit."

The Captain held up his palm to seal the deal.

Ratha lightly touched her five fingertips to his.

"By my daylights, Ratha, I am sorry for what I have done."

"Then save her," said Ratha. "That is your charge."

Calyphor and Deruda suddenly materialized behind them.

Ratha stepped back.

Deruda clutched Chase to her chest, as Calyphor fastened his arms around Captain Nate. Then, with nothing more than a slight ruffling sound, the Varunans soared into the air, headed west.

Chapter 18

QUARRY

By dawn, Evelyn, Knox, and the Melorians had gained the western edges of the Broomwash. Tree cover had all but disappeared, and their small band was forced to scrabble on hands and knees through dirt-colored grasses. Their progress was slow, and would soon be halted by the rising sun. In the harsh light of day, they would be too easy to spot by the Exorians.

Calla, in the lead, raised her palm to motion for them to stop. Seaborne and Duelle conferenced, their heads so close together, their hoods touched. Seaborne circled back to Evelyn and Knox.

"Too many eyes here to risk crossing open land; there's a place ahead where we will wait out the day. We'll try again at nightfall," he whispered.

His face was crusted with dirt, his expression grim.

"Try not to make a sound. *Tehuantl* have good hearing."

"*Tehuantl?*" Knox squeaked. "I thought they'd moved off."

He had been so worried about stumbling on an Exorian raiding party that the sleek, black killing machines of Exor had slipped his mind.

"The Broomwash is their main hunting ground now. Dankar relies on them to guard the border to spare his warriors."

"Where are the warriors sent?" whispered Evelyn.

A look of distress passed over Seaborne's face.

"Metria."

Calla began moving again, the tips of her knives raking the ground beneath her as she crawled. Her head swiveled underneath the hood, on guard for any movement in the grass. A distant roar, like a strangled scream, caused her to pick up the pace.

Within minutes, they reached a small outcropping of boulders, pitted and worn from exposure and assembled in such a way that there were several cracks between the rocks. Calla got to her feet, and, turning sideways, somehow inched her body through one of the small spaces between the rocks. Once she was inside, her hand became visible through the crack, gesturing for them to follow.

It seemed impossible to Knox that Seaborne and Duelle could fit through the small spaces, but one by one, they maneuvered their way in, contorting their bodies to squirm through. Evelyn and Knox copied the Melorians' movements, and, being smaller, had little trouble squeezing through.

Inside was a small enclosure, barely big enough to fit all five of them.

"Starvation has its benefits," Seaborne said with a grimace.

He pulled out a makeshift flask from his waistband filled with water from the Vossbeck. He passed it to Calla, who took a drink and passed it to Knox and Evelyn. The flask made two rounds before it was dry.

"We have to move at first light," murmured Duelle. "We won't last long here without water."

Another roar from a *tehuantl*, patrolling somewhere beyond the outcropping, reached their ears.

"It doesn't seem like we'll last long, no matter what," said Knox.

"Shhh, lad. We'll do what we can," Seaborne said, and drew his knees to his chin, sinking his head onto them. "Rest now."

✛   ✛   ✛

The sound of soft footsteps woke Knox. Calla, Seaborne, and Duelle were already awake and at attention. A golden, late-afternoon light poured through the long, vertical crack in the rocks. They had been sleeping for several hours.

Knox touched Evelyn's foot. She woke with a jolt.

"What?" she said out loud.

Calla put a finger to her lips.

The footsteps were coming closer, the sound of grass being rubbed together and steady, even breathing. A shadow and then the silhouette of a long, sleek *tehuantl* passed outside the crack in the rocks. The cat leapt effortlessly atop the outcropping and let out a tremendous roar.

Knox felt the hairs on the back of his neck stand up. The sound went straight to his heart.

Another halfhearted roar, and then the noise of the cat flopping its body down on the rocks.

"Great," whispered Knox. "It's sunbathing."

Seaborne leaned forward and whispered directly in his ear. "Do not speak or move."

They waited, keeping as still as possible while the shadow cast by the setting sun grew longer and longer, until the sky fell into twilight. In the distance, another *tehuantl* yowled. The one above them answered, and leapt from its perch onto the grass six feet in front of their hiding spot, landing with a light thud.

Knox could see most of the cat through the crack in the rock. It stretched, curling its back, and then rolled in the grass, looking as harmless as a big kitten. Knox admired how glossy the animal's fur was, shining black and smooth in the dying light. It was almost hard to believe it would hurt anyone. Once upon a time, before Dankar, the *tehuantl* were friendly. Maybe this one still was; maybe Dankar hadn't gotten to it like the rest.

Knox watched the cat roll playfully back and forth on the grass. He shifted slightly, trying to take the weight off his foot that was falling asleep. His ankle cracked, a small sound, but it was enough to alert the cat. It instantly jumped to its feet.

The Melorians exchanged glances and moved silently in front of Evelyn and Knox. The cat was sniffing loudly at the ground, a low growl emanating from its throat.

"It's caught our scent," whispered Calla.

The *tehuantl* moved directly in front of the crack, sniffing with its large pink nose. A yellow eye bore down on them through the slice in the rock. The cat blinked and then roared a warning. Its great jaws split open wide enough to fit any of their heads. A black paw batted at them through the crack, claws extended.

Calla tried to arm her bow, but in the small confines of the enclosure, she could not put any tension on the string. The cat batted at them again, narrowly missing Seaborne's thigh.

Knox lunged forward and stabbed at the paw with one of his throwing knives. The *tehuantl* roared in pain, then redoubled its efforts. It threw itself against the boulders in a frenzy, trying to get at them. A foot or two of granite and a narrow crack lay between them.

"It's waiting us out," said Seaborne.

"Or waiting for assistance," added Duelle. "Do we know how many could be out there?"

The *tehuantl* roared again into the enclosure, frustrated, and then leapt to the top of the outcropping. They could hear its sniffing above them. Seaborne and Calla shook their heads.

"We're stuck," said Calla. "We can't move and we can't signal for help."

Outside, night had fallen. Knox could see a small sliver of sky through the crack. A star brightened as the shadow of night grew deeper. In the tight space, the scent of sweat and fear seemed overpowering. The *tehuantl* could probably smell them a mile off.

"Do you think it knows how many of us there are?" he asked.

"Hard to say, lad," answered Seaborne. After a short pause, he added, "But I think I know where you're headed."

"What?" asked Knox, confused. He had no idea where he was headed.

Seaborne crawled to the narrow opening, peered out into the evening, and unsheathed his machete—a difficult thing to do in the small confines of the space. "I'll draw them off, and then you all make a run for it. Go back into the forest and wait for me there."

Calla grabbed his arm.

"You can't do this. The *tehuantl* have the high ground. You won't make it twenty feet."

Seaborne tightened his grip on his blade. "There's no other way. We can't stay here."

"There has to be," Calla implored.

"I might make it; you never know. Try and cover me with your bow."

"I can't get a good shot from in here."

"Don't, Seaborne," said Evelyn. "*Please.* Didn't you say there was another guard here? They'll find us."

"We don't know if they're coming. They might be dead . . . and, as much as I like you all, I'd rather have my end quick, thank you, than waste away in here with you," said Seaborne, trying to sound as if he meant it.

"If you go, we all go," said Knox.

"Don't be foolish, lad."

"He's not foolish," said Calla. "He's right."

"Agreed, Seaborne," added Duelle. "We fight as one or not at all."

Seaborne sighed. "All right. I see there's no sense in arguing with the lot of you. But once you get through the opening, run as fast as you can and keep a good distance between you. That beast can't be everywhere at once. And I *am* going first."

"Evelyn," Knox whispered. "Can cats see in the dark?"

"I think so."

"Can you?" said Knox, thinking of her skill with her knives.

"No."

"Your blades are useless then, huh?"

"I think so, unless the cat attacks straight on—"

"That's not going to happen," interrupted Calla. "Your job is to run. Let us worry about the *tehuantl*."

"*I* will worry about the *tehuantl*," snapped Seaborne, "and you will take your own advice, Calla. As soon as I'm out, you head back to the Wold. That's an order."

Seaborne leaned closer to her and whispered, "You must take the young ones to safety." Then he raised the crossbow and turned sideways. "We will see each other again," he said, and inched through the narrow opening.

The *tehuantl* screamed in the air above them. Knox felt his heart leap into his mouth at the sound. Seaborne shouted. The *tehuantl* leapt from the rocks, its paws making a dull thud when it hit the ground. Calla slipped through the opening, her bow at the ready, Duelle directly behind her. Evelyn hesitated a minute, then pushed herself through the crack. Knox pulled two of his knives from his harness, raised his hood, and followed.

Outside, it was strangely quiet. Either the *tehuantl* had already silenced Seaborne, or their friend had succeeded in drawing it off. A dark mass moved to Knox's right. He saw it in his peripheral vision and froze.

"Steady, friend," Duelle whispered, "it's me. Keep your knives harnessed." He crouched down. Knox copied him, shifting on his heels.

"The *tehuantl* is on the hunt. Be still."

Knox inhaled slowly, trying to calm his nerves. He looked up.

Overhead, the blue-black sky was freckled with stars. A bright waxing moon was rising to the east. His blood thumped through his veins and his ears twitched with every little sound. Normally, he would have been happy for the beautiful night, but tonight, he wished more than ever for clouds to obscure the moonlight.

Duelle shifted position. Knox's focus snapped back onto the grasses.

"Do you see it?" he breathed.

Duelle shook his head beneath his hood.

"Maybe Seaborne led it away?"

"No, it is here. Somewhere in the grass. It is stalking us."

Knox gulped.

"Stay close," said Duelle.

"Are we running?"

"No."

About two hundred yards away, the scrub and grass exploded in screams.

The silhouette of the *tehuantl* leapt into the air, snarling and spitting, a shadow against the moonlight. There was a shout—human—as the cat pounced.

Knox and Duelle broke into a run.

The cat tore and bit at a hooded figure on the ground. It was in a frenzy, its daylights ignited by the smell of blood.

A curved knife whizzed through the air from somewhere in the brush, slicing deeply into the cat's flank. The animal whipped around, forgetting its prey for a moment, leaving Duelle and Knox a window in which to attack.

Duelle armed his bow, but before he managed to launch an arrow, a heavy bolt whizzed through the air and hobbled the cat. It curled into itself, yowling and desperately trying to remove the bolt from its hind leg with its jaws.

Evelyn and Seaborne crashed through the grass. They circled the injured cat. The *tehuantl* alternated snarls and pitiful whimpers, baring its white fangs, its ears flattening back against its head.

Seaborne took a step forward. The *tehuantl* swiped angrily at his calf and hissed. It dragged itself a few yards off and let out a tremendous roar that thundered out across the Broomwash.

"It's calling for help," said Duelle urgently.

Seaborne raised the crossbow once more.

"May your daylights speed onward," he whispered, and released another bolt—this time, directly at the *tehuantl*'s heart. It landed deep inside the animal's glossy fur.

The cat whimpered in pain and lay back against the grass pathetically. It tried to drag itself away with its front paws, the shaft of the bolt driving deeper inside with each movement. Finally, it gave up and sank back into the grass, panting heavily. The grass around it flooded dark with blood. The *tehuantl* no longer looked lethal, but became, as it had earlier when it was rolling in the grass, something akin to a very large house cat. One that was sick, and in need.

Knox was stirred at the sight and moved toward it.

"Stay back, lad," ordered Seaborne.

He crossed quickly to the human figure on the ground, which lay motionless. It was Calla. Her quiver was in shreds around her and the back of her poncho was torn into pieces. She was bleeding from several deep gashes made by the *tehuantl's* claws.

He dropped to his knees and lifted her to his breast.

"Oh, no," he said. "Please, no! Not her!"

Calla moaned.

"Thank the daylights," he cried, and rocked her. "I thought you were dead."

"Just resting," she said weakly.

The *tehuantl* let out another whimper. Its yellow eyes had turned gray and glassy, and its jaws were spread open, gasping for air.

Knox ignored Seaborne's warning and knelt beside the dying creature.

"What are you doing?" hissed Evelyn.

Knox waved her off. Something about the *tehuantl* was drawing him in. Its smooth head glistened in the moonlight between its small, delicate ears. He had never seen anything more powerful, or more beautiful.

"I'm sorry," he said, raising his hand.

The *tehuantl* did not move.

Knox laid a few fingers on the cat's forehead and gently stroked the soft fur of its brow. It made a wet, ragged sound that was almost a purr. He scratched the cat's ears and stroked its neck, damp with blood.

"I'm sorry," he repeated.

The *tehuantl* took its last juddering breath and went limp. The life left its eyes.

Knox felt a loss that made no sense in light of the terror he'd just experienced. This cat had almost killed Calla. So why did *he* feel so guilty?

He understood now why Tinator had hesitated in killing these creatures. There was something fine and noble in them that could not be corrupted. Something good. Something that spoke to Knox and connected them in ways he did not have words for.

"Is it dead?" Evelyn's shocked voice rang out above him, then it changed. "Oh, Knox—"

Knox realized that tears were dripping off his cheeks. He scraped them away with the back of his hand.

"You were petting the *tehuantl*," said Evelyn.

"Yeah?" he shot back. "So what."

She dropped to her knees beside him. "That was good of you . . . it didn't have to die alone."

She looked at Knox with new appreciation.

"You are a lot kinder than you let people know."

Knox rocked back on his heels. "Don't tell Chase."

Evelyn patted him. "Our secret, I swear."

"Bloody fools! Did *nobody* listen to my orders?" groused Seaborne, helping Calla to her feet. Her daylights were already stanching the blood and giving her back some strength. She limped over to peer down at the cat.

"Such a shame," she lamented. "Such a waste."

"Aye," agreed Seaborne, "but between the two of you, I am grateful it is the *tehuantl*."

A great roar boomed out across the brush, as if they had conjured another one by speaking their name out loud; another roar followed, and then another.

"It's a pride," groaned Duelle, "come to answer this one's call."

"Can you run?" asked Seaborne, looking at Calla.

She shook her head. "Not yet, and not fast enough anyway. None of us could."

"I'll carry you on my back," said Seaborne.

"There's no point," she said. "They're too fast."

"Your father, Tinator, would not have given in so easily, Calla," admonished Seaborne. "They do not yet know where we are. If we crawl through the grass back toward the forest, we may yet avoid them."

"Crawling won't be necessary," said a gravelly voice, coming from what seemed to be the ground, "if you will follow me."

A small figure moved into their midst.

"Oi," croaked Seaborne. "What's this now?"

"Chantarelle," breathed Evelyn.

"To the rescue . . . again," said Chantarelle, bowing.

"We must move," said Calla, masking her surprise at the little man's appearance with urgent need. "Now."

She motioned with her chin at their refuge of boulders less than a quarter-mile from where they stood. A number of *tehuantl* had assembled there, their sleek fur turned silver in the moonlight. They yowled and roared plaintively into the night.

"They're calling for this one." Calla motioned to the cat at her feet.

"Are you alone?" asked Duelle, eyes combing the grass.

"Yes—and no," said Chantarelle.

Just then, Axl and Tar swept past their small group, leaving a trail of flattened grass in their wake. They ran toward the outcropping, teeth bared and growling, and began to circle the pride.

"What are they doing?" cried Knox.

"They know what to do, which is a sight more than you do," said Seaborne.

"Come," said Chantarelle, tugging on Knox's poncho. He set off into the grass, dragging him along. Evelyn and the Melorians followed. Calla limped along, leaning on Seaborne. They quickly put distance between themselves and the pride of *tehuantl,* which was, at least momentarily, being kept at bay by the hounds.

"Careful now," Chantarelle said from the grass. It was difficult to make him out, as small as he was. "We're almost there."

Within minutes, they found themselves at a spot in the Broomwash where the ground appeared to rise and fold into itself, like bread dough. At the seam where one layer met the other, there was a good-sized gap, hidden well by the grass and small rocks. If they hadn't been led there, they never would have seen it.

"In you go—all of you. The hounds can't be expected to hold those cats off for long," said Chantarelle.

"Another tunnel?" asked Knox.

"Yes," Chantarelle pointed. "Go."

"I don't know who you are, little man, but I don't need to be told twice," said Seaborne. He pushed past Knox, half carrying Calla. He lowered her into the gap, then eased himself in.

One by one, they all followed, with Chantarelle in the rear. At the bottom of the drop, they stopped, looking up at the last shred of light they would see for some time. Ahead of them was an inky blackness, deep and empty as the void between stars.

Seaborne hitched the crossbow over his shoulder.

"Come, Calla, behind me, hand on my shoulder. Evelyn, you take Calla's shoulder. Knox, you fall in behind, then Duelle. We'll go in a line. If someone stops or drops their hand, we all stop," Seaborne said.

"Wait, no—I can't do this again," said Evelyn, holding back. Her voice sounded as if it had already been swallowed by the tunnel. "I hate it down here. I feel like I'm suffocating."

Chantarelle tsked.

"I'm sorry, Chantarelle. I know it's your home, but it's true. I can't bear it. I'd rather take my chances with the *tehuantl.*"

"That is because you are only thinking of the tunnel. You do not think of what lies at either end, or how it is all connected. Use your daylights, Evelyn. They will show you."

Evelyn looked at Chantarelle, and then cocked an eyebrow at Knox.

"I don't see the point."

"You might as well try it," said Knox. "What do you have to lose?"

Chantarelle took her hand. "Close your eyes. Use your other senses. You have five of them for a reason."

She did as she was told and shut her eyes.

"Now, Evelyn, *listen*."

Evelyn reached out into the quiet of the tunnel with her ears. She heard the soft rustle of the Melorians' ponchos, the rhythm of Knox's breath. Her own breath.

"That's it," said Chantarelle.

The train of her thoughts began to slow and her mind grew quiet. She was aware of the air buffeting down from the entrance, and she smelled the animal scent of her skin. The dusty, rubber taste of the rattlesnake lingered at the back of her tongue.

Chantarelle squeezed her hand.

She felt a pulse of energy—a quickening—and opened her eyes.

She had to blink at the brightness of the aura that surrounded the little man. She looked up at Knox. He, too, was surrounded by a cocoon of light, though not as bright as Chantarelle's.

"Knox—you're glowing!" she said.

Knox stretched out his hands, turning them over.

"Where?"

Seaborne, Calla, and Duelle gathered around her. They, too, were cloaked in a bright, warm light. And beyond them, she saw that the walls of the tunnel were no longer dark, but cracked and lined and pulsing with light. She looked down at her own hands and saw the same light rushing through her veins. She was filled with a sense of peace and contentment—a feeling of rightness—she had never known before. Here they all were, all made of the same light.

"It's so beautiful," she breathed.

"It is," said Chantarelle, and removed his hand from hers. The regular darkness of the tunnel resumed, and her companions took on their normal dusky silhouettes.

"What was that?" she asked.

"Your daylights," explained Chantarelle. "They allow you to see the *atar* as it truly is."

It took a moment for this to sink in.

She knew that she could never look at her surroundings in the same way again. It was like seeing a strand of hair for the first time through a microscope—the delicate layers of cells and scales, invisible to the naked eye, but all part of an intricate system. Worlds within worlds existed in everything.

She looked up through the gap in the ground and saw the moon, encircled by its own aura of silver light, and then far beyond it, she saw a star, pulsing and radiant as her own veins had been only moments ago. The whole of everything was light, from the darkest depths to outer space.

"I think I'm ready now," she said.

"Aye, Evelyn, I think you are," said Seaborne, looking at Chantarelle with newfound respect.

Chapter 19

REMNANTS

Thirty miles to the north, Chase propped himself against a rock, watching the same moon whose light had just cast a final glow on Knox, Evelyn, and the Melorians. To the east lay the mountains of Varuna with their snowy peaks. To the west, the skirt of the mountain range fell away into the flat, barren Exorian plain.

The Captain had taken the first watch while Chase slept; now Chase was on guard. They would move when the moon had risen two hand lengths from the mountain peaks. Far off in the distance, Chase thought he heard the cry of a *tehuantl*. His eyes searched the ground. Nothing.

At present he and the Captain were safe enough, dug into a culvert that was walking distance from the border, where they had been dropped off earlier. Calyphor and Deruda had armed them with Metrian swords.

Chase extended his hands in a line to measure. The moon was at the knuckle of the top hand. He walked over and shook the Captain, careful not to cut himself on the Captain's sword, which lay at the ready against his hip.

The Captain was instantly awake.

"Time?" he said gruffly.

"Almost."

"We'll have about six hours to make it into Exor before the sun rises."

"That's it?"

"The days are long now. There is little rest for the creatures that prefer the dark—almost as if Dankar wills it to be so."

"Can he do that?" Chase asked, aghast.

Captain Nate gave him a sideways glance.

"I don't know. The power of the stones of Ayda is kept at the will of their Keepers. Who is to say what might happen should a Keeper's will grow unchecked? Perhaps the power of the stone and the Keeper they attend grows likewise; it is not for me to say. I am not a Keeper. Thank the daylights."

"Yeah, but you know one."

"So do you."

"Don't remind me," said Chase, thinking of Ratha's cold stare. "You wouldn't want to be a Keeper?"

Captain Nate exhaled sharply. "Never."

"But you'd live, like, forever, and get to do all this cool stuff—"

"Living forever is overrated, boy," said the Captain. "The world needs change. New beginnings. Imagine a world where the sun never set and everything stayed the same . . ." Captain Nate stood up, preparing to move. "Most people would call that hell."

Chase was quiet for a minute. The Captain had a point.

They descended quickly and quietly through the foothills, picking their way between boulders and rocky outcroppings. The going was different than Chase remembered from his last journey into Exor. As the mantle of rock gave way to shale and then coarse dirt, the ground grew spongier underfoot. Here and there, tiny pillows of moss and low-lying patches of ground cover clung to the ground's surface.

"The glacier is melting," Captain Nate observed, turning back to look at the Varunan mountain range. "Exor will not be a desert for long."

"That's a good thing, isn't it? Maybe Dankar will relax," said Chase.

"I don't think Dankar cares a nickel about Exor—or Ayda, for that matter. This is all just a means to an end. His interest lies far beyond Ayda, beyond the fog. It always has. He and his kin have a vein of ambition in their blood that knows no bounds. I should know; in my youth, I was a pawn of men with that same ambition. Human life is a currency for them, to be bought and sold and spent in their service."

"Captain, back there, when we were with Ratha, you made it sound like your whole life was a mistake."

Captain Nate looked away. "I'm not proud of much, that's true."

"But what did you do besides—this?" Chase gestured at the desert. "I mean, you've been around a long time."

"My crimes began long before I came to Ayda. I was an explorer then, as I have told you. I saw many lands and strange sights on my journeys. I laid claim to them all."

Chase shrugged a little. "That doesn't sound *so* bad."

"Remember your history books, Chase. Not only land was taken—"

Chase's jaw dropped. "You stole people, too?"

"Only as oddities at first: gifts for my king in exchange for another expedition. But soon they became my most precious cargo. Portugal needed laborers, and—to my everlasting shame—I was able to offer an unlimited supply." He sighed. "It was the making of me. I had any ship I chose at my disposal. My family grew rich. I was the king's favorite. I grew fat off the misery of others and called it contentment. But then one day I came ashore on a land that could not be plundered. I remember that day as a dream I see now with waking eyes. I should like to go back to that time."

"Ayda."

"Yes."

Chase fell silent in the face of Captain Nate's past. What was there to say? The Captain had transported slaves; he had trafficked in human souls. Made money that way.

"There must have been something else you could have done, rather than kidnapping people and selling them for profit," Chase blurted.

Captain Nate stopped in his tracks.

"I was an explorer," he said. "My heart's desire lay only in new vistas and strange lands. I could never settle in one place in those days. My skin would itch and my heart would ache beneath my ribs until I was given a ship and sent to sea. I could find no peace without it. But I already told you: Ships do not come free, and the price of these expeditions was paid by securing bounty from new lands."

"It's still disgusting," said Chase, moving past him.

"I agree."

Captain Nate walked in silence for several moments.

"It is more than that, Chase. It is a stain of evil I will never wash clean. I could say I was young, or just following orders, but the truth is, I didn't know any better. I had been schooled in a land ruled by those who claimed the Others as kin. When I came here, to Ayda, where all creatures are free to live as the nature of their daylights intends, I saw the world as it was meant to be, and I wished never to leave. I swore on the *atar* that I would never steal or take another human life again if I could be granted that wish."

"But you *did* leave."

"I did. It's true." His brow wrinkled. "Even here, I could not tame the nature of my daylights; they would not be contained. Rysta understood that my soul would wither if I stayed in one place, and because she loved me, she risked everything to grant me my wish. She gave me the freedom I needed, along with a way to return. We both thought it was the solution."

"It didn't turn out so well," said Chase.

"No," agreed Captain Nate. "And that is another permanent stain on my soul. But now, at least, I have a chance to return her gift. I will see her free if it is the last thing I do on this earth."

"There is one thing I still don't get," said Chase.

Captain Nate grunted, clearly not used to so much conversation.

"Rysta is an Other," continued Chase. "And so is Rothermel. They can't all be bad."

He purposely left out Ratha; he wasn't so sure about her.

"No, they aren't all bad, nor did they start out that way. After the fall of their fathers, they became twisted and damaged in time by the power and longevity bequeathed to them. But there does still exist a strain in mankind—very rare, very dilute—that holds true to the higher claims of their forefathers."

"The Watchers."

"Yes, the Watchers. Though all of the Watchers but Remiel were destroyed, their children were not. In time, many fell to the evil plots of their own kin, or unexpectedly, in wars they had begun to lose. But not all of them; some went on to beget lines that nurtured the humanity in their blood. Through their actions, the balance of the daylights has not completely expired.

"And, of course, we can take comfort in the fact that Ayda exists . . . in the fact that the Keepers always strive to undo the evil of the Others . . . and in the very existence of the Fifth Stone—as long as it is uncorrupted."

Chase grabbed his arm.

"You told Ratha you knew where it was; do you?"

"I told Ratha what she needed to know to get us on our way."

"So you *lied?*"

A hole opened up in Chase's stomach.

"It was all a big show? You know she's going to torture you to find out!"

"I told her I would give her all the knowledge I have, which is the truth. Besides, I seem to recall hearing about a similar situation where someone was not completely forthright in order to advance his objective."

He looked sideways at Chase.

Chase bowed his head. He had lied, too, to Knox and Evelyn, and to Seaborne. He'd allowed them all to get captured by the Exorians and taken prisoner because Ratha had told him it was the only way to go back home.

What he hadn't known was that part of the plan was Rysta's sacrifice. So Ratha had lied to him, he had lied to his brother and friends, and now the Captain was lying to Ratha. Full circle.

"It would have been a difficult choice for anyone to make, even for a Watcher—don't you think?" the Captain asked, changing the subject.

"What do you mean? What choice?"

"Remiel's."

Chase walked a few paces behind the Captain, mulling over what he knew about the legend of Remiel. The ground beneath his feet crumbled into fine particles. Soon they would be walking on sand.

Remiel and his brothers were meant to live among their charges as teachers and guides, following only one law: human and Watcher blood could never mingle. But Remiel had fallen in love with Rysta's mother, Rachel, despite his vow. Even so, his betrayal might have been kept secret, except that one by one, all the other Watchers followed his example, until each had found human mates and sired children.

When their betrayal was discovered, the punishment came in the form of a choice: sacrifice themselves and their families, and the rest of humanity would be saved. Refuse, and watch all they had wrought on Earth over one thousand years laid to waste.

Chase gazed out over the Exorian plain. As empty and silent as it was, marked only by tall rock spires and low, scrubby outcroppings of rock and brush, it was beautiful. He tried to imagine it ceasing to exist. It seemed impossible.

In the end, only Remiel made the sacrifice. The other Watchers stood aside, saving their own—or so they thought.

Chase shook his head.

It seemed so unfair. If only the Watchers had *known* that it was only a test. In the end, Remiel didn't die. He and his family were taken to Ayda.

Chase sighed.

"I probably would have made the wrong choice. I wouldn't have done what Remiel did," he admitted out loud. "I wouldn't have made the sacrifice."

"Alas, son, neither would I," said Captain Nate with a frown. "One's path is quickly decided based on such choices, yet most of the time we don't understand what the choice really is. And now we face yet another: how to get into Exor—south, by the Broomwash, or straight across the plain, due west."

They considered the landscape before them, lit by the half-moon. Going south was easily the safer move, but also the most roundabout. They could cling to the cover of the foothills a while longer and then come up to the Dwellings from the canyon. Due west, the plain that led straight toward the plateau looked awfully exposed and dangerous. It was riskier, but much shorter.

"Can we make it across the plain before sunrise?" Chase asked.

"If we move fast and stop yammering."

Chase pivoted his head back and forth. The moon had climbed higher in the sky. There wasn't much time.

"West?" he ventured.

"You sure?"

"No—"

Captain Nate nudged his sword up his hip and smiled.

"West it is."

Sometimes there just wasn't a good choice.

Chapter 20

THE ARENA

As usual, they came for Louis just before daybreak.

He lay huddled on the cool sandstone floor of his cell, drinking in the last few moments of darkness before his torment began anew. He heard the sound of the scribes' footsteps, the scrape of the key in the lock, felt the heat of their torches, and then he was on his feet, half carried, half dragged out into the low-slung hallway. Every fiber in his being rebelled at the idea of another day chained to the cliff, left to roast beneath the Exorian sun. He was reaching his limit. He had no idea how long Dankar would punish him, or if there would ever be an end to it. Perhaps his adopted uncle meant for him to die out there on that rock, however long it took.

He quickly quashed those thoughts. To give in to them was the path toward panic and certain death, and he had resolved not to die yet. He must help Rysta escape so they could find Frankie and the other outliers. He had not forgotten the dream of the little girl in the yellow T-shirt, the one from his initiation. He had memories that preceded this place. Somewhere out there, beyond the fog, was his home. His family. He was connected to Frankie and the other outliers by this fact. And this meant that he was not alone in Ayda, and never would be again.

Louis found the strength to walk without support, and angrily brushed off the hand of the scribe clutching his arm. The flames of their torches danced in the hallway, casting shadows on the wall and across the empty mouths of other, unoccupied cells. Louis's eyes were swollen and raw, but he managed to keep track of where he was going. He needed to know where Rysta was being kept.

He channeled his awareness to observe every detail of his surroundings. The feel of the air in the hallway; where was it freshest? The odor of the torches burning and the sweat from the bare skin of the scribes. How long had they had to walk to reach him? Where did they emerge from the dungeon outside? He used these details to sketch a mental picture of where he was being held in relation to what he knew about the Dwellings, which was less than he'd imagined.

He now knew the dungeons were extensive, and located directly below the main section of the Palace, part of a labyrinth of chambers and hallways belowground. The central passage to the storehouses and kitchens was located nearby. The hallway to the dungeons extended off the main passage, and if he could get there, it would eventually lead to the pit-houses, where perhaps he could find shelter and someone to help him.

The women and young children of Exor lived in the pit-houses, tasked with the daily food gathering, cooking, cleaning, and maintenance of the Palace. Louis had been too old when he came to Ayda to spend much time there, having passed the time of the Cleaving. In Exor, boys were taken from their mothers and sisters at an early age and tested. Depending on how a boy's daylights fared, he was deemed either a scribe or a warrior, and raised in separate lodgings among others of his kind. From that day on, the boy was to consider Dankar his parent, and the other scribes or warriors his tribe, and no one else.

Because of his weak daylights, Louis had not had the test until now, and had lived out his boyhood in the Palace with Dankar.

He had not questioned this arrangement before, but now he understood why Dankar was so strict with the orders of his kingdom—and it gave him hope. Dankar was afraid of the bond of family. If Louis could escape to the pit-houses, he might be able to convince the mothers and sisters there to help him. Surely they wanted their sons and brothers back?

Louis had no more time to ponder his plan. The great sandstone door that opened to the desert pivoted on its wheel and a gust of cool early-morning air blew into the passage. The torches danced and flickered with new life. Outside, the sky loomed dark purple. Predawn.

He was taken aback. This was different. He had not been outside in the cool of the darkness; usually Dankar preferred to bring him out when the heat of the day was building.

"What's going on?" he mumbled, dreading some new punishment.

"You'll see," said the scribe on his right.

Louis eyed the man carefully, trying to pick up any hidden meaning in his statement. The scribe's face was inscrutable, as always. They were trained to show as little emotion as possible.

They led him up the steps of the striated cliff onto the plateau that overlooked the pit-houses, to his left. To the north lay the warrior dormitories, and, in the far distance, the rust-colored hills where the *tehuantl* had their lair. To the east lay the great empty Exorian plain and the rising slope of the foothills that marked the boundary of Exor and Varuna. A low band of light glowed at the edge of the eastern horizon. Daybreak would soon follow.

The scribes took him on a path north that skirted the warrior dormitories, winding around deep depressions in the rock that had been scooped out to create storehouses and caches for any fortuitous rainfall that would be siphoned off to irrigate the gardens, so carefully cultivated by the inhabitants of the pit-houses. Their job had become easier with the capture of Rysta. Rain fell more regularly on Exor with her presence, and pools of water were not as rare as they used to be.

Passing by one of the depressions, Louis felt the heaviness of moisture seeping up from the cache and smelled the rare scent of water. He suddenly realized how thirsty he was, and slowed to drink in the scent. The scribes prodded him.

"Not here," one of them said.

They walked on, the glowing band of light to the east thickening as the sky faded from deep black to purple to gray. They led him along the steps that lay just west of the warriors' living quarters, silent and seemingly unpeopled at this hour.

But Louis knew different. In Exor, someone was always watching.

The scribes halted, eyes cast down.

"We go no farther," the one on the right said. "You must walk the rest of the way alone."

Louis knew approximately where he was. Just south of the warriors' living quarters was their training ground: a deep arena sunk into the cragged walls of the plateau—invisible to all but the birds that occasionally flew overhead. Only warriors were allowed this close to the periphery . . . and prisoners.

Sudden fear swept over him.

"You have no choice," said the other scribe, nodding his head in the general direction of the arena. "You must go down there, or we will take you back to the cliff edge, where you will stay until your bones are scoured clean by the sun. We will not come for you again."

Louis looked out across the plain. He knew by the scribes' tone that they were telling the truth. He could take his chances with whatever lay in wait for him down in the arena, or be taken back to the cliff and left until there was nothing more of him to hang.

"You were his favorite. Perhaps he will spare you," said the other scribe, who had been completely silent until now. "There is always opportunity in uncertainty."

Louis caught the man's eye. He saw pity there, and it took him by surprise. He had encountered so little of that in Exor.

It was pity that had stirred him into protecting the outliers, and Rysta. Perhaps if he had chosen a different course of action—if he had done as he had been asked and not interfered with his uncle's plans for the outliers—this man beside him might now be his friend, not his guard. They might walk together into the scribes' quarters with all the other scribes, ready to eat breakfast and attend to their duties, working alongside one another as brothers.

But it was too late for that now.

"Go now," the other scribe ordered.

Louis took his leave, stumbling a little, bone-weary from the exertion after so much time spent in a cell. His bare feet sensed the smooth contours of a path as his eyes adjusted to a deepening darkness that met him as he descended down a steep switchback cut into the plateau wall. After a few more switchbacks, he found himself at the end of the path, far below the lip of the rock face.

Here, it was still the blackest of night, but he had the sensation of a great space around him. He looked up to ground himself, and was comforted by the sight of dimming stars fading into morning. There would be a morning this day, and another, and another following that, whether he lived to see them or not.

Chapter 21

REINFORCEMENTS

All sense of time receded as Chantarelle led the Melorians, Knox, and Evelyn slowly through the darkness. They traveled almost blind, heeding only the dull thump of their footsteps, the dancing flame of Chantarelle's oil lamp, and the sound of their own breaths, distinct and audible in the close air.

At first, Knox felt certain they would not be traveling underground for long, which was a good thing. He was beginning to feel not so fond of tunnels either, and this one in particular. It felt different than the other. Drier, and less inhabited. He wondered if the fires aboveground had reached all the way down here. This thought filled him with dread. Chantarelle had said that the tunnels were built a long time ago as a sanctuary for people. If Dankar's power could wipe them out, too, would there be anywhere to hide?

He closed his eyes and concentrated on walking. That felt okay, but if he let his mind wander and started thinking about how deep under the ground they might be—how the roof of the tunnel might cave in—his panic would bloom.

He counted steps to calm his mind. He calculated it could not be more than a few miles until they were safely back under cover of the forest; but then again, Chantarelle's tunnels were deceptive.

He lost count around eight thousand steps, when, suddenly, the terrain beneath his feet changed. His arm tensed as Evelyn increased the distance between them. They were definitely climbing.

He heard Seaborne's voice from up ahead.

"Now that's a sight."

Knox opened his eyes to darkness, but the quality had shifted somewhat. Chantarelle extinguished his lamp.

Evelyn stopped.

"Look up," she said.

Knox craned his neck back. The ceiling of the tunnel was much higher than he had imagined, and it was lined with tiny pricks of glowing light, almost as if he were looking up at distant stars in a night sky. The light was faintly green.

"What is it?" asked Evelyn.

"*They,*" croaked Chantarelle from the depths, "are worms; well, worm larvae. They hatch from eggs laid along the walls and ceilings of these tunnels. It's a good sign. We are getting closer to the surface."

"But they're shiny," said Evelyn.

"Yes, that happens once they've hatched. The light attracts prey—small insects, including the mature insects of their own kind who come in here to lay their eggs. Each egg, once it's hatched, sends down a small, sticky string that serves as a web."

Knox squinted at the roof of the tunnel. It was true: he could see threads coming down from some of the glowing dots.

"So they lay a trap for their own parents?" he asked.

"After a fashion," replied Chantarelle.

"Cool!"

"That's sad," said Evelyn, shrugging Knox's hand off her shoulder.

"It's just how it is. The strong take from the weak. Life feeds on death. Down here there is not much to choose from. They must eat what they can catch."

Knox flashed back on eating the raw rattlesnake, and said as much.

"That's different, Knox," said Evelyn. "I would starve before I ate my own parents—or any other human—that's for sure."

"Be grateful you are not a worm then," said Chantarelle.

"Aye," interrupted Seaborne, impatient, "that is indeed something to be thankful for. You said we are close now. How much farther?"

"Not far," said Chantarelle. "You must be quiet as we surface. We don't know what is out there yet."

"What do you mean?" asked Knox. "Where are we?"

"Rothermel sent me to take you where you are most needed."

"And where is that?" cried Calla.

"Exor."

Evelyn gasped.

"You wee, bloody fool!" cried Seaborne. "Why in the daylights would you do such a thing?" He made to turn around. "We'll just go back then."

"I have led you to the very foot of the Dwellings, as Rothermel asked," stressed Chantarelle, the green light of the tunnel reflecting in his eyes. "If I have calculated correctly, we are somewhere beneath the plateau that surrounds the Palace. We must be careful not to take a wrong turn. I am not as familiar with these tunnels, as I do not travel them often. There are many; some lead directly to the Palace, some to the warriors' barracks. We must avoid those, of course."

"Are you daft, little man?" Seaborne roared. "What are we supposed to do here? Start explaining now, or I will catch you and eat you like those blasted worms up there."

"If you will follow me," said Chantarelle, "all will be made clear."

They trudged a bit farther until they came to a junction of several tunnel openings.

"Here we wait," said Chantarelle.

"Wait for what?" asked Seaborne.

"Maybe Rothermel wants us to find Rysta," Evelyn whispered.

"How do you mean?" asked Knox.

"If the tunnels lead to the dungeons, maybe she's there. You know, like we were. Do you think that's it?"

"You are very wise, Evelyn," said a man's voice.

A dark shape materialized at the opening to one of the other tunnels, darker than the glowworm-lit gray of the one they were in. He moved closer and lowered his hood.

"Adhoran," said Seaborne, and held up his palm. "What are you doing here? I thought you had taken your family to safety."

"I have, but cowering behind the walls of Metria is not where I belong. Thanks to Chantarelle, I have come to take back what was taken. And I do not come alone. I have brought all whom our Keeper can spare."

Behind him another tall shape emerged out of the gloom, and then another, and another. More Melorians crowded behind them, all fully armed. They wore full weapons harnesses, and bore bows and quivers and a single-blade ax on a long wooden shaft.

Seaborne's jaw dropped. Calla bowed her head.

"So this is it, then?" Seaborne croaked.

"We are to follow you into Exor, come what may," said Adhoran.

✛   ✛   ✛

Just before sunrise, the Melorians, Knox, and Evelyn emerged like a small army from Chantarelle's tunnel into a crevice in the sandstone canyon at the edge of the Dwellings. They followed it out until they found themselves on a shallow bank of the newly formed Exorian River, flowing green and muddied along the floor of the canyon. Along the riverbed, patches of vibrant green plants were growing, and vines snaked their branches up the canyon walls.

Seaborne was heartened by the sight.

"All is not lost," he said, pointing it out. "See how, when given a chance, the daylights balance themselves and life prevails."

Adhoran, Duelle, and Calla joined him.

"Where do you think Rysta is?" asked Knox, staring at the river.

"Dankar will keep her near, so I presume she is in the Palace, or beneath it in a cell," said Seaborne. "Chantarelle, do you know these cells we speak of?"

Chantarelle did not answer. The company searched the ground, but the little man was nowhere to be seen.

"Not tall enough for a fight, I warrant," said Seaborne, holding his hand about three feet from the ground.

Adhoran noticed Knox and Evelyn, and leaned in to say something to Seaborne.

"You did? You saw them? Where did they go?" asked Seaborne. "Knox, Adhoran has seen your brother, and the other one. The Captain."

"Where?" cried Evelyn.

"In Metria. They had just arrived. I did not see them long. They left with Urza, headed I know not where."

"Did they have the Fifth Stone?" asked Evelyn.

"Wow, way to get to the point," Knox muttered under his breath.

Evelyn gave him a look.

"I saw nothing," said Adhoran. "I queried Hesam about it later. I know she was a friend to the outliers."

"Hesam?" said Knox. "What did she say?"

"Only that they had moved north."

"But that makes no sense. Why would they go north?"

Evelyn chewed on her lip.

"Think about it, Knox," she said. "Who lives north of Metria?"

"Uh, Varuna is north, so . . . Ratha."

Evelyn nodded, keeping his gaze. "Ratha sent us back home so Chase could bring Captain Nate back here—"

"—and now she wants him delivered," finished Knox. "So does Ratha have the Fifth Stone now?"

They both looked at Seaborne, and then at Calla.

" 'Tis anyone's guess, but if Rothermel has sent us all here, it stands to reason that the time has finally come to give Dankar his due. Perhaps that is knowledge enough for now," said Seaborne.

Calla smiled. "Can it be true?" She turned to the Melorians massed behind them.

"Take heart, brothers and sisters!" she called. "A great day dawns! Today, we shall give back to Exor what they have dealt to us! Our daylights shall rise and lead us to victory!"

The Melorians raised their axes and their bows in a silent salute.

"We will ford the river here," said Seaborne, slinging his crossbow over his shoulder and wading into the water.

Chapter 22

BODI

Chase and the Captain had not spoken for hours. What initially seemed like a straight path toward the plateau, keeping the moon overhead or in front of them and slightly to the left, had turned out to be as deceptive as crossing ice. The seemingly solid ground of the desert plain undulated like the sea; ground winds shifted the dunes, and what appeared to be a safe footstep suddenly sank into a hidden crevice and mired them knee-deep in sand. The going was slow and arduous, and—more dangerous than anything—they had not brought enough water. Chase's throat and mouth felt like he had eaten his flannel pajamas.

"I'm so thirsty," he croaked.

"We are close now," said the Captain, gesturing toward a distant mesa that rose out of the sand and merged into a larger hillside. Beside it was a sunken area of sand that, in another lifetime, could have been a streambed. It lay flat and gray in the moonlight. Some distance beyond were the dark fingers of the rock spires that dotted the eastern outskirts of the Dwellings.

"See that," the Captain said, pointing to the sunken area. "That is a wadi, and we may find some relief there."

"A wadi?"

"Yes—a gully that is dry except in rainy seasons. In my days on Ayda, this desert had many wadis. It was not so devoid of life. There were horned bucks, monkeys, snakes, and other species that lived here. I see no signs of them now . . . but this is what happens when the daylights are out of balance. Extinction."

"I don't see any water," Chase said, using his far-reaching eyesight to search the contours of the wadi.

"It's our best bet," the Captain said.

He led the way, shuffling through the sand toward the wadi's depression.

"Keep an eye out for *tehuantl*," the Captain added. "They hunt at daybreak and sunset, and if they are around, they will be close to any source of water. They know it is where living things will gather—not that there are many of those out here."

"Great." Chase grunted. "*Perfect*. Just what we need. We can die of thirst, of a *tehuantl* attack, or by an Exorian spear. Good times."

He tried to lick his lips, but he had no saliva left.

"You sound just like your brother," said the Captain.

The wadi was a disappointment at first—just a cracked bed of sand and stone. However, the hardened streambed was easier to walk on, and they made good progress, passing the mesa until they could see in the distance a rising plateau of sandstone.

"The Dwellings," the Captain grunted, tossing his head in the direction of the plateau. "The stronghold of Exor. It's all built into that plateau."

Chase surveyed the darkened mass, noticing that the sky was turning purple around it. Sunrise wasn't too far off.

"How do we enter it from here?"

"That is a good question," the Captain said. Then he pointed, exclaiming, "Ah! Look, Chase—just ahead. A gifting tree."

An umbrella-like silhouette of a stunted tree stood alone on the bank of the wadi, maybe a quarter-mile ahead. Chase could make out many interwoven branches with short, spiked leaves and what looked to be long hanging pods.

"At last, some good luck!" said the Captain.

They picked up their pace, and soon they were standing beside the strange-looking tree. It was barely taller than Chase. Its bark was thick and gnarled, and its leaves looked lethal. Captain Nate used his sword to cut several pods from the branches. He gave a handful to Chase, and then stuffed a few into his mouth, crunching away.

"Eat it," he mumbled. "You'll see."

Chase sniffed at a pod and then bit into it. It tasted like a stick of kindling at first, but as he began to chew, the stringy shell gave way and his mouth was filled with juice from the seeds. The flavor was not sweet, but it wasn't awful, either. It tasted more like an herb than a fruit, dusty and pungent. Chase shoved another pod, and then another, in his mouth, spitting out the husk when he had savored all of the juice. It only took ten pods for him to feel all symptoms of thirst disappear.

"The Exorians in my time called this tree *katari*—or life-giver," said the Captain. "It survives in the harshest, driest climates and bears fruit that will see a traveler across the desert. Every part of the tree but its leaves is edible. It takes very little, and gives so much. That is why it is also known as a gifting tree."

He knelt by the roots and gently unearthed a taproot from the sand. He used his sword to slice off a small section, which he passed to Chase.

"Don't chew this; just keep it in your mouth."

Chase did as he was told and was surprised to feel liquid running down his throat. It was reenergizing and sweet-tart, like lemonade. He smiled at the sensation.

The Captain watched him, nodding,

"Quenchwater: the blood-sap of the *katari*. It will carry us a long way."

"Can we cut off more?" asked Chase greedily. "It could come in handy."

"No," the Captain said, shaking his head. "I wouldn't want to risk damaging the tree. It is a delicate thing, harvesting quenchwater. I will take a bit of the bark, however, in case you are hungry."

He flaked off a few chunks of bark and put them in a pouch he kept tied around his waist. Chase had not noticed it before.

"Now we honor the tree's gifts."

The Captain pulled another pod off one of the branches and used his sword to break it open. He removed the seed pods and stepped a few paces away from the tree. He dug a shallow hole and placed the seeds and the empty pod in it. He put a slice of root in his mouth, and spit the liquid onto the seeds. Then, to Chase's astonishment, he used his sword to cut into his hand, making a deep gash. He held his hand over the seeds and let his blood saturate them; then he used his other hand to cover the hole with sand. He bowed his head.

"I give thanks, and in doing so, I honor all daylights in all living things."

He made the sign of an X over the hole and stood up.

The sky behind the Captain was turning a pearly gray. Chase looked back toward the mountains where a thin line of lavender divided the snowy peaks from the darker night sky.

"The sun's coming up," he observed.

Captain Nate nodded, sucking on his cut, which had already begun to heal.

"We will pick up the pace now that the ground is firmer beneath our feet. Look." He pointed his chin toward the ascent onto the plateau. "It is not that far."

Chase's heart was thumping fast. Now that they were close, it occurred to him that they didn't have much of a plan.

"What do we do when we reach the outskirts?"

"We'll think of something," said the Captain, taking one last look at the gifting tree. He moved into the center of the wadi and began to trot.

"I hate running," groaned Chase, jogging behind him.

"Use your daylights and the energy from the *katari*. Don't complain."

Chase forced his feet to move in step with the Captain, wondering when he would have to stop. *If* he would have to stop.

So much had changed since he had come to Ayda. He decided to listen to the Captain's advice. He emptied his mind of all the reasons he'd ever had for why he couldn't run, and just ran. His muscles felt light and agile; his feet flew across the dried-up streambed. In no time, he and the Captain had crossed the few miles to the plateau. Above them, the sky had lightened to a purple predawn glow.

"Would you look at that!" the Captain gasped, reeling to a halt.

Chase skidded to a stop beside him.

To the left of the wadi, at the base of the plateau, was a grid of boulders the size of cars. They stood upright in the sand, spaced evenly apart from one another—almost as if they had been planted there. As light filled the sky, Chase realized they weren't boulders at all, but a field of giant stone heads—more than eight feet tall—carved out of rock and placed there. Each head had distinct features and an ornament on top, and they sprouted out of the ground like enormous sandstone buds. Their height, combined with the rosy light of the rising sun that flickered across their faces, made them seem eerily alive, as if they could be giants buried in the sand up to their necks.

He counted them: ten heads.

"Are they . . . uh . . . what I think they are?"

"I think so, yes, but I have no memory of them."

"Did Dankar put them here?"

"No."

"Well, who did? And why?"

"It is not uncommon. I have seen it before."

Chase raised his eyebrow. "Really? Giant stone heads?"

"Mount Rushmore?"

Chase smiled despite himself. "Okay, yeah, I get it. It's a monument."

"Ah, but what you don't get is that the heads of Mount Rushmore are carved in the Black Hills, sacred lands taken from the Lakota Sioux. For them, the faces of their conquerors are forever looking down upon them. Not an accident, eh? Perhaps this is similar."

Chase contemplated the stone head in front of him. Its lips were drawn in a tight, foreboding line. Its eyes were open, staring. It wore a tall helmet, not unlike the ones he had seen in Metria. It was all very confusing. He exhaled loudly through his nose.

"So, if this is like Exor's Mount Rushmore, is it here to scare us off? I mean, if these heads are here, and we're going there"—he pointed to the plateau—"this must be the place they're protecting. Isn't that, like, the worst place to go?"

"To answer your question, yes. I think these heads are here to warn people away. But I don't think Dankar put them here. I think they were put here by Ranu in the early days."

Chase looked up at one of the giant faces. It scowled down, its eyes boring into him. What would happen if the heads actually *were* connected to bodies underground, and if they all of a sudden came alive and pushed up out of the ground?

"Let's climb," he said, feeling an urgent need to get out of there. He nodded at the wall. "We can take our chances at the top."

The Captain frowned. "I'm not fond of those chances."

"Do you have any better ideas?"

The Captain shook his head.

They shot out from behind the stone head, running straight for the wall. A sudden movement—more a shift in the light than anything—stopped them short. The Captain froze and put a finger to his lips, unsheathing his sword.

A rustle and an exhale—definitely human—came from behind them.

Signaling with a look, the Captain whirled back toward the stone head, going one way; Chase split off along the other side.

"Who are you? Show yourself!" shouted the Captain, raising his sword.

No answer came from behind the stone head.

The Captain and Chase began to circle it, swords at the ready. As they converged around the opposite ends, there was a high-pitched squeak, and then a small figure dashed out, making a beeline for an outcropping of rubble that lay to the left, at the bottom of the plateau wall.

The Captain was on the runaway in three strides, swooping it up by the scruff of the neck, and realizing a second later that he was holding a kicking child—a little girl.

He dropped her in the sand, stunned.

She crab-crawled backwards, away from him.

"Are you a Melorian?" she cried, clearly more afraid of them than they were of her.

"A Melorian? No, I am . . . ah . . . a traveler," the Captain said evasively.

Her eyes traveled the distance between the Captain and Chase. The girl eyed the blade in the Captain's hand.

"Don't hurt me."

"Hurt you?"

"Is *he* a Melorian?" She indicated Chase.

The Captain squatted beside the girl. Lowering his voice, he said, "*He* is a valuable prize for Dankar."

"*Whaaa*—?" Chase spat.

The Captain shushed him with a hand signal.

"I found him wandering out here," the Captain continued. "Will you help me take him to the Dwellings? There could be a reward."

The little girl narrowed her eyes at Captain Nate, then at Chase. She dug into the sand with her bare feet. She had a long face with a prominent nose. Her eyes were dark and determined-looking. Her head was wrapped in an orange rag, and she was dressed in a clean white shift that Chase recognized as the same kind of tunic he had worn in Exor. Whoever she was, she looked clean and well taken care of.

"Well, speak up, child. Will you take me to the Palace or not?" the Captain barked.

The girl cowered. She couldn't be more than eight, not much older than Teddy. Chase remembered that the Captain really didn't have a way with kids.

"What's your name?" Chase asked, moving closer.

"Bodi," she answered after a pause. "Did you run away?" she asked Chase, peering up at him. "Lots of boys try when it comes time for the Cleaving."

Chase shot a puzzled look at Captain Nate.

"I'm Chase. I'm not from around here, so I don't know what a cleaving is."

"It's when they take you away from your mother to go live with the scribes. When it's time, you find out if you're going to be a scribe or a warrior. All of the boys in Exor have to do it, even if they don't want to."

"Why not the girls?" asked Chase.

Bodi shrugged. "I don't know. I wish I could go. I would be a great warrior." She gave him a fierce look.

"I bet you would. Who takes the boys away?"

Bodi shrugged again. "The scribes—at least, that's who took my brother away. His name is Emon."

Chase nodded. "I have two brothers. I'd be sad if they got taken away."

"Who are you anyway?" Bodi spat at him with sudden surprising venom. "Did you escape the cells?"

"*Yeesssss*," he said slowly, the gears in his head clicking. "I was with the Metrians, with Rysta, the prisoner. But I escaped . . ."

The little girl's eyes darkened with hate. "Then, you're a *Metrian?*"

"Uh, no. Actually, I'm a Varunan, if you really want to know."

Bodi's expression changed instantly from disdain to curiosity. She pinched herself in the arm, hard.

"Why are you doing that?"

"To wake myself up. Varunans only come in dreams. That's what my mother told me."

"You're not dreaming," he said. "If you don't believe me, feel for yourself."

He put her hand on his arm. She patted him and then gave his forearm a little tweak.

"Ow!" Chase yelped.

The girl was stunned into silence for a minute. Then she said, "Can you fly?"

Chase shook his head. "No, I don't fly."

Bodi looked crestfallen.

"Are you here all by yourself?" asked Chase, trying to get back to the point.

She nodded.

"Wow, that's brave of you. I was scared out here last night, and I'm a lot bigger than you. Weren't you afraid of the *tehuantl?*"

She shot him a look. "Why? They don't attack Exorians. Only filthy Melorians who want to steal our food and rich Metrians who keep all the water for themselves."

She glanced up at Chase.

"I don't know about Varunans. But the *tehuantl* will probably eat you, too."

"Is that what you've been told about the other people here on Ayda?" the Captain asked.

Bodi shrugged again. "They hate us and we hate them."

Captain Nate turned away, pressing his fingers into his eyes. "That is a word I have never heard on Ayda, let alone out of one so young."

Chase knelt down so he could be eye level with Bodi.

"Have you ever actually met a Melorian or a Metrian?"

She shook her head.

"Well, I have," he said. "And they are just the same as you and me. You have some ideas about them that aren't true, just like the idea you had that I could fly. In fact, the Melorians and Metrians I know would like you very much. One of my brothers—his name is Teddy—he is a Metrian."

And my other brother is a Melorian. His name is Knox. And we all get along really well—most of the time."

Chase grimaced, thinking about how much he and Knox used to fight. Bodi looked confused.

"You are all different tribes in one family?"

Chase nodded.

"You can be different and like different things and still be a family."

Bodi contemplated this. Her brow furrowed.

"We are all Exorian in Exor," she said with pride. "My brother and I come here—I mean, we used to come here . . . before he was taken—to play with them." She nodded in the direction of the stone heads.

"You *play* with them?" repeated Chase, trying to imagine how that would work.

Bodi nodded.

The Captain shifted impatiently. They needed to get moving.

"Uh . . . so, Bodi," Chase asked, "how do you usually get out here?"

"Over there," answered Bodi.

She pointed backwards toward the jumble of rocks at the bottom of the rock wall.

"Hmm," murmured Chase, pretending not to care all that much. "That's a long way to climb! Do you do that all the time? It must take all day."

Bodi looked at the ground. She shook her head again.

"Is there *another* way?" Chase lifted her chin so she was looking straight at him.

"It's a secret. My mother told me to never tell anyone."

"I know all about secrets, Bodi. Listen, if you show us your special way, I promise we won't tell *anyone*."

She hesitated.

"C'mon, Bodi." Chase smiled at her. "Show us the shortcut, and we'll take you back to your house, to breakfast and everything, before anyone finds out you're gone. You don't want your mother to be worried."

Bodi's eyes welled up. "She won't care. She only cares about my brother."

"I bet that's not true," said Chase.

"It *is* true. Ever since the Cleaving, all she does is cry. Everyone knows that's what happens, but she didn't want him to go. She wanted him to run away, but they came for him before he could go."

Captain Nate broke in.

"So your mother didn't want your brother to be a scribe? She was going to help him escape?"

Bodi nodded her head. "She didn't want him to take the test. Nobody knows if they're a scribe or a warrior until they take a test," she explained. "Sometimes boys die if their daylights aren't strong enough. And if they don't die, you hardly ever get to see them if they're scribes, and you *never* get to see them if they become warriors. My mother didn't want him to go."

She looked down again and said softly, "Neither did I."

"What about your father?" asked the Captain.

Bodi looked at him blankly, as if she had never heard the word.

"Don't you have a father?"

Bodi looked puzzled. "I have a lizard."

The Captain studied the hillside, and then Bodi, and spoke.

"Bodi, I'll make you a deal. If you take me to your mother by the secret way, I promise I will help her, and your brother, and I won't ever tell anyone else how you came here. I will not allow your brother to do anything that might get him into trouble. I will . . . uh . . . speak to Dankar on his behalf."

Bodi looked unsure.

"Plus, you could show me your lizard," added Chase. "My little brother has a turtle."

"A turtle?" asked Bodi. "What is that?"

"It's like a lizard with a shell. It can live in water. I'll tell you about him as we walk," said Chase, prodding her gently. "His name is Bob."

"That's a strange name."

She looked toward the hillside and then back at them, weighing the deal.

"You have to spit-swear that you won't tell."

"We spit-swear," the Captain said, making the sign of the cross over his heart. "Now let's go."

Bodi shook her head and held out her palm. When the Captain didn't react, she reached up and took his right hand and spit in his palm; then, she pushed her own hand up to the Captain's face.

Chase laughed.

"You have to spit in her hand and then shake."

"Mother, Mary, and Joseph," grumbled the Captain, but he managed to produce a small amount of moisture to spit into Bodi's palm. They shook. Chase did the same.

With the pact sealed, Bodi led them straight for the tumbled outcropping of rubble. She scrambled up the pile, her toes gripping the ridges of the rocks. Chase and Captain Nate heaved themselves up behind her. When they finally got to the top, Bodi pointed to a large opening hidden behind two slabs of rubble.

"There's a passage through here that takes you near my house."

She paused for a minute.

"You know, if you break a spit-swear, the dirty Melorians will find you and carve your heart out and eat it."

"We can only hope," the Captain muttered behind her.

Chapter 23

DOG STAR

Louis felt the level floor of the arena with his feet. Some instinct told him not to venture into the empty space, so he groped the air around him until his hand encountered the wall of rock he had just descended. He pressed himself against it, protecting his back, and slid sideways alongside the wall, away from the path. He continued to slide this way for several yards before sensing a change in the air. He froze. Somebody—*something*—was out there. He could feel it. Was it a *tehuantl?* It would be just like Dankar to delegate the dirty work.

He strained his eyes to see in the dark, and looked up again. This time, the sky was shading to pink and gray. Soon enough, he would come face-to-face with the fate Dankar had in store for him. He would not have to wait long.

He squatted down, resting his aching back and shoulders against the rock, and willed his heartbeat to return to normal. The space around him felt uncontained. He leaned back into the solidity of the wall and tried to quiet his trembling limbs. He looked up again, searching the sky for the morning star—any star—for orientation.

He remembered a night in the Broomwash with Frankie—how frightened she had been that he had left her alone in the dark. He recalled how light she was when he'd lifted her on his back. She hardly weighed anything at all. He could have run across the Broomwash with her if he'd had to.

Now he wished that he had done so . . . turned around and taken her straight back to Melor. But he had been trained to be a good errand boy, and so he had done as he was asked: delivered the child straight into the hands of Dankar. And, as Dankar had told him would happen, the others eventually followed—and in their wake, the water-hoarder, who had sacrificed everything to free them. It had all worked out according to his plan.

Dankar had used him—and all the other outliers—to his advantage. Well, *almost* all, thought Louis. Dankar had not expected his favorite to turn against him. He had not expected the children to escape.

Louis leaned his head back into the rock. Was Frankie safe? Were any of them safe?

He couldn't say for sure, although it seemed unlikely. Dankar was now more powerful than ever. He already had the stone of Exor. Surely he would use his powers to gain the stone of Metria, then the stone of Melor. And once he had those three, there was little the Varunans could do—regardless of their reputation. Perhaps the wind-talker would drive Dankar crazy with hallucinations.

Louis smiled despite himself. If only. Dankar was already a lunatic.

His eyes raked the lightening sky one last time and then returned to the stone-cold blackness before him. With utter certainty, he knew that he was breathing in the last moments of his life, and a channel of despair opened within, as black and shapeless as the space around him. It was hard for him to figure out at this point which was deeper: the void around him, or the one inside of him. He was treading a narrow bridge in his mind. One misstep and he could be lost forever. An almost hysterical urge to laugh came over him at the thought. Despite everything, not much had changed. Hadn't he *always* been lost? From the day he'd first set out on that sailboat so long ago, up to this moment.

He had found what he went off looking for that day, even though it was entirely different from what he had expected. Instead of discovering new harbors and bringing back small treasures for his sister, he had found a world so entirely different from his own that he had almost forgotten his first home. *Almost*, but not entirely. It was these small fragments of memory from that stranger shore where he was born that he would take with him in this final confrontation with Dankar.

Because he *did* remember. He knew who he really was: he was born Edward Henry Baker. And he had become the man known as Louis, friend and protector of Frankie. He had mattered to all of them, and that meant they would remember him. Were *already* remembering him.

The thought that Frankie—or maybe even his sister or his parents, if they were still alive—might be thinking of him at this very moment heartened Louis. He raised his head once more, and there, as if answering some unspoken wish, was the morning star, bright and reddish, squatting low on the black line that demarcated the farthest edge of the arena wall to the south.

Dankar called it the Dog Star, a holdover from his days as a king beyond the fog. There, the star was considered evil. It heralded the return of long, hot days and short tempers. But not in Exor. Here, the morning star was a blessing—a reminder of the power of the Exorian daylights that bound them as a people.

Louis chewed his shredded lip and tasted blood. There was a reason he had been sent down here at this moment, at sunrise. Dankar had wanted him to see the morning star, to know that even the stars were on the side of the Exorians.

His eyes adjusted to the light, just as an orange glow appeared over the wall of the arena, like a small ember in a sooty grate. Soon he would know what awaited him. Within moments it tipped the sky orange and red, and the few clouds that lingered above flamed russet. He had seen many sunrises before, but today it was as if the sun had decided to reveal to him the full beauty and power of Exor, as if to ask him why he could have ever doubted where he belonged.

A thud like a massive drumbeat shook the ground.

His head snapped to attention. The sun was high enough now to illuminate the grounds of the arena closest to him. He saw red dirt at his feet and the gold and umber striations of the rock wall he was leaning against. The rest lay in shadow yet, although straight ahead, he began to make out a large structure rising out of the ground at the westernmost point of the arena. It looked to him to be a large pyramid of steps peaking in a small, square building set on a flat terrace. Stone statues of *tehuantl*, their jowls distorted in grotesque snarls, were stationed on either side of the structure, facing out to gaze down on the arena. Steep steps led up to the building, too deep for anyone to walk. Those who approached the top were meant to crawl.

Thud.

Nothing moved in the arena. Whatever was coming, it would come soon.

Thud.

The ground beneath his feet shook. A blast of fire shot from the snarling mouths of the stone *tehuantl* at the top of the pyramid.

Thud.

The ground shook again, and the sun finally moved far enough overhead to reveal a full array of Exorian warriors standing massed in formation between Louis and the pyramid.

Thud.

The warriors raised their spears as one and drove them into the ground.

Thud. Thud. Thud.

Louis had never seen so many in one place before. Dankar must have emptied the barracks and the Dwellings. Their scarred, hide-like backs formed a wall that, for a moment, almost felt protective. They raised their spears again and slammed them down.

Thud.

And, as if to answer their call, a figure appeared in the open doorway of the building at the top of the pyramid. The warriors cheered. The figure stepped to the front, flanked by the flaming statues. It wore a mask in the shape of the sun, made from a human skull and feathers dipped in gold. The shining jet-black pelt of a *tehuantl* was draped around broad, perfectly formed shoulders. The figure carried a glass bowl filled with a gold-colored liquid. The moisture glistened enticingly in the sun.

Louis was once again aware of how thirsty he was. He stared at the bowl, which beckoned to him from across the full length of the arena. He licked his bloodied, sunburnt lips. The need to drink became overwhelming.

The figure at the top of the pyramid raised the bowl between his hands, as if to offer it to Louis. As he did, the wall of warriors split seamlessly in two, creating a straight path for Louis to approach the pyramid.

Louis knew nothing now except his thirst. He stumbled toward the shining figure holding out the bowl. It called to him. On either side, the warriors resumed their drumbeat.

Thud, thud, thud, thud, urging him toward his fate.

The sun reached his bare back, already burnt, but he no longer cared. Whatever the bowl contained, he would drink it. He *had* to drink it. When he reached the foot of the pyramid, the figure in the mask peered over the edge of the terrace, looming over him from above like a giant. The eyes in the sun-mask glittered. The gold liquid rippled enticingly.

Louis began to crawl.

Chapter 24

THE PIT-HOUSES

The passage Bodi led them through was ceremonial by the looks of it. Great care had been taken to create a wide tunnel that all three of them could walk in, side by side. It never grew truly dark in the tunnel. As in Metria, holes had been drilled into the walls at specific places to allow a dusky light to filter through. Intricate patterns of circles with interweaving designs and points radiating out in all directions had been carved into the walls. Many of them had once been painted with bright colors, barely visible now.

"How old is this tunnel?" whispered Chase.

The Captain took in the breadth of the passage, the detailed designs on the wall. His eyes were troubled. "Pre-Dankar."

"So, like, when Ranu was alive?"

The Captain nodded once.

"Who's Ranu?" Bodi piped in, her high voice echoing in the passage.

Chase put a hand on her shoulder to quiet her.

She shrugged it off and repeated, "Who's Ranu?"

"He was the original Keeper of the stone of Exor, before Dankar killed him and stole it."

Bodi gave him a puzzled look. "You are wrong."

"Sorry, but I'm not," said Chase. "Dankar killed Ranu in the Great Battle more than five hundred years ago, and took your people's stone. That's why all of this is happening. That's why your brother was taken away."

Bodi shook her head defiantly.

"You are wrong. Dankar is an Exorian, and if Ranu was an Exorian, then Dankar couldn't have killed him. It's impossible. No Exorian can ever kill another, not even the *tehuantl*. Our daylights won't allow it."

Chase stopped mid-stride, absorbing what she had just said.

"Exorians can kill everything else on Ayda, but not each other?"

Bodi nodded.

"So that's why you were unafraid to go out into the desert by yourself? The *tehuantl* can't hurt you. Nothing in the desert can?" asked Captain Nate.

"Except you," she replied.

"Ah, but I've made you a spit-swear."

Bodi turned back toward him, her mouth curling into a small grin, her first attempt at a smile that they had seen.

The passage grew broader and the thin light of sunrise spread across the floor and walls. The drawings etched on the sides of the tunnel grew more distinct. Chase saw now that the intricate designs of circles and rays were connected to create one large mural that also included pictures of *tehuantl*, snakes, spearheads, and faces. In some places, the original colors used to stain the drawings were visible, and in others, he could see traces of gold.

"This is a fancy tunnel considering it goes nowhere," he muttered.

"No tunnel goes nowhere," said Captain Nate. "This one happens to connect the Dwellings with what must have been a sacred site for Ranu. Or perhaps his father. Remember the stone heads. There were ten, the same as the number of original Watchers. Perhaps Remiel built this tunnel to honor his kin."

"Remiel lived in Exor? Why? It's a dustbowl."

Captain Nate sighed.

"You fall prey to the same assumptions as our new friend. Exor was not always so dry or deserted, nor was it cut off from the rest of Ayda as it is today. In Remiel's day, when the daylights were in balance—before Dankar came to these shores—Ayda was one land, with one people . . . and one stone. When I first arrived here, so long ago, there were no Metrians or Melorians or Exorians—only Aydans, and that was enough."

"What about Varunans?" asked Chase, thinking about himself.

"Always a solitary sort, perhaps, but no, back then even those whose daylights leaned toward the heights did not consider themselves as separate from their brothers and sisters on Ayda."

"One big happy family, then?"

"It would appear not, given the way things are now," said Captain Nate.

Bodi was walking a couple of steps ahead, quietly listening.

"Without the Fifth Stone to balance the daylights, the people of Ayda have had years to nurse their preferences—and their hatred for those who do not share those preferences. It is no different where we come from. People choose a tribe and then look suspiciously on all those not in that tribe. It always leads to bloodshed, as it has done for all of our history. The difference on Ayda is that these people did not choose to be divided; it was forced upon them."

The light in the tunnel grew stronger and cast a deep yellow glow, the color of butter. The other end was near, just around the next curve of the tunnel wall. A distant thud, like that of a great mallet, reverberated through the ground. Dust flew off the sides of the tunnel.

Bodi stopped.

Another thud unsettled the dust.

Chase and the Captain exchanged nervous looks.

"Bodi, what is that?"

"A new warrior is being initiated. Wait here."

She disappeared around the bend.

Chase squatted with his back against the wall. His throat was dry. He reached into his satchel for his canteen. It was empty. He shook it dramatically at Captain Nate. Before the Captain could say anything, Bodi was back.

"Come quick," she whispered. "Everyone is up early, making preparations. There is to be a celebration."

They followed her, blinking in the light as they emerged from the tunnel into what appeared to be a sizable village of mud huts, rounded and domed, rising off the desert floor like loaves of unbaked bread. The huts were identical in appearance and, though there were no windows, the position of their doors faced the same direction: east. A sandstone cliff loomed some ways behind the huts, and smoke rose from the center of a few. There was a yeasty smell of baking in the air, and small groups of people moved in between the gaps of the huts.

Chase traced the cliff behind them with his eyes and noticed evenly spaced apertures that faced down toward the village. *Windows.* Anyone could be in there, watching them.

"We have to get out of sight," he said, indicating their problem to Captain Nate. The early shadows of morning created pockets for them to hide in, but not for long.

"Where is your home, Bodi?" the Captain said urgently.

"Over here," she whispered. "Follow me."

She led them between several huts, walking without sound past simple rectangular doorways covered by blue cloth that hung to the ground. She bore left, skirting the edges of a garden shaded by a gauzy canopy, from which they heard voices. From what could be seen, the plants appeared to be well watered and thriving, with brilliant green leaves that contrasted with the monochrome of their surroundings.

They crept along the edge of the garden, trying to stay out of view of the Palace windows, and away from any villagers. Bodi signaled for them to stop at the back of a hut and disappeared around the curve of the wall.

Chase touched it. It was hard as cement, and thick. He put his ear to it, trying to hear voices inside. Nothing.

In minutes, Bodi returned and ushered them through the blue cloth that was the door. Both Captain Nate and Chase had to stoop a little to pass through, and what met them was a cool, dark room illuminated only by a square hole cut in the center of the roof. The makings of a small fire pit lay directly below the square, at the center of the one room.

From this small amount of light, Chase could see that the hut was actually a four-sided room made of interlocking logs woven together until they formed a kind of upside-down basket—only this house wouldn't be easy to knock down. Mud had been packed between the logs in thick layers. The walls were airtight and well insulated against both cold and heat.

"Who are you?" a voice whispered from the dark recesses of the room.

Captain Nate bowed deeply, a gesture so unfamiliar to him—and Chase—that Chase couldn't help smirking.

"I was sent for by Dankar to find this young captive and return him to the Palace," Captain Nate lied, gesturing toward Chase.

"Come into the light, so I may see you."

Captain Nate took Chase's arm and pretended to push him closer toward the fire pit.

"Easy now," he whispered into Chase's ear.

"He is not from here," the woman said simply, her voice monotone. No emotion in it at all.

"He is a Varunan. Separated from his tribe in the mountains and captured by an Exorian scouting party in the foothills of the Voss. He escaped his guard as they were crossing the plain and I was sent to retrieve him. Dankar has great interest in him."

The woman was silent.

"He has brothers. And a turtle," added Bodi.

Her mother shifted in the dark, getting to her feet and moving into the light, closer to Chase. She was small and compact, and wore a simple shift dyed the same blue as the cloth on the door. Her eyes were dark and clear.

"You are not from here, either," she said to Captain Nate, but her eyes remained glued to Chase. "If you were, you would know it is against the law of Exor for males beyond the age of Cleaving to enter the pit-houses unless they are scribes. It is a crime punishable by torture. Leave now, before they see you. If you are who you say you are, you have less to fear from Dankar than me or my daughter."

"It is for you and your daughter that we are here," said Captain Nate. "And your son. His name is Emon, am I right?"

The woman's eyes darted to Captain Nate's, suddenly fearful.

"Why? Who asks?"

Captain Nate held the woman's gaze.

"You are right," he said. "We are not exactly who we claim to be. We are outliers, come from beyond the fog to stand here before you. I was once a regular visitor to this land, but have been exiled beyond the fog. I come back now to reunite all Aydans."

The woman snorted in disbelief.

"There have been signs of late—storm clouds gathering across the plains, and the river, swollen with rain—but this . . . this is truly a trick to test me. *Outliers*. They are the stuff of stories told to babies."

Captain Nate put a hand on Chase's shoulder.

"Stories they may be, but they are nonetheless true. And as for what I told you, this boy *is* a Varunan. An emissary of Ratha herself. He is here at her behest."

Bodi's mother took a step back into the shadow, gathering Bodi to her hip, and hissed, "Be gone from my house, bad spirits."

Captain Nate raised his voice.

"We are not spirits. We are flesh and blood as you are, and we come because you and all of Ayda stand on the edge of disaster. All is not as

Dankar would have you believe. I don't know what you know of Varunans, or what you have been taught, but they are a people with great insight; their daylights give them the ability to sense that which is not visible to others."

He squeezed Chase's shoulder.

"Tell her."

Chase spun his head around to question Captain Nate. What the heck was he supposed to say?

"Tell her how Dankar has kept the water-keeper from bringing her gifts to Exor; how he plans to wage a great war that will destroy Ayda and cost the daylights of many Exorians. Tell her his plans to take this war beyond the fog, and how many Exorians will be sent to do his bidding far from here."

Chase was stunned. "You mean, tell her the truth?"

"Yes. Quick, now."

He recited an extremely abbreviated version of how he and his brothers and Frankie and Evelyn had come to be captured by Dankar, and how Dankar had told them of his plans to lay siege to Ayda and gain control of all four stones. He told Bodi and her mother how Dankar planned to use the stones to dispel the fog and take his warriors (and whomever else he needed) away from Ayda to wage a bigger battle in the lands beyond the fog. The lands where they *all* had once come from.

When he was finished, he heard Bodi's mother sigh.

"My own mother, may her daylights shine, told me such made-up tales of a land beyond the fog where she was born. She described a great vessel that carried her across a wide body of water. She did not want to go, but cruel men bound her and forced her on this vessel. It was to take her to another land—one she feared. But then, it took her to Ayda, to Exor, and she had nothing more to fear. At least, that's what she said. I thought it was just a story, but you are telling me now that there is truth in it. What is it to me?" she asked. "From what you say, if Dankar gets what he wants, it will be good for Exorians."

"Do you believe that?" asked Captain Nate. "Do you remember hearing in any of your mother's stories about a time when Exor was a greener land, and the people of Ayda were free to live wherever they pleased? A time when families, and tribes, were not divided, and children were allowed to stay with their parents until they chose to leave?"

Bodi's mother waved a dismissive hand in front of her face.

"You speak of legend. It has no bearing on the danger you have put me and my daughter in. These words will not comfort us in a cell."

Captain Nate grunted in frustration.

"Then, these signs you spoke of—you see that things are changing, do you not? It is because Dankar holds the water-keeper captive in his dungeon."

"If that is the reason it rains now, then all the better for us."

"No!" exclaimed the Captain. "It is not better! She will die here, separated from her lands and her stone, and then what do you think will happen? Do you think Dankar can march into Metria and use their stone like a toy? The stones of Ayda are not playthings for a spoiled child. He thinks of them as jewels to collect in his crown, but they are not so. They are more powerful than he can imagine. Without Rysta, the essence of the *atar* that resides in the stone of Metria will fade, and the imbalance that Dankar has begun in Exor will spread. What happens to one will eventually happen to all. Ayda shall grow barren and dry, and no one—not you, or me, or Bodi, or your son, or this boy here—shall survive. No one can live off rocks and sand."

"The Exorians have been doing so for as long as we can remember."

Captain Nate stared at her helplessly; then, with a heave, he slumped to the ground, defeated.

"I cannot convince a mind so set in its own ways."

The woman stared at him.

"How do you come to know these things anyway, stranger?"

"Because he was here when Dankar came," interrupted Chase. "He remembered what Ayda was like before all of this."

The woman shook her head.

"It cannot be so. I am asleep still and dreaming."

"No, sadly, you are awake," said the Captain. "And your children are in danger. Let me ask you this: Where do you think Dankar will find the forces he needs to conquer Ayda and the lands beyond the fog? Do you think he will spare *any* of you in his greed? He has one objective, and he does not care who is fragmented in the pursuit of it. He will come for Bodi, he will come for you, as he will come for everyone else in Exor. You will fight for him or you will be fragmented. He knows no other way. Do not be mistaken about this. The grief you have experienced up to now will be nothing in comparison."

The woman was quiet. Outside, footsteps could be heard along the pathways between the huts, punctuated by the occasional throb of conversation.

"If I leave my senses for a minute and say I believe you, still, I have to ask, why did you come all this way just to stand here in *my* home? How can I possibly help you?"

Chase shot a look toward Bodi, who was still hanging on her mother's hip, just like Teddy did with his mom. A pang of missing his little brothers stabbed him.

Captain Nate answered for both of them.

"I came because this boy asked me to. Like your son, he has left his mother to do his duty. I am sure she longs for him as much as you long for your own—" He was interrupted by a sharp noise outside the door.

"If you do not want to help me, then call out and have us discovered," he whispered, holding his hands up, "but whatever you do, be quick about it. We are running out of time."

The woman paced into the square of light. Her face was crumpled in worry.

This time, Chase knew what to say.

"It's not fair what Dankar is doing. Why should there be a—whaddya call it—a Cleaving, anyway? And scribes and warriors and people forced to live apart and do stuff they don't want to do. Who is he to take away anybody's kid and make them fight or serve him? And look at you and Bodi—why should you have to stay here in the pit-houses, and never see Emon?"

"*Shhh* . . . Lower your voice when you speak of Dankar in that manner," said Bodi's mother, but her tone had changed. She faced the Captain.

"Do you think that if this water-keeper were freed, she could defeat Dankar, and my son could come back to me? That *all* of our sons could come back to us?"

"Should that come to pass, and Dankar were defeated, I think there would be no one to keep your son from you ever again."

"Mama," said Bodi. "I want Emon to come home."

"Lead us to the dungeons," Captain Nate insisted. "Get us closer to where they are holding the water-keeper, and we will make our own way from there. Should we get caught, you can say you are turning us in."

Bodi's mother considered his answer, then sprang into action, moving quickly around the interior of the hut, grabbing at bundles of cloth. "If we are to move around the village at this time," she said, "we must figure out a way to hide you in plain sight."

"Varunans are good at that," said Chase, grinning slightly at Captain Nate.

Chapter 25

FIREWATER

Louis used the last of his energy to drag himself up the final series of steps to the top of the pyramid. He lay facedown, without moving, at the feet of the man in the sun-mask. At the corner of his vision he saw flames pouring out of the mouth of the stone *tehuantl* to his left.

He felt movement above him, and was aware that the man was now standing over him, holding the bowl of golden liquid.

He pressed his cheek into the smooth rock of the terrace and looked out across the arena at the rows of Exorian warriors below. The morning sun shone in his eyes, not yet at its full strength but enough to make him dizzy. A cool hand touched his face. He opened his eyes and the face of the water-keeper swam into his field of vision. Her blue eyes were dark and hollow.

"Rysta," he croaked.

"*Shhh*, save your strength," she said. She lifted him up and leaned him against her. He heard the sound of chains when she moved and knew she was shackled.

"He is going through with the ceremony. You are to become a warrior today." She smiled at him as she said it, but her tone was lifeless.

"I'm not Aydan," said Louis. "I'm an outlier. My daylights will fragment."

"Perhaps you are stronger than you think," said Rysta.

Her hand moved to her breast, where her necklace lay: a simple chain upon which hung a purple-tinged stone wrapped in silver.

Louis recognized it from the last time he had seen her, at the canyon's edge.

Rysta's fingers moved to the stone pendant. At her touch, the stone began to radiate a soothing silver light, like the sky behind a full moon.

The man in the mask shoved Rysta aside and lifted the bowl so that Louis could see it. The rim of the bowl was cool and wet.

Louis was overcome with a need to drink it. The man held it nearer, but still too far out of reach, teasing him with it. The glass eyes in the *tehuantl* pelt reflected the flames spewing out of the mouth of the stone statue behind where Louis lay.

"Initiate," the man intoned, "you have been brought here to answer the sacred call of the stone of Exor. Will you offer your daylights in return for the bond that unites the warriors of Exor? Will you live on to see days of glory and victory, in service to Dankar?"

The bowl twinkled in the sunlight. The reflection in the *tehuantl* pelt's eyes glowed. Louis's thirst raked at his insides, demanding he quench it. Below, the warriors began to chant.

Ex-or. Ex-or. Ex-or.

The man in the mask held the bowl in the air like a sacrament.

"The elixir of Exor, the fire of new life!" he yelled. "You have all drunk from this bowl and know its power. Very few, only the chosen, are strong enough to contain it!"

A wild roar went through the mass of warriors. Their chanting grew louder.

The man in the mask paced the edge of the plateau and raised the bowl with both hands, encouraging the warriors below to chant louder.

Louis followed the bowl with his eyes. His thirst was all-consuming. He needed to drink from the bowl. Either way he was dead. If he didn't drink, he would die slowly—painfully—of thirst, and if he did, his daylights would most likely fragment in a quick, merciful death.

Rysta used the seconds when the man in the mask's back was turned to yank the chain of her necklace and break it. She dragged herself back over to Louis and pressed the stone pendant into his hand, wrapping his palm tightly around it.

"Whatever happens," she whispered into Louis's ear, "do not let go of the stone. It will protect you."

The man in the mask turned back toward Louis. His eyes were cold and glittering behind the gleaming mask. Louis recognized them now. They were Dankar's eyes.

"Son of Exor, the time has come to find your strength."

The gold liquid shone like life itself, sparked by the sun.

"Do you wish to drink of the fire of new life? Do you vow to relinquish all that has come before and forswear any attachments but to Exor, until the fragmentation of your daylights?" Dankar asked, pushing the bowl closer to Louis.

Louis glanced at Rysta. Her head was bowed. The bones in her face stuck out through skin the color of bleached tree bark. Wisps of dried, white hair escaped her hood. She seemed to have aged a lifetime in mere minutes. Giving the necklace to Louis had cost her.

Louis gripped the stone pendant tightly and furtively wrapped the broken chain around his hand. His palm throbbed with a surprising coolness, as if he had just stuck that hand into a pool of cold water.

Dankar's eyes were locked on Louis.

Rysta crawled to one of the stone *tehuantls* and leaned against it.

"Answer me, son of Exor!" cried Dankar.

Louis pressed the fist that hid Rysta's pendant to his bare chest. He felt braver holding it.

"All right," he whispered. "I'll do it."

"Drink, then, and seal your bond!"

Dankar tipped the bowl toward Louis's lips.

Fumes evaporating off the top of the liquid stung his eyes, but he gulped the liquid down. It burned his already damaged throat and blazed into his stomach as if he had swallowed a lit torch.

Dankar retreated a few steps, lifting his mask.

The firewater spread through Louis's chest and into his limbs, scorching his body from the inside. He writhed on the ground, but he did not lose his grip on Rysta's necklace. Its cold pressure against his heart permeated his skin and gave him some measure of relief. For several moments it felt as if a battle were being waged inside him: the cool sensation brought on by Rysta's pendant was trying to beat back the raging heat of the firewater. He clenched his fist around the stone pendant, willing it to prevail, but it was not enough. The firewater chased the cold up his chest and into his arms, and then—in an agonizing flash—took over, burning away the coolness, melting it, until all he could feel was a hot, stinging pain.

The warriors below clashed their spears together and chanted in a wild frenzy. The air seemed to pulsate around him as if the earth were breathing. The walls of the arena telescoped and the sky above was no longer blue, but overcast in roiling gray, like boiling water. His mind played tricks. He saw birds—vultures—circling overhead, waiting to breakfast on his remains. A flash of yellow danced between the ranks of warriors. The little girl in pigtails and a yellow T-shirt was skipping between the rows of warriors. He heard Frankie humming her song. The one with the bell. The little girl wove between the warriors. He reached out to her.

"Grace," he groaned, but she had already skipped out of sight.

The heat of the firewater reached his brain and burned all remaining thought and memory away. He scrabbled at the ground, writhing in pain.

Rysta's necklace dropped out of his hand, the stone pendant now a smoking, ruined husk. Rysta had given him the only remaining connection she had had to the stone of Metria—the last remnant of her power—and it had not saved him. In an instant he knew that Ayda would burn. There was nothing to stop Dankar from invading Metria now.

A single tear welled up from within him. It rolled off his cheek and landed with finality on the dust-colored earth.

"Kill me," he pleaded. "Please."

Then, mercifully, everything went black.

Chapter 26

THE PALACE

Knox ran pell-mell through the hallway abutting the courtyard in the Palace, cursing his heavy poncho. A deep gash on his knee was gushing blood. Evelyn was somewhere up ahead with Adhoran and a pointguard of Melorians, trying to retrace their old route—from the room where they had first seen Dankar, back down to the cells beneath the Palace.

Seaborne, Calla, and Duelle rallied behind him once again, after having dispatched a small band of Exorian warriors who were protecting the front doorway. It had not been much of a fight, considering the Melorians had caught the guard in the dark and completely by surprise. Knox had forgotten how foul the Exorian warriors looked—as if they'd been roasted.

He tripped clumsily on the steps up to the doorway and slammed his knee on the dusty rock, the only Melorian blood that had been shed so far. Already the blood was thickening, he noticed as he ran—a sign that his daylights were getting stronger from being on Ayda.

Seaborne, Calla, Duelle, and the rest moved quickly beside him through the Palace, going from room to room and meeting little to no resistance. Besides the guard outside, the only people they ran into were a couple of unarmed scribes, clearly servants of Dankar, and not equipped to fight. They fled at the sight of the Melorians appearing like ghosts out of the dusk, hooded and menacing, with full harnesses of weaponry. Knox strained his ears to hear the sound of any alarm or warning being issued, but the Palace was eerily quiet, the way most houses feel just before sunrise. It felt almost deserted.

The Melorians used hand signals to communicate the same question: *Where is everyone?*

An owl hoot echoed through the vaulted ceilings of the hallway, stopped, and then echoed again. They followed it back into the recesses of the Palace, until it led them to a side hallway that branched off into a series of smaller rooms. Bedrooms, all strangely empty. For such a large dwelling, it seemed to Knox that nobody really lived here except for Dankar. No wonder he liked kidnapping people; it was probably his only source of company.

They took turns scoping out each bedroom, and in the very last one, they found Adhoran and Evelyn, stooped by a small window. The first light of daybreak turned the sand-colored walls a glowing orange. Knox, Duelle, and Calla approached the window; the remaining Melorians and Seaborne stood guard in the hall.

From their vantage point, Knox could look down into some kind of village filled with small, round clay huts. Beyond the village was another rock face that rose in steps to a plateau. To the far right and far left, the plateau rose to meet the cliff from which the Palace had been constructed, so that the village below was contained as if it had been built at the bottom of a bowl. As far as he could tell, there was no way to get out of the village except by passing through the Palace or climbing up the cliff walls—and even then, there was nowhere to go. Beyond the rock plateau was desert, and far, far beyond that lay the mountains, lit with a reddish-orange glow.

He suddenly felt sorry for the people of Exor. He thought again about the *tehuantl* Seaborne had killed. Maybe the Exorians—and the *tehuantls*—were suffering as much as the Melorians; they just didn't know because it was their daylights that Dankar held hostage.

"The village is already moving," whispered Adhoran, looking out the window.

"How many are there?" Knox whispered back.

Adhoran grimaced, and gestured for the rest of the Melorians to join them in the room. He pointed to the assortment of huts.

"We do not know what lies in wait for us down there, but I caution you to use your weapons wisely. We are here to challenge Dankar and his army and find Rysta, not lay waste to Exor."

"Why not?" asked Calla. "Have they given Melor such leeway?"

A few of the other Melorians muttered their agreement.

Adhoran scowled and faced them.

"There are children in that village! I will not spill their blood, nor will I allow you to do so. Have your daylights become so muddled?"

"You have been too long in Metria, Adhoran," scoffed one of the Melorians. "You might not be so high and mighty if you had spent these last moonrises without a full belly."

"I am not so soft that I have forgotten who I am. Who we are. Killing without regard is not the Melorian way. We will find the dungeons and scale north of the village here, along the plateau."

"Those huts could be hiding a legion of warriors," whispered Seaborne. "How do we know?"

"We don't," said Adhoran. "But what does your instinct tell you?"

Seaborne gazed down at the village, still in shadow. The scent of woodsmoke lingered lightly in the air. "That everyone down there is asleep in their own beds, unaware of our quest."

Adhoran nodded. "Mine as well." Then he looked pointedly at Evelyn and Knox. "Can you take us to the dungeons from here?"

Evelyn nodded. "I think so. I think I remember."

Knox resisted the impulse to chew on his Melorian shirt collar. The most obvious thing in the world was bothering him. He raised a hand, sheepishly, as if he were in school.

Seaborne raised one of his bushy eyebrows at him. "Yes, Knox?"

"I hate to bring it up, but where the heck is Dankar?"

"Maybe he's gone on a raid," said Calla. "Maybe we got lucky."

Seaborne scratched his lip. "I do not think he is one to fight his own battles. He would not go far from his lair."

"If we don't know where Dankar is, what's to stop us from bumping right into him?" asked Evelyn.

"Nothing," replied Seaborne. A finger of light from the window caught his attention. "But something tells me we need to find Rysta before the sun rises much higher."

⊹   ⊹   ⊹

Chase and Captain Nate were ready to follow Bodi's mother out of the hut and into the village. Chase was dressed in a long blue tunic that fell past his knees and a hastily assembled veil and hood that almost completely hid his face. Both Metrian swords were lashed to his torso, hidden by the tunic. Captain Nate was bare-chested and barefoot. Bodi's mother had done her best to make him look like a scribe. His newly shaven head shone like a beacon in the dusky light of the hut.

"You'll have to leave those here," she told them, pointing to their Metrian boots. "No Exorian has such things."

They stripped them off. Their feet looked soft and white. Chase never went anywhere barefoot. The small toe on each foot was much shorter than the other toes, and he didn't like the way it looked—like he was missing half a little toe.

"Scuff your feet in the dirt a little," she said, frowning. "They are too pale."

Bodi went out first to create a distraction. A rattle of clay pots and a cry of distress from the garden area quickly followed. Chase heard Bodi apologizing in a loud voice.

Her mother took this moment to push back the blue cloth at the door and lead Captain Nate and Chase around the hut and into the back alley that wove its way around the windowless sections of the other huts. She was headed straight for the passageway that connected the pit-houses to the kitchen of the Dwellings. It was not much of a plan, but if they moved fast, it might be enough. Bodi would go back to the hut once they were safely away.

They made their way through the back of the village, finally coming into a broader, more populated avenue.

"Walk ahead of me," she whispered to Captain Nate. "To the left. Walk like you know where you are going. And you"—she shoved a large basket hanging from the back of one of the huts into Chase's arms—"carry this. Keep your head down."

Ahead, women dressed in gauzy tunics and brightly dyed turban-like scarfs tended to their morning work. A small flock of young children played at their feet. A few older girls, maybe Evelyn's age, were kneading dough into flat circles on smooth rocks dug into the sand. They wore the same shapeless dresses as their mothers, and were protected from the sun with blue veils, like the one that covered Chase. The low hum of human activity filled the air, along with the scent of baking. It was a colorful, reassuring sight, and it made Chase wish he could stop and talk to one of them—which, when considering his past aversion to talking to anyone he didn't know, felt like a new thing. A good thing.

The Exorians were too absorbed in their routine to notice there were strangers in their midst until Captain Nate was only a few yards away. It was a measure of how few scribes came into the village. All noise and activity stopped immediately. The women scooped up their children, hushing them. The young girls making bread lowered their eyes, huddling behind their coverings.

Chase lowered his head, too, not sure how much of his face could be seen through the veil. He was not that much shorter than Bodi's mother, but he figured he could pass for a girl. He shortened his steps and tried to hide his feet. A few of the smaller children peered past their mother's shoulders at the strangers.

Bodi's mother stayed close, not making eye contact with any of her neighbors. They swept past the small crowd. There was no break in the dead silence that followed them until they were well away.

"Where are the fathers of the children?" whispered Captain Nate. "The boys are taken away to be initiated, I understand that. But where are the fathers of the younger children?"

Bodi's mother looked at him strangely.

"What do you mean? The father of all Exorians is always with us." She pointed with two fingers to the sky and said, "We are children of the sun."

"The sun?" Chase cut in. "How is that possible?"

He was old enough to know how babies were made.

Bodi's mother shrugged, as if the answer were as plain as the dirt they were treading on.

"It simply is. The sun is the source of all life, as it has always been. There is no life here without it—in a seed, in a womb, in . . . anything. Without the sun, there is only"—she sighed and held up her hands, searching for words—"space: cold, empty, without form. This is why Exorians are superior to all other tribes. This is why we are told we must protect and serve Dankar: He is the true Keeper of all the daylights, and father to all children of Exor."

She looked at Chase out of the corner of her eye.

"Do not be confused, Varunan. We can live, even thrive, without much influence from the other daylights. Whereas your tribe"—she turned to look at Chase directly—"how many of you are left up there in the mountains?"

Chase opened his mouth to argue, to defend his daylights, but he didn't know what to say. He'd only ever met a few Varunans; maybe those were all there were. Maybe being a Varunan was like being able to read Latin—not much use to anyone anymore.

Captain Nate exhaled sharply.

"Dankar is the father of all those babies? Exorians are superior to all other tribes?" He grabbed Chase's elbow. "Is this what it has come to? The sooner we stop this madness, the better it will be for everyone."

He quickened his step.

Bodi's mother touched a seam in the rock wall, and as if it were on a hinge, a large slab swung inward revealing a wide passage, lit by flaming torches. It looked clean and well-traveled.

"This is where I leave you. I must return to my daughter," she declared, stepping aside to allow Captain Nate and Chase to enter the passageway.

"Where does this go?" asked Chase.

"To the kitchen and storage rooms. From there you will have to find your own way. It is all I know of the Palace."

"Are there guards, or scribes, or anyone we need to be aware of?"

"There may be scribes, and perhaps work has begun in the kitchen. There is to be a great celebration here today. A great victory is at hand, we've been told." She shrugged. "I do not know; my work is not in the Palace. I tend the gardens."

Captain Nate turned to her, saying, "Thank you. I will not forget your kindness."

Bodi's mother nodded. "You said if I helped you to find the water-hoarder, you would bring my son back to me, and that all sons and daughters of Exor would be reunited when Dankar is deposed. I will hold you to your word."

The Captain bent his head in acknowledgment.

Bodi's mother retreated, pressing the seam on the outside of the door. She turned back once.

"If I can, I will send word to Emon. Not all scribes who serve Dankar do so willingly." She acknowledged Chase. "Take care, Varunan. I will see you in my dreams."

The rock slab swung shut.

Chase flung aside the gauzy blue shroud that he—and their weapons—had been hiding under. He threw Captain Nate his sword.

"Only one way to go now," the Captain grimaced.

They took off down the passageway.

Chapter 27

BEYOND RECOGNITION

Louis rose from the ground. The skin on his knees was thick and cracked and mottled, as if deeply bruised and burnt. The hand that propelled him up looked the same: deep gashes of pink at the knuckles beneath a tough, hide-like pelt. The other hand, the one that had held Rysta's stone pendant for as long as it could, was pink, and looked small and frail in comparison. He felt ashamed of it and hid it behind the other palm.

"Son of Exor, Warrior of Fire—all of Ayda awaits you," said a voice behind him.

He turned to see the mask radiant and blazing, filling his vision, as if it were the face of the sun itself. It blinded him and he was aware of a strange pulling in his chest. A burning, and then, a deep and abiding thirst. His mind felt empty except for this thirst.

"You are still thirsty, I know. From here on you will always thirst for firewater. It is the sustenance of the warrior."

Dankar turned away to retrieve something from the small building behind them, and in that moment, Louis became barely aware of something else, something light and cool, like a tickle or a fine mist, running up his right arm. He slapped at it, but it did not stop. It ran the full length of his arm and into his torso, creating a strange opposing sensation to the heat that burned inside him.

Dankar returned bearing a small flask.

Louis's mind felt scoured—all thought and memory burned away by the firewater. Instinctively, he looked down at his right hand: small and pink and ugly to his eyes.

"Your own supply of firewater," said Dankar, handing the flask to him. "You are a warrior now; you may refill it as you desire."

A low moaning noise from behind Louis caught his attention. He turned back to see the prostrate figure of a woman. His right hand tingled. Above her, the jaws of the *tehuantl* breathed fire.

Dankar followed his gaze.

"Bring her to me," he ordered.

Louis snapped into action, his body obeying almost before his mind had taken in the command. He strode over to the figure in a few quick, strong paces and lifted the woman and slung her over his shoulder as if she were a bag of twigs.

"Louis," she whispered.

He stopped short at the sound of her voice. The tingling in his arm intensified and he felt doubt. He searched his mind for the source, but could not remember anything.

"You are not lost," the woman said to him. "Find your way back to them. To the outliers. *To Frankie*. You are one of them."

"Bring her here," Dankar roared.

The doubt subsided. He shouldered the woman and delivered her to Dankar's feet.

Dankar knelt beside her to speak directly in her ear. "This is where it ends, cousin."

The woman smiled. A strange sight.

"Ah, but you are wrong, Dankar," said the woman. "It never ends."

She put a hand on the black fur of the pelt he was wearing.

"It is a crime for you to wear the skin of the *tehuantl*. You will be cursed for it."

"I think not," said Dankar. "From now on, Rysta, I'll wear the skin of anything I want—including yours."

Dankar dug under the *tehuantl* pelt and brought forth a twisted knife with a black blade. He spit on it once, rubbing the saliva into the blade with his thumb. Then he lifted it above his head and addressed the crowd below him.

"Brothers of Fire, children of the Sun, you are here to witness a new beginning for Ayda. Today, we stand as conqueror of all, afraid of none! I will soon lay claim to the stone of Metria and all those who align themselves with it. For here, I have its Keeper. The stone is no longer protected."

He knelt down by Rysta and opened the folds of her robe, his hands searching for her necklace.

"I don't have it anymore," she said. "I lost it."

Dankar's nostrils flared. He lowered his voice.

"It matters not, Rysta. I will go to Metria and find its stone, if I have to drain every drop of blood and water from your lands. It would go easier on you and your people if you would simply tell me where it is. This is your last chance to protect them—the same chance I gave to your brother Ranu so long ago. Just tell me where the stone is, and I will spare the Metrians."

Rysta shut her eyes, refusing to speak.

Dankar shook his head.

"Then you go to your death knowing you were not as merciful as your brother. He, at least, tried to save his people. He was willing to sacrifice his stone for them. You are not so generous."

Dankar raised the knife, and spoke again to the crowd.

"Warriors of Exor, today you will leave this place and set fire to the rivers and pools of Metria! You shall burn its lands and the city to the ground. Leave no one alive. Today marks the end of Metria"—his lips curled back in a snarl—"and its Keeper."

The knife sliced the air, aimed at Rysta's heart.

Louis's right hand—the small one—shot out instinctively to stop it.

"WHAT!" Dankar screamed, turning the dagger on Louis. "You *still* defy me!"

Louis's eyes, still the same blue in his ruined face, stared in surprise at his hand—the naked human hand gripping Dankar's wrist.

"I'm not *trying* to do anything," Louis grunted. "It's got a mind of its own."

Dankar snorted with rage, ripping Louis's hand off his wrist. He glared at his newly fashioned warrior, at Rysta, then down at the crowd below.

He took a step back, squaring his shoulders beneath the *tehuantl* pelt.

"Give it to me," he ordered, holding out his palm.

Louis was confused.

"Your obscenity of a hand. Give. It. To. Me."

Louis surrendered his right hand.

"I should cut it off"—Dankar growled in disgust—"but considering you are an experiment, and a largely successful one, I will overlook this . . . *imperfection*."

He pressed the hilt of the knife into Louis's extended palm and gestured at Rysta.

"Kill her," he said.

The tingling, cool sensation surged up his arm from the hand where Louis held the knife. Again, he felt doubt. He did not move.

Dankar pulled down the sun mask to cover his face. The morning sun caught and reflected the gold in the mask, so that all Louis could see was a great, shining beam of light.

Louis's thirst returned, even more powerful than before. He took his flask of firewater and sipped. The liquid coursed through his body with a shock that was not altogether unwelcome. It erased any doubt of who he had become.

"Do it," hissed Dankar, from behind the mask.

Louis gripped the knife and turned on Rysta.

Chapter 28

IN THE DUNGEON

"**W**hat is that?" Calla barked in a whisper.

The Melorians stopped in their tracks. Evelyn had successfully led them down into the dungeon, mentally retracing the route they'd taken the last time she'd had the misfortune to be in Exor. The cells, however, were empty. No sign of life.

"Where *is* she?" grumbled Seaborne. "I don't like the feel of this. Something's wrong."

Murmurs of agreement rose up from the other Melorians. Everyone was jumpy in the tight space—and the dimly lit emptiness. It was unnerving. Bows and arrows would be useless here.

A swift pattering sound reverberated in the tunnel.

"Bare feet," said Adhoran, lifting his ax. "Exorians. We've been found out."

Seaborne unsheathed his broadsword. The Melorians, Evelyn, and Knox scattered as best they could and crouched down, disappearing into the shadows, ready to spring at whoever was coming at them.

The footsteps grew clearer, feet slapping against sandy rock. Knox held his breath, easing one of the throwing knives from his harness. There was barely any light to see by, but he would try to aim well.

Seaborne gave the signal. The Melorians at the head of the passage sprang, seizing each of the Exorians and throwing them to the ground.

Calla kneeled on the back of one—a scribe, by his dress—and pulled his head up, her curved blade at his throat.

"How goes it, Exorian?" she whispered. "Burnt any Melorians lately?"

"No, not lately—in fact, never," said a gruff voice.

Knox thought he recognized it. He bent down to get a closer look.

The other Exorian was shorter and was lying facedown on the tunnel floor, a battle-ax pressed against the back of his neck to keep him that way. He was dressed in a white undergarment and wore a Metrian sword. Not a scribe or a warrior.

"Look at their feet," said Evelyn.

"Ev?" asked the muffled voice of the Metrian-clad Exorian.

"What the heck?" said Knox. He looked down. Both of the Exorians had clean, white feet. He knelt down to examine one of them more closely, then rocked back on his heels, letting out a low whistle. He would know those feet—and those tiny little toes—anywhere.

"Is that you, Chase?"

"Yeah, Knox, can you tell them to let me up?"

"That's my brother!" cried Knox, knocking the battle-ax away with his hand.

Chase sat up, rubbing his jaw. "Ow—"

Knox hurled himself at Chase. "What are you doing here—and what the heck are you wearing?"

"I could ask you the same thing," said Chase. He tossed his chin toward Captain Nate. "I'm here with him."

Knox spun his head over to look at the other man.

Calla withdrew her knife from his throat, and he, too, sat up, raising his hand in the traditional Aydan greeting.

"I come in peace," he said to Calla.

"Who are you?" Knox asked.

"You would know me as Captain Nate."

Knox whistled again and shot Chase a confused look.

The Melorians eyed this new development warily; they did not lower their weapons.

"What the heck is going on, Chase? That is so *not* Captain Nate. He's way too young."

Adhoran pushed his way into the group and caught sight of Captain Nate and Chase.

"I have seen these two before—in Metria. He speaks the truth."

"It's the fog," explained Chase. "We passed through it, and, he just got —I don't know . . . younger."

"Hohhh-ly crap," Knox exhaled.

Chase smiled at the familiar expression.

Knox grabbed his brother's chin and gave him the once-over.

"You look the same. Still ugly." He punched Chase lightly in the arm and smiled back. "I'm glad to see you!"

"So am I," said Evelyn, coming into Chase's view. She hesitated a moment, then hugged him. Chase hugged her back, noticing that she felt small in his embrace, and even thinner than he remembered, and she smelled like earth and pine—and something else. Something bitter. It took him a minute to name it: soot.

Evelyn's large eyes were shining at him, and for a small, infinitesimal moment, Chase had the sense that everything might turn out okay if she could just go on looking at him like that for the rest of time.

"I knew you were worth your salt, lad!" boomed Seaborne, extending his hand to help Chase up, and ruffling his hair on the way. "You did what you set out to do, and that means something in this world, I warrant. We could have used you when we were beating back that mewling pack of *tehuantls*."

Chase shot Knox a look. "A whole pack?"

Knox grinned.

"Yeah, Chase, you've missed a lot. *Seriously*." He elbowed Evelyn in the ribs. "Underground tunnels that I had to carry Evelyn through, and this huge whirlpool that sucked us up and spit us out, like the best water-park ride you have ever been on, and Rothermel's Keep, which is very cool—"

"Don't forget Chantarelle," said Evelyn. "And you did not have to carry me." She rolled her eyes and smiled at Chase. "Some things don't change. Knox is still a brat."

"Hey, now," said Knox, faking injury. "That hurts."

"What's a chantarelle?" Chase asked, feeling unreasonably happy to be with Evelyn and Knox again, even if it was in a dungeon beneath Dankar's palace.

"It's not a *what*—it's a guy. A little dude! He's a guide between Ayda and . . . well, everywhere!" Knox spluttered. "Remember the cave in the woods at Summerledge—where we used to hide? I *told* you something was in there! It was Chantarelle. He has all these tunnels and this crazy underground city, and he's been watching us the whole time. And then when you ran off, Evelyn and I went looking for you, and we found *him*. Stupid note, by the way. Chantarelle brought us back here, to find you."

"He has a tunnel to Summerledge?"

"Yeah, that's what I'm trying to tell you."

Chase flashed back to the vision Ratha had put in his head: the one of Teddy on his hands and knees crawling through a tunnel, with their mother following him. Could it be real? If such a tunnel existed, maybe Teddy had found it, or maybe Chantarelle had gone back for him, and their mother had insisted on going with Teddy?

"Knox, I gotta tell you something. I think Mom and Teddy might be—" He was distracted from finishing his sentence by Captain Nate, who had stood up to address the Melorians.

"The boy has done as he promised—he has fulfilled his oath. Now it is my turn."

Seaborne stepped forward, with Calla hovering at his side.

"Tell us, then—do you bring the Fifth Stone with you, or did you only bring more misery? We have had more than our share since you left."

Captain Nate lowered his palm.

"The Fifth Stone is not mine to bring anywhere."

"What do you mean?" Calla objected. "How is it that you come to be here if you do not have the stone? What use are you to us then?" She turned away, frustrated. "We were counting on you."

"Wait," said Chase. "He *has* come back to help! He didn't have to. He came back because I asked him to, and because he still loves Rysta."

Seaborne sighed. "Chase, sentiments are not weapons. If love is all he brings, he is on a fool's errand. Look around you."

For the first time, Chase took note of the band of heavily armed Melorians.

"We have come here to fight to the last man and woman because we have nothing else. Melor is spent. We would rather die fighting here in Exor for our home than watch Exor take over our lands."

"But Rothermel is alive? The stone of Melor is safe?" asked Chase.

"For now, we presume."

"Then all is not yet lost," said Captain Nate. He bent down to pick up his sword.

The Melorians were instantly alarmed, weapons raised to strike.

The Captain left the sword where it lay, holding his hands up in surrender.

"I have made many terrible mistakes in this life," he said, eyeing the Melorians. "And I do not ask your pardon for them. But I *will* retrieve Rysta from this place and bring her back to Metria if I have to fight through you to do it."

Adhoran grimaced and cradled his ax. "I should like to see you try."

Seaborne moved between them.

"That won't be necessary. We are here for Rysta, as well."

"Then we have no quarrel."

"But where is the Fifth Stone, then, if you don't have it?" asked Calla.

Captain Nate sighed.

"I will tell you what I have told Ratha and the Varunans: Should I live through this day, I shall help you to see the Fifth Stone returned to these shores if it is in my power to do so. I possess knowledge and a sword, and the will to do what I can to right the wrongs I have committed. It is less than you have asked for, but I give it in the service of Melor."

He bowed deeply to her.

Seaborne allowed a moment of silence to pass before extending his hand, palm out, fingers splayed.

"Then I welcome you as a brother in battle."

Captain Nate brushed Seaborne's fingertips with his own.

The Melorians lowered their weapons.

Adhoran caught Chase's eye, his lips pressed together in a tight smile. "And so we meet again, outlier."

Seaborne picked up Captain Nate's sword from the ground and handed it to him.

"We'll take two roads," he said. "I will lead my company along the plateau. You follow these tunnels and search for Rysta. She is not in the Palace—of that we are sure—so she must be here somewhere. We will divert any resistance from above and move east, toward the plains. We must make haste and take advantage of our unexpected presence."

He looked directly at Chase and Captain Nate.

"I pray to the daylights we meet again."

Chapter 29

RAIN OF FIRE

A great roar rose up to meet Louis as he raised the knife to slay the water-hoarder.

Rysta did not open her eyes. She lay motionless, as if already dead.

The cries of his Exorian brothers carried on the rising wind, bringing with them a blast of cooler air. A spasm of joy went through him as he looked down at Rysta. He was ready to do Dankar's bidding without any regret. His right hand twitched suddenly, and he covered it in shame with his left. He was a warrior-hero of Exor, subject to no one but Dankar.

Below, the tenor of the roar suddenly shifted. He heard the unmistakable twang of a crossbow releasing a bolt, and the sound of spears clashing with swords.

A horde of hooded invaders poured into the arena off the walls of the plateau. They jumped and slid lightly down the switchbacks, graceful as *tehuantls*, and heavily armed. Upon hitting the ground, they separated into three flanks. One went straight through the middle, led by a tall man wielding a heavy ax. One skirted the cliff wall, scouring the outside of the battlefield with bows and arrows and knives. And the last stood by the archway to the tunnel leading to the warriors' barracks, guarding the escape.

"MELORIANS!" roared Dankar from somewhere behind Louis. "Leave her to me, and go deal with them!"

Louis watched from the pyramid as the Melorians set upon the rows of warriors. They had surprise in their favor. The Exorians had not had time to light their spears. It never occurred to any of them that they might be attacked here, in the heart of Exor. A hot flame of anger propelled him, half running, half falling, down the tiers of steep stone stairs and into the fray.

Louis himself was unarmed except for the obsidian knife, and he used it to slash at whatever enemy target he could find. No other thought came to him but to defend his fellow warriors; his new skin was like its own armor, and the fury of the firewater burned through his muscles, making him strong.

The scene on the arena floor was pandemonium. The eastern wind had picked up, swooping down into the arena in hot and cold gusts, stirring up the dust and raking tiny pebbles into the air. Small rumbles shook the ground and sent little avalanches of rock off the cliff face and into the arena, adding to the confusion.

"*Aargh!*" Louis growled, clapping a hand on the back of his thigh, suddenly aware of a sharp sting. It met the small hilt of a knife, now embedded in one of the crevices of his thick skin. He whirled around to face his attacker and saw a small Melorian darting away. The hood of the Melorian's poncho had dropped back to reveal the face of a boy. He had short, spiked hair and freckles.

Louis's right hand began to throb at the sight of him. He transferred the knife to his left, aware that the other had become a liability. One swipe of a Melorian blade could remove it. The boy disappeared into the rising swirl of sand and grit. Louis gripped the knife and went after him.

✢   ✢   ✢

Captain Nate and Chase emerged from a small hatch through the floor of the pyramid and into the small building at the top. They had run through a maze of tunnels that funneled from the Palace to the scribes' quarters, and then to a small antechamber at the base of the cliff. From there, a spiral staircase led up the back of the pyramid to the building at the top. They had taken the stairs three at a time. The hatch flew back. The building was small, with only one door facing the arena.

"Wait here for my signal," Captain Nate ordered, taking up a position on one side of the door. He brandished his Metrian sword behind his back, and his freshly shaven scalp was shiny with sweat.

"Aye, aye, Captain," whispered Chase, hiding behind the opposite side of the door.

They peeked out and quickly withdrew, startled at the sight of a hideous gold skull staring back at them. It took a moment for them to realize that the face was just a mask, hanging off the back of Dankar's head, and that Dankar actually had his back to them. He stood at the edge of the terrace, the black fur of a *tehuantl* pelt wrapped around his shoulders.

Rysta lay motionless at Dankar's feet, and before Chase knew it, Captain Nate had leapt out of the doorway and crossed the space between them in two strides.

"WHAT HAVE YOU DONE?" he screamed.

Dankar twisted around just in time to sidestep a vicious swipe of the Captain's sword. He looked stunned, unable to conceive of what was happening. It took a moment for Chase to realize that Dankar believed a scribe was attacking him—an impossibility in Dankar's mind.

Dankar stumbled and fell, narrowly avoiding a tumble off the edge of the dais.

Captain Nate pounced, but Dankar was quick. He scrambled toward one of the stone *tehuantl* statues, grabbing the glass bowl that lay on the ground. With a quick strike, he broke the bowl on the statue and used the broken shard as a weapon, slashing wildly at Captain Nate's bare skin.

"You . . . murdering, evil . . . *relic!*" seethed Captain Nate. "You will pay for what you've done here!"

Chase heard Rysta groan. She was alive!

"RYSTA!" he yelled, forgetting his orders.

She sat up and pushed back her hood. Long spools of white hair streamed over her shoulders, and her face, once luminous as starlight, was gray and ashen, the skin parched and shrunken like paper over her cheekbones.

"Caspar," she moaned.

At the sound of his name, the Captain froze.

Dankar took advantage of the reprieve to scramble behind the statue.

Chase ran to Rysta's side and began to drag her toward the building.

"Caspar," she cried again, scrabbling back toward the Captain. "I have waited so long for you! Chase, please, let me go to him!"

Chase pulled her into the building. Her chains were heavy.

"I'm so sorry, Rysta—you just have to wait a little bit longer. It's not safe." He leaned in to whisper in her ear. "Seaborne is here, and the Melorians. We've come to take you back to Metria."

She gave him a weary smile.

Dankar stepped out from behind the statue, his beady eyes fixed on Captain Nate.

"So, it is you then, is it? Come back from the dead?" he sneered.

Captain Nate took a step toward Dankar, jabbing his sword. Dankar retreated back behind the statue. His oily laugh hovered above the sound of battle below.

"You humans are so . . . *suggestible*. But I am intrigued, most certainly. I had thought you were long gone. There is only one power that I know of on this Earth that can strengthen the daylights so, and now you have finally given me the last piece of the puzzle. It is out *there*, as I suspected . . . unless"—Dankar peered out from behind the statue at Captain Nate—"you have brought it here?"

"Come out and fight me fair," growled Captain Nate.

"Fair? How is this fair, when you have a sword and I have a piece of broken glass? We shall fight, Caspar, bane of Ayda, I assure you!"

Dankar snarled, and in a shimmering explosion of light, he transformed himself into a giant, black *tehuantl* that leapt across the terrace. The creature roared and raised itself up on two legs, pummeling Captain Nate, and pinning him to the ground. It opened wide its massive jaws with dagger-sharp teeth and took the Captain's head in its mouth.

Chase yelled at the same time Rysta screamed. Her body arched. She clutched the spot on her chest where once her necklace had lain and, with one tremendous heave, she released a beam of white light streaming straight from her center. It struck the *tehuantl* in the flank. The *tehuantl* roared in pain, then toppled over the side of the pyramid steps.

Chase sprinted to the Captain, just in time to see the cat twist gracefully in mid-air and land lightly on all four paws, sauntering down the rest of the stairs into the arena. It paused and looked back up, then unleashed another bloodcurdling roar and leapt into the battle on the ground.

Captain Nate struggled to his feet, disoriented. Rysta clutched at the frame of the doorway, trying to stay upright. He ran to catch her and dropped his sword. With one sweep of his arm, he lifted her to him and carried her through the hatch to safety.

Chase took out his own sword with one hand, picked up the Captain's sword with the other, and charged down the steps of the pyramid to find Knox and Evelyn.

⁜   ⁜   ⁜

Knox was darting back and forth between the warring parties, throwing his knives when he saw an opportunity. In the gritty haze kicked up by the sand eddies in the arena, it was hard to keep track of Seaborne and Evelyn.

Evelyn seemed to be everywhere, moving so quickly the Exorians had little time to react. The knives Mara had given her spun lightly in her hands. She made the most of them, and the Exorians' lack of shields. Calla was at the archway to a tunnel protecting their exit, while Seaborne cut a swath into the center. Once there, he and the Melorians circled back to take on the enemy. Adhoran and what was left of the Melorian guard patrolled the sides of the arena, weeding out as many Exorians as they could from the outer edges.

They hadn't had much time to plan, having basically stumbled on the arena while they were patrolling the plateau. The relative emptiness of the rest of the Dwellings made sense now: Dankar's warriors had been assembled here.

Finally, Knox thought. The surprise of their attack was having an impact. The Exorians were falling by the handful. Knox had time to lean against the cliff wall of the arena and catch his breath. He wasn't used to fighting in this heat, and the grit in the air made his mouth taste like a dirt road. He wiped the sweat out of his eyes with the hem of his poncho. The air was yellow and thick, and small showers of pebbles rained down on his head every few moments.

Three dark figures clashed and whirled out of the sand-induced haze. Knox rearmed himself and pushed off the wall, ready to join in.

The tremendous roar of a *tehuantl* sent his heart skittering into his mouth. It ricocheted off the wall of the arena. He moved to the left, trying to find Seaborne so they could make their way to the exit. His ears strained to hear every sound. A *tehuantl* could pounce and kill him before he even knew it was there, but there was something that made him want to see one again. He caught sight of Seaborne in the distance, fighting two-handed with both his sword and machete, and made to sprint, when he felt a strong hand grip his arm.

The hand spun him around and he was face-to-face with a large Exorian warrior. The thick ridges and bloody scabs that formed like scales on the warrior's skin looked fresh and raw and painful up close.

Knox tried to squirm out of the warrior's grip, but it held fast. The Exorian raised his other hand; it held a black knife with a paper-thin edge. Knox flinched—more at the sight of the hand than the knife. It was flesh-colored and healthy-looking. He stared at it and then at the warrior's mottled face, trying to make sense of it. There was something strange about this guy. He had blue eyes, not the orange-flecked dark color of most Exorian warriors. Something deep and instinctual told him that this warrior was different. He hesitated.

The Exorian took the opportunity to tip his knife toward Knox's heart. Knox grabbed it with both hands. The blade cut into his skin.

"You don't want to do that!" he shouted.

"But I do," said the warrior, in a voice Knox knew he recognized.

They struggled. Knox used all his strength to keep the knife from moving forward, but his grip was slipping because of the blood pouring out of the gashes in his hands. The tip of the blade pressed into his chest, piercing through the poncho and leather harness as if they were made of paper. Knox felt a sting, then a deeper pain. In seconds the blade would find his heart.

He bent down and sank his teeth hard into the normal-looking hand—until he tasted blood, or something like it. The warrior's blood was more bitter than regular blood.

The warrior had not expected the pain, and the knife jolted, giving Knox time to push it backwards. The warrior used both hands to press the knife back toward Knox.

Knox knew he would not be able to hold it off much longer. From some deep recess inside his head, he heard Tinator's voice: *Anytime you want this to end, lower your sword.*

His first lesson.

Why not give up?

"No!" Knox shouted.

Then use your daylights! Tinator's voice shouted, just as a great force pulsed through his feet from the ground, propelling Knox up and forward. He smashed his forehead as hard as he could into the bridge of the warrior's blackened nose. The warrior staggered back in surprise, overcome, just as Evelyn swooped in, her knives spinning. She leapt on the warrior from behind, locking her legs around his torso and crossing her knives over his throat for a killing blow. The warrior instinctively put his mismatched hands up to ward off the end.

"Evelyn, don't!" cried Knox, still reeling from the force of what had just happened.

He grabbed the hand of the warrior that held the knife—the one that still looked human—and quickly disarmed him.

Evelyn stared at the warrior's hands in confusion, but kept her knives in position.

Knox looked directly at the warrior's face, into his blue eyes. There was something in them—something so familiar and known that he could barely look away. He had seen those eyes before.

A dread rose up in his chest. He couldn't name it, but he was absolutely certain that something terrible had happened here.

"We have to let him go, Ev."

"Why? He'll kill us!"

"I took his knife, so he can't do much. Not with you and your helicopter blades around. Let him go."

Knox didn't have time to explain. All he knew was that he was having the same feeling he'd had during the fight with the *tehuantl*. He knew if they killed this warrior, it would be an evil act—one they would never be able to wash away.

"Knox! Look at him; he'll knock us flat, and then one of his friends will light us on fire."

Knox stared again into the disturbing blue of the warrior's eyes. Where had he seen those eyes before? Then it came to him. In Exor, at the edge of a canyon.

"I don't think he will—will you, Louis?"

"Louis?" said Evelyn, relaxing her knives. "This is Louis?"

"I think so, yes."

The warrior stared at Knox.

"Louis?" Knox demanded.

Evelyn released her grip on Louis, and darted to his front. She peered up at his face, and then down at his hands.

"I think it is," she breathed. "What has he done to you, Louis?"

She looked out across the arena at all the other Exorian warriors, fighting for their lives.

"This is what Dankar was talking about—his experiment! He told us about it the day we first saw him, remember?"

She lowered her knives.

Louis swiveled his eyes between Evelyn and Knox. He took a few unsure steps backwards, then grabbed his right hand as if it were hurting. He made no move to run or attack.

"What should we do with him?" asked Knox. "We can't just leave him like this. He'll get himself killed. He's not even armed."

"Louis, you need to come with us," said Evelyn, speaking loud over the din of the battle. She took a step toward him.

Louis removed a small flask from his waistband and took a sip. His eyes darkened and his lips curled back. He snarled at them from the back of his throat and ran off.

Knox shook his head, watching him disappear into the yellow haze.

"I can't believe it. Dankar actually did it. His transformation thing that he was going to do to Seaborne. And it worked . . . at least, sort of."

He thought about the hand, the warrior's eyes. He searched the haze again.

"This is bad, Evelyn, really bad."

She wiped her face with her arm, leaving a swipe of clean skin beneath the layers of dust and sweat that had formed a paste on her face.

"How can it get any worse than this?" she said.

"Because if we get caught, Dankar will do it to us."

✢   ✢   ✢

Chase stumbled down the steps of the pyramid, hitting the ground hard. He sprang up, gripped the sword, and was instantly assaulted by the air, spinning with grit and sand. His first thought was that Ratha was lending a hand from afar. The *tehuantl*—Dankar—roared again somewhere in the distance.

Chase took off after it. Above the swirl of yellow haze, he could see a bank of storm clouds rolling in on the wind. Rain was coming.

"Yes!" he cried out loud.

Thunder boomed through the arena, quickly followed by a bolt of lightning. The ground rumbled and the wind picked up, pelting his face with dirt.

Chase tore a swatch of fabric off the end of his garment and wrapped it tightly around his mouth. The path of the *tehuantl* was easy to follow. Chase leapt gingerly over the fallen soldiers—Exorian and Melorian both—in hot pursuit. Within moments he was at the center of the fighting. Using the sword defensively, he pushed through a skirmish and narrowly avoided being struck by a Melorian arrow. Dressed as he was, he suddenly realized the Melorians might mistake him for an Exorian.

Not good, he thought to himself.

Above, the storm clouds opened and a light rain began to fall. The dust settled enough for Chase to make out a cluster of Melorians standing back to back, fighting off an advancing throng of Exorians. He made straight for them. Rain fell to the ground in thick drops, and the dirt floor of the arena quickly turned muddy. Using the sword, he beat his way through the Exorians and hurled himself into the Melorian huddle.

"It's Chase!" he yelled. "I'm on your side!"

A Melorian pulled him into the huddle.

"We found Rysta!" he yelled to whomever he was fighting next to. "We need to get out of here, now! Dankar's here—he's the *tehuantl*."

"Easier said than done!" cried one of the Melorians.

A deeper voice called out. "Break for—"

The roar of a *tehuantl* stopped the order short. The hair on the back of Chase's neck stood up. It was close.

"Get to the exit!" the deep voice shouted. "Any way you can!"

The huddle shattered in all directions. Chase was running again, beating off Exorian spears. In the confusion, he had lost all sense of direction. The smell of sulfur filled his nose.

"CHASE! OVER HERE!" It was Evelyn.

He ran toward the sound of his name. She and Knox were huddled under their hoods.

All around them the drops of rain were catching fire in mid-air. His own exposed skin exploded in tiny, painful bursts, as if he were being stung by a swarm of bees. He saw a spark land on Knox's hood and burn into the fabric before going out, then another, and another.

"Looks like Dankar is turning the tables," grunted Knox, stomping on the sparks as they fell to the ground. "And the *tehuantls* are here."

"It's him!" panted Chase. "Dankar is the *tehuantl*. He changed."

Knox whipped his head around in a panic. "Where's Seaborne, and Calla?"

Chase slapped at the sparks landing on his skin.

"There's no time left to make it to the exit. We have to climb out of here," he said, looking up at the sides of the arena.

Knox glanced at his brother, and back at Evelyn.

She nodded. "He's right."

A fresh shower of sparks rained down on them. Knox brushed them off with his poncho, then held it up like a tent over Chase's bare head.

"We gotta go!"

"Follow me!" cried Evelyn.

They ran to the closest side of the arena, using their ponchos to shield Chase. The fighting had quieted now. The Melorians were intent on escape, while the Exorians allowed the fire rain to do its work.

Evelyn grabbed a handhold of rock and pulled herself a few feet up the arena wall. Chase and Knox copied her, feeling their way up and across the face of the cliff.

Chase made the mistake of looking up.

"It's so high!" he yelled. "We'll never make it."

"Don't think about it," Knox yelled back. "Just keep climbing."

The fire rain pelted them. Chase ducked it as best he could.

About halfway up, they heard a great rumbling coming from the arena floor, followed by another echoing roar from the *tehuantl*—Dankar. They stopped to look down.

Below, Dankar, in *tehuantl* form, was squaring off with a tall, helmeted Melorian, barring him from the exit.

"Oh, no," squeaked Knox.

"It's Adhoran!" cried Evelyn.

"We have to go back!" yelled Chase. "He has a little boy!"

He took a step down and his foot slipped. He scrambled to hold on to the cliff wall, but swung out of control. Evelyn grabbed his arm and slammed him back into the wall.

"We can't! We'll fall!"

A scrabbling sound and a small shower of pebbles fell on them. They looked up. Two vultures had landed on a small ledge just above them. Their beady eyes surveyed the scene below.

Dankar paced back and forth in front of the exit.

Adhoran leaned on the butt of his ax, looking worse for wear. His poncho had been torn off and he was bleeding in several places. Massed behind him, like some kind of misshapen chorus, were the surviving Exorian warriors. They stood stock-still, not advancing, as if they already knew they had won. Bodies of both Melorian and Exorian warriors littered the arena. The vultures fluffed their wings and preened. They would have a good meal today.

Knox pressed his face into the rock wall. "I can't watch this," he moaned.

Dankar roared suddenly, with such force that it shook the arena walls. He reared back on his hind legs. A hooded figure darted from the archway like a missile, placing itself between Adhoran and Dankar. The figure lowered her hood; knives spun from her hands.

Calla.

The tehuantl leapt. Evelyn shrieked.

Adhoran swung his ax and let go of the handle. It sang through the air with a metal hiss and hit the cat on the shoulder, forcing it to miss its mark.

Seaborne, Duelle, and several of the remaining Melorians rushed from the archway back into the arena. The Exorian warriors advanced.

The *tehuantl* screamed and attacked Adhoran, hitting him square in the back with his front paws and knocking him to the ground.

Calla and Seaborne beat at the cat's flank with their blades, causing it to explode in a frenzy of teeth and claws. The Exorians joined the attack, and the Melorians were easily surrounded.

The vultures took off flying into the arena, circling the fray in anticipation.

Motion at eye level, across the arena, caused Chase to look up. There, on the terrace of the pyramid, stood Captain Nate, surrounded by a group of young scribes.

"Evelyn, Knox—look!" he called. "Captain Nate!"

The jaws of the *tehuantl* statues were still blazing. The Captain stood before one and lit a torch. The scribes came forward, pushing waist-high balls of woven dried branches. The Captain held the torch to the dried wood, setting each ball alight, and with a great sizzling sound, the scribes launched the balls one by one off the terrace, down the steps, and into the arena.

A fresh gust of wind tore into the arena. It caught the flaming trails left behind the balls and fanned them, spreading fire across the floor. At the same time, a rumbling sound came up from the ground, and the cliff wall that Evelyn, Knox, and Chase held onto began to shake.

"Oh no," cried Evelyn.

A shuddering jolt was followed by a tremendous groan, and the arena opened up with a giant *whooooosh*, like a massive vacuum cleaner.

Their fingers scrambled to dig into the rock. The rock wall shook beneath their fingertips. It began to disintegrate. A giant suck of air was peeling them off the cliff.

"I—I CAN'T HOLD ON!" yelled Chase.

"NEITHER CAN I!" screamed Evelyn.

Knox swung his body to get a better handhold, but it was too late. The wall beneath them gave way. They hurtled straight down, plummeting to the ground, sucked toward the chasm that had opened below. One of the vultures screamed by, its wings on fire.

A loud *boom* shook the air and the earth groaned again. Heat pulsated from the ground.

Chase, Knox, and Evelyn soared back up into the air, spewing up from the flames and dust like a geyser, caught in the updraft as the floor of the arena snapped shut as suddenly as it had split open. Flames licked at their backs. They were catapulted up, lofted high as if they were caught in the draft of a great bellows, and thrown far across the plateau. The walls of the arena crumbled into rubble beneath them.

Chapter 30

SURVIVORS

Chase came to lying facedown with a mouth full of grit. He had no idea how long he'd been unconscious. Every bone in his body felt broken.

He moved his foot around carefully and used an arm to push himself up to a sitting position. His spine wasn't snapped, at least. He searched around a little for both swords—his and Captain Nate's. They were gone, lost in the explosion.

Evelyn lay on her back just a few yards from him, out cold. He scrambled over to her.

"Ev . . . Evelyn!" He shook her hard, but she didn't move.

He cast around wildly, looking for Knox. He didn't see him. He looked back down at Evelyn. First things first. He felt her neck for a pulse. Blood thumped against his fingers.

Chase was feeling better by the second—so much so that he was able to stand and get his bearings.

They had been thrown out of the arena and onto the top of the cliff. If he looked east, to the mountains, the Dwellings and the pit-houses were behind and below him, to his right. To his left, then, would be the wadi and the field of stone heads. He turned 180 degrees and faced, approximately, where he thought the arena should be.

An enormous cloud of sand mushroomed in the air in that direction, obscuring his view. He focused his mind, thinking of Seaborne, Calla, and the Melorians, and tried to see through the dust cloud, but it was too dense. His daylights weren't that strong.

The unmistakable sound of spitting came from somewhere behind him.

"Knox—," he started, and stopped mid-sentence.

Bodi and a scribe were standing side by side, holding the reins of two fully saddled camels.

Chase didn't know what to say.

Evelyn began to stir.

One of the camels leaned its long, curved neck toward her and sneezed, showering her with a spray of camel exhaust. Her eyes flew open.

"It's okay, Ev," said Chase quickly.

He turned to Bodi. "What are you doing here? And who is this?"

Bodi eyed Evelyn, whose face was coated in a thick rime of dust.

"This is Emon, my brother. He and some of the other scribes have escaped to the pit-houses. Dankar was going to make them fight."

Chase's heart fell. "So Dankar is still alive?"

Bodi nodded.

"He is very angry," added Emon. "He does not like disobedience."

"Yeah, I kinda know that about him."

"Mama sent us," said Bodi. "You are in danger. Take the camels to the wadi right away. You have very little time."

Evelyn sat up, rubbing camel spit and dust off her face with her poncho.

"What happened to the Melorians?"

Emon answered, "We do not know. But some have escaped. And the Captain and the water-keeper, Rysta. They are in need of you. That is why you must go to the wadi. My mother says they are there. You must go quickly."

"I can't go anywhere without my brother," said Chase. "I won't."

"You don't have to," said Knox's voice, and then Knox himself appeared, climbing out of a deep depression in the rock, looking none the worse for having been pitched through the air like a bean bag. He had found some water, because both his face and hair were dripping wet.

"Whoa—camels. Cool," he said.

"Knox! You're okay!" cried Chase, more relieved than he wanted to admit that his brother was in one piece.

"Chase!" mimicked Knox, grinning. "I am okay." Then his face dropped. "I hope the others are."

Chase's thoughts spooled out like rope, falling in all different directions.

His first instinct was to go back to the arena and check for survivors. It seemed impossible that anyone could come out alive after what had just happened, but he had. And so had Evelyn and Knox, and by the looks of them, without injury. None of them were even in shock. And the Melorians were ten times stronger—heck, even Seaborne was a thousand times stronger—than they were. If he and Knox and Evelyn had made it, why wouldn't they? He said a silent thanks to his daylights and took a deep breath.

"So Dankar lives?" he asked Bodi and Emon again, wanting absolute confirmation.

Emon shook the reins impatiently at Chase. "Yes—that's why you need to go."

"I'm ready to get out of here," said Evelyn.

She jumped up and took a set of reins from Bodi. Knox grabbed the other set. The two camels knelt to allow them to mount.

"You two lovebirds take that one; this ride's mine," said Knox, swinging a leg over the back of the camel.

"Fine by me," said Evelyn, shooting a sharp look at Knox and patting the saddle. "I need a new traveling companion. You were getting boring."

Knox mimed being crushed.

Chase let Evelyn get settled in the saddle before he climbed on. The camel was not all that different from a horse, except its neck was farther away and its back was broader.

The animals both stood up at the same time. Bodi patted a lump in the blue padded blanket underneath one of the saddles.

"Mama put food and drink in here."

"Thank her for us," said Chase, looking down at them from what seemed to be a great height. They looked small and defenseless and very much like brother and sister. In another world, Bodi and Teddy would be playmates—and he could teach Emon to skateboard. Their mothers might even be friends. Guilt stabbed at him. He didn't want them to get punished.

"Will you get in trouble for helping us?"

Emon shrugged.

"We are all in trouble anyway. Dankar lost a great many warriors in the arena. He now looks to all Exorians to fight. He has already given the call. My mother is frightened. She does not want all-out war. She hopes that the Captain will keep his word."

"What word is that?" Knox cut in. "I don't like it when you make private deals," he said, looking at his brother.

"I'll tell you later," said Chase.

A shout reverberated up from one of the lower steps.

Emon shaded his eyes. "So long, Varunan; I hope we never meet again, so I won't have to kill you."

He took out a grass switch from beneath his tunic and handed it to Bodi.

"The camels are drawn to water; they will take you."

Before they could say anything else, Bodi flicked the camels' rumps with the switch and they lurched forward in a trot.

The edge of the plateau loomed not far ahead. From astride the camel, it appeared that the ground just dropped off into thin air, but the camels charged over it and onto a narrow ledge that descended in switchbacks to the desert floor.

Chase, Evelyn, and Knox swayed precariously on this slender track, holding on to the looped rope attached to their camels' saddles. On one side, their elbows scraped the cliff; on the other side was a free fall.

"I hate heights!" whined Knox, closing his eyes. "This is worse than being back in that pit with Dankar."

"Don't say that," Evelyn called back to him.

Chase smiled a little.

Despite the danger they were in, it was great to have his brother and Evelyn with him again. He wasn't bothered at all by the ride, and when the pitch got steep, Evelyn had to lean her weight back into him, which was a nice feeling. It made him wonder about Knox's comment before. Maybe Evelyn had said something to Knox while they were in Melor. Maybe Evelyn liked him—like, *liked* him.

The camels trudged along. The only sound was from their labored breathing and the tiny pebbles that shook loose as they passed, cascading with a tinkle off the drop.

"What's that?" Evelyn asked, interrupting Chase's reverie. She was pointing north, toward a green patch in the sea of rust and brown.

"That's where we're headed."

He looked east, orienting himself by the pillars of rock that stood up like towers against the flat sky. If he was right, they would come down south of the field of stone heads. This was a double-edged sword: they could use the stone heads as cover, but it also meant that the Exorians might use Bodi's secret passage to ambush them. He tensed.

"What?" asked Evelyn. "Do you see something?"

There was no use freaking her out until they knew for sure which way the blade was going to fall.

"No; just want to be prepared."

She was quiet for a moment, then said, "Do you think we would know if something had happened to Seaborne, or the others? You know . . . do you think we would *feel* it?"

Chase glanced over his shoulder at Knox.

His brother sat bolt upright in his saddle, the hood of his poncho pulled up. He rode with the calm alertness of a trained Melorian soldier, and if

Chase hadn't already known it was Knox, he might have mistaken him for one. Knox certainly would have felt something. His daylights would know.

"Yeah, I think so," Chase said. "I hope so."

Evelyn grew very still.

"Chase, I heard the call of my daylights down in Chantarelle's tunnels. Well, it's more like I felt them, or saw them—I don't know. He showed them to me. The only problem is, I don't know what to do with them. I don't know how what he showed me can help. They're different than yours or Knox's or Teddy's . . ."

Her voice drifted off. She was unable to explain.

Chase listened, not sure what to say.

"That's okay, Ev. I'm sure you'll figure it out when the time comes. I'm glad you finally heard them."

Evelyn sighed and sank a little in her saddle.

"There is no time, Chase. You haven't been to Melor; you don't know how bad it is. The Melorians came into this fight with nothing left to lose. And now Dankar's going to move into Metria. He leaves nothing standing. He burns it *all*. If people don't die in the fighting, they die from starvation."

She turned in the saddle to look at him sideways. "That means us, too."

Chase thought about the faces of the Exorians he had seen at the pit-houses that morning. Some of those women and children had lost sons and brothers today, and would never know it. And if they did know it, their minds would be filled with revenge. Dankar would get plenty of replacements for his army.

Chase remembered the images Ratha had shown him the first time he had seen her atop her aerie—the ones of dead soldiers lying on battlefields. The arena floor had not looked very different today.

The ledge took another zigzag and hit flat land. The camels veered left, following the rim of the plateau. Chase saw the stone heads and pulled on the reins, slowing their camel so Knox could come abreast of them.

"Ranu put those there. The wadi is beyond them."

Knox frowned. "Good place for a trap."

"I know."

Evelyn slid easily from the saddle and dropped on the ground. "I'll scout."

"No," both boys cried in unison.

She put her hands on her hips. "Why—because I'm a girl? Don't be idiots. I am faster than both of you—and my knives go farther."

She whipped out her curved blades and spun them to make her point. Chase and Knox shrugged at each other.

"She's right," said Knox. "Scout away, Ev."

Evelyn shot out of the shade of the plateau wall, darting straight for the first stone head. She gained it easily, circled it, and moved to the next.

Chase and Knox advanced. They had almost reached the first head when a spear whizzed toward them. The camels instinctively avoided it and it landed harmlessly in the sand.

"Evelyn!" shouted Chase.

He and Knox quickly brought the camels under cover of the first head.

"I'm on it," she yelled back.

She sprinted, weaving through the third and fourth heads, her knives in position.

"Give me your slingshot!" Chase shouted to Knox.

There was no way he could reach anybody on the ground with his sword. The camel was too tall.

Knox unhooked his slingshot from his harness and chucked it to Chase, along with his bag of rocks.

"It's all right—I have it under control," Evelyn called.

They followed her voice and found her at the back of the seventh head, two confused-looking scribes, a little younger than Emon, cowering beneath her pointed knives. One held on to an Exorian spear, which looked odd and oversized in his hand.

"No wonder they couldn't hit us," said Knox, sliding off his camel and gesturing toward the spear. "Don't you guys know you're supposed to fight close-up with those spears, not by throwing them?"

One of the scribes shook his head.

"We aren't trained to fight, but Dankar has ordered all the scribes to leave their duties and aid the warriors."

"Are you here with warriors?" asked Evelyn, immediately alert.

The other scribe answered, pointing with his chin toward the direction of the wadi.

"They went ahead; we were supposed to keep a lookout."

"I wish I still had Captain Nate's sword," Chase said to Knox and Evelyn, joining them on the ground. "If Captain Nate and Rysta are ahead, they are unarmed. We have to move."

"What about them?" asked Knox, indicating the scribes.

"Leave them, they aren't a threat."

"What if they come after us?"

"We have camels, they can't run very fast, and"—he said this loudly for the benefit of the scribes—"we have Evelyn; you know she never misses."

Evelyn twirled her knives again to cement his point, then climbed up in front of Chase on their camel. Knox took a menacing step toward the scribes and ran a hand down his harness, stocked with throwing knives.

"Yeah, well, neither do I"—he grabbed a spear out of the scribe's grasp—"and I'll take *this,* just for kicks." He looked it up and down before mounting his camel. Then he pointed it toward the Exorians. "Good weapon for camelback. So don't get any ideas."

The scribes squatted against the rock, their hands up.

Knox snorted. "You guys are too young to fight; you should go home."

"Look who's talking," said Evelyn.

Knox ignored the comment as their camels fell into a swift jog.

Chase looked back at the scribes huddled behind the stone head. He felt sorry for them. If they were the future of Dankar's army, the Metrians and Melorians would have little trouble defeating them. Then his heart spasmed with a strange little twist. If those scribes were being sent to war, untrained and unprepared, what might happen to Bodi and Emon?

Chapter 31

DISSOLUTION

The wadi made itself known by a stark change in landscape. The rusts and browns of the desert erupted instantly into a deep green. The ground was wet and stuck to the camels' hooves, making a sucking gulp when they lifted them. A thicket of thorn bushes obscured the view, but once they'd passed through them, they were able to ride in the canal bed, following it down into the gully.

There, a tranquil scene awaited them: a silver pond surrounded by new foliage and red banks of sandstone. At the edge of one of the banks was Captain Nate. Rysta's head was in his lap. He was dipping his hand into the pond over and over to pour water on her. Strewn beside him on the riverbank were the bodies of three Exorian warriors. He had taken them bare-handed.

The camels raced toward the pond.

The Captain's head shot up in alarm.

"It's us," yelled Chase, quickly dropping to the ground. "We're here!" Evelyn dropped beside him.

Rysta's head lolled in the crook of the Captain's arm. He continued to pour water over her, saturating her robes, skin, hair. She didn't move.

"Can I help?" asked Evelyn, wide-eyed, kneeling beside the wadi to gather more water. She used both hands to bathe Rysta's feet.

"She's still alive—barely. She's spent most of her daylights," the Captain croaked. "If she stays in Exor much longer, she will fragment. There's little left now to bind her vessel."

Chase flashed back on the torrent of light that had poured out of Rysta like a laser, knocking Dankar off the pyramid.

"What can we do?" he asked. "We have camels."

"We must get her to the Voss. It's her only chance." His eyes narrowed at Chase. "I won't lose her again."

"I know," said Chase. "Knox, get the food and water that Bodi's mother packed for us."

Knox ran over with a small wrapped package and a stoppered dried gourd filled with liquid. The Captain pulled the cork from the gourd and sniffed at its contents. A light flickered in his eyes for the first time since they had crossed into Exor.

"Bless you," he muttered.

He lifted Rysta's head, tipping the mouth of the gourd to her lips.

"Drink this, my darling."

He wet her lips with the liquid, letting it drip into the deep cracks at the corners. Her lips parted and he drizzled in a few more drops, then a few more, like feeding a kitten with an eyedropper. It was slow going, but the drink was having an impact. Rysta's limbs stirred and her eyelids fluttered.

"What is it?" Knox asked.

"Quenchwater from the roots of the gifting tree. It is very rare, very hard to distill, and it takes time and patience to gather this much without killing the tree—but once you consume it, you can walk for miles in the desert without thirst. It feeds the daylights. Chase has tasted it."

He continued to drip the nectar into Rysta's mouth. A low moan escaped her.

"Rysta," the Captain whispered into her hair. "You are safe now. I have come for you."

Her eyelids cracked open, showing the whites of her eyes.

The Captain hugged her to him.

"I am so sorry," he said. "I should have come before . . ." He hid his face in the folds of her robes. "I promise you, I will never leave you again."

Rysta lifted her hand, scorched red from the sun, and brought it to his face. Her eyes opened fully, the irises filmy. They caught sight of Evelyn.

"How are you here?" Her voice was thin, barely even a whisper.

The Captain lifted her up so she could sit. Evelyn looked between the two of them, not sure who Rysta was addressing.

"We came here to rescue you, just like you rescued us," Evelyn began. "Me, the Captain, Chase, Knox—your brother, Seaborne, and any other Melorians we could find."

"Here?" Rysta asked, swinging her head around in search of them.

"Easy," said the Captain, as she fell back into him, dizzy. "Drink more of this."

He held up the gourd and Rysta drank a few swallows. When they had sunk in, she was strong enough to sit unaided. Her movements were still as graceful and languid as they had been when Chase, Knox, and Evelyn had first encountered her in her grotto in Metria, but her features were barely recognizable as the same. Her time in Exor had aged her. She was old now—a strange sight in Ayda.

"How is this possible?" Rysta asked. "How is it you have returned?"

She gazed at them in wonder, lingering longest on Captain Nate.

He brought her hands to his lips and kissed them.

"The children—Ratha sent them back for me. I couldn't let you rot in this place," said the Captain. "I had to come back—"

"My sister?"

"Your brother and sister love you, Rysta. They always have," the Captain said tenderly. "As do I."

This statement sank in and had its effect. She leaned against the Captain to rise to her feet.

"Is my brother alive?" she asked. "I cannot feel him."

The Captain looked away. "I do not know."

Rysta let the wet outer layer of her robes fall to the ground. Beneath them, she wore a simple dress, the pink shade of a shell. Her shoulder blades jutted out the back of the thin fabric, and her long white hair fell to her fingertips.

She swiveled her gaze to take in all of the glittering wadi, the bodies of the dead warriors, the green of the resurrected stream bank, and the flat blue sky above. She beckoned to Chase, Evelyn, and Knox to come closer. They did. Her blue eyes, once so clear, now veiled and veined with red, sought each of them. Her fingers groped vainly for the lost pendant at her breast.

"I have nothing to give you but my thanks," she said finally. "I had hoped my necklace might save the outlier, Louis, but I do not think it made much difference. He is lost to us now. It is a pity I only had my necklace and not the full strength of the stone of Metria at my disposal—but at least the real stone is safe."

"No," said Knox. "I think it did help. Evelyn and I saw him. He has a normal hand, and his eyes are the same. He's not lost. Not entirely."

"Well, then, maybe it did some good."

She looked into Captain Nate's eyes.

"I have no way to contact the stone of Metria now. The power in my necklace that connected us was spent in the exchange at the pyramid. I fear the fate of Metria is beyond me now."

To Chase and Knox's surprise, Evelyn burst into tears.

"I'm so sorry I took your necklace, Rysta," she sobbed. "It's all my fault. If I hadn't taken it, we wouldn't be here. We'd all be safe in Metria. I shouldn't have taken it; I know that now."

Rysta pulled her into a trembling embrace. When Evelyn's cries had subsided a bit, Rysta tipped Evelyn's face up to look at her.

"Had you not taken the necklace, we might have faced far worse. We will never know. Fate is a crossroads, and there is no guide but what is most true at the moment of crossing. Do not curse yourself by holding on to the past," said Rysta. "You chose to help your sister. Are you so very different than my own kin then?"

Evelyn shook her head.

"And then you chose to come back here, to help me—am I right?"

Evelyn nodded.

"Well, then, you see, your debt is paid. No more tears, especially here, where you must save your water."

Rysta looked over Evelyn's shoulder at Chase and Knox.

"Where is Teddy?" she asked.

Chase gulped. "I'm not sure."

Knox shot him a startled look.

"What do you mean, you're not sure?"

Chase explained the vision of his mother and Teddy that Ratha had shown him, and the one of Frankie.

"So you think Mom and Teddy are on their way—or that they might already *be* here?" Knox said. He whirled around, looking at the ground, as if he expected them to pop up out of nowhere.

"Evelyn, you gotta get in touch with Chantarelle. Use your thingie, your connection-vision, or whatever it is, and get him here!" he cried. "We can't let them come up in Exor! He needs to take them somewhere safe!"

"Connection-vision?" asked Chase.

"My daylights," Evelyn corrected. "And I don't think they work that way."

Rysta's knees began to buckle and she swayed into the Captain.

"Take me to the water."

The Captain half carried her to the wadi's edge. She leaned on him to wade in knee-deep; the water danced and licked at her robes, as if to welcome her. Her fingers strayed again to her breast, out of habit, then to the surface of the water.

"The Exorians will be coming after us," said Chase. "That's why we have the camels. We have to cross the border by nightfall. If you are strong enough, we should leave soon."

Rysta cupped her hands and splashed water over her face. The beads of moisture stuck to her skin, and, for a moment, her features returned to their former youthful look. She faced the Captain, who beheld her with such affection that Chase flushed in embarrassment. Knox and Evelyn instinctively turned toward the camels to give the Captain and Rysta some privacy.

The Captain kissed her. Light skipped off the small ripples in the water and spangled the air around them.

"In my heart, I never left you. Not for a moment."

Rysta smiled at him.

"I know," she said. "Nor I, you. There is a room in my heart where we live, together, and always shall live. It is a peaked room with great, tall windows that look out to the sea. Waves beat on the shore and wash the air; they fill our hearts with joy."

The Captain stroked her white hair. "You fill my heart with joy."

"It is the same thing."

His hand stopped mid-stroke. "What do you mean?"

Rysta looked straight at him. "My vessel is spent; my daylights long for freedom."

"Rysta—," the Captain gasped.

Chase, Evelyn, and Knox whipped around in alarm.

A golden haze surrounded the Captain and Rysta, as if a funnel of dust motes were circling them in the light. Rysta's shape was barely discernible through the swirling particles. She touched the Captain's jaw, then placed her hand on the water. Ripples undulating from it caused a small wake.

"You must go back to Metria. Take the children with you. Do what you can," she said.

"No!" cried the Captain. "You must come with me!"

He tried to embrace Rysta, but she had become too insubstantial.

"Caspar, my love, do not grieve," her voice said. "Do we cry for a cloud that comes to Earth as rain? No—for we know that the rain will run to the sea and return to the sky again as a cloud. It is an endless cycle. I am here with you, in every drop of rain, in every river, in every wave. There are no endings. You and I shall live in that room in my heart forever."

A *swoosh* of water erupted in the air, meeting the swirl of light particles to create a shimmering, golden geyser. It hovered above the Captain, dappling the air, and then fell like gentle rain into the wadi. The Captain stood there, knee-deep, and alone, the pink fabric of Rysta's dress grabbing at his knees like a castaway net.

"*Noooo!*" he cried, and fell forward, submerging himself underwater with the dress.

The surface turned eerily calm.

Chase, Evelyn, and Knox sat in shocked silence for a minute, gazing after Rysta, before realizing that the Captain had yet to emerge. They splashed into the wadi to drag him out. The water was as warm as blood, and shimmered golden as fresh honey. The camels gazed at them placidly from the water's edge.

A small rainbow rose and spread across the water's surface.

Chapter 32

SANDSTORM

Captain Nate was catatonic when they pulled him out. He lay on his back on the sand, Rysta's pink dress wrapped around him like a shroud, his eyes staring blankly up at the sky.

"What just happened?" Knox wailed. "Did she just, like, *poooff*?"

He made a sound like air expelling, throwing his fingers apart.

"I think she fragmented," said Evelyn, sweeping the wadi with red, swollen eyes. She was looking for signs of a rose-colored fish. "If we were in Metria, she might have been able to transform, but the Keepers don't have the strength if they aren't in their own lands."

Chase stared across the wadi. What were they supposed to do next? How could they fight Dankar without Rysta? He buried his head in his hands.

Knox shot up, smelling a change in the air. He put his ear to the ground.

"We gotta go," he barked.

"What is it?" said Evelyn.

"Don't know. Maybe the scribes reported us, but somebody's coming. And they're coming fast."

He looked at the Captain sprawled on the ground.

"What are we going to do with him?"

Chase lifted his head. His eyes fell on the gourd. It was still half full. He tipped it into the Captain's mouth, then passed it around to Knox and Evelyn. He took a big swallow, and the quenchwater hit him like a shot of adrenaline.

"Wow, that's powerful stuff," said Knox. "Way better than Chantarelle's beer. Let me have another slug." He reached for the gourd, but Chase had taken it to the water's edge, and carefully submerged it, filling it back up again with water.

"Diluted quenchwater is better than none," he explained. "Hand me Rysta's dress."

Evelyn unwrapped the garment from the Captain's hands and tossed it to Chase. It was light and fragrant, and sailed through the air like a flag. A vision of Rysta as he had first seen her—white and shining, standing barefoot in the starlight—overwhelmed him. He remembered her kindness to them; how much she had loved his little brother; how she had longed to mother and protect them; how desperately sad she was.

A lump rose in his throat and tears welled up. One had the nerve to cross his lower lid and drip off his cheek, landing in the wadi with a tiny splash. He looked down at where it landed. There, reflected in the water, was an image of his house—of Summerledge—with its porch and bottle-green lawn bending off into a pink granite ledge.

"Get over here!" he shouted to Evelyn and Knox. "Look at the water! Do you see it?"

They both looked down where he was pointing.

"I don't see anything, Chase," said Evelyn.

Chase looked again and saw only the reflection of their faces, dusty and grim. Chase's had a single tear track smudged along one cheek, like a scar.

"I saw Summerledge."

Evelyn looked back down at the water.

"I think that I saw something like that back home. I was with Teddy and we jumped over a puddle, and when I looked down, I saw the city of Metria. I didn't know what it was then; I hadn't remembered yet. But do you think it's possible that we can see our world here through the water, and they can see ours?"

"At this point, I think anything is possible."

"Teddy saw it, too!" said Evelyn excitedly. "He told me he saw pictures in the puddles!"

At the mention of Teddy's name, Chase and Knox exchanged looks.

"We have to find Chantarelle," said Knox. "He'll know if Teddy and Mom are here."

He splashed out of the water and hooked his arms under Captain Nate's armpits, lugging the man's dead weight toward the camels.

Chase and Evelyn helped load Captain Nate on the saddle behind Knox, then mounted their own.

"We'll go back across the plains, into Varuna, then head south to the Voss," said Chase. "From there we can make it into Melor and look for Chantarelle—"

"Chase," Knox cut in. He looked worried. "We can't let anything bad happen to Mom. We have to keep the Exorians away. They can't follow us."

"I know, Knox. Let's cross the desert first."

Evelyn slapped the rump of her camel, and they set off in a trot on a straight course for the mountains.

They sprinted past the field of stone heads. The quenchwater had done its job, and the riders—except for Captain Nate—felt alert. Chase veered them left, and west, and set out into the deepening plain of the desert. The sun was now behind them, sinking.

They had put more than three hundred meters between themselves and the stone heads when they heard a whooping call and the sound of pounding hooves behind them.

Evelyn glanced back over her shoulder.

A host of Exorian camel riders was tearing across the desert, gaining on them.

"We have company, and they ride camels better than we do!" she warned Chase.

"WE HAVE TO GIVE IT ALL WE'VE GOT!" Chase shouted to Knox.

"C'mon, baby! RUN!" Knox shouted, and dug his heels into his camel.

Chase slapped the reins and dug his heels into the camel's flank. The camel lurched forward, sand flying in great thundering spurts behind them.

Knox was bending low, urging his camel on with his voice. Behind him, Captain Nate seemed to be coming back to life.

The camels raced ahead past the first outcropping of rock spires, lit like a match at their top and eerily dark below.

The Exorians came galloping on, closing the gap.

They passed the second outcropping, and then the third, and now had more than two miles between them and the Dwellings, but the camels were flagging. Their ears lay back on their heads, their tongues hung from their mouths, and sweaty foam dripped from their flanks. The sound of their hooves beat the ground.

"THEY'LL DIE RIGHT UNDER US IF WE RIDE THEM LIKE THIS THE WHOLE WAY!" shouted Evelyn.

"I KNOW, BUT WHAT DO YOU WANT ME TO DO?" Chase yelled back.

"ASK RATHA TO HELP!"

Evelyn had never met Ratha, Chase reminded himself, or she would not be telling him to do this. Ratha was the least empathetic Keeper he had met.

"What do you have to lose?" asked Evelyn directly in his ear. "Please! Chase, they're right behind us!"

Chase heard the panic in her voice.

He looked over his shoulder. A force of about twenty-five Exorians, a few scribes and more warriors, were on camelback, racing across the desert, in flat-out pursuit. Their spears caught the afternoon sun and threw it back on their faces, like flashbulbs. Then, as if the Exorians were already assured of their victory, their spears ignited.

"HOLY CRAP!" Chase heard Knox yell.

The Exorians were gaining on them, moving apart in a wide V to come along either side.

Evelyn was right. What did they have to lose now? They couldn't outrun the Exorians, and if they were caught, Dankar had no more use for them. He was already winning.

Ratha had heard him once before, back at Lake Voss. Maybe she was listening now.

Chase closed his eyes and focused on the sensation of the camel swaying beneath him, the air rushing across his face, the shuffling fall of the sand as they galloped across it. He wiped his mind of all other thoughts and concentrated on an image of Ratha as he had met her first, in Varuna, on the terrace in the mountains, her cauldron burning orange and purple and blue beside the four-sided building. A nebula of color spun around the image, dipping in and out and then coalescing into a tube through which his awareness slipped. The reins dropped out of his hands, and the sound and smell of the desert fell away.

Help us, Ratha! he thought, over and over.

And then he was standing at the edge of the terrace once again.

Ratha stood a few paces off, her robe pulsating in that nauseating strobe-like way.

"Chase," she said. Her eyes glowed with renewed ferocity.

"You heard me," he croaked.

"Of course."

"Can you help me?"

"As you have helped me?"

"I did what you asked: I brought Captain Nate back. I did my best."

"Yes, but without the Fifth Stone, the Captain is of little use. And now my sister is dead."

"He told you he'd tell you all he knows; if we die now, he won't do it."

Ratha cocked her head in that funny way she had, like a bird.

"True, but then, he may never come back. Better he die now, where I can watch."

"But what about me, and my brother, and Evelyn! And my mom and Teddy?!"

"The tethers of loved ones pull tightly, do they not?" Ratha looked off in the distance, then squared up with him again.

"I have felt them myself—but, as you see, my loved ones are dropping like petals from a flower after frost."

She was on him in three flashing steps.

"You were *too late*. My father, my sister, my brother, my mother—all gone. Tell me why I should save you and yours?"

A throb of anger went through Chase.

"BECAUSE YOU'RE MY KEEPER, THAT'S WHY!" he shouted. "You're supposed to protect me—but instead you brought me, brought *all* of us here, to do your dirty work! And now that it's all gone wrong, you want to blame someone. I'll tell you why you should do it: It's your job!"

Ratha looked as if she had been slapped. She flickered off to a far side of the terrace.

"Well?" said Chase. "What's it going to be? We don't have much time!"

"You have as much time as I grant," Ratha snapped from her side of the terrace.

She paced for a moment, then turned on him.

"Family is a funny thing, isn't it, Chase? Bound by blood and duty to people you might not otherwise care to know. This is why following your own daylights will guide you to your own kind—your real kin. Blood is an accident of nature; choice is fate."

She gave him that cockeyed look.

"But, as you say, I brought you here without *giving* you a choice, so perhaps I do owe you something."

She paused.

"Here is my offer: I am your Keeper, and as such, I demand your presence here in Varuna, with me, in exchange for getting you out of this mess. No more wandering. Do you understand? I will help you, but in return, you shall come here. You will learn our ways and take up your true birthright."

Chase stared at her. He couldn't think of a fate worse than dying—except maybe living here with Ratha. Everything about the idea repelled him. She was a monster. He had no doubt she would kill Captain Nate—or him, if the mood struck her. He remembered how easily she had ripped into his head and made his nose bleed. If Captain Nate hadn't intervened, she might have killed him then.

But Captain Nate did intervene. He had offered his own life in exchange for Rysta's and Chase's. Just as Rysta had offered her life to Dankar so that Chase and his brothers and Evelyn and Frankie could be free. Just as Remiel had sacrificed his family for the sake of all humankind so long ago. And Tinator. Tinator had died to protect them.

It dawned on Chase that everything truly important happened between people because somebody somewhere gave up something that mattered, even when they really didn't want to.

His thoughts strayed to his parents.

Had his father *wanted* to take the job that had moved their family from Indiana to Sherwood Forest? Had Evelyn and Frankie *wanted* to come to Fells Harbor? He had never even bothered to ask them; he'd just assumed they were happy about it. Maybe his dad was as sad as they were to be uprooted. Maybe Evelyn had felt the exact same way he felt now: afraid and angry at the thought of leaving Haiti.

He had never really noticed how much other people had given up—had never cared that much about how they felt. He'd been too consumed with his own feelings.

The blood rushed to his face. With a pang, he remembered how Knox had jumped in to save him from the bullies at their new school.

"You must decide!" Ratha said urgently. "The Exorians have caught up with your brother and the Captain. Their camel has just been speared through the flank. It is stumbling—and—ah, *interesting*—this force is led by the new warrior. The blue-eyed one."

She gave Chase a funny look.

Chase shuddered. His teeth clenched, as if his body were trying to stop him from saying the words. But the time had come for Chase to do something for everyone else.

"Okay, fine! YES!" he shouted.

Bang!

The door on the far side of the square building blew open with such force that it hit the wall like a shot. A freezing cold wind came billowing out of the aperture and spilled across the terrace in a gale force. It sped past Chase, flattening his cheeks, and into the atmosphere, headed west.

"Before you go," cried Ratha over the wind, "ask yourself why the Exorian warrior has blue eyes—just like yours. *Exactly* like yours. Remember—you are not the only outlier I brought here."

Chase slammed back into his body. A blast of cold air hit him in the face.

"They're right behind us!" cried Evelyn.

Chase looked back. Ratha had done her time-bending thing and slipped him back in time to the point when the Exorians were still many paces behind. The only difference was the cold air blowing directly in their direction.

The camels, reenergized by the bracing air, strained against the reins and sprinted ahead. The north wind buffeted and curled around them, saving its strength to lift up the sand that lay between them and their attackers. The wind began to shriek. Sand rose up behind them in a churning tornado and swept toward the Exorians.

The Exorian camels balked and reared, dumping some of their riders in the sand. Then, the tornado split into several whirling columns, which joined together to form a boiling wall of sand, as tall as a mountain, and impossible to pass through.

"Yes!" said Chase, lifting his eyes to the mountains. "Thank you!"

Maybe Ratha was not a complete monster. She'd kept her end of the deal; the only problem was, now he would have to keep his.

✛   ✛   ✛

They left the camels at the border and crossed into Varuna on foot, the sun a flat orange nub on the horizon behind them. The Captain, still mute, trudged alongside.

Knox sniffed the air, and smiled a little. "I smell plants."

Evelyn took a sniff, too. "You do? I don't smell anything."

"If we turn south from here, we should be in Melor by morning," Knox said. "We need to find Chantarelle."

"I know, Knox. I know." Chase didn't know how to break it to them that he couldn't go with them—that he was staying in Varuna.

"How about we go to the Voss and figure out our next step," said Chase. "Rothermel told us to meet there, remember?" He turned to face the Captain. "You remember, right, Captain?" he repeated, trying to engage him.

The Captain just stared ahead, his eyes devoid of any feeling.

Evelyn sidled up to Chase.

"Leave him alone, Chase. He needs to grieve. My father told me I didn't speak for a year after my mother died."

She dropped back to walk next to Captain Nate.

Knox trotted ahead, swinging his head back and forth, taking in any notable landmarks.

In time, a fat moon rose to the east.

Chase was mulling over Ratha's last words. What did she mean?

"Knox, do you know the blue-eyed warrior? The one you think is Louis."

"The one with the hand?" Knox asked.

"I don't know; I never saw him—but Ratha told me something about him. She said he had blue eyes just like me—like us. And that we weren't the only outliers she'd brought here. Do you think, maybe . . ."

Chase stopped and shook his head.

"He's definitely Louis, the guy we met at the canyon's edge," said Knox. "Frankie's friend. Dankar did his little experiment on him, but it didn't totally work."

Chase gave Knox a pointed look.

"I believe you, but now I'm wondering if maybe he's also somebody else. He's an outlier, like us, right? So maybe he was brought here, too. Like, maybe he went out for a sail one day and got caught up in Ratha's grand plan? Landed in Exor?"

Knox finally caught on.

"Are you thinking he's Uncle Edward?"

"Do you think it's possible? Do you think it's him?"

Knox thought for a long minute. "Yeah, I think it is," he said slowly.

"I do, too," agreed Chase, looking directly at Knox. "It makes sense. Ratha told me to ask myself why he had blue eyes. Like you. Like me. Like Mom."

Knox whistled under his breath.

"Mom's long-lost brother. She's going to freak. He looks like a gargoyle, and I wouldn't exactly call him friendly."

He described his encounter with Louis in the arena.

Chase was silent for a minute, thinking over this new information.

"I doubt Louis remembers much—the fog and all, plus whatever Dankar's done to him. Gorked his daylights," said Chase. "He messes with people and gives them all these rules and duties they have to follow. The Exorians have been doing it for so long, they don't even bother to ask why. He treats them like they aren't even people; they are just his slaves, to do with as he pleases."

Knox thought again about the *tehuantl*.

"Poor Louis—I mean, Uncle Edward, or whatever we're gonna call him. He saved our lives, and he didn't even know who we were. And now he's . . ."

Knox shrugged, unable to come up with a word for the terrible thing that had happened.

"Yeah," said Chase. "I know."

"But you're right—if he truly is Uncle Edward, Mom *is* going to freak." They walked together in brooding silence.

"You know what, Chase?" said Knox. "All we know for sure is that if Louis really is our uncle, then he's not who he was—but, then again, Dankar's experiment wasn't a total success. He still has that one human hand. Maybe it's a sign that some of him is still—I don't know—*here*. With us. Maybe he can be turned back. I think that's why Rysta gave him her necklace."

"Maybe," said Chase. He wasn't convinced.

He turned to face his brother, saying firmly, "We have to tell the others. We can't let anyone hurt him." He was thinking about their mother. "No matter who Louis is now, Mom will want to see him. She'll want to know if he's her brother, even now. And if he is, she will be happy to know he's alive, no matter what he looks like."

Knox pulled back his hood.

"Why?"

"Because that's how I'd feel if it were you."

Chapter 33

NEW DIRECTIONS

By the next day they noticed the land had begun to slope downward. The morning sun rose, glowing like a furnace, over the tips of the snowy mountains, and with it came a bird's-eye view of what remained of the forest of Melor. Ash particles swam in the fresh-hatched streaks of sunlight, great strokes of forest were blackened and destroyed, and the odor of smoke and burning pitch was strong.

Chase, Evelyn, Knox, and the Captain had walked through the night without tiring, using their Melorian training. The Captain seemed oblivious to all things except his own desolation. Lack of food, however, was once again becoming a problem.

"I can't remember the last meal I ate," groaned Knox. "I mean, a *real* meal: like a hamburger and fries. I'm starving."

He looked as if he were about to stomp his foot in a tantrum.

"That's the thing I liked most about Metria. All the food, everywhere we went. There's nothing to eat in Varuna, or Melor, except"—he made a face—"snakes."

"Snakes?" said Chase, raising an eyebrow.

"Don't ask," said Evelyn. "And Knox, don't be a baby. Think about Seaborne and Calla and the rest of the Melorians. They've been hungry a lot longer than we have."

That cowed him.

They trudged along, stomachs rumbling loud enough to be heard.

The Captain came out of his trance long enough to pull out the leather pouch he had tied around his waist. He threw it to Chase, who uncinched it. Inside was the bark they'd taken from the *katari* tree. Chase put a flake in his mouth and gave one to Evelyn and Knox. The Captain held up his hand to block Chase from giving him any. It tasted like roasted cardboard splinters, but it lasted a long time, and their hunger pains began to abate. They chewed and walked as the sun rose higher and higher over Varuna.

By mid-day, fields of shale and hardpan gave way to softer, more leafy ground. They stopped a moment at an overlook and there lay the Voss twinkling below, nestled at the heart of Ayda like a shining platter. At one end, the head of the Vossbeck curved west into the charred landscape of Melor, and far to the east, the Hestredes flowed, wide and bubbling, into the meadows and lush lowlands of Metria, still seemingly unsullied by Dankar's hand.

The sight of it made the Captain stoop, as if pulled to the ground by an unseen weight. He raised an arm to cover his eyes.

Chase felt a similar pang. They were looking at a sight Rysta would never see again, yet it spoke powerfully to them of her. The water caught the light from the sun and spread it across its surface, spangled and playful.

If joy was a physical thing, Chase thought to himself, it would look like light dancing across water. But he felt no joy in the sight of it. Their presence here without Rysta felt wrong—as if they had trespassed into a place where they didn't belong. The permanence of Rysta's absence sank into him, leaden and dull.

He spoke to the Captain. "I'm sorry. She should be here."

The Captain lowered his arm to give Chase a look so full of pain that, for a moment, Chase felt afraid.

"We tried," the Captain said. "We did our best." His voice cracked. "I know it wasn't enough. But you did try. She knew we came back."

"I'm sorry I lost your sword."

"It doesn't matter now, Chase," said Captain Nate.

His voice was tinny, as if it came from behind a closed door.

"I have no use for it. I will no longer protect my life. I am weary of it."

Chase was going to object, but Evelyn cut in.

"Hey, Chase, what's that?" She was pointing at the Voss.

Chase followed her finger to see a small speck on the surface of the lake, followed by a V-shaped wake.

Knox squinted. "A bird or something, probably."

Chase shook his head. "No. It's too big to be a bird."

The Captain stiffened. He followed the progress of the speck for a moment.

"It's a ship," he said, giving Chase a knowing look. "From Metria. They've come for Rysta—I must tell them."

He leapt from the overlook and hastened down the slope at a dead run, making a beeline for the shore.

"They're gonna go on the warpath when they find out she's gone," said Knox.

He leapt off the overlook after the Captain, Evelyn and Chase right behind him.

"Well, at least you'll get your meal now," said Evelyn, running next to Knox. "The Metrians will have food on the ship."

"Yeah, well, I've lost my appetite," he said sadly.

✛   ✛   ✛

They emerged onto the northeast shore of the Voss along a promontory of land that poked into the water and formed the boundary line between Melor and Varuna. Almost directly across the lake foamed the headwaters of the Hestredes.

The Metrian ship sailed toward them full tilt, its red sails billowing in the southeasterly, the kindest of winds. It was a smaller ship than the one the children had sailed on, on their first trip to Metria, but large enough for a sizable cabin and three sails. There would be room for all of them.

The Captain paced the shore as they waited for the ship to throw anchor. Two dories, manned by six fully armored Metrians, rowed ashore. When they were just feet from land, a lithe figure sprang from the first dory and removed her helmet.

"Hesam!" cried Chase, instantly recognizing her clear blue eyes and pale hair. It was their old friend and navigator.

"Here I am, as always, sailing you out of trouble," she said, raising her palm, fingers splayed. Her expression was blank, and her eyes roamed across them and over the beach, searching.

The Metrians pulled the dories ashore.

Another familiar figure stepped onto the beach. This one wore no armor, but was dressed in the flowing garb of Rysta's personal attendants. It was Urza. She wasted no time with greetings, and addressed the Captain.

"Where is she?"

"She is not here," he choked out. His shoulders began to heave.

"Is she still in Exor?" Urza looked alarmed.

She cast an inquisitive eye over Chase, Evelyn, and Knox.

"Did the rescue fail? We have heard no word except to set sail here to meet you."

The Captain tried to speak.

"She's not in Exor," Evelyn jumped in. "She . . . she—"

"She's fragmented, Urza," the Captain said, voice breaking. "She had nothing left. She knew her vessel couldn't make it back across the desert. She left me. She left us. I—I couldn't save her. I was too late."

Urza, Hesam, and the other Metrians took this in with a troubled silence. All motion on the lake appeared to cease, as well as sound—as if the volume knob of the world had been snapped off. The wind dropped and the lake became as still as a mirror. For a moment, all time and being and sound halted to grieve the passing of Rysta.

Urza broke the spell.

"Rysta's necklace," she said to the Captain. "She would have given you that."

He shook his head. "It is ruined."

Urza recoiled as if she'd been stung.

"Then we have less time than we thought. Already Exorians push into our lands. We must return to Metria immediately and call on all those who can to protect our stone."

She signaled Hesam with a look.

The Metrians dragged the dories back toward the water.

"Dankar will waste no time now. He will come straight to Metria, and we must be there to meet him—"

She was distracted by the sight of a flaming arrow slicing through the air from behind a boulder. It whizzed past their heads and landed with a thud in the wooden hull of one of the dories. Flames began to consume the small boat.

The Metrians quickly doused it with water, but more arrows rained down on them. Hesam pulled the arrow out of the hull.

"This is a Melorian arrow," she said, confused.

"The fireworms took them from us," cried Knox. "In the arena."

"They aren't worms, Knox; they're people, just like us. They've been misled," said Captain Nate.

Knox cut him off.

"Right now, they're people who want us to die, and I'm not interested in that—are you?"

A swarm of Exorian warriors, some on camelback, were advancing on them from the Melorian side of the lake.

Evelyn pulled out her knives and shouted to Chase. "You don't have a weapon. Get on the boat!"

The Metrian regiment swept past him, fueled by revenge, their curved swords blazing in the sun. Hesam secured her helmet and joined the line.

The Captain, Urza, and Chase were left behind, with nothing to fight with. The Captain motioned to Chase.

"You and Urza must go to the boat, like Evelyn says. The others will meet you there. Urza must be protected. She knows where the stone of Metria is hidden."

"And what about you?" asked Chase.

"I will fight in my own way."

"You don't have your sword; you'll never make it!"

"Who said that was the objective?"

"Don't be stupid," cried Chase. "Rysta wouldn't want you to die! She told you to go back to Metria."

He guessed this wasn't the time to tell the Captain about his own deal with Ratha.

The Captain didn't reply. He sped down the beach to join the others, leaving Urza and Chase dumbfounded. Three more sizzling arrows winged by their heads, one almost striking Chase.

"Help me move this into the water," said Urza, bending down to move the dory. "We must get to the ship."

Chase watched his brother and Evelyn and the Captain, moving with the Metrians in a phalanx up the beach. The Exorians—the same ones they had outrun in the desert—were coming on fast, spears lit and shields up. Chase could see panic in the camels' eyes.

Then, he remembered: his uncle—Louis—might be part of the group. He had been leading them, or so Ratha had said. He and Knox hadn't told Evelyn or the Captain what they had discovered.

"KNOX!" he yelled.

Knox quarter-turned, not wanting to risk taking his eyes off the oncoming Exorians.

"LOOK FOR LOUIS!"

Chase pushed the dory into the water. He and Urza boarded and they put oars to water.

Chapter 34

MERCY

The Exorians and Metrians met in a slashing, clanging fury, throwing pebbles and grit up off the beach.

Chase watched from the relative safety of the boat, Urza beside him.

Evelyn and Knox were having trouble with the Captain, who kept trying to leap into the middle of the battle, barely dressed and without any way to defend himself. They had positioned themselves on either side of him, between the fighting and the boat.

An Exorian on camelback charged through the line, straight at them, eyes glowing orange and spear tip flaming. Knox hurled one of his throwing knives at the warrior's unguarded shin. It glanced off the thick hide and fell onto the beach. Evelyn's knives were spinning in her hands.

"GO FOR THE CAMEL!" screamed Knox.

Evelyn looked horrified. Before she let go, the Captain launched himself at the Exorian. The Exorian threw his spear at the easy target, but the Captain dove and rolled on the pebbles at the last minute, and the spear overshot its mark. The Captain sprang and grabbed it, just as the warrior and his camel thundered down on top of him.

Evelyn attacked, hacking at the warrior's leg and forcing him to defend himself with the shield.

The Captain took the opportunity to throw himself at the warrior from the other side, pushing him off the saddle and dismounting him. The Exorian fell at Evelyn's feet, her knives pointed at his mottled, scabbed chest. The Captain quickly took the Exorian's place astride the camel and rode off.

Knox sprang to help Evelyn, even though it was clear that she had the situation under control. One swipe and the Exorian would be done for.

She hesitated.

"Ev—what are you doing?" asked Knox.

She looked at him sideways. Her dark eyes flashed.

"I'm just sick of it, Knox. I'm tired of death. It follows me everywhere I go."

"It's us or them," said Knox, but he, too, sounded less sure. He was thinking about Louis. And Bodi and Emon. This could be their dad, for all he and Evelyn knew.

The Exorian stared up at them, listening.

Evelyn pulled back her knives. "Enough of this. I don't want to hurt him. Let's tie him up."

"With what?"

"Look for some rope."

Knox ran to the dory left on the beach and found a line. Evelyn jerked the Exorian to a sitting position. They bound his arms behind his back, and his legs, and dragged him to the water's edge.

"We'll throw you in there face-first, if you don't behave!" threatened Knox.

The Exorian nodded once and hung his head.

Knox swept his eyes over the battle, searching.

"Evelyn, stay here with this guy and don't let anyone get near the boat. I gotta go look for someone."

Knox sped toward the fracas.

The Exorians were gaining the upper hand. They had more men, and a height advantage on the camels.

Still, the Metrians were not giving up. Their armor stood up well against the Exorian spears, and it was not easily set on fire, so the fighting had become hand to hand.

The Captain, on his stolen camel, tried to peel off the other camel riders by taunting them with the spear and then riding down the beach a ways. It seemed to be working.

Knox circled the fighters on the ground, trying to catch sight of the Exorians' faces. The transformation made them all look so similar: broad and muscled and hidebound. It was only the shape of their limbs, their lips, and their eyes that gave any clue to possible differences. He thought again about Louis, and the man he'd been. For all Knox knew, every one of these scarred Exorians had once been a man. Somebody's son, maybe even someone's brother or father. Dankar had changed them, just like he'd changed Louis.

"What in the name of all the blessed daylights do you think you are doing?" cried a familiar voice, coming from the Melorian side of the beach. "Research?"

Knox whipped his head around. Seaborne and Calla were sprinting down the beach toward him, and beside them—Knox honestly could have wept with relief—ran Axl and Tar.

The Captain was farther down the beach. He had led the Exorians on camelback quite a ways onto the Melorian side of the shore, and it was here that the hounds went on the offensive, snarling and barking and biting at the camels' legs.

The camels were having none of it, and took off into the hills, carrying their helpless riders along with them.

Seaborne and Calla splashed into the water and made their way toward Knox. They both were the worse for wear, thinner than ever, and clearly exhausted.

"We came straight here from the Dwellings, back through the tunnel. Chantarelle led us. We came out at the Broomwash. We knew you would come to the Voss. Do you have Rysta?"

Knox shook his head. "I'm sorry, Seaborne. She's gone. Fragmented."

"No, it's not possible," said Seaborne. His face crumpled. "She's a Keeper. She's stronger than all of us. This is horrible news." He brought his hands to his face. "She was like a mother to me."

"She was too tired," said Knox. "And she gave her necklace to Louis. It got wrecked. Plus, all that time in Exor—her daylights weren't strong enough to heal her."

"This is terrible," cried Calla. "We have to get back to the Wold. We must tell my mother and Rothermel." She made a motion to go back, but Seaborne stopped her.

"Nay, Calla. We need to drive these Exorians into the Voss, and then see where we are. Rothermel already knows, I warrant, if I understand anything about the daylights."

He surveyed the fierce fighting on the beach. "Well, at least Metrians know how to hold their own!"

The Captain came splashing toward them, still on the camel.

Seaborne gave him a once-over, and, noting that he'd lost his spear, threw him his machete. Then he unsheathed his broadsword from the scabbard on his back.

"Let's drive these devils into the lake. Let the stone of Metria have her revenge."

Knox couldn't help but smile a little at the thought. Metrians could swim, but the Exorians—that was a different story.

They sprang apart to circle the fighters and come at them from behind. In a short time, the fighting had been inched to the water's edge. The Metrians, understanding now what the tactic was, left off their attack and dove headfirst into the waters of the Voss, swimming straight for their ship. They quickly put distance between themselves and the Exorians with wide strokes. The Melorian hounds returned from chasing the camels into the hills and helped to herd the surrounded Exorians into the water.

Knox, Seaborne, Calla, and the Captain rounded up any stray Exorians and drove them into the shallows of the Voss. At the first lick of cold, mountain springwater, the warriors hollered as if in pain. Evelyn unbound and marched her prisoner up the shore to join his company.

The Exorians were tormented by the water. Their strange mutated flesh pulsated and bubbled when it came in contact with it, and they hopped up and down on either foot, trying to keep at least one of their feet out of the water. Seaborne and Calla pushed them deeper in. Their howls grew louder.

Knox searched their faces frantically, looking for Louis.

A cold wind picked up from the northeast and blew across the lake. Ripples of chop started to break over the Exorians' midriffs. A wild panic grew in their orange-flecked eyes. The chop became real waves. The Exorians punched at the water, making matters worse. A few of them stumbled and submerged beneath the surface of the lake.

"I can't watch this," muttered Evelyn. She turned away.

Knox, still searching, did a double take.

There! He saw a flash of normal-looking flesh: a hand, slicing through the water. A lone Exorian was separating himself from the group, making choppy strokes through the waves, swimming back across the lake, nearer to the Exorian border.

"Blimey, will you look at that! One of them can swim," said Seaborne. "What is this world coming to?"

The Captain charged forward on his camel, his machete raised. "Shall I?"

"NO!" Knox yelled.

The Captain lowered his weapon, surprised. "What's this—sympathy for the devil?"

"He's not a devil," argued Knox. "Look, I don't have time to explain right now, but . . . but . . . I think he's my uncle!"

"What?" asked Evelyn, turning back around. "Your *uncle?* Are you out of your mind?"

"It's true," said Knox, following the swimming Exorian with his eyes. "I think that's Louis, and Chase and I think Louis is our uncle. Chase is pretty sure. Ratha said something about it that makes him think it's true, and we can't risk hurting him. It's not his fault that Dankar turned him into—*that!*"

He gesticulated toward the throng of spluttering, splashing, half-drowned Exorians.

"None of them are to blame! Louis was like us, and then Dankar did something to him. He was going to do it to you, Seaborne. He probably did it to all of them, too. They were probably just normal Exorians, scribes or something, and then he mutated them."

"Crikey," said Seaborne, shaking his head.

Knox watched the Exorians struggle in the water a moment longer, feeling suddenly sorry for them.

"We need to let them go," he said.

"Are you mad?" cried Seaborne. "Calla, are you hearing this?"

"I am," she said, throwing a peculiar look at Knox. "Tell me, Knox, why?"

"What if it was you, or me, or Seaborne? It could be, someday. They didn't ask for this. Dankar just did it, just like he corrupted the daylights of the *tehuantls*. It's not their fault. It's Dankar's."

A few of the Exorians were scrambling into shallower waters.

"DON'T GET ANY IDEAS!" roared Seaborne, waving his sword. "I don't care whose mother's sons you are—you'll stay there until we're well away, or I *will* drive you into the depths myself, until you all drown!"

The Exorians fell back.

"What should we do with them, then?" asked Calla.

"I have no earthly idea," sighed Seaborne.

They pondered the Exorians. Standing waist-high in the water, the warriors looked chastened, and more like hapless, wet lizards than the terrifying warriors they appeared to be on dry land.

Evelyn had been quiet a long time before she spoke.

"If Dankar did this to them, maybe it can be undone." Some of her reasoning had to do with Frankie. "If the Exorians' daylights are damaged or unbalanced because of Dankar—or whatever—maybe they can be rebalanced. Maybe they can be transformed back to who they were before. They won't want to fight us then. We have to take them prisoner," said Evelyn, struck with an idea. "We'll take them to Metria and see if we can heal them there. There's room on the boat."

Seaborne looked at her as if she were mental. "*Heal* them," he repeated.

"Yes. Heal them. Like Chase and Knox's dad is trying to heal Frankie."

Seaborne shook his head at her. "No."

The Captain cut in.

"Respectfully, I disagree—she may be on to something. Perhaps it's a spell that can be removed; and if not, we can always use them as hostages."

Seaborne and Calla traded looks.

"Do you really think it's wise?" asked Seaborne.

"I think Knox and Evelyn have a point," said the Captain.

Seaborne sighed in protest, but set off to speak with Urza anyway. When he came back, he returned with the Metrian guards. They disarmed the Exorians, shackled them, and led them to the dories to be taken to the boat.

"I don't know what you're driving at, the two of you, but Urza also seems to think you might be on to something. 'Make friends of our enemies,' is how she put it."

Knox smiled at the woebegone expressions of the Exorian warriors as they were loaded onto the dories. He had never seen a sorrier-looking group.

"Well, Seaborne, if it makes you feel any better, I don't think they're too happy about it."

"Aye, I hope they get seasick, the lot of them," he snorted. "Come now, we must prepare to leave. Knox, round up your brother. We head for the Wold."

Chase was already walking toward them down the beach.

Knox gestured to him.

"C'mon, Chase. We need to get back to the Wold as quickly as possible and talk to Chantarelle. Find out if Mom and Teddy are here."

"Teddy? Here?" cried Seaborne.

"Yeah. It's a long story. Chase will tell you."

Chase caught up with them. The skin on the back of his neck was already tingling. His ears twitched. He detected the shuffling whisper of feathers in the air.

"You'll have to tell them, Knox; I can't."

"What are you talking about?" cried Knox.

Chase pointed down the beach. A ways off were Calyphor and Deruda, hands clasped quietly across their middles.

"I'm not coming with you. I'm going to Varuna."

Knox swung his head back and forth.

"Oh no, Chase, that is *not* okay."

"It's part of the deal, Knox. I don't have a choice. Ratha and I have an agreement."

"That's not true; you always have a choice. A Keeper can't make you do anything you don't want to do."

"I made my choice already, Knox. Remember the sandstorm in the desert? It didn't come out of nowhere."

"But what about me?" Knox's voice had turned younger, pleading.

Chase's heart gave a little thud. He tried to sound confident.

"You have your own job to do. You need to find out about Mom and Teddy. You need to make sure they are okay. You have to keep them safe until we can all be together again."

Knox swallowed hard.

"What, no sassy comeback?" Chase chided his brother.

Knox shook his head.

"I don't want you to go, Chase."

Axl reared up on her back legs and jumped on Knox, placing her front legs on either of his shoulders, almost knocking him down. She licked his cheeks with her great, raspy tongue, trying to comfort him.

"It won't be forever, Knox. If you miss me, just look to the mountains." He gestured behind him vaguely. "I'll be there. In the meantime, you need to go to Melor. Find Chantarelle. Find Mom and Teddy. They are going to need you. So will the Melorians."

"Aye, Knox, your brother is right," Seaborne agreed. "There comes a time when the call of the daylights must be abided—and besides, I do need you. You are a true asset in battle, m'lad. I am very proud of you."

Knox looked pleased, despite the lump in his throat.

Chase turned to Evelyn. Without warning, she catapulted into him and threw her arms around him.

"I know you have to go, but I don't want you to," she said into his neck. "I'll miss you so much."

"Careful, Ev. You'll stab me with those knives of yours."

"Don't stay away too long!" she said in his ear, then pressed her lips awkwardly on the corner of his mouth.

Chase put his hand to the spot, stunned.

Seaborne and Calla laughed.

Calyphor and Deruda came up behind Chase. A sound like wind rustling through leaves filled the air as they moved. The rustling grew louder until it coalesced into words that only Chase could understand.

You are not the only one with a promise to fulfill.

"Do you hear that?" Chase asked.

" 'Tis the wind, lad," said Seaborne. "She's expecting you."

Tell him, said the rustling.

The Captain put a hand on Chase's shoulder. He was speaking, but Chase could not make out what he said, the voice in his head was blowing so loudly.

Tell him now!

Chase grabbed the hand on his shoulder and shot his eyes up to the Captain's.

"I'm supposed to tell you that I'm not the only one with a promise to fulfill."

The Captain's eyes drifted to Calyphor and Deruda, who stood motionless just beyond Chase, their lips unmoving. They stared back at him with empty, clear eyes.

"Ratha will know where to find me," the Captain said to them. "I will not disappoint her, but for now I go to Metria, as Rysta requested. It was her dying wish. I will not disregard it."

Calyphor stepped directly behind Chase.

"Until we meet again, then," said the Captain, then added in a low voice only Chase could hear: "It will not be long, I promise you."

Chase nodded.

Calyphor wrapped his arms around Chase's torso. Then, with a giant *whoosh,* the ancient Varunans extended their wings and blasted off the beach.

Chase was flying again, up into the clouds and out of sight.

Chapter 35

WHAT REMAINS

The party on the beach watched the sky long after Chase had disappeared.

The Metrians had finished loading the Exorian prisoners in the hold of the boat, and were anxious to set sail.

Axl nudged Knox in the knees with his snout, pushing him toward Calla. When Knox tried to object, the hound bared its teeth and growled.

"He wants you to come with us, Knox. Back to Melor, to the Keep," Calla urged, as if Knox might object and take off after Chase. The hound pushed his knees again. Axl was not going to take no for an answer.

Knox held up his hands.

"She doesn't have to get so pushy about it; that's where I'm going. Jeez, Axl—I'm going, I'm going."

Seaborne spoke to the Captain.

"What did the lad mean: *He's not the only one with a promise to fulfill?*"

The Captain's gaze fell on the Metrian ship. His face looked caved in on itself.

"It is a reminder from Ratha that I have one more duty to carry out."

"And what would that be?"

"I must keep my promise to her and reveal all knowledge I have of the Fifth Stone. It is not a prospect I relish. I have vowed to protect it with my life, and I know Ratha will not hesitate to spare one to get at the other."

"I am beginning to believe those who say the Fifth Stone is a dream," said Calla. "It's gone, just as the legend says. Enough of us have died in the hope of its return. We are the only ones who can save Ayda now; best learn to live with that," said Calla. "We are on our own."

The Captain shook his head.

"You are wrong. The Fifth Stone still exists—and so does its Keeper."

"If you *know* that," Knox cut in, "why did you let us risk our lives? Why didn't you just . . . I don't know, make a phone call or something?"

The Captain hung his head.

"I am a seeker, Knox. It is my true nature to find what has been hidden. Long ago, during the Great Battle, after Remiel created the four stones of power from the Fifth, I was exiled from Ayda, far away from Rysta, to accompany the Fifth Stone and its Keeper into oblivion. You were told the Fifth Stone was destroyed, or lost, But it wasn't. It was sent purposefully from these shores with its Keeper, and with me as their sworn protector.

"I did not want to go. I did not want to leave Rysta. But I had caused the strife in Ayda by leading Dankar to these shores, and it seemed to me the only way to keep Ayda—and the ones I loved—safe.

"The Fifth Stone must *never* fall into Dankar's hands. That fact has not changed in five hundred years. And I will tell you this much: The only way the Fifth Stone will come back to Ayda is when its Keeper decides it is time, only when all other hope has failed."

His tone was so solemn that the Melorians, Knox, and Evelyn caught it, like a chill passing through them.

"It has not come to that yet," said the Captain, noticing their stricken faces. "We have achieved much on our own. Dankar has been dealt a blow he did not expect in the arena. We have taken many of his soldiers hostage, and may discover more of his weaknesses. We may yet turn his arrogance against him, for he does not hold sway over all of Exor. There are those who would see things renewed. Our strength has not wavered. There is hope yet."

"But what are you going to do about Ratha?" asked Knox.

The Captain frowned.

"Before I settle with her, I will go to Metria, and by any means possible, try to get the Keeper a message. After that, it is out of my hands. It is out of all of our hands."

He turned without another word and headed toward the Metrian ship. His shoulders were stooped, his gait crooked—as if all the years had finally taken their toll. He made a sad, solitary figure as he receded down the beach.

Evelyn followed him with her eyes. Something stirred in her heart, and, almost as if a lens had been dropped over her vision, the second sight brought on by her daylights bloomed. Every living thing before her blossomed in a sudden radiance; only this time, she saw something else. She saw lines—channels—of glowing light connecting her to Knox, and then to Seaborne, and to Calla. The lines spread out like meridians on a map and crossed to Axl and Tar, and across the beach, to the Captain, piercing the hull of the boat to connect her to the Exorian prisoners and the Metrians.

She knew without having to think about it that whatever happened to the Captain would happen to all of them, and vice versa. She almost laughed out loud at how simple it was.

Her normal vision clicked back into place.

"I'm going with him," she announced.

Knox did a double take. "Are you serious? No, you're not."

"Yes, I am," she said in a sharp tone. "Don't argue with me, Knox. You go to Melor and find Teddy and your mother. I'm going to Metria, with the Captain. I want to help him."

Knox frowned at her. "Are you sure?"

Evelyn nodded.

"Bring everyone to Metria if it gets bad in Melor." She glanced at Seaborne and Calla and the hounds. "All of you—don't be heroes."

"Too late for that," said Knox, grinning.

"I'll be on the lookout for you!" Evelyn shouted, and took off down the beach after the Captain. Her poncho flew back in the wind and her hood fell down around her shoulders. The sun glinted off her chestnut hair. She turned once and gave them a wave, then caught up to the Captain.

Seaborne took a deep breath.

"We'd best be going as well."

Knox turned from watching Evelyn and the Captain make their way to the ship.

"Yeah, agreed. It's a two-day march from here, at least."

Calla reached over and ruffled his hair in an uncharacteristic show of affection.

"You sound like my father, Knox."

"Off we go then," said Seaborne, breaking into a sprint. The hounds galloped ahead, releasing three long howls.

Evelyn raised her head at the sound. She saw their three hooded figures moving across the shore with the speed of a deer. Knox was having no trouble keeping up. She smiled at the sight. His Melorian daylights were in full force.

She lifted her hand as if the light she knew was beneath it all might show through her skin, like a flashlight beam under a sheet. She saw only coppery skin covered in a fine layer of dust. Her own powers were less obvious than Knox's.

A wave of exhaustion washed over her. She pulled up her hood and wrapped her poncho around her and sank low on the deck of the Metrian ship. The steady beat of the lake against the hull lulled her to sleep.

✛   ✛   ✛

The sun was setting when Evelyn awoke, and the ship was stationary.

In the golden-tinged air the surroundings looked familiar. They had anchored in the bay outside of the caverns in Metria where she and the boys had first been sent. It had the hollow feeling of a ghost town now, and the sounds of the monkeys and birds that usually filled the air in Metria were absent. News of Rysta's fate must have traveled quickly.

The Metrians were disembarking, disgorging their prisoners from the hold, making little sound. An Exorian raiding party had been spotted on the western shore of the Hestredes. She joined the Captain in one of the dories. Hesam leaned against her own oars, making swift time.

They rowed through the wide tunnel that created the mouth of the lagoon and into the cavern itself. It was different than her last time here. Cold and empty as a cathedral left in ruin—and something else. She cocked her head to pinpoint it, and then she named it: the sound of falling water that had once been a hallmark of the cavern was no longer there. The curtain of water that had once fallen from a great height into the lagoon had disappeared. The only sound came from the soft dip of the Metrian oars.

They made straight for Rysta's enclosure and landed on the beach where Evelyn and the boys had first seen Rysta. She remembered the sight of Rysta kneeling, arms open, to welcome them, her pale hair shining in the moonlight like a starry veil.

Hesam and the Metrian guard stationed themselves on the shore of the small island. Urza disembarked from her own dory and waited for the Captain and Evelyn to join her. Above, the open sky fell dark.

"Thank you, Hesam," said Urza. "There are food and weapon stores in the back rooms, should you need them. Enough for all of you, and the prisoners. Take them deep inside the caverns."

"They aren't coming with us?" asked Evelyn.

"The prisoners will stay here for the time being. The Metrian guard will defend the cavern and the northern boundaries. The Exorians are upon us, and I do not dare risk traveling over land or across open water."

"Then how are we going to get to the city?"

By way of an answer, Urza led them through the leafy vegetation to the edge of Rysta's pool. She nodded.

"Through there."

Evelyn glanced at the placid pool. She remembered its magical qualities—how it could show you things you wanted to see.

Urza stooped at the edge of the pool and dipped her hand into the water, making a circling motion.

The skin of water trembled at first, then began to spin faster and faster. It rose up in a tube and spread out in the space over their heads, forming a liquid canopy. The subterranean rocks that contained the waters of the pool became visible, and beyond them, a dark and narrow tunnel. A small head emerged from the depths.

"More of you lately than I've had in centuries," he grumbled.

Chantarelle.

"Follow me," he said, beckoning to Evelyn, Urza, and the Captain with his hand. They jumped beside him into the empty pool.

An idea struck Evelyn as she descended into yet another tunnel: if Chantarelle could get outliers here, surely he could send a message back there. Then, at least the Keeper of the Fifth Stone would know what the Aydans were facing, beyond any doubt. What the Keeper decided to do from there was anyone's guess, but the message would be sent.

"Chantarelle," she said, "the Captain has something he wants to ask you when we get to the city."

"Very well," said Chantarelle. "I hope it is a good question."

"It is," she said, "it really is."

Their heads disappeared underground.

The waters that hovered above the pool hesitated a moment longer, then cascaded back into their rightful place, shimmering in the silver light of dusk as if they had never been disturbed. An image of Rysta, luminous and pale, swam slowly to the surface. The waters of the pool trembled once more and the image dissolved.

Somewhere to the south, a gull called out, searching for the sea.

•

About the Author

G. A. MORGAN is the author of *The Fog of Forgetting*, the first book in The Five Stones Trilogy, and several nonfiction works under her full name, Genevieve Morgan. She grew up in New York City and spent every summer of her childhood in Maine. She lives and works in Portland, Maine. The conclusion to the trilogy, *The Kinfolk*, will be released in July 2016.

THE FIVE STONES TRILOGY

GA-MORGAN.COM